* * * *

"Detective adventure rich in action and suspense, seen through the eyes of a characteristic Stewart heroine, and surely there are few more attractive young women in today's popular fiction."
The New York Times

* * * *

MARY STEWART
One of the world's most beloved story tellers

MY BROTHER MICHAEL
One of her most famous and satisfying best sellers

My Brother Michael

by Mary Stewart

FAWCETT CREST • NEW YORK

FOR KIM
IN LOVING MEMORY

A Fawcett Crest Book
Published by Ballantine Books

Copyright © 1959, 1960 by Mary Stewart

ISBN 0-449-20735-8

This edition published by arrangement with
William Morrow & Co., Inc.

Printed in Canada

First Fawcett Crest Edition: May 1961
First Ballantine Books Edition: April 1985
Third Printing: January 1989

AUTHOR'S NOTE

The quotations from Professor Gilbert Murray's translation of the *Electra* of Euripides appear by kind permission of Messrs. Allen & Unwin. I am also indebted to the editors of the Penguin Classics for permission to use extracts from Sophocles and Euripides in translations by E. F. Watling and Philip Vellacott; to Messrs. Faber and Faber for their leave to use the lines from Dudley Fitts' translation of *The Frogs* of Aristophanes; and to the Clarenden Press, Oxford, for the lines from Ingram Bywater's translation of Aristotle *On the Art of Poetry*.

If it were possible to do so adequately, I should like here to thank my friends in Greece—especially Electra and her family—for their very great kindness to me during my visits to their country; and I must add a particular note of thanks to those people in Delphi itself who helped me to gather information for this book: Mr. George Vouzas, of the Apollon Hotel; Mario, who showed me round; "Pete" Gerousis, who patiently answered all my questions; and the caretaker of the studio, who assured me that "things like that could never happen in Delphi." I believe him. At any rate, they never did.

M. S.

MY BROTHER MICHAEL

If you do not love the Greeks, you cannot love anything.

REX WARNER

CHAPTER

1

Why, woman,
What are you waiting for?

SOPHOCLES: *Electra*
(tr. E. F. Watling).

"Nothing ever happens to me."

I wrote the words slowly, looked at them for a moment with a little sigh, then put my ballpoint pen down on the café table and rummaged in my handbag for a cigarette.

As I breathed the smoke in I looked about me. It occurred to me, thinking of that last depressed sentence in my letter to Elizabeth, that enough was happening at the moment to satisfy all but the most adventure-hungry. That is the impression that Athens gives you. Everyone is moving, talking, gesticulating—but particularly talking. The second one remembers in Athens is not the clamour of the impatiently congested traffic, or the perpetual hammer of pneumatic drill or even the age-old sound of chisels chippng away at the Pentelic marble which is still the cheapest stone for building . . . what one remembers about Athens is the roar of talking. Up to your high hotel window, above the smell of dust and the blare of traffic it comes, surging like the sea below the temple at Sunium—the sound of Athenian voices arguing, laughing, talk-talk-talking, as once they talked the world into shape in the busy colonnades of the Agora, not so very far from where I sat.

It was a popular and crowded café. I had found a table at the back of the room near the bar. All along the outer wall big glass doors gave on to the pavement, standing open to the dust and din of Omonia Square, which is, in effect, the commercial centre of Athens. It is certainly the centre of all the noise and bustle of the city. The traffic crawled or surged past in a ceaseless confusion. Crowds—as jammed as the traffic—eddied on the wide pavements. Knots of men, most of them impeccably dressed in dark city clothes, discussed whatever men do discuss at mid-morning in Athens; their faces were lively and intent, their hands fidgeting unceasingly with the little loops of amber "nervous beads" that the men of the Eastern Mediterranean carry. Women, some fashionably dressed, others with the wide black skirt and black head-covering of the peasant, went about their shopping. A donkey, so laden with massed flowers that it looked like a moving garden, passed slowly by, its owner shouting his wares in vain against the hurly-burly of the hot morning streets.

I pushed my coffee cup aside, drew again at my cigarette, and picked up my letter. I began to read over what I had written.

"You'll have had my other letters by now, about Mykonos and Delos, and the one I wrote a couple of days ago from Crete. It's difficult to know just how to write—I want so much to tell you what a wonderful country this is, and yet I feel I mustn't pile it on too thick or you'll find that wretched broken leg that prevented your coming even more of a tragedy than before! Well, I won't go on about *that*, either. . . . I'm sitting in a café on Omonia Square—it's about the busiest place in this eternally busy city—and calculating what to do next. I've just come off the boat from Crete. I can't believe that there's any place on earth more beautiful than the Greek islands, and Crete's in a class by itself, magnificent and exciting and a bit grim as well—but I told you about it in my last letter. Now there's Delphi still to come, and everyone, solo and chorus, has assured me that it'll be the crown of the trip. I hope they're right; some of the places, like Eleusis and Argos and even Corinth, are a bit disappointing . . . one leaves oneself open to the ghosts, as it were, but the myths and magic are all gone. However, I'm told that Delphi really is *something*. So I've left it till last. The only trouble is, I'm getting a bit worried about the cash. I suppose I'm a bit of a fool where money is concerned. Philip ran all that, and how right he was. . . ."

Here a passing customer, pushing his way between the tables towards the bar-counter, jogged my chair, and I looked up, jerked momentarily out of my thoughts.

A crowd of customers—all male—seemed to be gathering at the bar for what looked like a very substantial mid-morning snack. It appeared that the Athenian businessman had to bridge the gap between breakfast and luncheon with something rather more sustaining than coffee. I saw one plate piled high with Russian salad and thick dressing, another full of savoury meatballs and green beans swimming in oil, and innumerable smaller dishes heaped with fried potatoes and small onions and fish and pimentos and half a dozen things I didn't recognize. Behind the counter was a row of earthenware jars, and in the shadow of their narrow necks I saw olives, fresh from the cool farm-sheds in Aegina and Salamis. The winebottles on the shelf above bore names like Samos and Nemea and Chios and Mavrodaphne.

I smiled, and looked down again at the page.

". . . but in a way I'm finding it wonderful to be here alone. Don't misunderstand me, I don't mean *you!* I wish like anything you were here, for your own sake as well as mine. But you know what I do mean, don't you? This is the first time for years I've been away on my own—I was almost going to say 'off the leash'—and I'm really enjoying myself in a way I hadn't thought possible before. You know, I don't suppose he'd ever have come here at all; I just can't see Philip prowling round Mycenae or Cnossos or Delos, can you? Or letting me prowl either? He'd have been all set to dash off to Istanbul or Beirut or even Cyprus—anywhere, in short, where things are *happening*, not centuries ago in the past, but *now*—and even if they weren't happening, he'd make them.

"Fun—yes, it was always fun, but—oh, I'm not going to write about that either, Elizabeth, but I was right, absolutely right. I'm sure of it now. It wouldn't have worked, not in a million years. This trip on my own has shown me that, more clearly than ever. There's no regret, only relief that perhaps, now, I'll have time to be myself. There, now I've admitted it, and we'll drop the subject. Even if I am quite shatteringly incompetent when I am being myself, it's fun, and I muddle along somehow. But I do admit . . ."

I turned the page, reaching forward absently with my left hand to tap ash from my cigarette. There was a paler circle showing still against the tan at the base of the third finger, where Philip's ring had been. In ten days of Aegean sunshine, it had begun to fade . . . six long years fading now without regret, leaving behind them a store of gay memories that would fade too, and a sneaking curiosity to know if the beggar maid had been really happy once she was married to King Cophetua. . . .

"But I do admit there's another side to this Great Emancipation. Things do seem a trifle dull occasionally, after so

many years spent being swept along in Philip's—you must
admit—magnificent wake! I feel just a little bit high and
dry. You'd have thought that something—some sniff of an
adventure—would have happened to a young woman (is one
still young at twenty-five?) marooned on her own in the
wilds of Hellas, but no! I go tamely from temple to temple,
guidebook in hand, and spend the rather long evenings
writing up notes for that wonderful book I was always going
to write, and persuading myself I'm enjoying the peace and
quiet. . . . I suppose it's the other side of the picture, and I'll
adjust myself in time. And if something exciting did happen,
I wonder just what sort of a showing I'd make—surely I've
got *some* talent for living, even if it looked feeble beside *his*
overplus? But life never does seem to deliver itself into the
hands of females, does it? I'll just finish up as usual in the
hotel bedroom, making notes for that book that'll never get
written. Nothing ever happens to me."

I put down the cigarette, and picked up my pen again. I
had better finish the letter, and on a slightly different note,
or Elizabeth was going to wonder if I wasn't, after all, re-
gretting the so-called emancipation of that broken engage-
ment.

I wrote cheerfully, "On the whole, I'm doing fine. The
language wasn't a difficulty after all. Most people seem to
speak a bit of French or English, and I have managed to acquire about six words of Greek—though there have been
difficult moments! I haven't managed the money quite so
well. I won't pretend I'm exactly broke yet, but I rather let
myself go in Crete—it was worth it, ye gods, but if it means
passing up Delphi I shall regret it. Not that I *can* miss
Delphi. That's unthinkable. I must get there somehow, but
I'm afraid I may have to scamp it in a one-day tour, which
is all I can afford. There's a tour bus on Thursday, and I
think I'll have to be content with that. If only I could afford
a car! Do you suppose that if I prayed to all the gods at
once—?"

Someone cleared his throat just above me. A shadow crept
half-apologetically across the page.

I looked up.

It wasn't the waiter, trying to winkle me out of my corner
table. It was a little dark man with patched and shabby
dungarees, a greasy blue shirt, and a hesitant smirk behind
the inevitable moustache. His trousers were held up with
string, which it appeared he didn't trust, because he held
on to them firmly with one grimy hand.

I must have looked at him with a chilly surprise, because the apologetic look deepened, but instead of going away he spoke in very bad French.

He said, "It is about the car for Delphi."

I said stupidly, looking down at the letter under my hand, "The car for Delphi?"

"You wanted a car for Delphi, *non?*"

The sun had probed even into this corner of the café. I peered at him against it. "Why, yes, I did. But I really don't see how—"

"I bring it." One grimy hand—the one that wasn't holding up his trousers—waved towards the blazing doorway.

My eyes followed the gesture, bemusedly. There was indeed a car, a large shabby-looking black affair, parked at the pavement's edge.

"Look here," I said, "I don't understand—"

"*Voilà!*" With a grin, he fished what was patently a car key from his pocket, and dangled it above the table. "This is it. It is a matter of life and death, I understand that—oh, perfectly. So I come as quick as I can—"

I said with some exasperation, "I haven't the remotest idea what you're talking about."

The grin vanished, to be replaced by a look of vivid anxiety. "I am late. This I know. I am sorry. Mademoiselle will forgive me? She will be in time. The car—she does not look much but she is good, oh, a very good car. If mademoiselle—"

"Look," I said patiently, "I don't want a car. I'm sorry if I misled you, but I can't hire one. You see—"

"But mademoiselle said she desired a car."

"I know I did. I'm sorry. But the fact is—"

"And mademoiselle said it was a matter of life and death."

"Madem—I didn't. You said that. I'm afraid I don't want your car, monsieur. I regret. But I don't want it."

"But mademoiselle—"

I said flatly, "I can't afford it."

His face lighted at once with a very white-toothed and singularly attractive grin. "Money!" The word was contemptuous. "We do not speak of money! Besides," he added with great simplicity, "the deposit is already paid."

I said blankly, "Deposit? Paid?"

"But yes. Mademoiselle paid it earlier."

I drew a breath that was three parts relief. It wasn't

witchcraft after all, nor was it an intervention of the ironic gods of Greece. It was a simple case of mistaken identity.

I said firmly, "I'm sorry. There has been a mistake. That is not my car. I didn't hire it at all."

The dangling key stilled for a moment, then swung in front of me with unimpaired vigour. "It is not the car mademoiselle saw, no, but that one was bad, bad. It had a—how do you say?—a crack in it that the water came out."

"A leak. But—"

"A leak. That is why I am late, you see, but we get this car, oh so good, since mademoiselle say it is so urgent a matter that Monsieur Simon have the car at Delphi straightaway. You leave straightaway you are in Delphi in three hours—four hours"—his look lingered on me momentarily, summing me up—"five hours maybe? And then perhaps all is well with Monsieur Simon and this matter of life and—"

"Death," I said. "Yes, I know. But the fact remains, monsieur, that I don't know what you're talking about! There is some mistake, and I'm sorry. It was not I who asked for the car. I gather that this, er, Monsieur Simon's girl was to have been in this café waiting for the car? . . . Well, I can't see anybody here at present who might fill the bill. . . ."

He spoke quickly, so quickly that I realized afterwards that he must have followed my rapid French only sketchily, and was pouncing on a phrase that made sense—the sense he wanted to hear. The key still swung on his fingertip as if it were hot and he wanted to drop it. He said, "That is it. This café. A young lady sitting alone. Half past ten. But I am late. You are Simon's girl, yes?"

He looked, with that bright brown uncomprehending gaze, so like an anxious monkey that my near-exasperation vanished, and I smiled at him, shaking my head, and summoned up one of my six hard-learned words of Greek. "*Ne*," I said, as forcefully as I could. "*Ne, ne, ne.*" I laughed and held out my cigarette case. "I'm sorry there's been a muddle. Have a cigarette."

The cigarette seemed to be an amazing cure-all for worry. The lines vanished magically from his face. The vivid smile flashed. The key dropped with a jingle in front of me while the hand that wasn't holding up his pants reached for my cigarette case. "Thank you, mademoiselle. It is a good car, mademoiselle. Have a good journey."

I was feeling in my bag for matches, and not until I raised my head did I really take in what he'd said. And by then it was too late. He had gone. I caught a glimpse of him sliding through the crowd at the café door like a whippet let off a string, then he vanished. Three of my cigarettes had gone too. But the car key lay on the table in front of me, and the black car still stood outside in the violent sunlight.

It was only then, as I sat gaping like an idiot at the key, the car, and the sunlight on the cloth where a moment ago the little man had cast a shadow, that I realized that my momentary piece of showing-off was likely to cost me pretty dear. I remembered a little sickly that in Greek, *"ne"* means "yes."

Of course I ran after him. But the crowd surged and swayed on the pavement, regardless, and there was no sign in any direction of the shabby messenger of the gods. My waiter followed me anxiously onto the pavement, ready to grab, I suppose, if I showed signs of taking off without paying him for my coffee. I ignored him and peered earnestly in all directions. But when he showed signs of retreating to bring up reinforcements to escort me personally back to my table and the bill, I judged it time to give up the search. I went back to my corner, picked up the key, threw a quick, worried smile at the still-pursuing waiter, who didn't speak English, and pushed my way towards the bar-counter to seek out the proprietor, who did.

I elbowed my way through the crowd of men, with a nervously reiterated *"Parakalo,"* which apparently, was the right word for "Please." At any rate the men gave way, and I leaned anxiously over the counter.

"Parakalo, kyrie—"

The proprietor threw me a harassed sweating glance over a pile of fried potatoes, and placed me unerringly. "Miss?"

"Kyrie, I am in difficulty. A queer thing has just happened. A man has brought that car over there—you see it, beyond the blue tables—to deliver it to someone in the café. By a mistake he appears to think I'm the person who hired it. He thinks I'm driving it up to Delphi for someone. But I know nothing about it, *kyrie;* it's all a mistake, and I don't know what to do!"

He threw a dollop of dressing over some tomatoes, pushed them towards a large man perched on a small stool at the counter, and wiped a hand over his brow. "Do you wish me to explain to him? Where is he?"

"That's the trouble, *kyrie.* He's gone. He just left me the key—here it is—and then went. I tried to catch him but he's vanished. I wondered if you knew who was supposed to be here to collect the car?"

"No. I know nothing." He picked up a large ladle, stirred something under the counter, and threw another look at the car outside. "Nothing. Who was the car for?"

"Monsieur, I told you, I don't know who—"

"You said it was to be driven somewhere—to Delphi, was it? Did this man not say who it was for?"

"Oh. Yes. A—a Mr. Simon."

He spooned some of the mixture—it seemed to be a sort of bouillabaisse—into a plate, handed it to a hovering waiter, and then said, with a shrug, "At Delphi? I have not heard of such a one. It is possible somebody here saw the man, or knows the car. If you wait a moment I will ask."

He said something then, in Greek, to the men at the counter, and became on the instant the centre of an animated, even passionate discussion which lasted some four or five minutes and involved in the end every male customer in the café, and which eventually produced, with all the goodwill in the world, the information that nobody had noticed the little man with the key, nobody knew the car, nobody had ever heard of a Monsieur Simon at Delphi (this though one of the men was a native of Crissa, only a few kilometres distant from Delphi), nobody thought it in the least likely that anyone from Delphi would hire a car in Athens, and (finally) nobody in their senses would drive it up there anyway.

"Though," said the man from Crissa, who was talking with his mouth full, "it is possible that this Simon is an English tourist staying at Delphi. That would explain everything." He didn't say why, merely smiling with the great kindness and charm through a mouthful of prawns, but I got his meaning.

I said apologetically, "I know it seems mad, *kyrie*, but I can't help feeling one ought to do something about it. The man who brought the key said it was"—I hesitated—"well, a matter of life and death."

The Greek raised his eyebrows; then he shrugged. I got the impression that matters of life and death were everyday affairs in Athens. He said, with another charming smile, "Quite an adventure, mademoiselle," and turned back to his plate.

I looked at him thoughtfully for a moment. "Yes," I said slowly, "yes." I turned back to the proprietor, who was struggling to scoop olives out of one of the beautiful jars. It was apparent that the rush hour and the heat were beginning to overset even his Athenian good manners and patience so I merely smiled at him and said, "Thank you for your goodness, *kyrie*. I'm sorry to have troubled you. It seems to me that if the matter really is urgent, then the person who wants the car will certainly come and get it as arranged."

"You wish to leave the key with me? I will take it, and then you need have no more worry. No, it will be a pleasure, I assure you."

"I won't trouble you yet, thanks. I must confess"—I laughed—"to a little curiosity. I'll wait here for a bit, and if this girl comes, I'll give her the key myself."

And to the poor man's relief, I wriggled back out of the press and returned to my table. I sat down and ordered another coffee, then lit another cigarette, and settled down to a pretence of finishing my letter, but in reality to keep one watchful eye on the door, and the other on the shabby black car that should—surely—by now have been hurtling along the Delphi road on that matter of life and death. . . .

I waited an hour. The waiter had begun to look askance again, so I pushed aside my untouched letter and gave an order, then sat playing with a plateful of beans and some small pink fish while I watched, in an expectancy that gradually gave way to uneasiness, the constant coming-and-going at the café door.

My motive in waiting hadn't been quite as straightforward as I had suggested to the proprietor of the café. It had occurred to me that, since I had become involved in the affair through no fault of my own, I might be able to turn it to advantage. When "Simon's girl" arrived to claim the car, it might surely be possible to suggest—or even ask outright—that I might be her passenger as far as Delphi. And the possibility of getting a lift up to Delphi was not the only one which had occurred to me. . . .

So the minutes dragged by, and still no one came, and somehow, the longer I waited, the less possible it seemed to walk out of the café and leave everything to settle itself without me, and the more insidiously did that other possibility begin to present itself. Dry-mouthed, I pushed it aside, but there it was, a challenge, a gift, a dare from the gods. . . .

At twelve o'clock, when nobody had appeared to claim the car, I thrust my plate aside, and set myself to consider that other possibility as coolly as I could.

It was, simply, to drive the car up to Delphi myself.

It was apparent that, for whatever reason, the girl wasn't coming. Something must have prevented her, for otherwise she would simply have telephoned the garage to cancel the order. But the car—the urgently wanted car—was still there, already an hour and a half late in starting. I, on the other hand, wanted very badly to go to Delphi, and could start straightaway. I had come straight up from Piraeus off the Crete steamer, and had everything with me that I needed for a short stay in Delphi. I could go up today, deliver the car, have two days there with the money saved on the bus fare, and come back with the tourist bus on Thursday. The thing was simple, obvious, and a direct intervention of providence.

I picked up the key with fingers that felt as if they didn't belong to me, and reached slowly for my only luggage—the big brightly coloured hold-all of Mykonos weaving—that hung on the back of a chair.

I hesitated with my hand touching it. Then I let the hand drop, and sat, twisting the key over and over, watching with unseeing eyes the way the sun glinted on it as it turned.

It couldn't be done. It was just one of those things that couldn't be done. I must have been mad even to consider doing it. All that had happened was that Simon's girl had forgotten to cancel the order for the car and claim the deposit. It was nothing to do with me. No one would thank me for intervening in an affair that, in spite of my silly mistake, had nothing whatever to do with me. That phrase "a matter of life and death," so glib a chorus, so persuasive an excuse to interfere—it was only a phrase, after all, a phrase from which I had built up this feeling of urgency which gave me (I pretended) the excuse to act. *In any case, it had nothing to do with me.* The obvious—the only—thing to do was to leave the car standing there, hand over the key, and go away.

The decision brought with it a sense of relief so vivid, so physical almost, that it startled me. On the wave of it I stood up, picked up the car key, and swung my hold-all up to my shoulder. The unfinished letter to Elizabeth lay on the table. I reached for it, and as I folded it over to thrust it into my bag, the sentence caught my eye again. "Nothing ever happens to me."

The paper crackled suddenly as my fingers tightened. I suppose moments of self-knowledge come at all sorts of odd times. I have often wondered if they are ever pleasant. I had one such moment now.

It didn't last long. I didn't let it. It was with a sort of resigned surprise that I found myself once more at the counter, handing a slip of paper across it to the proprietor.

"My name and address," I said rather breathlessly, "just in case someone does come for the car later on. Miss Camilla Haven, the Olympias Hotel, Rue Marnis. . . . Tell them I —I'll take care of the car. Tell them I did it for the best."

· I was out in the street and getting into the car before it occurred to me that my last words had sounded uncommonly like an epitaph.

CHAPTER

2

It's a long way to Delphi.

EURIPIDES: *Ion*
(tr. Philip Vellacott).

Even if it wasn't Hermes himself who had brought me the
key, the hand of every god in Hellas must have been over
me that day, because I got out of Athens alive. More, un-
scathed.

There were some sticky moments. There was the shoeblack
who was so urgent to clean my shoes that he followed me to
the car and clung to the side and would certainly have been
hurt when I started off, if only I'd remembered to put the
car into gear. There was the moment when I turned—at a
cautious ten miles per hour and hugging the left-hand pavement—out of Omonia Square into St. Constantine Street,
and met a taxi almost head-on on what I thought was his
wrong side, till the volume and fervour of his abuse shocked
me back onto my own right. Then there was the encounter in
the narrow alley with two furious pedestrians who stepped off
the pavement without a single glance in my direction. How
was I to know it was a one-way street? I was lucky with my
brakes that time. I wasn't so lucky with the flower-donkey,
but it was only the flowers I touched, and the driver was
charming about it. He refused the note I hastily held out to
him and he actually gave me the flowers I'd knocked out of
the donkey's pannier.

All things considered, people were very forgiving. The
only really unpleasant person was the man who spat on the
hood as I came hesitatingly out from behind a stationary
bus. There was no need for such a display of temper. I'd
hardly touched him.

By the time I got to the main road that leads out of
Athens along the Sacred Way I'd found out two things. One

was that a few weeks spent in punting around the English
country roads in Elizabeth's old Hillman (Philip, under-
standably, had never let me touch his car) was not really an
adequate preparation for driving through Athens in a strange
car with a left-hand drive. The other was that the shabby
black car had an unexpectedly powerful engine. If it had
been less shabby and ancient-looking—if it had been one of
the sleek winged transatlantic monsters commonly used as
taxis in Athens—I should never have dared myself to drive
it, but its shabby façade had reassured me. Almost it could
have been the old Hillman I'd learned on. Almost. I hadn't
been in it three minutes before I discovered that it had an
acceleration like the kick of a jet, and by the time I'd as-
sessed its possibilities as a lethal weapon—which were
limitless—it was too late. I was out in the traffic and it
seemed safer to stay there. So I hung on grimly to the wheel,
changing hands now and again as I remembered that the
gear levers were on the right, and prayed to the whole
Olympian hierarchy as we jerked and nudged our terrified
and apologetic way out through the city suburbs, turning at
length into the great double road that runs along the coast
towards Eleusis and Corinth.

After the packed and flashing streets, the road seemed
open and comparatively empty. This was the Sacred Way;
down this wide sea-bordered road the ancient pilgrims had
gone with songs and torches to celebrate the Mysteries at
Eleusis. This lake now lying to the right was the holy lake of
Demeter. Across that bay on the left, the island of Salamis
lay like a drowned dragon, and there—*there*—Themistocles
had smashed the Persian fleet. . . .

But I looked neither to right nor left as I drove. I had
been this way before, and had got the first sharp disillusion
over. There was no need, here, to leave oneself open to the
ghosts; they had long since gone. Now, the Sacred Way ran
straight and wide (the tar sweating a little in the sun) between the cement factories and the ironworks; the holy lake
was silted up with weeds and slag; in the bay of Salamis lay
the rusty hulks of tankers, and the wine-dark water reflected
the aluminum towers of the refinery. At the other side of the
bay belched the chimneys of Megara, and above them a trio
of Vampire jets wheeled, screaming, against the ineffable
Greek sky. And this was Eleusis itself, this dirty village almost hidden in the choking clouds of ochreous smoke from
the cement works.

I kept my eyes on the road, my attention on the car, and

drove as fast as I dared. Soon the industrial country was behind us, and the road, narrower now and whitening with
dust under the pitiless September sun, lifted itself away
from the shore and wound up between fields of red earth set
with olives, where small box-like houses squatted, haphazardly it seemed, among the trees. Children, ragged and brown
and thin, stood in the dust to stare as I went by. A woman,
black-clad, and veiled like a Moslem, bent to lift bread from
the white beehive oven that stood under an olive tree.
Scrawny hens scratched about, and a dog hurled itself yelling
after the car. Donkeys plodded in the deep dust at the road's
edge, half hidden under their top-heavy loads of brushwood.
A high cart swayed along a track towards the road; it was
piled with grapes, gleaming waxily, cloudy green. The flanks
of the mule were glossy, and bloomy as dark grapes. The air
smelt of heat and dung and dust and the lees of the grape
harvest.

The sun beat down. Wherever the trees stood near the
road the shade fell like a blessing. It was not long past noon,
and the heat was terrific. The only relief was the breeze of
the car's movement, and the cloudy heads of the great olives
sailing between the road and the great brazen bowl of the
sky.

There was very little traffic out in the heat of the day, and
I was determined to take full advantage of the afternoon
lull, so I drove on through the hot bright minutes, feeling
confident now, and even secure. I had got the feel of the
car, and I was still steadfastly refusing to think about what
I had done. I had taken a "dare" from the gods, and the results would wait till I got——if I got—to Delphi.

If I got to Delphi.

My confidence in myself had been steadily growing as I
drove on through an empty landscape, through country that
grew wilder and more beautiful as the road shook itself clear
of the olive groves and climbed the hills that lie to the north
of Attica. It even survived the series of frightening hairpin
bends that sink from the summit of these hills towards the
flat fields of the Boeotian plain. But it didn't survive the bus.

This was the service bus from Athens and I caught up with
it halfway along the dead-straight road that bisects the plain.
It was small, evil-looking, and smelly. It also seemed to be
packed to the doors with people, boxes, and various livestock,
including hens and at least one small goat. It was roaring
along in a fifty-yard trail of dust. I drew carefully out to the
left, and pressed forward to pass.

The bus, which was already in the middle of the road, swung over promptly to the left and accelerated slightly. I moved back, swallowing dust. The bus went back to the crown of the road and settled back to its rackety thirty miles an hour.

I waited half a minute, and tried again. I crept cautiously up to its rear wheel and hoped the driver would see me.

He did. Accelerating madly, he surged once again into my path, got me well and truly behind him, then settled back complacently into the centre of the road. I went back once more into the choking dust-train. I was trying not to mind, to tell myself that when he had had his joke, he would let me safely by, but I could feel my hands beginning to tighten on the wheel, and a nerve was jumping somewhere in my throat. If Philip had been driving . . . but then I told myself, if Philip had been driving, it wouldn't have happened. Women drivers are fair game on the roads of Greece.

Here we passed a board which said, in Greek and English letters: THEBES 4 km.; DELPHI 77 km. If I had to stay behind the bus all the way to Delphi. . . .

I tried again. This time as I pulled out to approach him I sounded the horn decisively. To my surprise and gratitude, he drew over promptly to the right, and slowed down. I made for the gap. There was just room, no more, between the bus and the verge, which was of deep, crumbling dry soil. Taut with nervous concentration, I pressed forward and accelerated.

I wasn't getting past. The bus rocked and roared alongside, travelling faster, keeping pace with me. My car had the speed of it, but the gap was narrowing and I wasn't sure enough of my judgment to force the big car past. The driver of the bus closed in more sharply. I don't know if he would actually have forced me off the road, but as the swaying dirty-green enamel rocked nearer, I lost my nerve, as he had known I would. I stood on the brakes. The bus roared on. I was left once more in the dust.

Ahead of us I could see the first scattered houses of Thebes, the legendary city that, I knew, was gone even more irrecoverably than Eleusis. Where Antigone led the blind Oedipus out into exile, the old men of Thebes sit on the concrete pavements in the sun, beside the gas pumps. The game of *tric-trac* that they sit over, hour after hour, is probably the oldest thing in Thebes. There is a fountain somewhere, beloved of the nymphs. That's all. But I had no time then to mourn the passing of the legends. I wasn't thinking about

Oedipus or Antigone, or even about Philip or Simon or my own miserable prelude to adventure. I just drove on towards Thebes with my eyes fixed in hatred ahead of me. There was nothing left in life at that moment but the desire to pass that filthy bus.

Presently the chance came. A knot of women, waiting by the roadside, signalled him to stop, and he slowed down. I closed up behind, my eyes on the strip to the left of him, my hands slippery on the wheel, and that nerve beginning to jump again.

He stopped, right in the centre of the road. There was no possible space to pass. I stopped behind him and waited, then, as he drew away from me again, and I let in the clutch, I stalled the engine. My hand shook on the ignition. The engine wouldn't start. At the edge of my vision I caught sight of a face at the rear window of the withdrawing bus, a dark young face, split in a wide grin. As I started the car and followed I saw the youth turn as if to nudge someone on the back seat beside him. Another face turned to stare and grin. And another.

Then, close behind me—so close that it nearly sent me into the ditch with fright—I heard a horn. As I swerved automatically to the right a jeep, driven fast on its wrong side, roared up from behind, overtook me rather too wide, with the nearside wheels churning dust, and charged straight, at the same headlong pace, for the rear of the bus, with its horn still blasting like a siren. I caught a fleeting glimpse of a girl driving, a young, dark face, with lashes drooping over her eyes and a bored, sulky mouth. She was lounging back in her seat, handling the jeep with casual, almost insolent, expertise. And, woman driver or no, the bus made way for her, whipping smartly over to the right and staying there respectfully while she tore by. I didn't consciously decide to follow her; in fact I'm not sure yet whether I trod on the accelerator deliberately, or whether I was feeling for the brake, but something hit me in the small of the back, and the big black car shot forward, missed the bus by inches, and stormed past in the wake of the jeep, with two wheels on the crown of the road and the other two churning up enough dust to have guided the children of Israel straight into Thebes. Where the bus had its offside wheels I neither knew nor cared. I didn't even look in the mirror.

I swept into Thebes and dived smartly down the wrong side of the dual carriageway which is the road through to Levadia and Delphi.

The hand of Hermes, god of wayfarers, was over me still. There was a horse fair at Levadia, which, with its accompanying trappings of fiesta, jammed the streets; but after that I met nothing, except slow little caravans of country people on their way by mule and donkey-back to the fair; and once a train of gypsies—real Egyptians—on the move with mules and ponies covered in bright blankets.

Soon after I had passed Levadia the country began to change. The grim banalities of Attica, the heavy Technicolour prosperity of the plains, sank back and were forgotten as the hills crowded in. The road reared and twisted between great ribs of brown hill that thrust the landscape up into folded ranges. At the foot of the steep waterless valleys dead streams curled white along their single beds, like the sloughed skins of snakes. The sides of the valley were dry with the yellowish growth of burned grass, and drifts of stones and crumbling soil.

Bigger and bigger grew the circling hills, barer the land, drawn in with great sweeps of colour that ran from red to ochre, from ochre to burnt umber to lion-tawny, with, above all, the burning, the limitless, the lovely light. And beyond all, at length, a grey ghost of a mountain massif; not purple, not faintly blue with distance like the mountains of a softer country, but spectre-white, magnificent, a lion silvered. Parnassus, home of the ghosts of the old gods.

I stopped only once to rest, some way beyond Levadia. The road, which wound high along the hillside, was in shadow, and the air, at that height, was cool. I sat for about fifteen minutes on the parapet that edged the road. Below me, deep in a forked valley, was a place where three tracks met; the ghost of an ancient crossroads where once a young man, coming from Delphi to Thebes, struck an old man down out of his chariot, and killed him. . . .

But no ghosts moved today. No sound, no breath, not even the shadow of a hanging hawk. Only the bare lion-coloured hills, and the illimitable, merciless light.

I got back into the car. As I started the engine I reflected that the god of wayfarers, who had done very well by me so far, had only some twenty miles' more duty to do, and then he could abandon me to my fate.

In fact, he abandoned me just ten kilometres short of Delphi, in the middle of the village of Arachova.

CHAPTER

3

But if I don't get out from under pretty damned soon, there'll
be a disaster in the rear.

ARISTOPHANES: *The Frogs*
(tr. Dudley Fitts).

Arachova is a showplace. It is not self-consciously so, but its
setting is picturesque in the extreme, and the Greek style of
building does the rest.

The village is perched on a precipitous hillside, and the
houses are built in tiers, one up behind the other, the floor of
one level with the roof of the next. The whole village looks
as if it were just about to slide into the depths of the valley
below. The walls are white and the roofs are rose-red, and
over every wall hang flowering plants, and vines rich with
grapes, and great dollops of wool dyed the colours of amber
and hyacinth and blood. Along the short main street are
places selling rugs which hang out in the sunlight, brilliant
against the blinding white walls. The street itself has some
corners, and is about eight feet wide. On one of these corners
I ran into a truck.

Not quite literally. I managed to stop with the hood of my
car about nine inches away from his, and there I stayed, paralyzed, unable even to think. The two vehicles stood headlamp to headlamp, like a pair of cats staring one another out,
one of them preserving a mysterious silence. I had, of course,
stalled the engine. . . .

It became apparent all too soon that it was I, and not the
truck driver, who would have to back. The whole village—
the male portion of it—turned out to tell me so, with gestures. They were charming and delightful and terribly help-
ful. They did everything except reverse the car for me. And
they obviously couldn't understand why anyone who was in
charge of such a car shouldn't be able to reverse it just like
that.

Eventually I reversed it into somebody's shop doorway. The whole village helped to pick up the trestle table, re-hang the rugs, and assure me that it didn't matter a scrap.

I straightened up the car and reversed again, into a donkey. The whole village assured me that the donkey wasn't hurt and it would stop in a kilometre or so and come home.

I straightened up the car. This time I churned out a reasonably straight course for ten yards while the village held its breath. Then came a bend in the road. I stopped. I definitely was not prepared to chance reversing over the two-foot parapet into somebody's garden twenty feet down the hillside. I sat there breathing hard, smiling ferociously back at the villagers, and wishing I had never been born and that Simon hadn't either. My bolt was shot.

I had stopped in a patch of sunlight and the glare from the white walls was blinding. The men crowded closer, grinning delightedly and making gallant and—no doubt fortunately—incomprehensible remarks. The truck driver, also grinning, hung out of his cab with the air of a man prepared to spend the whole afternoon enjoying the show.

In desperation, I leaned over the door of the car and addressed the most forward of my helpers, a stout, florid-looking man with small twinkling eyes, who was obviously vastly delighted with the whole business. He spoke a fluent if decidedly odd mixture of French and English.

"Monsieur," I said, "I do not think I can manage this. You see, it's not my car; it belongs to a Monsieur Simon, of Delphi, who requires it urgently, for business. I—I'm not very used to it yet, and since it's not mine I don't like to take risks. . . . I wonder, could you or one of these gentlemen back it for me? Or perhaps the driver of the truck would help, if you would ask him? You see, it's not my car. . . ."

Some rag of pride led me to insist on this, until I saw he wasn't listening. The smile had gone from the cheerful sweating face. He said, "Who did you say the car was for?"

"A Monsieur Simon, of Delphi. He hired it from Athens, urgently." I regarded him hopefully. "Do you know him?"

"No," he said, and shook his head. But he spoke a little too quickly, and as he spoke his eyes flickered away from mine. The man at his elbow looked at me sharply, and then asked a question in rapid Greek, where I thought I caught the word "Simon." My friend nodded once, with that swift flicker of a sidelong look back at me, and said something under his breath. The men near him stared, and muttered, and I thought I saw a new kind of curiosity, furtive, and perhaps even avid, replacing the naïve amusement of a moment ago.

But this was only the most fleeting of impressions. Before
I could decide whether to pursue the inquiry or not, I realized that none of the men were looking at me any more.
There was some more of that swift and semi-furtive mutter-
ing; the last of the cheery grins had disappeared, and the
men who had been crowding most closely round the car were
moving away, unobtrusively yet swiftly, bunching as sheep
bunch at the approach of the dog. One and all, they were
looking in the same direction.

At my elbow came the fluttering click of "nervous beads,"
and the stout man's voice said softly, "He will help you."

I said "Who?" before I realized he was no longer beside
me.

I turned my head and looked where they all were looking.

A man was coming slowly down a steep-stepped alley that
led uphill between the houses on my right.

He was about thirty years old, dark-haired and tanned
like all the others in the group near the car, but his clothes,
no less than his air and bearing, made him look unmistak-
ably English.

He was not tall, an inch or two under six feet, perhaps,
but he was broad in the shoulder, and held himself well, with
a sort of easy, well-knit movement that spoke of training
and perfect physical fitness. I thought him good-looking; a
thinnish sun-browned face, black brows, straight nose, and a
hard mouth; but just at the moment his expression was what
Jane Austen would have called repulsive—meaning that,
whatever thoughts held him in that slightly frowning ab-
straction, it was obvious that he didn't intend them to be
disturbed.

He seemed to be hardly aware of where he was, or what he
was doing. A child scampered up the steps and pushed by
him, apparently unnoticed. A couple of hens flapped across
under his feet without making him pause. A hanging plant
splashed petals in a scarlet shower over the white sleeve of
his shirt, but he made no move to brush them away.

When he reached the foot of the alleyway, he paused. He
seemed to come abruptly out of his preoccupation, whatever
it was, and stood there, hands thrust into the pockets of his
flannels, surveying the scene in the street. His eyes went
straight to the group of men. I saw the slight frown disap-
pear, and the brown face became a mask, remote, cold, reflecting oddly the wariness that I had seen in the villagers.
Then he looked straight at me, and it was with something of

a shock that I met his eyes. They weren't dark, as I had expected. They were grey, very clear and light, and violently
alive.

He came down the last step and crossed to the door of the
car. The group melted away from us. He took no more notice
of them than he had of the hens, or the falling geranium
petals.

He looked down at me. "You seem to be in trouble. Is
there anything I can do?"

"I'd be terribly grateful if you *could* help me," I said. "I—
I've been trying to back the car."

"I see." I thought I heard amusement behind the pleasant
voice, but his face still expressed nothing. I said bleakly, "I
was trying to get it to go *there*." "There" was a space beyond
the curve of the road which, about fifty yards back, looked
as remote as the moon.

"And she won't go?"

"No," I said shortly.

"Is there something wrong with her?"

"Just," I said, "that I can't drive."

"Oh." It was amusement. I said quickly, "It's not my car."

Here the truck driver leaned out of his cabin and shouted
something in Greek, and the Englishman laughed. The laugh
transformed his face. The mask of rather careful indifference
broke up, and he looked all at once younger and quite ap-
proachable, even attractive. He shouted something back in
what sounded to me like excellent Greek. At any rate the
driver understood, because he nodded and withdrew into his
cab, and I heard the truck's engine begin to roar.

The newcomer laid a hand on the door.

"If you'll allow me, perhaps I can persuade her to go."

"I shouldn't be surprised," I said bitterly, as I moved over.
"I was told this was a man's country. It's true. Go ahead."

He got into the car. I found myself hoping that he would
miss the gears, forget to start the engine, leave the handbrake
on—do even a single one of the damned silly things I'd been
doing all day, but he didn't. To my fury the car moved
quietly backwards, slid into the cobbled space beyond the
corner, paused about two inches away from a house wall, and
waited there politely for the truck to pass.

It approached with an appalling noise and a cloud of black
smoke. As it drew level, its driver, leaning out of his cab,
yelled something at my companion and sent a grinning black-
eyed salutation to me that somehow, without a word being
intelligible, made me understand that, though incompetent,

I was female and therefore delightful, and that was just how it should be.

The truck roared on its way. I saw its driver glance back and lift a hand to the men who still stood in a little group near the café door. One or two of them responded, but most were still watching, not the car, but my companion.

I glanced at him. I knew then that I was right. He was aware of it too. His eyes, narrowed against the sun, showed none of that vivid aliveness that I had surprised in them. He sent the group a look, slow, appraising, utterly without expression. I thought he hesitated. A hand went to the car door, as if he were going to get out, then it dropped back onto the wheel, and he turned to me in inquiry.

I answered his look before he spoke. "Don't give a thought to my *amour-propre*, will you? Of course I should love you to drive the beastly thing through the village for me. I haven't a rag of pride left, and as long as I get this car to Delphi in one piece, my self-respect can be salvaged later. Believe me, I'm terribly grateful."

He smiled. "You must be tired, and it's dreadfully hot. Have you come far?"

"From Athens."

His brows shot up, but he said nothing. The car was moving with the minimum of noise and fuss through the narrow street. The little group of men had disappeared, melting chin-on-shoulder into the café as the car approached them. He didn't glance aside after them.

I said defiantly, "Yes, all the way. And not a scratch."

"Congratulations. . . . And here we are. Clear of the houses and all set for Delphi. You did say Delphi?"

"I did." I regarded him thoughtfully. "I suppose you wouldn't by any chance be going that way yourself?"

"As it happens, yes."

"Would you——?" I hesitated, then took the plunge. "Would you like a lift? In a manner of speaking, that is?"

"I should be delighted. And if the manner of speaking means will I drive—with pleasure, ma'am."

"That's wonderful." I relaxed with a little sigh. The car purred round the last corner and gathered speed up a long curling hill. "I've really quite enjoyed myself, but you know, I've missed half the scenery."

"Never mind. You brought some of it with you."

"What d'you mean?"

He said coolly, "The feathers on the hood. Very original they look, and quite striking."

"The—oh!" My hand flew to my mouth. *"Feathers?* Honestly?"

"Indeed yes. Lots of them."

I said guiltily, "That must be the hen just outside Levadia. At least, it was a cockerel. White ones?"

"Yes."

"Well, it was asking for it. I even hooted the horn, and if you'd heard this horn you'd know that cockerel was bent on death. I didn't kill him, though, really I didn't. I saw him come out the other side and dash away. It *is* only feathers, truly it is."

He laughed. He, too, seemed in some indefinable way to have relaxed. It was as if he had left his preoccupations behind him in Arachova, and with them that impression he had given of a rather formidable reserve. He might have been any pleasant, casually met stranger on holiday.

"No hen'll look at that chap till he's grown a new tail," he said cheerfully, "and you don't have to make excuses to me. It wasn't my cockerel."

"No," I said, "but I've a feeling this is your—" I stopped.

"This is what?"

"Oh, nothing. Merciful heavens, what a view!"

We were running along a high white road that hugged the side of Parnassus. Below us to the left the steep hillside fell away to the valley of the Pleistus, the river that winds down between Parnassus' great flanks and the rounded ridges of Mount Cirphis, towards the plain of Crissa and the sea. All along the Pleistus—at this season a dry white serpent of shingle beds that glittered in the sun—all along its course, filling the valley bottom with the tumbling, whispering green-silver of water, flowed the olive woods; themselves a river, a green-and-silver flood of plumy branches as soft as sea spray, over which the ever-present breezes slid, not as they do over corn, in flying shadows, but in whitening breaths, little gasps that lift and toss the olive crests for all the world like breaking spray. Long pale ripples followed one another down the valley. Where, at the valley's end, Parnassus thrust a sudden buttress of gaunt rock into the flood, the sea of grey trees seemed to break round it, flowing on, flooding out to fill the flat plain beyond, still rippling, still moving with the ceaseless sheen and shadow of flowing water, till in the west the motion was stilled against the flanks of the distant hills, and to the south against the sudden sharp bright gleam of the sea.

I said, after a while, "Are you staying in Delphi?"

"Yes. I've been there a few days. Have you come for long?"

I laughed. "Till the money gives out, and I'm afraid that won't be long enough. I only hope there'll be a room for me somewhere. I came up unexpectedly and haven't booked. Someone told me the Apollon was good."

"It's very nice. Delphi's fairly full just now, but you'll get a room somewhere, I'm sure. Perhaps we can persuade the Apollon to throw someone out for you." A pause. "Hadn't we better introduce ourselves? My name's Lester."

"I'm Camilla Haven." I hesitated. Could I possibly be right in my guess about him? I thought over it again: the villagers' reaction to the name Simon in Arachova; their de-meanor when this man appeared; the voice at my elbow murmuring, "He will help you. . . ." Together, they seemed to add up to the solution of my problem. I said slowly, watching him, "I've got a sort of alias today, though. You might say I'm . . . 'Simon's girl.' "

The dark brows shot up. One of those quick, light, electri-fying glances, then he was watching the road again. He said evenly, "How very gratifying. But why? Because I rescued you in Arachova?"

I felt the blood coming into my cheeks. I hadn't thought of that one. I said quickly, "No. I only meant I'd been deputiz-ing for her—the other girl—since Athens. With the car."

"The car?" he said blankly.

"Yes." I swallowed and shot a glance at him. This was going to sound even sillier than I had imagined. "This is—oh, dear, I've begun at the wrong end but . . . well, this is your car. The one from Athens."

I could see nothing in his glance this time except puzzle-ment, with possibly a dash of doubt about my sanity.

"I'm afraid I don't follow. My car? From Athens? And what 'other girl'? Forgive me, but—just what are you talking about?"

"I'm sorry. I shouldn't have jumped it on you like that. I'd better begin at the beginning. I—I've done a rather silly thing, and I hope you're not going to be too angry with me, Mr. Lester. I'll explain exactly how it happened in a moment, if you'll let me, but the important thing is that this is the car you're expecting. The girl you sent to hire it didn't turn up to claim it, and I was handed the key by mistake, so—well, I brought it up here for you. I—I hope it's all right. It was the most marvellous luck to find you—"

"Just a moment. Forgive me for interrupting, but—well, I

still haven't the remotest idea what you're talking about. You say someone hired this car in Athens and you were given the key, and drove it up here?"

"Yes." This time it was my voice that sounded flat and blank. "It wasn't—it wasn't you?"

"Decidedly not. I know nothing about a car from Athens or anywhere else."

"But back there in Arachova—" I hesitated, feeling more than ever confused and foolish.

"Yes?" The car slowed, dipped onto a little bridge set at an angle over a narrow gorge, then accelerated up the curling hill beyond. His tone was casual, but somehow I got the impression of sharp interest. "Just what made you think I ought to know about it?"

I said quickly, "Was I wrong? I thought . . . look, you *are* called Simon, aren't you?"

"That is my name. They told you in Arachova? Those men?"

"No. That is, yes, in a way. But . . . never mind that now. You did say you were staying in Delphi?"

"Yes."

I said flatly, stupidly, "Then it *must* be you! It must be!"

"I do assure you it isn't." The quick appraising glance he gave me must have shown him the distress in my face, because he smiled then, and said gently, "But I'm afraid I still don't quite see where the mystery comes in. Surely the garage also gave you the hirer's name and address? Have you lost it, or forgotten to write it down, or something?"

I said in a very small voice, "That's just it. I never knew it."

He looked startled, and then, I thought, amused. "I see. You never knew it. Except, I take it, that his name was Simon?"

"Yes. I told you I'd done something silly. It seemed all right at the time, and I thought in Arachova that it had turned out beautifully, like a story, but now . . ." My voice trailed away. I looked away from him across the blue depths of the valley, and spoke my thoughts with artless and quite unguarded emphasis. "Oh dear, and it would have been so *wonderful* if it *had* been you!"

The words were hardly out before I realized what they sounded like. For the second time in a few minutes I felt the heat wash scarlet into my cheeks. I opened my lips to say something, anything, but before I could speak he said pleasantly, "I wish it had. But look, don't worry so about it.

It can't be as bad as you think, and perhaps, if you'll let me, I can help you. Would you care to tell me just what's happened?"

I told him. I kept to a bare recital of the facts, from the moment when the little man approached me with the key, to the fateful second of decision which had landed me—so neatly, as I had thought—at Simon Lester's feet in Arachova. Only the facts: nothing of the miserable tangle of motive; the fear and self-questioning and uneasy bravado . . . but somehow, as I finished the story, I had a feeling that I had told him rather more than I intended. Oddly, I didn't mind. I had told him. He had said he would help. It was over to him. It was a familiar feeling, and yet not quite familiar. . . .

I sat back, relaxed and at ease for the first time since eleven that morning, while below us the breeze ran with white feet over the billowing olives, and beside us, along the high hot road, the sun beat the smell of dust out of the red earth, and the rock glowed and sent the heat back like a blast.

He had made no comment on the silly story as I told it. Now he merely said, "I see. So it really only amounts to this: that you've brought up an unknown car for an unknown man who wants it for something unspecified, and you don't know where to find him."

"That's not a very kind way of putting it, but—yes. I told you it was silly."

"Maybe. But in your place I'd have done exactly the same."

"*Would* you?"

He laughed. "Of course. What right-minded person could resist a challenge like that?"

"Honestly?"

"Honestly."

I let out a long breath. "You've no idea how much better you've made me feel! But at least you'd have managed the adventure properly! It seems to me that it's not enough to be bold; one has to be competent as well. *You'd* never have got stuck in Arachova—and if you had, you'd have been able to back the car!"

"Ah, yes," he said, "Arachova." The shutters were up once more. He added, half under his breath, "Simon, of Delphi. . . ."

I said quickly, "It does seem odd, doesn't it? That there should be two? I told you that the man from Crissa didn't know anyone of that name hereabouts. Delphi's small, isn't it?

"Lord, yes."

"Then he'd know, wouldn't he? That was why I was so sure it must be you."

He didn't answer. There was that look again, smooth, blank; the unclimbable wall with spikes at the top. I gave him a doubtful glance he didn't see, and said, tentatively, "Could there have been some kind of mistake? I mean, suppose it *is* you; suppose someone got a message wrong, and the whole thing is just a mix-up? Do you know anyone in Athens, perhaps, who might have—?"

"No." The syllable was definite to the point of curtness. "It's quite impossible. I've had no communication with Athens during the last week at all, so it's hard to see how any message can have gone astray. And you say it was a girl who did the hiring. I've no idea who that could be. No, I'm afraid it's nothing whatever to do with me." A pause, then he added in a different voice, as if he felt he had been too abrupt, "But please don't worry about it any more. We'll soon get it straightened out, and then you can settle down and enjoy Delphi. I think you'll vote it's been worth it."

"It'll have to be pretty good."

"It is." He nodded, almost idly, ahead of the car. "You can't see the village from here, but the ruins are this side of the bluff, in the curve of the mountain under those high cliffs. There—that's Apollo's temple, below the cliffs they call the Shining Ones. You see?"

I saw. Ahead of us the mountain thrust that great buttress out into the valley, the river of olive trees swirling round it as the water swirls round the prow of a ship, to spread out beyond into a great flat lake that filled the plain. High up, in the angle where the bluff joined the mountain, I saw it, Apollo's temple, six columns of apricot stone, glowing against the climbing darkness of the trees behind. Above them soared the sunburned cliffs; below was a tumble, as yet unrecognizable, of what must be monument and treasury and shrine. From where we were the pillars seemed hardly real; not stone that had ever felt hand or chisel, but insubstantial, the music-built columns of legend: Olympian building, left floating—warm from the god's hand—between sky and earth. Above, the indescribable sky of Hellas; below, the silver tide of the olives everlastingly rippling down to the sea. No house, no man, no beast. As it was in the beginning.

I realized then that Simon Lester had stopped the car. We must have stood there for some minutes, at the edge of the road, in the shadow of a stone pine. He didn't speak, and neither did I.

But I noticed that it wasn't Apollo's shining columns that held him. His gaze was on something nearer at hand, away up the side of Parnassus above the road. I followed his look, but could see nothing; only the bare rock shifting and flowing upwards with the liquid shimmer of the heat.

After a bit I said merely, "And the village is just the other side of the bluff?"

"Yes. The road runs through those trees below the ruins and then round that shoulder into Delphi. Beyond the village it drops rather steeply to the plain. Crissa—where your friend in the café comes from—is about halfway down. At the bottom the road forks for Amphissa and Itea."

"Itea? That's the fishing port, isn't it? Where the pilgrims used to land in the old days when they were making for the shrine?"

"Yes. You can just see the houses away over there at the edge of the sea." He turned the subject abruptly, but so smoothly that I realized that he was following his own thoughts, and that these had not been about the view, or the road to Itea. "I'm still rather curious to know how you knew my name. I understand it was from those men in Arachova. Was . . . something said?"

"Not really. I'd been trying to explain to the men why I really didn't dare try and reverse the car there—I'd never reversed it before, of course, and it *is* such a length. I told them it wasn't mine, but that it was for someone called Simon, at Delphi. I thought they looked as if that meant something. . . . Then one of them said something to the others, and they all turned and stared at you. It was just the way they looked, somehow. I don't know if you noticed?"

"I noticed."

"Well, that was all. I suppose, when you arrived, they assumed that you were the person to deal with the car. Then, when you told me you came from Delphi, I guessed you might be Simon—my 'Simon.' They . . ."—I hesitated—"they seemed to assume you were the right one, too."

There was an infinitesimal pause before his hand went to the ignition. "Ah, well," he said smoothly, "the sooner we get to Delphi and find your man, the better, don't you think?"

"I do indeed." I laughed. "After all this, we'll probably find him watching beside the road and dancing with impatience; that is, if the little man was right and it really is a matter—" I stopped. Until I repeated the words, half-automatically, I'd forgotten them myself.

"It is what?"

I said slowly, looking at him, "A matter of life and death. . . ."

We were moving again, quickly now. Below us the sea of olives flowed and rippled like smoke. Above, the pitiless sun beat down on the rock with a heat like the clang of brass.

He said, "Is that all he told you?"

"Yes. But he repeated it."

" 'A matter of life and death'?"

"Just that. Only of course we were speaking in French. The phrase was *'il y va de la vie.'* "

"And you got the impression he meant it seriously?"

I said slowly, "Yes. I believe I did. I don't know if I took it in really urgently at the time, but you know, I think that's really why I did this silly thing with the car."

"You took the car, and the risks with it, because of some subconscious feeling of urgency about the affair?"

I said, "That makes it sound more definite than it was, and there were—other reasons. . . . But yes. Yes."

The car roared up a long incline, swept round and down a curling hill. I leaned back against the hot leather, folded my hands in my lap, and said, not looking at him, "If the little man was right, it's just as well you're not 'Simon,' isn't it?"

He said, quite without expression, "Just as well. And here we are. What comes first? Simon, or the hotel?"

"Both. I imagine the hotel people are as likely to know of him as anyone, and at least I expect they speak English. My six words of Greek won't get me very far alone."

"On the other hand," said Simon gravely, "they might get you a good deal further than you intended."

CHAPTER

4

"And thou camest to Crissa under sow-clad Parnassus, to its foot that faces west, and rocks overhang the spot, and a hollow, stony, wood-clad vale stretches beneath it."

Homeric *Hymn to Apollo*.

To my relief the hotel had a room to offer.

"But only for tonight, I'm afraid," said the proprietor, who spoke, after all, excellent English. "I deeply regret, but I cannot be certain about tomorrow. I have had a—what do you call it? A provisional booking. Perhaps I can take you, perhaps not. If not, there is the Kastalia further along the street, or the Tourist Pavilion at the other end of Delphi. It has a magnificent view, but," he smiled charmingly, "it is very expensive."

"It couldn't have a better view than this," I said.

This was true. The village consists only of two or three rows of flat-topped houses, washed ochre and pink and dazzling white, set in their tiers along the steep side of the hill. At the beginning of the village the road divides into a Y that makes the two main streets, and at the junction stands the Apollon Hotel, facing over the valley towards the distant gleam of the Corinthian Gulf.

Outside the hotel, on the edge of the road which was used as a terrace, two big plane trees made a deep island of shade for some wooden tables and chairs. Simon Lester had parked the car just beyond these, and was waiting there. When I had completed the formalities of booking I went out to speak to him.

"It's all right. They can take me for tonight, and just at the moment that's all I care about." I held out my hand. "I have to thank you very much, Mr. Lester. I don't quite know where I'd have been without your help. I've a feeling it might have been somewhere at the bottom of the valley, with the eagles of Zeus picking my bones!"

"It was a pleasure." He was looking down at me, measuringly. "And now what are you planning to do? Rest and have some tea first, or is that"—a gesture indicated the car—"worrying you too much?"

I said uncertainly, "It is, rather. I think I'd better go right ahead and do what I can."

"Look," he said, "if you'll forgive my saying so, you look as if you'd better have that rest. Won't you please leave this to me, at any rate for the time being? Why don't you go and lie down, and have tea brought to your room—they make excellent tea here, by the way—while I make a few inquiries for you?"

"Why, I—you mustn't—I mean, it's absurd that you should be landed with my difficulties," I said, a little confusedly, and conscious only of a strong desire that he should, in fact, be landed with them all. I finished feebly, "I couldn't let you."

"Why not? It would be too cruel if you turned on me now and told me to mind my own business."

"I didn't mean it like that. You know I didn't. It's only—"

"That it's your affair and you want to see it through? Of course. But I must confess I'm seething with curiosity myself by now, and after all it's partly my affair too, since my alter ego has managed to involve me. I really would be very grateful if you'd let me help. Besides," he added, "wouldn't you honestly much rather go and have a rest and some tea now, while I do the detecting for you in my fluent but no doubt peculiar Greek?"

"I—" I hesitated again, then said truthfully, "I should adore to."

"Then that's settled." He glanced at his wrist. "It's about twenty past four now. Shall we say an hour? I'll report back at five-thirty. Right?"

"Right." I looked at him a little helplessly. "But if you do find him, and he's angry—"

"Well?"

"I don't want you made responsible for what's happened. It wouldn't be fair, and I'd much rather face my own music."

"You'd be surprised," he said cryptically, "how responsible I feel already. All right, then. See you later."

With a quick wave of the hand he was gone down the steps to the lower road.

My room overlooked the valley, and had a long window with a balcony. The shutters were closed against the sun, but even so the room seemed full of light, globed in light, incandescent with it. As the door shut behind the maid who had shown me upstairs, I went across to the window and pulled back the shutters. Like a blast the heat met me. The sun was wheeling over now towards the west, full across the valley from my window, and valley and plain were heavy with sleepy heat. The tide of olives had stilled itself, and even the illusion of coolness created by those rippling grey leaves was gone. In the distance the wedge of shining water that showed at the edge of the plain struck at the eyes like the flash from a burning-glass.

I closed my eyes against it, pulling the shutters to again. Then I slipped off my dress, and had a long, cool wash. I sat on the edge of the bed for some minutes after that, brushing my hair, till I heard the maid coming back with the tea. I had my tea—Simon Lester had been right about its excellence—propped against pillows, and with my feet up on the bed. I don't think I thought any more about Simon —either of the Simons—or about the car, or about anything except the shadowed quiet of the little white room.

Presently I put the tray off my knees onto the table by the bed, and lay back to relax. Before I knew it was even near, sleep had overtaken me. . . .

I woke to a feeling of freshness and the incongruous sound of rain. But the light still drove white against the shutters, and when I opened them a crack I saw that the sun still blazed, deeper now and lower, but at full power. Half my window was in shadow now, where the plane trees put a bough or two between it and the falling sun. The sound of rain, I realized, was the sound of their leaves, pattering and rustling in the breeze that had got up to cool the evening.

I glanced down at the terrace below the balcony. He was there, sitting under one of the plane trees, smoking. His chair was pulled up to the railing that edged the terrace, and one arm lay along this. He sat there, relaxed, looking at nothing, completely at ease. The car was standing where he had parked it before. If—as appeared to be the case—he had not located another "Simon" to deliver it to, the fact didn't appear to worry him unduly.

I reflected, as I looked down at him thoughtfully, that it would probably take a good deal to worry Simon Lester. That quiet manner, that air of being casually and good-temperedly on terms with life . . . with it all went something that is particularly hard to describe. To say that he knew what he wanted and took it, would be to give the wrong impression; it was rather that whatever decisions he had to make, were made, and then dismissed—this with an ease that argued an almost frightening brand of self-confidence.

I don't know how much of this I saw in him on that first day; it may be that I simply recognized straightaway the presence of qualities I myself so conspicuously lacked; but I do remember the immediate and vivid impression I got of a self-sufficiency harder and more complete than anything conveyed in years of Philip's *grand-seigneur* gasconading, and at the same time quite different in quality. I didn't see yet where the difference lay. I only know that I felt obscurely grateful to Simon for not having made me feel too much of a fool, and, less obscurely, for having so calmly undertaken to help me in the matter of the "other Simon. . . ."

I wondered, as I closed the shutters again, if he had even bothered to make the gesture of looking for him.

On the whole, I imagined not.

In this, it seemed, I had done him less than justice.

When I went downstairs I found him, hands thrust deep in trouser pockets, in earnest contemplation of the car, together with a Greek to whose bright blue shirt was pinned the insignia of a guide.

Simon looked up and smiled at me. "Rested?"

"Perfectly, thank you. And the tea *was* good."

"I'm glad to hear it. Perhaps you're strong enough, then, to bear the blow?" He jerked his head towards the car.

"I thought as much. You've not found him?"

"Not a sign. I've been to the other hotels, but there's no visitor of that name. Then I went along to the Museum to meet George here. He tells me that he doesn't know anyone called Simon in Delphi, either."

The Greek said, "Only yourself, *Kyrie* Lester."

"Only myself," agreed Simon.

I said, rather helplessly, "What shall we do?"

"*Kyrie* Lester," said the Greek, watching him rather curiously, "could it not be, perhaps, that there *is* no other Simon? And that it is not a mistake? That someone is—how do you put it?—using your name?"

"Taking my name in vain?" Simon laughed, but I knew that this had already occurred to him. It had occurred to me, too. "It doesn't seem likely. For one thing, who would? And for another, if they did, and it was urgent, they'd surely have appeared by now to claim the damned thing."

"That is probably true."

"You can bet it's true. But I'm going to get to the bottom of this very odd little affair—and not only for the sake of Miss Haven here, who's worried about it. Look, George, you are sure about it? No Simons at all, however unlikely? A grandfather with a wooden leg, or a mule-boy aged seven and a half, or one of the men working up on the exacavations?"

"About the last I do not know, of course, though assuredly you are right and they would have come to look for it. In Delphi, nobody. Nobody at all."

"Then the places nearby? You're a native, aren't you? You'll know a fair number of people all round here. Crissa, for instance. It might be Crissa . . . that's only a few kilometres away. What about that?"

George shook his head. "No. I am sure. I would have remembered. And in Arachova . . ."

Simon ran a finger along the wing of the car, then contemplated the tip for a moment. "Yes?"

George said, regretfully, "No, I do not remember anyone in Arachova, either."

Simon took out a handkerchief and wiped his fingertip clean again. "In any case I can find out. I'm going back there tonight."

The Greek gave him a quick bright glance that held, I thought, curiosity. But he only said, "Ah. Well, I regret, but that is all I can tell you, except—oh, but that is not the same; it is of no use to you."

"We'll have it, though, please. You've thought of someone?"

George said slowly, "There is a Simonides at Itea. I do not think this is the man, but he is the only one I know of. But perhaps, *kyrie*, you would like to ask someone else? I do not know everybody, me. Elias Sarantopoulou, my cousin, he is also in the Tourist Police. He is at the office now, or perhaps he is at the cafe . . . if you like to come with me I will show you the place; it is opposite the Post Office."

"I know it," said Simon. "Thanks, but I really doubt if your cousin will know any more than you. This is an irritating little problem, isn't it? It'll probably solve itself very soon, but meanwhile I suppose we must do something. We'll try your Simonides at Itea. Who is Simonides, what is he?"

George, of course, took him literally. "He has a little

baker's shop near the cinema in the middle of the main street, facing the sea. Giannakis Simonides." He glanced at his wrist. "The bus goes in ten minutes. The shop is not far from the place where the bus stops."

Simon said, "We have a car," then grinned as he caught my eye. My answering smile was a rather brittle one. The car stood there like a mockery. I hated the sight of it.

Simon nodded to George, said something in Greek, then pulled open the car door for me.

I said doubtfully, "Ought we to?"

"Why not? This is a quite legitimate attempt at delivery. Come along, the sooner we get down to Itea the better. It'll be dark in an hour. Are you tired?"

"Not now. But—you'll drive, won't you, Mr. Lester?"

"You bet I will. You haven't seen the Itea road. And please call me Simon. It's more euphonious than 'Mr. Lester,' and besides . . ." his grin, as he slid into his seat beside me, was malicious ". . . it'll give you an illusion of comfort."

I didn't answer that one, except with a look, but as we drove off I said suddenly, and almost to my own surprise, "I'm beginning to feel frightened."

The glance he gave me held surprise but, oddly enough, no amusement. "That's a strong word."

"I suppose so. Perhaps it isn't, either, from me. I'm the world's most complete coward. I—I wish I'd had the sense to let well enough alone. The beastly thing should still be standing there in Omonia Square, and —"

"And you'd still be wishing madly you were in Delphi?"

"There is that," I acknowledged. "But you do see, don't you?"

"Of course I do."

The car had crept carefully through Delphi's narrow upper street, topped the rise opposite the presbytery, and then dived down to meet the lower road out of the village.

I said abruptly, "Do you suppose for a moment that this Simonides is the man we're looking for?"

"It doesn't seem very probable." Perhaps he felt this to be a little brusque, for he added, "We might as well try it, all the same."

"Something to make me feel progress is being made?" No answer to this. I said, "You know, it really would be carrying coincidence a bit too far to suppose there are two Simons in Delphi."

"It's not," he said evenly, "a very common name."

I waited, but he didn't speak again. We had left the village behind, dropping in a gradual descent between dykes of red earth and stones where the road had been recently widened. The ditches and mounds showed raw as wounds in the sunburnt earth. The rich rays of the now-setting sun flooded it with strong amber light against which the dry thistles that grew everywhere stood up delicate and sharp, like intricate filigree of copper wire. Above the road the new hotel, the Tourist Pavilion, showed as raw and new and wounding as the torn ditches alongside us. The curved windows flashed as we passed beneath and wheeled into the first hairpin of the descent to the plain of olives.

I said casually, "Are you just holidaying here in Delphi?"

I had meant it as a non sequitur, a conversational makeweight, the normal casual query with which you might greet anyone you met in such a place; but even as I said it I could hear how it pointed back to my last remark. I started to say something else, but he was already answering without any indication that he saw my question as other than innocent.

"In a way. I'm a schoolmaster. I have a house at Wintringham. Classics is my subject."

Whatever I had expected it wasn't this; this seal and parchment of respectability. I said feebly, "Then of course you're interested in the classical sites. Like me."

"Don't tell me you're a colleague? Another beggarly usher?"

"Afraid so."

"Classics?"

"Yes. Only in a girls' school that just means Latin, to my sorrow and shame."

"You don't know Ancient Greek?"

"A little. A very little. Enough sometimes to catch a word and follow what's being said. Enough to know my alphabet and make a wild guess at what some of the notices mean, and to have had a queer feeling at the pit of the stomach when I went to see *Antigone* in the Herodes Atticus Theatre in Athens and heard the chorus calling on Zeus against that deep black sky that had heard the same call for three thousand years." I added, feeling slightly ashamed of what I'd let him see, "What a ghastly road."

The car heeled yet again round a hairpin curve and plunged on down the great shoulder of Parnassus that sticks out into the Crissa Plain. Below us was a village, and below it again the flood of olives, flowing mile-wide now down to the sea.

Simon said cheerfully, "The buses all have icons stuck up in front of the driver, *and* with a little red light in front, run off the battery. On this road the icon swings madly from side to side at the bends and everybody crosses themselves."

I laughed. "Including the driver?"

"This is true. Yes, including the driver. I have a feeling that sometimes," said Simon, "he also shuts his eyes." He pulled the big car round an even sharper bend, missed an up-coming truck by inches, and added, "You can open yours now. This is Crissa."

I felt the colour come into my cheeks. "I'm sorry. I must be losing my nerve."

"You're still tired, that's all. We'll have something to drink in Itea before we seek out this Simonides."

"No, please," I protested, almost too quickly.

He eyed me for a moment. "You really are scared, aren't you?"

"I—yes, I am."

"I shouldn't worry; I really shouldn't. It can't matter, or it'd have been settled long before this."

"I know. I know it's nonsense. It's silly and it's trivial and it doesn't mean a thing, but I told you I'm the world's worst coward. It's true. I've been persuading myself for years that I'd be as competent and self-sufficient as anyone else, given the chance, but now I know. . . . Why, I can't even bear *scenes,* so why I ever thought I could get away with this sort of mayhem I have no idea." I stopped. It occurred to me with a queer little shock that I would never have said anything like that to Philip, not in a hundred years.

Simon was saying calmly, "Never mind. I'm here, aren't I? Whatever we get into, I'll talk you out of it, so sit back and relax."

"If," I said, "we find Simon."

"If," said Simon, "we do."

I was glad enough, when we got to Itea, to leave everything to him.

Itea is the port which in ancient times saw the landing of the pilgrims bound for the shrine of Apollo at Delphi. The shrine was a religious centre for the whole ancient world for many hundreds of years, and to us nowadays, used to modern transport, it is astonishing to contemplate the distances that men travelled on foot and on horseback or in small ships, to worship the God of light and peace and healing, or to ask the advice of the famous Oracle enshrined below the temple. The easy way was by Itea. The sea journey, for all its hazards, was less exhausting and dangerous than the journey by road

through the mountains, and here into the little port of Itea
the pilgrims crowded, to see from the harbour the winding
river valley of the Pleistus and, beyond the shoulder of Parnassus where modern Delphi stands, the bright cliffs of the
Shining Ones that guard the holy spring.

Today Itea is a grubby little fishing village, with one long
street of shops and *tavernas* facing the sea and separated from
it by the road and then perhaps fifty yards of dusty boulevard
where pepper trees give shade and the men of the village
gather for the usual drinks and ices and sticky honey-cakes.

Simon stopped the car under the trees and led me to a
rickety iron table which seemed to have fewer attendant
wasps than the others. I would have liked tea again, but felt
so ashamed of this insular craving—and so doubtful of getting anything approaching what I wanted—that I asked for
fresh lemonade, and got it, delicious and cold and tangy with
the real fruit, and with it a *pasta* something like shredded
wheat, but frantically oversweet with honey and chopped
nuts. It was wonderful. The wasps loved it too. When we had
finished it, I defiantly asked for another, and stayed to eat
it while Simon went off to look for the baker's shop of
Simonides.

I watched him go, thoughtfully beating off an extra-large
and persistent wasp.

Somehow I didn't think Giannakis Simonides was our man.
"Monsieur Simon, at Delphi . . ." And there was only one
Monsieur Simon at Delphi.

There was that queer reserve, too, in Simon's manner; there
was Arachova; and the way he had shelved my question as to
what he was doing in Delphi. The thing had ceased to be a
slightly awkward puzzle. It was fast becoming a mystery,
with Simon Lester at its centre. And Simon's girl . . .

I finished my cake now and got up. Simon had paid the
waiter before he had left me. I could see him standing in a
doorway some distance up the street. The place was apparently a restaurant, for outside it stood the big charcoal
stove, and over this a whole lamb revolved slowly on the
spit, which was being turned by a stout woman in a blue
apron. Simon appeared to be questioning her; she was nodding vigorously, and then, with a wave of her free hand,
seemed to be directing him further up the street.

He looked back, saw me standing under the pepper trees,
and raised a hand in salute. Then he made a vague gesture
towards the other end of the street, and set off that way, walking fast.

Taking his gesture to mean that he had some information, but that he didn't expect me to follow him, I stayed where I was and watched him. He went perhaps a hundred yards, hesitated, then glanced up at a billboard and plunged into the darkness of a deserted cinema. As he vanished, I turned in the opposite direction and began to walk along the boulevard. I was only too thankful to leave the enquiry to him. If he really was in the centre of the mystery, he could keep it to himself, and welcome. . . .

Meanwhile I would do what I had come to Delphi for. Since chance had brought me down to Itea, the start of the ancient pilgrimage, I would try and see the shrine as the old pilgrims had seen it on their first landing from the Corinthian Gulf.

I walked quickly along the harbour's edge. On my right the sea paled towards sunset, and across the opal shimmer of the bay came a fishing boat, turquoise and white, with her prow raked in a proud pure curve above its liquid image. Under a sail of that same scarlet had the worshippers come into harbour when the God was still at Delphi.

I left the sea's edge and walked rapidly across the street. I wanted to get behind the ugly row of houses, back into the old olive woods, where I could look straight up towards the Pleistus valley with nothing but immemorial rock and tree and sky between me and the shrine.

Behind the main street were a few sorry alleys of concrete, with houses, as usual, scattered seemingly at random in the dust patches between the trees. I passed the last house, skirted a building that looked like a ruined warehouse, and followed a cracked stretch of concrete which appeared to lead straight into the outskirts of the forest of olives. The concrete was criss-crossed with cracks, like crazy paving, and thistles grew in the fissures. I startled a browsing donkey, and it plunged off under the trees in a smother of dust, to be lost in the shadows. Soon the concrete came to an end, and I found myself walking through soft earth in the deeper twilight of the trees. The breeze had strengthened with the approach of evening, and overhead the olives had resumed their liquid rippling.

I hurried on towards a space ahead where stronger light promised a clearing. I was lucky. There was a slight rise in the ground, and to the north of it the great olives thinned. From the top of the little ridge, across the ruffling crests of the trees, I could see the old Pilgrims' Way, unscarred by my own century. I stood for a few minutes, gazing up towards the shrine in the now rapidly fading light.

The temple columns were invisible behind the curve of the Crissa bluff, but there was the black cleft of Castalia, and above it the great cliffs whose names are Flamboyant and Roseate, the Shining Ones. . . . The dying sun ran up the Flamboyant cliff like fire.

This was, I thought, the way to come to Delphi . . . not straight up into the ruins in the wake of a guide, but to land from a small boat in a bay of pearl, and see it as they would have seen it, flaming in the distance like a beacon, the journey's end.

Something like a fleck of darkness went by my cheek. A bat. It was deep twilight now, the swift-falling Aegean dusk. I turned to see lights pricking out in the houses behind me. I could just see the streetlamps, faint and far between, along the sea front. They looked a long way away. Where I stood the shadow of a huge olive brooded like a cloud. I turned to go back to the village.

Instead of returning the way I had come, I took what I judged to be the direction of the car, and, plunging down from the ridge into the depths of the wood, I set off quickly through the twisted and shadowy trunks.

I had gone perhaps a hundred yards before the trees began to thin. Some way off to my left I saw the lights of the first house, an outpost of the village, and was hurrying towards it through the soft dust when a sudden flash of light quite near me, and to my right, brought me up short, startled. It was the flash of an electric torch, deep in the trees. Perhaps my adventures of the day had worked on my imagination rather too well, or perhaps it was the ancient mystery that I had been attempting to call up, but the fact remains that I felt suddenly frightened, and stood very still, with the trunk of an enormous olive between me and the torch-light.

Then I realized what it was. There was a house set by itself deep in the grove, the usual two-windowed box of a place with its woodpile and its lean-to shed and its scrawny chickens gone to roost in the vine. The flash I had seen showed me a man bending over a motor vehicle of some sort which was parked close to the side of the house. It looked like a jeep. As I watched he jerked the hood open, shone the light into the engine, and leaned over it. I saw his face highlighted by the queerly refracted light, a very Greek face, dark, with hair crisping down the wide cheekbones in the manner of the heroes, and a roundish head covered with close curls like a statue's.

Then somebody in the cottage must have kindled the lamp, for a soft oblong of light slanted out of one of the windows, showing the dusty clutter outside—a woodman's block with the axe still sunk in it and gleaming as the light caught it, a couple of old gasoline cans, and a chipped enamel bowl for the hens' food. My causeless fear vanished and I turned quickly to go.

The man by the jeep must have seen the movement of my skirt in the darkness, because he looked up. I caught a glimpse of his face before the torch went out. He was smiling. I turned and hurried away. As I went, I thought the torch-beam flicked out to touch me momentarily, but the Greek made no move to follow.

Simon was sitting in the car, smoking. He got out when he saw me and came round to open my door. He answered my look with a shake of the head.

"No go. I've asked all the questions I could and it's a dead end." He got into the driver's seat and started the engine. "I really think we'll have to call it a day—go back to Delphi and have dinner and leave it to sort itself out in its own good time."

"But will it?"

He turned the car and started back towards Delphi. "I think so."

Bearing in mind what I had been thinking before about the "mystery," I didn't argue. I said simply, "Then we'll leave it. As you wish."

I saw him glance at me sideways, but he made no comment. The lights of the village were behind us, and we gathered speed up the narrow road. He dropped something into my lap, a leafy twig that smelt delicious when my fingers touched it.

"What is it?"

"Basil. The herb of kings."

I brushed it to and fro across my lips. The smell was sweet and minty, pungent above the smell of dust. "The pot of basil? Was it under this stuff that poor Isabella buried Lorenzo's head?"

"That's it."

There was a pause. We passed a crossroads where our lights showed a sign, AMPHISSA 9. We turned right for Crissa.

"Did you go to look for the Pilgrims' Way back there in Itea?" asked Simon.

"Yes. I got a wonderful view just before the light went. The Shining Ones were terrific."

"You found the ridge, then?"

I must have sounded surprise. "You know it? You've been here before?"

"I was down here yesterday."

"In Itea?"

"Yes." The road was climbing now. After a short silence he said, with no perceptible change of expression, "You know, I really don't know any more about it than you do."

The basil leaves were cool and still against my mouth. At length I said, "I'm sorry. Did I make it so obvious? But what was I to think?"

"Probably just what you did think. The thing's slightly crazy anyway, and I doubt if it'll prove to matter at all." I saw him smile. "Thank you for not pretending you didn't know what I meant."

"But I did. I'd been thinking about very little else myself."

"I know that. But nine women out of ten would have said 'What d'you mean?' and there we'd have been, submerged in a lovely welter of personalities and explanations."

"There wasn't any need of either."

Simon said, " 'O rare for Antony.' "

I said involuntarily, "What d'you mean?"

He laughed then. "Skip it. Will you have dinner with me tonight?"

"Why, thank you, Mr. Lester—"

"Simon."

"Simon, then, but perhaps I should—I mean—"

"That's wonderful then. At your hotel?"

"Look, I didn't say—"

"You owe it to me," said Simon coolly.

"I owe it to you? I do not! How d'you work that out?"

"As reparation for suspecting me of—whatever you did suspect me of." We were climbing through the twisting street of Crissa, and as we passed a lighted shop he glanced at his wrist. "It's nearly seven now. Could you bear to dine in half an hour's time—say at half past seven?"

I gave up. "Whenever it suits you. But isn't that fearfully early for Greece? Are you so very hungry?"

"Reasonably. But it's not that. I—well, I've things to do and I want to get them done tonight."

"I see. Well, it won't be too early for me. I only had a snack for lunch, and I was too frightened to enjoy that. So thank you. I'd like that. At the Apollon, you said? You're not staying there yourself?"

"No. When I got here the place was full up so I got permission to sleep in the studio up the hill. You won't have seen it yet. It's a big ugly square building a couple of hundred feet up behind the village."

"A studio? An artist's studio, do you mean?"

"Yes. I don't know what it was used for originally, but now it has a caretaker, and is let out to visiting artists and bona fide students who can't afford to pay for a hotel. I suppose I'm up there under slightly false pretences, but I wanted to be in Delphi for some days and I couldn't find a room. Now that I'm settled into the studio I find it'll do me admirably. There's only one other tenant at present, an English boy, who's a genuine artist . . . and good, too, though he won't let you say so."

"But surely you've a perfectly good claim on the studio, too?" I said. "After all, you count as a student. And as a classicist you've a bona fide claim on any concession. It's not a question of 'false pretences' at all."

He sent me a sideways look that I couldn't read in the darkness. He said rather shortly, "I'm not here to pursue my classical studies."

"Oh." It sounded lame, and I hoped it hadn't sounded like a question. But the syllable hung there between us like a dominant awaiting resolution.

Simon said suddenly, into the darkness straight ahead, "My brother Michael was here during the war."

Crissa was below us now. Far down to our left as we climbed along the face of the bluff the lights of Itea were strung along like beads under the thin moon.

He said, still in that expressionless way, "He was in the Peloponnese for some time, as B.L.O.—that's British Liaison Officer—between our chaps and the *andartes*, the Greek guerrillas under Zervas. Later he moved over into the Pindus region with ELAS, the main resistance group. He was in this part of the country in nineteen forty-four. He stayed with some people in Arachova; a shepherd called Stephanos and his son Nikolaos. Nikolaos is dead, but Stephanos still lives in Arachova. I went over to try and see him today, but he's away in Levadia, and not expected back till this evening—so the woman of his house told me."

"The woman of his house?"

He laughed. "His wife. You'll find everyone has to belong,

hereabouts. Every man belongs to a place, and I'm afraid that every woman belongs to a man."

"I believe you," I said, without rancour. "I suppose it gives meaning to her life, poor thing?"

"But of course. . . . Anyway I'm going down to Arachova again tonight to see Stephanos."

"I see. Then this is a—a sort of pilgrimage for you? A genuine pilgrimage to Delphi?"

"You could call it that. I've come to appease his shade."

I caught my breath. "Oh. How stupid of me. I'm sorry. I didn't realize."

"That he died? Yes."

"Here?"

"Yes, in nineteen forty-four. Somewhere on Parnassus."

We had wheeled up onto the last stretch of the road before Delphi. To our left blazed the lighted windows of the luxurious Tourist Pavilion. Far down now on the right the thin moon was already dying out in a welter of stars. The sea was faintly luminous beneath them, like a black satin ribbon.

Something made me say suddenly, into the dark, "Simon."

"Yes?"

"Why did you say 'appease'?"

A little silence. Then he spoke quite lightly. "I'll tell you about that, if I may. But not just at this moment. Here's Delphi. I'll leave you and the car at your hotel, and I'll meet you on the terrace here in half an hour. Right?"

"Right." The car drew up where it had stood before. He came round and opened my door for me. I got out, and when I would have turned to repeat some words of thanks for his help in my afternoon's quest he shook his head, laughed, raised a hand in farewell and vanished up the steep lane beside the hotel.

With a feeling that things were moving altogether too fast for me, I turned and went indoors.

CHAPTER

5

> "But enough of tales—I have wept for these
> things once already."
>
> EURIPIDES: *Helen*
> (tr. Philip Vellacott).

Any fears I might have had that Simon's melancholy pilgrimage would be allowed to cloud my first visit to Delphi
were dispelled when I came down at length to dinner, and
walked out to the hotel terrace to find a table.

Seven-thirty was certainly an outrageously early hour for
dining in Greece, and only one other of the tables under the
plane trees was occupied, and that, too, by English people.
Simon Lester wasn't there yet, so I sat down under one of
the trees from whose dark boughs hung lights, which swung
gently in the warm evening air. I saw Simon then below the
terrace railing, making one of an extremely gay and noisy
group of Greeks which surrounded a fair boy in the garb of
a hiker, and a very small donkey almost hidden under its
awkwardly loaded panniers.

The fair young man looked very much as if he had just
completed some arduous trek in the wilds. His face, hands,
and clothes were filthy; he had a generous stubble on his
chin, and his eyes—I could see it even from where I sat—
were bloodshot with fatigue. The donkey was in rather better case, and stood smugly beside him, under its load of what
appeared to be the paraphernalia of an artist—boxes, roughly
wrapped canvases, and a small collapsible easel, as well as a
sleeping bag and the rather unappetizing end of a large black
loaf.

Half the youth of Delphi seemed to have rallied to the
stranger's welcome, like the wasps to my honey-cake. There
was a great deal of loud laughter, atrocious English, and
back-slapping—the last an attention which the stranger
could well have done without. He was reeling with tiredness,
but a white grin split the dirty bearded face as he responded

to the welcome. Simon was laughing too, pulling the donkey's ears and exchanging what appeared to be the most uproarious of jokes with the young Greeks. Frequent cries of "Avanti! Avanti!" puzzled me, till I realized that they coincided with the jolly slaps under which the donkey, too, was reeling. At each slap a cloud of dust rose from Avanti's fur.

Eventually Simon looked up and saw me. He said something to the fair boy, exchanged some laughing password with the Greeks, and came swiftly up to the terrace.

"I'm sorry, have you been waiting long?"

"No, I've just come down. What's going on down there? A modern Stevenson?"

"Just that. He's a Dutch painter who's been making his way through the mountains with a donkey, and sleeping rough. He's done pretty well. He's just here from Jannina now, and that's a long way through rough country."

"He certainly got a welcome," I said, laughing. "It looked as if all Delphi had turned out."

"Even the tourist traffic hasn't quite spoiled the Greek *philoxenia*—the 'welcome' that literally means 'love of a stranger,'" said Simon, "though goodness knows Delphi ought to be getting a bit blasé by now. At least he'll get the traditional night's lodging free."

"Up at the studio?"

"Yes. This is the end of his trek. Tomorrow, he says, he'll sell Modestine—the donkey Avanti—and get the bus for Athens."

I said, "I thought when I saw the easel and what-not that he must be your English painter friend from the studio."

"Nigel? No. I doubt if a venture like that would ever occur to Nigel. He hasn't the self-confidence."

"You said he was a good painter, though?"

"I think he's good," said Simon, picking up the menu and absently handing it to me. It was in Greek, so I handed it back again. "But he's convinced himself—or else some fool has told him—that his own particular style is no good any more. I admit it's not the fashion, but the boy can draw like an angel when he likes, and I should have thought that was a gift rare enough to command attention even among some of today's more strident talents." He handed me the menu. "He doesn't use colour much—what will you have to start with?—but the drawing's very sure and delicate, and exciting at the same time."

I gave the menu back to him. He scrutinized the scrawled

columns. "Hm. Yes. Well, some fool's told Nigel that his style's *vieux jeu,* or something. 'Emasculate' was one of the words, I believe. It's got him on the raw, so he's hard at work trying to form a style that he thinks will 'take,' but I'm terribly afraid it won't work. Oh, he's clever, and it's arresting enough, and it may catch on and find him a market of a sort—but it's not his own, and that never works fully. Another pity is that he's been here in Delphi a bit too long and got tied up with a girl who wasn't very good for him. She's gone, but the melancholy remains." He smiled. "As you see, it's with me, rather. I'm all the company Nigel's had up at the studio for the last three days, and I've been playing confidant."

"Or housemaster?"

He laughed. "If you like. He's very young in many ways, and habit dies hard. One takes it for granted one is there to help, though I'm not just sure how much anyone can do for an artist at the best of times. And at the worst they go into a kind of wilderness of the spirit where the best-intentioned listener can't even follow them."

"As bad as that?"

"I think so. I told you he was good. I believe the agony is in proportion to the talent. . . . Look, what are you going to eat? Why don't you choose something?" He handed me the menu.

I gave it patiently back. "I shall die of hunger in a minute," I told him. Have you *looked* at this dashed menu? The only things I recognize are *patates, tomates,* and *melon,* and I refuse to be a vegetarian in a land which produces those heavenly little chunks of lamb on sticks with mushrooms between."

"I'm sorry," said Simon penitently. "Here they are, see? *Souvlaka.* Well, so be it." He ordered the meal, then finally cocked an eyebrow at me. "What shall we drink? How's the palate coming on?"

"If that means can I swallow retsina yet," I said, "the answer is yes, though what it has to do with a palate I cannot see." Retsina is a mild wine strongly flavoured with resin. It can be pleasant; it can also be rough enough to fur the tongue with a sort of antiseptic gooseflesh. It comes in beautiful little copper tankards, and smells like turpentine. To acquire—or to pretend to acquire—a taste for retsina is the right thing to do when in Greece. As a tourist, I'm as much of a snob as anyone. "Retsina, certainly," I said. "What else, with *souvlaka?*"

I thought I saw the faintest shade of irony in Simon's eye. "Well, if you'd rather have wine—"

I said firmly, "They say that once you've got used to retsina it's the finest drink in the world and you won't ever take anything else. Burgundies and clarets and—well, other drinks, lose their flavour. Don't interrupt the process. The palate is faint yet pursuing and I expect I'll like it soon. Unless, of course, *you'd* like a nice sweet Samian wine?"

"Heaven forfend," said Simon basely, and, to the waiter, "Retsina, please."

When it came, it was good, as retsina goes—and the dinner along with it was excellent. I'm not a person whom the sight of olive oil repels, and I love Greek cooking. We had onion soup with grated cheese on top; then the *souvlaka,* which comes spiced with lemon and herbs, and flanked with chips and green beans in oil and a big dish of tomato salad. The cheese, and *halvas,* which is a sort of loaf made of grated nuts and honey, and is delicious. And finally the wonderful grapes of Greece, bloomed over like misted agates and cooled with water from the spring above the temple of Apollo.

Simon talked entertainingly through the meal without once mentioning Michael Lester or his purpose in visiting Delphi, and I myself forgot completely the cloud that was still hanging over my day, and only recollected it when a truck, chugging up past the terrace, slowed down to pass the car which stood parked at the edge of the narrow road.

Simon followed my look. He set down his little cup of Greek coffee, and then looked across the table at me.

"Conscience still active?"

"Not so active as it was. There's not so much room. That was a heavenly meal, and thank you very much."

"I wondered—" said Simon thoughtfully, and then stopped.

I said just as thoughtfully, "It's a long walk to Arachova. Is that it?"

He grinned. "That's it. Well? It's your car."

I said fervently, "It's not, you know. I never want to touch it again. I—I've renounced it."

"That's a pity, because—with your permission which I take it I have—I'm going to drive down to Arachova in a few minutes' time, and I was rather hoping you'd come too."

I said, in very real amazement, "Me? But you don't want me!"

"Please," said Simon.

For some reason I felt the colour coming hot into my

cheeks. "But you don't. It's your own—your private affair, and you can't possibly want a stranger tagging along with you. This may be Greece, but that's carrying *philoxenia* a bit too far! After all—"

"I promise not to let anything upset you." He smiled. "It's a long time ago, and it's not a present tragedy any more. It's just—well, you can call it curiosity, if you like."

"I wasn't worrying about its upsetting me. I was thinking only that—well, dash it, you hardly know me, and it *is* a private matter. You said it could be called a 'pilgrimage,' remember?"

He said slowly, "If I said what I really want to say you'd think I was crazy. But let me say this—and it's true—I'd be terribly grateful if you'd give me your company this evening."

There was a little pause. The group of Greeks had long since dispersed. Both artist and donkey had vanished. The other English diners had finished and gone into the hotel. Away over the invisible sea the thin moon hung, apricot now among the white scatter of stars. Above us the breeze in the plane trees sounded like rain.

I said, "Of course I'll come," and got to my feet. As he stubbed out his cigarette and rose I smiled at him with a touch of malice. "After all, you did tell me I owed you something."

He said quickly, "Look, I never meant—" and he caught my look and grinned. "All right, ma'am, you win. I won't try and bully you again." And he opened the car door for me.

"Michael was ten years older than me," said Simon. "There were just the two of us, and our mother died when I was fifteen. My father thought the sun rose and set in Michael—and so did I, I suppose. I remember how dead the house seemed when he was drafted off to the Med. . . . and Father just sat every day with the papers and the radio, trying to learn what he could." A little smile touched his lips. "It wasn't easy. I told you Michael came over here with the S.A.S.—the Special Air Service—when Germany occupied Greece. He was doing undercover work with the resistance in the mountains for eighteen months before he was killed, and of course news came very thinly and not always accurately. Occasionally men managed to get letters out. . . . If you knew someone was going to be picked up at night and taken off you did your damnedest to get a letter to him in the hope that he in his turn would get through, and the letter might eventually be mailed home from Cairo . . . but it was chancy, and no one in those days carried any more papers on him than he could help. So news was sparse and not very satisfactory. We only ever got three letters from Michael in all that time. All he told us in the first two was that he was well, and things were going according to plan—and all the usual formulae that you don't believe, but that just tell you he was alive when he wrote the letter four months before you got it."

He paused while he negotiated a sharp bend made more hair-raising than ever by the dark.

"We did eventually find out a certain amount about his work in Greece from chaps who'd been with him here in Force One Thirty-three, and had been in touch with him off and on through the fighting. I told you he was a B.L.O. attached to guerrillas. Perhaps I'd better tell you the set-up in Greece after the German invasion—or do you know all about it?"

"Not a great deal. Only that ELAS was the main guerrilla organization, and was more concerned in feathering its own Commie nest than in fighting Germans."

"So you do know that? You'd be surprised how many people never grasped it, even in nineteen forty-four when the Germans got out of Greece and ELAS turned on its own country—tried to stage a Communist *coup d'état*—and started murdering Greeks with the arms and cash we'd smuggled to them, and which they'd hidden safely away in the mountains till they could use them for the Party."

"But there were other guerrillas who did an honest job, surely?"

"Oh, yes. To begin with there were quite a few groups, and it was Michael's job among other things to try and bring them together in a more or less coherent plan of campaign. But it broke his heart as it broke the heart of every B.L.O. in Greece. ELAS set to work and smashed every other guerrilla organization it could get its filthy hands on."

"You mean actually fought its own people *during* the German occupation?"

"Indeed, yes. Smashed some groups and assimilated others until eventually there was only one other important resistance group, EDES, under a leader called Zervas, an honest man and a fine soldier."

"I remember. You said he was in the Peloponnese."

"That's it. ELAS tried hard to liquidate him too, of course. Don't mistake me, there were some brave and good men with ELAS too, and they did some damned good work, but there was rather a load of . . ." he paused fractionally, "infamy . . . to counteract the better things. It doesn't make good reading, the story of the resistance in Greece. Village after village, raped and burned by the Germans, was thereafter raped and burned by ELAS—their own people—for whatever pathetic supplies they could produce. And the final abomination was the famous battle of Mount Tzoumerka where Zervas with EDES was facing the Germans, and ELAS under Ares—of all the damned arrogant pseudonyms for one of the most filthy sadistic devils that ever walked—ELAS waited till Zervas was heavily engaged, and then attacked him on the flank."

"Attacked *Zervas?* While he was fighting the Germans?"

"Yes. Zervas fought a double-sided battle for several hours, and managed to beat off the Germans, but he still lost some of his valuable supplies to ELAS, who stashed them away, no doubt, against the end of the German war and the day of the New Dawn."

There was a silence, underlined by the humming of the engine. I could smell dust, and dead verbena. The autumn stars were milky-white and as large as asters. Against their mild radiance the young cypresses stood like spears.

"And that brings me to the reason for my visit to Delphi," asid Simon.

I said, "Michael's third letter?"

"You're quick, aren't you? Yes, indeed, Michael's third letter."

He changed gear, and the car slowed and turned carefully onto a narrow bridge set at right angles to the road. He went on in his pleasant, unemotional voice, "It came after we had had news of his death. I didn't read it then. In fact, I never knew Father had had it. I suppose he thought it would bring the thing alive again for me, when I'd just got over the worst. I was seventeen. And later, Father never talked about Michael. I didn't know of the letter's existence till six months ago, when Father died, and I, as his executor, had to go through his papers. The letter . . ."

He paused again, and I felt a curious little thrill go through me—the inevitable response (conditioned by tales told through how many centuries?) to the age-old device of fable: the dead man . . . the mysterious paper . . . the frayed and faded clue leading through the hills of a strange land. . . .

"The letter didn't say much," said Simon. "But it was—I

don't know quite how to describe it—it was excited. Even the writing. I knew Michael pretty well, for all the difference in our ages, and I tell you he was as excited as all-get-out when he wrote that letter. And I think it was something he'd found, somewhere on Parnassus."

Again that queer little thrill. The night swooped by, full of stars. On our left the mountain loomed like the lost world of the gods. All of a sudden it didn't seem possible that I was here, and that this—this ground where our tyres whispered through the dust—was Parnassus. The name was a shiver up the spine.

I said, "Yes?" in a very queer voice.

"You must understand," he said, "that when I read that letter in the end, I read it against a background of information picked up after the war. We'd found out, my father and I, just where and how Michael had been working, and we'd talked to some of the fellows he'd met here. We were told that he'd been sent up into this area in the spring of nineteen forty-three and for over a year before he was killed he was working with one of the ELAS bands whose leader was a man called Angelos Dragoumis. I couldn't learn very much about this Angelos—that was the name he was generally known by, and I gather that it was desperately inappropriate; only one of the other Force One Thirty-three chaps had actually met him, and the few enquiries I've made here in the last day or so have been quietly stone-walled. The Greeks aren't proud of men like Angelos. I don't mean that his group didn't do one or two brilliant things: they were with Ares and Zervas when the Gorgopotamos viaduct was destroyed in the teeth of the Germans, and there was the affair of the bridge at Lidorikion, where they—oh, well, that doesn't matter just now. The thing is that this man Angelos seems to have rather modelled himself on the ELAS Commander, Ares, and he made himself felt in the country hereabouts just as Ares did."

"You mean he plundered his own side?"

"That and worse. The usual beastly record of burning and rape and torture and smashed houses, and people—where they weren't murdered—left to starve. The extra unpleasant touch is that Angelos came from this district himself . . . yes, I know. It's hard to take, isn't it? He's dead, anyway . . . at least, that's the assumption. He vanished across the Yugoslav border when the Communist *putsch* failed in December, nineteen forty-four and he hasn't been heard of since."

"I imagine that in any case he'd not dare reappear in these parts," I said.

"True enough. Well, anyway, that was the man Michael was working with, and, as I say, they did get some pretty good results in the military line—but then the Germans arrived here in force, and Angelos' band scattered and went into hiding in the hills. Michael, I gather, was on his own. He evaded capture for some weeks, hiding somewhere up here on Parnassus. Then one day a patrol spotted him. He got away, but one of their bullets hit him—not a bad wound, but enough to disable him, and with no attention it might have proved serious. One of his contacts was Stephanos, the shepherd from Arachova that we're going to see tonight. Stephanos took Michael in, and he and his wife nursed and hid him and would, I think, have got him out of the country if the Germans hadn't descended on Arachova while Michael was still here."

Along the road the young cypresses stood like swords. They had come along this very road. I said, "And they found him."

"No. But they'd been told he was here, and so they took Stephanos' son Nikolaos out and shot him, because his parents wouldn't give Michael away."

"Simon!"

He said gently, "It was a commonplace. You don't know these people yet. They stood and let their families be murdered in front of them rather than betray an ally who'd eaten their salt."

"The other side of the picture," I said, thinking of ELAS, and Angelos.

"As you say. And when you think harshly of ELAS, remember two things. One is that the Greek is born a fighting animal. Doesn't their magnificent and pathetic history show you that? If a Greek can't find anyone else to fight, he'll fight his neighbour. The other is the poverty of Greece, and to the very poor, any creed that brings promise has a quick way to the heart."

I said, "I'll remember."

"Perhaps we've forgotten," he said, "what poverty means. When one sees . . . ah, well, never mind now. But I think that most things can be forgiven to the poor."

I was silent. I was remembering Philip again, and a beggar under the ramparts at Carcassonne; Philip saying "Good God!" in a shocked voice, dropping five hundred francs into the scrofulous hand, and then forgetting it. And now here

was this quiet, easy voice, talking in the dark of past in-
famies, expressing as a matter of course the sort of enormous
and tolerant compassion that I had never met—in the flesh
—before. . . .

"Poor naked wretches, wheresoe'er you are,
That bide the pelting of this pitiless storm,
How shall your houseless heads and unfed sides,
Your looped and windowed raggedness, defend you . . . ?"

It came to me with a shock like an arrow out of the dark
that—mystery or no mystery—I liked Simon Lester very
much indeed.

He said, "What is it?"

"Nothing. Go on. The Germans shot Nikolaos and Michael left."

"Yes. Apparently he moved out again into the mountains.
After this point I know very little about what happened.
So far I've pieced together the bare facts from what we were
told after the war by one of the other B.L.O.'s who was over
here, and from the priest at Delphi, who wrote to my father
some time back, when he was making his first enquiries."

"Didn't Stephanos write?"

"Stephanos can't write," said Simon. "What happened
next we can only guess at. Michael went off back into the
hills after the tragedy of Nikolaos' death. His shoulder
wasn't fully healed, but he was all right. Stephanos and his
wife wanted him to stay, but Nikolaos had left a small son
and a daughter, and . . . well, Michael said he wasn't risking
any more lives. He went. And that's all we know. He went
up there"—a gesture towards the shadow-haunted mountain—"and he was caught and killed there, somewhere on
Parnassus."

I said after a minute or two, "And you want to talk to
Stephanos and find out where he is?"

"I know where he is. He's buried at Delphi, in a little
graveyard not far from the studio, above the shrine of Apollo.
I've been to the grave already. No, that's not what I want
from Stephanos. I want to know just where Michael died on
Parnassus."

"Stephanos knows?"

"He found the body. It was he who sent Michael's last letter off, together with the other things he found on the body.
He got them smuggled somehow to this other B.L.O. and we
got them eventually. We didn't know who'd sent them until

later we were officially told that Michael was buried at Delphi. We wrote to the *papa*—the priest. He told us the simple facts, so of course my father wrote to Stephanos, and got a reply through the priest again, and—well, that seemed to be that."

"Until you saw Michael's letter."

"Until I saw Michael's letter."

We had rounded a shadowy bluff and there ahead, pouring down the mountainside like a cascade, were the steep lights of Arachova.

The car drew gently in to the side of the road and stopped. Simon switched the engine off and reached into an inner pocket for a wallet. From this he took a piece of paper and handed it to me.

"Wait a moment till I get my lighter to work. Would you like a cigarette?"

"Thank you."

After we had lighted our cigarettes he held the little flame for me while I unfolded the flimsy paper. It was a scrawl on a single sheet of cheap paper, smudged as if with rain, a bit dirty, torn here and there along the old folds, and dog-eared from being read and re-read. I opened it gently. I had the queerest feeling that I shouldn't have been touching it.

It was fairly short. "Dear Daddy," it began . . . why should there be something so very endearing about the thought of Michael Lester, a tough twenty-seven, using the childhood's diminutive? . . .

"Dear Daddy, God knows when you'll get this, as I see no chance of its getting taken off in the near future, but I've got to write. We've been having a bit of a party, but that's over now and I'm quite all right, so don't worry. I wonder, do you find this code of army-slang clichés as bloodily maddening as I do? At the best of times I suppose it has its uses, but just now —tonight—there is something I really want to say to you; to record, somehow, on paper—nothing to do with the war or my job here or anything like that, but still impossible to commit to paper and how *the hell* can I get it across to you? You know as well as I do that anything might happen before I see anyone I can send a private message by. If my memory were a little better—and if I'd paid a bit more attention to those classical studies (oh God, a world ago!) I might send you to the right bit in Callimachus, I think it's Callimachus. But I've forgotten where it comes. I'll have to leave it at that. However, I'm seeing a man I can trust tomorrow, and I'll tell him, come what may. And all being well, this'll be over some day soon, and we'll come back here together to the bright citadel, and I can show you

then—and little brother Simon too. How is he? Give him my
love. Till the day—and what a day it'll be!

> "Your loving son,
> "Michael."

The signature was a scrawl, running down almost off the
page. I folded the paper carefully, and gave it back to Simon.
He snapped the lighter out, and put the letter carefully away.
He said, "You see what I mean?"

"Well, I don't know your brother, but I take it that wasn't
his usual style."

"Far from it. This reads very oddly to me. Queer, rapid,
allusive; almost—if I didn't know Michael so well—hysterical. A feminine type of letter."

"I see what you mean."

He laughed, and started the engine. "Sorry. But it's my
guess he really was under some strong emotion when he
wrote that letter."

"I think I'd agree. Of course he was in a tough spot,
and—"

"He'd been in dozens before. And then all that about a
private message, and 'getting it across.' He really had something to say."

"Yes. I take it you've had a look through your Callimachus, whoever he may be?"

"I have. He wrote a deuce of a lot. No, there's no clue
there."

"And the 'bright citadel'?"

"That's a translation of a phrase the Delphic Oracle once
used to Julian the Apostate. I think that must be the one he
means. It refers to Apollo's shrine at Delphi."

"I see. That doesn't get us much further."

We were moving again towards the lights of Arachova. I
said, "You used the word 'clue.' Just what are you hoping
to find, Simon?"

"What Michael found."

After a little pause I said slowly, "Yes, I see. You mean
the bit about 'we'll come back here together to the bright
citadel and I'll show you'?"

"Yes. He'd found something and he was excited about it
and he wanted to 'record' it—he uses that word, too,
remember?"

"Yes. But don't you think that perhaps—?" I stopped.

"Well?"

I said, with some difficulty, "Might you not be seeing

something that isn't there? I do agree it's an odd letter, but there's another way of reading it, isn't there? A quite simple way. It's the way that I'd have taken it myself . . . except of course that I didn't know your brother Michael."

"And that way?"

"Well, say it *was* excitement, or rather emotion, of a sort, wouldn't there be a reason for it? Might he not quite naturally have things he wanted to say to your father and to you? I mean . . ." I stopped again, embarrassed.

He said simply, "You mean it was plain and simple affection? That Michael may have had a premonition he'd not get out of the jam he was in, and wanted to say something to my father . . . a sort of farewell? No . . . no, Camilla, not Michael. If he felt very deeply about people he kept it to himself. Nor do I think he'd dabble in 'premonitions.' He knew the risks and he didn't fuss. Besides he does say he wants to 'show' Father something, and me . . . here, in Greece."

"Perhaps the country itself. Heaven knows it's exciting enough. Would your father have been interested?"

Simon laughed. "He was a classicist too. He'd been here half a score of times before."

"Oh. Oh, I see. Yes, that does make a difference."

"I think so. No, I'm right. He'd found something, Camilla." A tiny pause, and that electric thrill again, which quivered to nothing as Simon added flatly, "I'm pretty certain I know what it was, too, but I could bear to make sure. And for a start, I'd like to know just where Michael died, and how. . . ."

Another pause. He must have been thinking back to my remarks about the letter, for he said thoughtfully, "No, all things taken together, I know I'm right. Though it does seem a little odd. . . . You may be right about the 'emotion'— though it wouldn't be like Mick. He was the most casual-seeming devil to talk to that you ever knew. It took quite some time before you guessed that he was probably the toughest too, and the most self-sufficient."

Like little brother Simon. . . . The thought came so pat and so clearly that for one terrible moment I was afraid I had said it aloud. And I had an uncomfortable feeling that he knew just what I was thinking.

I said quickly and idiotically, "Here's Arachova."

It was one of the rather less necessary remarks. Already we were hemmed in by the crowding walls, and the coloured rugs—still hanging outside the vividly lit shops—almost

brushed the sides of the car. There were two or three donkeys, freed from rope and saddle, wandering loose in the
street. I saw a goat on someone's garden wall. It gave us an
evil, gleaming glance before it leaped away into shadow and
vanished. There was the familiar smell of dust and dung and
gasoline fumes and the lees of wine.

Simon parked the car in the place where it had been that
afternoon. He stopped the engine and we got out. We walked
back towards the steep alleyway, where I had first seen him.
Opposite the foot of it was one of the village cafés, a dozen
tables in a whitewashed room open to the road. Most of the
tables were full. The men watched us . . . or rather, they
didn't look at me. They all watched Simon.

He paused at the foot of the alley and put a hand under
my elbow. I saw that light, wary look touch the groups of
dark-faced men, linger, leave them. He smiled down at me.

"Up here," he said, "and watch where you go. The steps
are tricky and the donkeys have provided a few extra natural
hazards. Stephanos, naturally, lives at the very top."

I looked up. The alley was about four feet wide and had a
gradient of one in three. The steps were just too far apart and
were made of sharp chunks of Parnassus with the minimum
of dressing. The donkeys—a herd of healthy donkeys—had
been that way many times. There was one dim light halfway
up.

For some reason it occurred to me at that moment to wonder just what I had got myself into. ELAS, Stephanos, a man
called Michael dying on Parnassus and lying bleaching to
earth again above Delphi . . . all this, out of nowhere, and
now a steep dark little alley and the pressure of Simon's
hand on my arm. I wondered sharply just what we were going to learn from Stephanos.

And suddenly, I knew that I didn't want to hear it.

"*Avanti*," said Simon beside me, sounding amused.

I pushed the coward impulse aside, and started up the
alleyway.

CHAPTER

6

> . . . Seek
> Thy brother with a tale that must be heard
> Howe'er it sicken.
>
> EURIPIDES: *Electra*
> (tr. Gilbert Murray).

Stephanos' house was a small two-storied building, set at the top of the stairway. Its bottom storey opened straight on the alley, and housed the beasts—a donkey and two goats and a gaggle of skinny hens—while stone stairs led up the outer wall of the house to the top storey where the family lived. At the head of the steps a wide concrete platform served as porch and garden in one. Its low parapet was crowded with pots full of greenery, and roofed with a trellis of rough branches which formed a pergola for the vine. I saw Simon stoop to avoid a loaded bough, and a hanging bunch of grapes brushed my cheek with a cold gentle touch. The top half of the door was open, and the light streamed out to gild the vine tendrils. There was a hot oily smell from the family's supper, mixed with goat, and donkey, and the furry musk-smell of geraniums where I had brushed a hand against one of the flowerpots.

We had been heard coming up the steps. As we crossed the platform the lower half of the door opened, and an old man stood there, large against the weak light from within.

I paused. Simon was behind me, still in shadow. I moved aside to let him pass me, and he came forward, hand outstretched, with some greeting in Greek. I saw the old man stiffen as he peered out. His mouth opened as if to make some involuntary exclamation, then he seemed to draw back a little. He said formally, "Brother of Michael, you are welcome. The woman of the house said you would come tonight."

Simon withdrew the hand which the old man hadn't appeared to notice, and said, with equal formality, "My name

is Simon. I'm glad to meet you, *Kyrie* Stephanos. This is
Kyria Haven, a friend who has brought me down in her car."

The old man's look touched me, no more. He inclined his
head, saying slowly, "You are both welcome. Be pleased to
come in."

He turned, then, and went into the room.

I should perhaps make it clear here that this and most of
the subsequent conversation was in Greek, and that therefore I didn't understand it. But afterwards Simon gave me
as exact a translation as he could, and at the time I was
able to follow what I may perhaps call the emotional movements of the conversation. So I shall set the interview
down as it occurred.

It seemed apparent to me, from the first short exchange
on the balcony, that our welcome wasn't exactly a glowing
one, and this surprised me. I had seen during my stay in
Greece so much of the miracle of Greek hospitality, that I
was both disconcerted and repelled. It didn't worry me that
Stephanos hadn't spoken to me—I was only a woman, after
all, and as such had pretty low social rating—but his rejec-
tion of Simon's outstretched hand had been quite deliberate,
and his gesture now, as he invited us to follow him in, was
heavy and (it seemed) reluctant.

I hesitated, glancing at Simon doubtfully.

He didn't appear to be in the least put out. He merely
lifted an eyebrow at me, and waited for me to precede him
into the house.

The single living and sleeping room of the house was high
and square. The floor was of scrubbed boards, the walls
whitewashed and hung with vivid holy pictures in appalling
colours. Light came from a single naked electric bulb. In
one corner stood an old-fashioned oil stove, and above it
shelves for pans and a blue curtain that no doubt concealed
food and crockery. Against one wall was an immense bed,
covered now with a brown blanket and obviously used during the day as a sofa. Above the bed hung a small icon of
the Virgin and Child, with a red electric bulb glowing in
front of it. A Victorian-looking cupboard, a scrubbed table,
a couple of kitchen chairs and a bench covered with cheap
oil cloth made up the rest of the furniture. A note of vivid
colour was supplied by the one rug on the boarded floor. It
was locally woven, in brilliant scarlet and parrot green. The
room had the air of great poverty and an almost fierce clean-
liness.

There was an old woman sitting over near the stove on

one of the hard chairs. I took her to be Stephanos' wife—the
woman of the house. She was dressed in black, and even in
the house wore the Moslem-looking headscarf, which veils
mouth and chin, and which gives the field workers of Greece
such an Eastern look. It was pulled down now below her
chin, and I could see her face. She looked very old, as the
peasant women of the hot countries do. Her face had lovely
bones, fine and regular, but the skin had dried into a thousand wrinkles, and her teeth had decayed. She smiled at me
and made a gesture of shy welcome, to which I responded
with a sort of bow and an embarrassed "Good evening" in
Greek, as I took the chair she indicated. She made no further
move to greet us, and I noticed that her look in reply to Simon's greeting was uneasy, almost scared. Her gnarled hands
moved in her lap, and then she dropped her eyes to them
and kept them there.

Simon had taken the other chair near the door, and the old
man sat down on the bench. I found myself staring at him.
So much a part of the land of myth was he that he might
have come straight out of Homer. His face was brown,
wrinkled like the woman's, and in expression patriarchal and
benevolent. The white hair and beard were curled like those
of the great Zeus in the Athens Museum. He was dressed in
a sort of long tunic of faded blue, buttoned close down the
front and reaching to his thighs; beneath it he wore what
looked like white cotton jodhpurs bound at the knees with
black bands. On his head was a small soft black cap. The
knotted, powerful hands looked as if they were uneasy without a crook to grasp.

He looked at Simon under thick white brows, ignoring me.
The look was grave and—I thought—measuring. In the corner beside me, the old woman sat silent. I could hear the
animals moving about below us, and the quick tread of someone coming up the alley from the street.

Stephanos had just opened his mouth to speak, when there
was an interruption. The quick steps outside mounted the
stone stairs at a run. A youth came across the balcony with a
rush and paused in the doorway, one hand on the jamb of
the door, the other thrust into his waistband. It was a very
dramatic pose, and he was a very dramatic young man. He
was about eighteen, lean and brown and beautiful, with thick
black curls and a vivid, excited face. He wore ancient
striped flannels, and the loudest and most awful shirt I
have ever seen.

He said, "Grandfather? He's come?"

Then he saw Simon. He didn't appear to notice me at all, but I was getting used to that, and merely sat quiet, like the woman of the house. The boy flashed a delighted smile at Simon, and a flood of rapid Greek, which was interrupted by his grandfather's saying repressively, "Who told you to come, Niko?"

Niko whirled back to him. All his movements were swift like those of a graceful but restless young cat. "They told me at Lefteris' that he had come again. I wanted to see him."

"And now you see him. Sit down and be silent, Niko. We have much to say."

I saw Niko throw a quick appraising glance at Simon. "Have you told him?"

"I have told him nothing. Sit down and be silent."

Niko turned to obey, but his look lingered on Simon. The dark eyes glinted with something that could have been excitement mixed with amusement—or even malice. Simon met it with that masked indifferent look that I was beginning to know. He had taken out his cigarette case and now he glanced at me. I shook my head. "Niko?" The boy put out a hand, then stopped, drew it back, and sent Simon another of his vivid smiles. "No, thank you, *kyrie*." A glance at his grandfather, then he crossed to the big bed and threw himself on it. Simon found his lighter, lit a cigarette with a certain deliberation, then put his lighter carefully back in his pocket before he turned to Stephanos.

The latter was sitting motionless. He still didn't speak. The silence came back, heavy, charged, and the boy stirred restlessly on the bed. His eyes never left Simon's face. Beside me the woman hadn't moved, but as I glanced at her I saw her eyes slide sideways to meet mine, only to drop swiftly to the hands in her lap as if in an ecstasy of shyness. I realized then that she had been covertly studying my frock, and the knowledge came to me suddenly, warmingly, that Stephanos, too, was shy.

Perhaps Simon had divided this too, for he didn't wait for Stephanos, but spoke easily, bridging the moment.

"*Kyrie* Stephanos, I'm very glad to meet you at last, and the woman of your house. My father and I wrote to you to thank you for what you did for my brother, but—well, letters can't say it all. My father is dead now, but I'm speaking for him too when I say thank you again. You'll understand it isn't always possible to put into words all that one feels—all one would like to say, but I think you will understand what I feel, and what my father felt." He turned his head to smile at the woman. She didn't smile back. I thought she made a little sound as if of pain, and she moved in her chair. Her narrow lips worked in and out, and her fingers gripped each other painfully.

Stephanos said, almost roughly, "There is nothing for you to say, *kyrie*. We did no more than we should."

"It was a very great deal," said Simon gently. "You couldn't have done more if he, too, had been your son." A quick glance at the old woman. "I shan't say much about that, *kyria*, because there are memories that you won't want to revive; and I shall try not to ask any questions that might distress you. But I had to come and thank you, for my father, and for myself . . . and to see the house where my brother Michael found friends in the last days of his life."

He paused, and looked round him slowly. There was silence again. Below us the animals shuffled and one of them sneezed. There was nothing in Simon's face to read, but I saw the boy's speculative glance on him again before it turned as if in impatience to his grandfather. But Stephanos said nothing.

At length Simon said, "So it was here."

"It was here, *kyrie*. Below, behind the manger, there is a gap in the wall. He hid there. The dirty Germans did not think to look behind the sacks of straw, and the dung. Would you like me to show you?"

Simon shook his head. "No. I told you I don't want to remind you of that day. And I don't think I need ask you anything much about it, as you told us most of it in the letter that the *papa* wrote for you. You told me how Michael had been wounded in the shoulder and had come here for shelter, and how, after . . . later on, he went back into the mountains."

"It was just before dawn," said the old man, "on the second of October. We begged him to stay with us, because he was not yet well, and the wet weather comes early in the mountains. But he would not. He helped us to bury my son Nikolaos, and then he went." He nodded towards the intent youth on the bed. "There was that one, you understand, and his sister Maria, who is since married to Georgios who has a shop in the village. When the Germans came the children were out in the fields with their mother, or who knows? They too might have been killed. *Kyrie* Michael"—he pronounced it as a trisyllable, Mi-ha-eel—"would not stay, because of them. He went up into the mountains."

"Yes. A few days later he was killed. You found his body somewhere over between here and Delphi, and you took it down to be buried."

"That is so. What I found on his body I gave after three weeks to Perikles Grivas, and he took it to an Englishman who was going by night from Galaxeidion. But this you know."

"This I know. I want you to show me where he was killed, Stephanos."

There was a short silence. The boy Niko watched Simon unwinkingly. I noticed that he had taken out a cigarette of his own and was smoking it.

The old man said heavily, "I will do that, of course. Tomorrow?"

"If it's convenient."

"For you, it is convenient."

"You're very good."

"You are the brother of Michael."

Simon said gently, "He was here a long time, wasn't he?"

Beside me the woman moved suddenly and said in a clear soft voice, "He was my son." I saw with a wrench of discomfort that there were tears on her cheeks. "He should have stayed," she said, and then repeated it almost desperately, "He should have stayed."

Simon said, "But he had to go. How could he stay and put you and your family in that danger again? When the Germans came back—"

"They didn't come back." It was Niko who spoke, clearly from the bed.

"No." Simon turned his head. "Because they caught Michael in the mountains. But if they hadn't caught him—if he had still been hiding here—they might have come back to the village, and then—"

"They did not catch him," said the old man.

Simon turned back sharply. Stephanos was sitting still on the bench, knees apart, hands clasped between them, his heavy body bent slightly forward. His eyes looked fathoms dark under the white brows. The two men stared at one another. I found myself stirring on my hard chair. It was as if the scene were taking place in slow motion, silent and incomprehensible, yet powered with emotions that plucked uncomfortably at the nerves.

Simon said slowly, "What are you trying to tell me?"

"Only," said Stephanos, "that Michael was not killed by the Germans. He was killed by a Greek."

"By a Greek?" Simon echoed it almost blankly.

The old man made a gesture that might have come straight from *Oedipus Rex*. To me, still not understanding anything except that the men's talk had an overtone of tragedy, it conveyed a curiously powerful impression of resignation and shame.

"By a man from Arachova," he said.

It was at this moment that the light chose to go out.

The Greeks were obviously accustomed to the whims of the electric system. With scarcely a moment's delay the old woman had found and lit an oil lamp, and placed it on the table in the middle of the room. It was a frightful-looking lamp of some cheap bright metal, but it burned with a soft apricot light and the sweet smell of olive oil. With the heavy shadows cast on his face, Stephanos looked more than ever like a tragic actor. Niko had rolled over on his stomach and was watching the other men bright-eyed, as if it were indeed a play. I supposed that, for him, his father's death and Michael's seemed so remote that this talk of them was no more than a breath from an exciting past.

Simon was saying, "I . . . see. That makes a lot of things a lot plainer. And of course you don't know who it was."

"Indeed we do."

Simon's brows shot up. The old man smiled sourly. "You are wondering why we have not killed him, *kyrie*, when we called Michael our son?"

From the bed Niko said in a smooth voice that was certainly malicious, "That is not the way the English work, grandfather."

Simon flicked him a look but said, mildly, to Stephanos, "Not exactly. I was wondering what had happened to him. I gather he's alive."

"I'll explain. I should tell you first of all that the man's name was Dragoumis. Angelos Dragoumis."

"Angelos?"

The old man nodded. "Yes. You know of him, of course. I told you in the letter the *papa* wrote for me that Michael had worked with him. But I should never have told you this of Angelos, if you had not come. Now that you are here, these things cannot be hidden. It is your right to know."

Simon was carefully extinguishing his cigarette in the lid

of a matchbox. His face was still and shuttered, his eyes
hidden. I saw the boy Niko roll over again on the bed and
grin to himself.

"You know that Angelos was the leader of the ELAS troop
that Michael was working with," said Stephanos. "When
Michael left here he went up, I think, with the intention of
rejoining them. They had scattered when the big German
search operation started in the hills, and most of them had
moved north, Angelos with them. What brought Angelos
back in this direction I don't know, but certain it is that he
fetched up against Michael over on Parnassus and murdered
him there."

"Why?"

"I do not know. Except that such murders were not rare
in those days. It may be that Michael and Angelos had had
some quarrel over the action of Angelos' troops. Perhaps
Michael was putting too much pressure on him; we know
now that Angelos was anxious to save his men and his supplies for a different battle—after the Germans had gone."

I saw Simon look up sharply, those light-grey eyes vividly
intent. "Angelos was one of them? Are you sure?"

"Certain. He played for high stakes, did Angelos Dragoumis. He was in Athens soon after the Germans had left
Greece, and we knew he was active in the massacre at
Kalamai. Oh yes, you may be sure that he was betraying
the Allies all the time."

He smiled thinly. "I do not think that Michael can have
known. No, this was some other quarrel. It may simply have
been that two such men could never come together, and
agree. Angelos was bad, bad from the heart, and Michael
. . . he did not like having to work with such a one. They
had quarrelled before. He told me so. Angelos was an arrogant man, and a bully, and Michael—well, Michael could
not be driven either."

"True enough." Simon was selecting another cigarette.
"But you said he was 'murdered.' If two men quarrel and
there's a fight, that isn't murder, Stephanos."

"It was murder. It was a fight, but not a fair one. Michael
had been wounded, remember."

"Even so—"

"He was struck from behind first, with a stone or with
the butt of a gun. There was a great mark there, and the
skin was broken. It is a miracle that the blow didn't kill
him, or stun him, at least. But he must have heard Angelos
behind him, and turned, because in spite of the traitor's

blow from behind, and Michael's wounded shoulder, there was a fight. Michael was—a good deal marked."

"I see." Simon was lighting his cigarette. "How did Angelos kill him? I take it he wasn't using a gun. A knife?"

"His neck was broken."

The match paused, an inch from Simon's cigarette. The grey eyes lifted to the old man's. I couldn't see their expression from where I sat, but I saw Stephanos nod, once, as Zeus might have nodded. Niko's eyes narrowed suddenly and glinted between their long lashes. The match made contact. "It must have been quite a scrap," said Simon.

"He wouldn't be easy to kill," said the old man. "But with the wounded shoulder, and the blow on the head . . ."

His voice trailed off. He wasn't looking at Simon now; he seemed to be seeing something beyond the lamplit walls of the room, something remote in place and time.

There was a pause. Then Simon blew out a long cloud of tobacco smoke. "Yes," he said. "Well. And the man Angelos . . . what happened to him?"

"That I can't tell you. He has not been back to Arachova, naturally. It was said that he went with many of his kind into Yugoslavia, when their bid for power failed. In fourteen years, nobody has heard of him, and it is probable that he is dead. He had only one relative, a cousin, Dimitrios Dragoumis, who has had no news of him."

"A cousin? Here?"

"Dragoumis lives now at Itea. He also fought in Angelos' troop, but he was not a leader, and—well, some things are best forgotten." The old man's voice roughened. "But the things that Angelos did to his own people, these are not forgotten. He was at Kalamai; it is said he was also at Pyrgos, where many hundred Greeks died, and among them my own cousin Panos, an old man." The gnarled hands moved convulsively on his knees. "No matter of that. . . . But I do not speak merely of his politics, *Kyrie* Simon, or even of what such as he do in war. He was evil, *kyrie,* he was a man who delighted in evil. He liked the sight of pain. He liked best to hurt children and old women, and he boasted like Ares of how many he himself had killed. He would put a man's eyes out—or a woman's—and smile while he did it. Always that smile. He was an evil man, and he betrayed Michael and murdered him."

"And if he has not been seen here since my brother died, how can you be sure he murdered him?"

"I saw him," said the old man simply.

"*You saw him?*"

"Yes. It was he beyond doubt. When I came on them he turned and ran. But I couldn't follow him." He paused again, one of those heavy terrible little pauses. "You see, Michael was still alive."

I saw Simon's eyes jerk up again to meet his. The old man nodded. "Yes. He lived only a minute or so. But it was enough to hold me there beside him and let Angelos get away."

"Angelos made no attempt to attack you?"

"None. He, too, had been badly mauled." There was satisfaction in the old shepherd's eyes. "Michael died hard, even with that traitor's bash on the back of the head. Angelos might have shot at me, but later I found his revolver lying under a boulder, as if it had been flung there in the struggle. The countryside was full of Germans, you see, and he must have counted on killing Michael quietly, after he'd stunned him, but he wasn't quick or clever enough, and Michael managed to turn on him. When I came to the head of the cliff and saw them below me, Angelos was just getting to his feet. He turned to look for his gun then, but my dog attacked him, and it was all he could do to get clear away. Without his gun, he could have done nothing." He wiped his mouth with the back of a knotted brown hand. "I took Michael down to Delphi. It was the nearest. That's all."

"He didn't speak?"

Stephanos hesitated, and Simon's glance sharpened. Stephanos shook his head. "It was nothing, *kyrie*. If there had been anything I would have put it in the letter."

"But he did speak?"

"Two words. He said, 'The Charioteer.' "

The words were "*O Eniochos*," and they were classical, not modern, Greek. They were also familiar to me, as to many visitors to Delphi, because they refer to the famous bronze statue that stands in the Delphi Museum. It is the statue of a youth, the Charioteer, robed in a stiffly pleated robe, still holding in his hands the reins of his vanished horses. I glanced at Simon, wondering where, in an exchange bristling with the names "Angelos," and "Michael," the Charioteer could have a place.

Simon was looking as puzzled as I. " 'The Charioteer'? Are you sure?"

"I am not quite sure. I had run hard down the path to the foot of the cliff, and I was out of breath and much distressed. He lived only a matter of seconds after I got to him.

But he knew me, and I thought that was what he said. It is a classical word, but of course it is familiar because it is used of the statue in the Delphi Museum. But why Michael should have tried to tell me about that, I do not know. If indeed that was what he whispered." He straightened his back a little. "I repeat, I would have told you if I had been sure, or if it had meant anything."

"Why did you not tell us about Angelos?"

"It was over then, and he had gone, and it was better to let Michael's father think he had died in battle and not at the hand of a traitor. Besides," said Stephanos simply, "we were ashamed."

"It was so much over," said Simon, "that when Michael's brother comes to Arachova to find out just how his brother died, the men in Arachova avoid him, and his host won't shake his hand."

The old man smiled. "Very well, then. It is not over. The shame remains."

"The shame isn't yours."

"It is that of Greece."

"My country's done a thing or two lately to balance it, Stephanos."

"Politics!" The old man made a gesture highly expressive of what he would wish to see done to all politicians, and Simon laughed. As if at a signal, the old woman got to her feet, pulled back the blue curtain, and brought out a big stone jar. She put glasses on the table and began to pour out the dark sweet wine. Stephanos said, "You will drink with us, then?"

"With the greatest of pleasure," said Simon. The old woman handed him a glass, then Stephanos, Niko, and finally me. She didn't take one herself, but remained standing, watching me with a sort of shy pleasure. I sipped the wine. It was as dark as mavrodaphne and tasted of cherries. I smiled at her over the glass and said tentatively, in Greek, "It's very good."

Her face split into a wide smile. She bobbed her head and repeated delightedly, "Very good, very good," and Niko turned over on the bed and said in American-accented English, "You speak Greek, miss?"

"No. Only a few words."

He turned to Simon. "How come you speak such good Greek, eh?"

"My brother Michael taught me when I was younger than

you. I went on learning and reading it afterwards. I knew I would come here one day."

"Why you not come before?"

"It costs too much, Niko."

"And now you are rich, eh?"

"I get by."

"*Oriste?*"

"I mean, I have enough."

"I see." The dark eyes widened in a limpid look. "And now you have come. You know about Angelos and your brother. What would you say if I told you something else, *kyrie?*"

"What?"

"That Angelos is still alive?"

Simon said slowly, "Are you telling me that, Niko?"

"He has been seen near Delphi, on the mountain."

"What? Recently?" said Simon sharply.

"Oh, yes." Niko flashed that beautiful mischievous smile up at him. "But perhaps it is only a ghost. There are ghosts on Parnassus, *kyrie*, lights that move and voices that carry across the rocks. There are those who see these things. Myself, no. It is the old gods, not?"

"Possibly," said Simon. "Is this the truth, Niko? That Angelos was seen?"

Niko shrugged. "How can I tell? It was Janis who saw him, and Janis is—" he made a significant gesture towards his forehead. "Angelos killed his mother when the *andartes* burned his father's farm, and ever since then Janis has been queer in the head, and has 'seen' Angelos—oh, many times. If ghosts are true, then he still walks on Parnassus. But Dimitrios Dragoumis—that is true enough. He has asked many questions about your coming. All the men here in Arachova know that you are coming and they talk about it and wonder—but Dragoumis, he has been to Delphi and to Arachova and has asked questions—oh, many questions."

"What is he like?"

"He is a little like his cousin. Not in the face, but in the—what do you say?—the build. But not in the spirit either." His look was innocent. "It may be that you will meet Dragoumis. But do not be afraid of him. And do not worry yourself about Angelos, *Kyrie* Simon."

Simon grinned. "Do I look as if I was worrying?"

"No," said Niko frankly, "but then, he is dead."

"And if Janis is right, and he is not dead?"

"I think," said Niko almost insolently, "that you are only an Englishman, *Kyrie* Simon. Not?"

"So what?"

Nike gave a charming little crack of laughter and rolled over on the bed. Stephanos said suddenly and angrily, in Greek, "Niko, behave yourself. What does he say, *Kyrie* Simon?"

"He thinks I couldn't deal with Angelos," said Simon idly. "Here, Niko, catch." He threw the boy a cigarette. Niko fielded it with a graceful clawed gesture. He was still laughing. Simon turned to Stephanos. "Do you think it's true that Angelos has been seen hereabouts?"

The old shepherd slanted a fierce look at his grandson under his white brows. "So he has told you that tale, has he? Some rumour started by an idiot who has seen Angelos at least a dozen times since the end of the war. Aye, and Germans too, a score of times. Don't pay any attention to *that* moonshine."

Simon laughed. "Or to the lights and voices on Parnassus?"

Stephanos said, "If a man goes up into Parnassus after sunset, why should he not see strange things? The gods still walk there, and a man who would not go carefully in the country of the gods is a fool." Another of those glowering looks at his grandson. "You, Niko, have learned a lot of folly in Athens. And that is a terrible shirt."

Niko sat up straight. "It is not!" he protested, stung. "It is American!"

Stephanos snorted and Simon grinned. "Aid to Greece?"

The old man gave a gruff bark of laughter. "He is not a bad boy, *kyrie*, even if Athens has spoiled him. But now he comes home to work, and I will make a man of him. Give *Kyrie* Simon some more wine." This to his wife, who hurried to refill Simon's glass.

"Thank you." Simon added, in a different tone, "Is it true that this man Dragoumis has been asking questions about me?"

"Quite true. After it was known that you were coming, he asked many questions—when you came, for how long, what you meant to do, and all that." He smiled sourly. "I don't speak much to that one, me."

"But why? Why should he be interested? Do you suppose he had anything to do with Michael's death?"

"He had nothing to do with it. That much we found out after the war, before he came back here. Otherwise he would not," said Stephanos simply, "have dared come back. No, he knew nothing about it. Once before, a year—more—eighteen months ago—he spoke to me and asked me what had happened, and where it was that Michael was killed. He showed a decent shame and he spoke well of Michael; but I do not talk of my sons to every man. I refused to speak of it. And no one else knew the whole truth except the priest at Delphi who is since dead, and my own brother Alkis who was killed in the war."

"And now me."

"And now you. I will take you there tomorrow and show you the place. It is your right."

He looked up under the white brows at Simon for another considering moment. Then he said slowly, irrelevantly, "I think, *Kyrie* Simon, that you are very like Michael. And Niko—Niko is even more of a fool than I had thought. . . ."

CHAPTER

7

The Oracles are dumm,
No voice or hideous humm
   Run through the arched roof in words deceiving
Apollo from his shrine
Can no more divine . . .

MILTON: *Nativity Hymn.*

Simon didn't speak on the way back to Delphi, so I sat
quietly beside him, wondering what had been said in that
sombre and somehow very foreign-seeming interview. Nothing that Stephanos—exotically Homeric—had said could
have been ordinary, while about Niko's racy intelligent
beauty there was something essentially Greek—a quick-
silver quality that is as evident today under the cheaply
Americanized trappings of his kind as it was in the black
and red of the classical vase paintings.

When at length, as we neared Delphi, trees crowded in
above the road blocking out the starlight, Simon slowed the
car, drove into a wide bay, and stopped. He switched
the engine off. Immediately the sound of running water filled
the air. He turned out the lights, and the dark trees crowded
closer. I could smell the pines, cool and pungent. They
loomed thick in the starlight, rank on rank of scented stone
pines crowding up towards the cleft where the water sprang.
Beyond the trees reared the immense darkness of rock, the
Shining Ones no longer shining, but pinnacles and towers of
imminent blackness.

Simon took out cigarettes and offered one to me. "How
much of that did you understand?"

"Nothing whatever, except that you were talking about
Michael and the ELAS leader Angelos." I smiled. "I see now
why you didn't mind my sitting in on your private affairs."

He said abruptly, "They've taken a very queer turn."

I waited.

"I'd like to tell you, if I may."

"Of course."

So we sat there in the car and smoked, while he told me, fully and accurately, what had passed in the shepherd's cottage. So vivid were my own visual impressions of the recent scene that I was able without difficulty to impose my picture, so to speak, over his, and see where movement and gesture had fitted in with the words.

When he had finished I didn't speak, for the sufficient reason that I could find nothing to say. The instinct that had halted me at the foot of the alley steps had been a true one: these waters were too deep for me. If I had felt myself inadequate before—I, who had been afraid of a mild skirmish over a hired car—what was I to feel now? Who was I, to offer comfort or even comment on a brother's murder? The murder might be fourteen years old, but there's a kind of shock in the very word, let alone the knowledge of the deed, however many years lie between it and the discovery. I didn't know Simon well enough to say the right thing, so I said nothing.

He himself made no comment, beyond telling me the story of the interview in that give-nothing-away voice of his that I was beginning to know. I did wonder fleetingly if he would say anything more about Michael's letter, or about the "find" which he, Simon, had said he knew of. . . . But he said nothing. He threw his finished cigarette over the side of the car into the dust, and it appeared that he threw the story with it, because he said, with a complete change of tone and subject:

"Shall we walk up through the ruins? You haven't seen them yet, and starlight's not a bad start. Unless, of course, you'd rather wait and see them for the first time alone?"

"No. I'd like to go."

We went up the steep path through the pines. Now that my eyes were used to the darkness it was just possible to see the way. We crossed the narrow rush of water and were on a track soft with pine needles.

After a while we came out from under the trees into an open space where fallen blocks made treacherous walking, and dimly in the starlight I could see the shape of ruined walls.

"The Roman market place," said Simon. "Those were shops and so on over there. By Delphi's standards this is modern stuff, so we by-pass it quickly. . . . Here we are. This is the gate of the temple precinct. The step's steep, but there's a wide smooth way up through the buildings to the temple itself. Can you see?"

"Fairly well. It's rather . . . stupendous by starlight, isn't it?"

Dimly I could make out the paved road that zigzagged up between the ruined walls of treasuries and shrines. The precinct seemed in this light enormous. Everywhere ahead of us, along the hillside, below among the pines that edged the road, above as far as the eye could reach in the starlight, loomed the broken walls, the spectral pillars, the steps and pedestals and altars of the ancient sanctuary. We walked slowly up the Sacred Way. I could make out the little Doric building that once housed the Athenian treasure, the grim stone where the Sybil sat to foretell the Trojan War, the slender pillars of the Portico of the Athenians, the shape of a great altar . . . then we had reached the temple itself, a naked and broken floor, half up the mountainside, held there in space by its massive retaining walls, and bordered with the six great columns that even in the darkness stood emphatic against the star-crowded sky.

I took a little breath.

Beside me, Simon quoted softly, " 'The gods still walk there, and a man who would not go carefully in the country of the gods is a fool.' "

"They *are* still here," I said. "Is it silly of me? But they are."

"Three thousand years," he said. "Wars, treachery, earthquake, slavery, oblivion. And men still recognize them here. No, it's not silly of you. It happens to everyone with intelligence and imagination. This is Delphi . . . and, well, we're not the first to hear the chariot wheels. Not by a long way."

"It's the only place in Greece I've really heard them. I've tried to imagine things—oh, you know how one does. But no, nothing, really, even on Delos. There are ghosts at Mycenae, but it's not the same. . . ."

"Poor human ghosts," he said. "But here . . . I suppose that if a place was, like Delphi, a centre of worship for—how many?—about two thousand years, something remains. Something inheres in stone, I'll swear, and here it's in the very air. The effect's helped by the landscape; I suppose it must be one of the most magnificent in the world. And of course this is just the setting for the holy place. Come up into the temple."

A ramp led up to the temple floor, which was paved with great stone blocks, some broken and dangerous. We picked our way carefully across this until we stood at the edge of the floor, between the columns. Below us was the sheer drop of the retaining wall; below that the steep mountainside and the ghosts of the scattered shrines. The far valley was an immensity of darkness, filled with the small movements of the night wind, and the sound of pine and olive.

Simon's cigarette beside me glowed and faded. I saw that he had turned his back on the spaces of the starlit valley. He was leaning against a column, gazing up the hill behind the temple. I could see nothing there but the thick shadows of trees, and against them more pale shapes of stone.

"What's up there?"

"That's where they found the Charioteer."

The word brought me back to the present with the tingle of a small electric shock. I had forgotten, in the overpowering discovery of Delphi, that Simon would have other preoccupations.

I hesitated; it was he, after all, who had sheered away from the story onto the neutral ground of Delphi. I said a little awkwardly, "Do you suppose Stephanos was right? Does it make any kind of sense to you?"

"None at all," he said cheerfully. His shoulder came away from the pillar. "Why don't you come up to the studio now, and meet Nigel, and have some coffee or a drink?"

"I'd like to, of course, but isn't it awfully late?"

"Not for this country. As far as I can make out nobody goes to bed at all, except in the afternoons. When in Greece, you know. . . . Are you tired?"

"Not a bit. I keep feeling I ought to be, but I'm not."

He laughed. "It's the air, or the light, or the simple intoxication of being alive in Hellas. It lasts, too. Then you will come?"

"I should love to."

As I picked my way across the temple floor with his hand under my arm I had time to feel surprise at myself, and a sort of resignation. Here I went again, I reflected. . . . Just in this way I had drifted along at Philip's bidding, in Philip's wake. But this was different. Just what the difference was I didn't stop to analyze.

I said, "Aren't we going down to the road? Why this way?"

"We don't need to go down. The studio's away up above the temple, just over the mountain's shoulder towards Delphi. It's easier to go up through the rest of the shrine."

"But the car?"

"I'll go and get it later when I've seen you down to your hotel. It's no distance from there by the road. This way, and watch your step. It's easier here. . . . These steps lead up towards the little theatre. That thing on the right was put up by Alexander the Great after a narrow escape in a lion hunt. . . . Here's the theatre. It's tiny compared with Athens or Epidaurus, but isn't it a gem?"

In the starlight the broken floor looked smooth. The semi-circular tiers of seats rose, seemingly new and unbroken, towards their backdrop of holly and cypress; it lay, a little broken marble cup of a theatre, silent except for the tiny scuffling of a dry twig that the breeze was patting idly along the empty flags.

I said on an impulse, "I suppose you wouldn't—no, I'm sorry. Of course not."

"What do you suppose I wouldn't do?"

"Nothing. It was silly, under the circumstances."

"The circumstances? Oh, that. Don't let that worry you. I suppose you want to hear something recited here in Greek, even if it's only *thalassa! thalassa!* Is that it? . . . What's the matter?"

"Nothing. Only that if you go on reading my thoughts like that you're going to be a very uncomfortable companion."

"You ought to practise too."

"I haven't the talent."

"Perhaps that's just as well."

"What d'you mean?"

He laughed. "Never mind. Was I right?"

"Yes. And not just *thalassa,* please. Some lines of verse, if you can think of anything. I heard someone reciting in the theatre at Epidaurus and it was like a miracle. Even a whisper carried right up to the topmost tier."

"It does the same here," he said, "only it's not so stupendous. All right, if you'd like it." He was feeling in his pockets as he spoke. "Half a minute; I'll have to find my lighter. . . . If you want to get your voice properly carried you have to locate the centre of the stage . . . it's marked by a cross on the flagstones. . . ."

As he pulled the lighter from his pocket I heard the small musical chink of metal on stone. I stooped quickly after the sound. "Something fell; some money, I think. Here . . . not far away, anyway. Shine the light down, will you?"

The lighter flicked into flame and he bent with it near the ground. Almost immediately I saw the sharp gleam of a coin. I picked it up and held it towards him. The orange-coloured flame slid alive and sparkling across the little disc in my palm. I said, "That's surely—*gold?*"

"Yes. Thank you." He took it and dropped it into his pocket. He might have been discussing a lost halfpenny, or at most a threepenny stamp. "That was one of the souvenirs that Stephanos sent us. I told you he sent what was on Michael's body when he died. There were three of these gold sovereigns." He moved away from me, holding the lighter low over the flags, searching for the central mark. You'd have thought there was nothing in his mind except the pleasant task of showing a girl over the Delphic ruins.

"Simon . . ."

"Here it is." He straightened up, the lighter still burning in his hand. He must have seen my look, because he smiled at me, that sudden, very attractive smile. "You know, I did tell you it was no longer a present tragedy, didn't I? I told you not to worry. Now, come here to the centre, and hear how your voice is picked up and carried high over those tiers of seats."

I moved forward to the spot. "I know you did. But when you told me that, you didn't know that your brother Michael had been murdered. Doesn't that make a difference?"

"Perhaps. There, do you hear the echo?"

"Glory, yes. It's weird, isn't it? As if the sound were coming back at you from those crags up there, and swirling all round you. It's like something tangible; like—yes, like sound made solid. . . . Are you really going to recite something, or would you rather not?"

I thought he misunderstood me deliberately. "With this lack of audience, I think I might. What'll you have?"

"You're the classicist. I leave it to you. But wait a moment. I'm going up into the back stalls."

I climbed the narrow aisle and found a seat two thirds of the way up the amphitheatre. The shaped marble of the seat was surprisingly comfortable, and the stone was still warm from the day's sun. The circular stage looked small below me. I could just make out its shape. Simon was nothing but a bodiless shadow. Then his voice came up out of the well of darkness, and the great rolling Greek lines rose and broke and echoed, rounding like a wind among the high crags. A phrase, a name, swam up from the flood of sound, giving directions to the music, like flights to an arrow. "Hades, Persephone, Hermes. . . ." I shut my eyes and listened.

He stopped. There was a pause. The echo went up the cliff, hung like the murmur of a gong, and died. Then his voice came clearly and softly, speaking in English; music translating music.

> ". . . Hades, Persephone,
> Hermes, steward of death,
> Eternal Wrath and Furies,
> Children of gods,
> Who see all murderers
> And all adulterous thieves, come soon!
> Be near me, and avenge
> My father's death, and bring
> My brother home!"

He had stopped speaking again. The words died into silence high above me, and in the wake of the echo, it seemed, the night wind moved. I heard the hollies rustle behind me, and then, further up the hill, a scatter of dust and pebbles under the foot of some wandering beast, a goat, perhaps, or a donkey; I thought I heard the clink of metal. Then the night was still again. I got up and started down the steep aisle.

Simon's voice came, pitched quietly and perfectly clear. "That do?"

"Beautifully." I reached the bottom and crossed the stage. "Thank you very much; but—I thought you said the tragedy was over?"

For the first time since I had known him (some seven hours? Could it possibly be only half a day?) he sounded disconcerted. "What d'you mean?" He left the centre of the stage and came to meet me.

"That speech was a bit—immediate, wasn't it?"

"You recognized it?"

"Yes. It's from Sophocles' *Electra*, isn't it?"

"Yes." There was a pause. He had a hand in his pocket, and now as he withdrew it I heard the chink of coins. He jingled them absently up and down. Then he said, "I was wrong, then. It's not over . . . at least not until Stephanos shows us the place tomorrow, and—"

He stopped. I reflected that Simon Lester seemed to have a remarkably royal habit of using the first person plural. I should have liked to say " 'Show *us?* ' " but didn't. I said merely, "And?"

He said abruptly, "And I find what Michael found—what he was killed for. The gold."

"The gold?"

"Yes. I told you I'd an idea what it was that Michael

might have found. I thought that, as soon as I read his
letters, and remembered the sovereigns he was carrying. And
after what Stephanos told us, I'm sure. It was gold he found,
Angelos' little hoard of British gold, stashed away against
the day of the Red Dawn."

"Yes, but Simon . . ." I began, then stopped. He knew
Michael better than I did, after all.

The sovereigns clinked together as he thrust them back
into his pocket. He turned away towards the side of the amphitheatre.

"This is the way up to the path. I'd better go first, perhaps; the steps are badly broken in places."

He reached a hand back to me, and together we mounted
the steep flight. At the top he paused and seemed to reach
up into the darkness. I heard the rustle of leaves. He turned
back to me and put something round and polished and cool
into my hand. "There you are. It's pomegranate. There's a
little tree growing behind the topmost seats, and I've been
longing for an excuse to pick one. Eat it soon, Persephone;
then you'll have to stay in Delphi."

The path led us out at last above the trees, where we could
see our way more clearly. It was wide enough now to walk
side by side. Simon went on, speaking softly, "I think I'm
right, Camilla; I think that's what Michael found. I'd
suspected it before, but now I know he was murdered by his
man Angelos, I'd bet on it for a certainty."

I said rather stupidly, still following my own thoughts,
"But Stephanos said he was killed in a quarrel. Angelos and
he—"

"If Michael had been quarrelling with a type like that he
wouldn't be very likely to turn his back on him," said
Simon. "I'm surprised Stephanos didn't think that one out
for himself."

"But if it was an old quarrel, and Michael thought it was
forgotten, but Angelos—"

"The same applies. I just don't see Michael trustfully
turning his back on a man who'd once had—or thought he
had—the sort of grudge that leads to murder."

"I suppose not."

"But take all the bits of the picture and put them together," said Simon, "and what d'you get? I told you that we
—the British—were flying in arms and gold during the Occupation, for the use of the *andartes*. Angelos, as we now
learn from Stephanos, was working for the Communist
putsch at the end of the German Occupation of Greece;

therefore, we can assume that he had an interest in holding back arms and supplies for later use. That's an assumption; but what facts have we? Angelos, when his men scatter northwards to avoid the Germans, comes south—alone. He meets Michael and kills him. He is interrupted before he can search the body, and on Michael are found gold sovereigns, and a hastily scribbled letter indicating that he has found something."

"Yes," I said, "but—"

"If Angelos had such a cache of guns and gold, and Michael, the B.L.O., had found it, would it not be the complete motive for Michael's murder?"

"Yes, of course it would. You mean that Michael, when he met him, tackled him about it and—oh, no, that won't do, will it? There's the same objection—that Angelos wouldn't have had the chance to hit him over the head."

"I can't help thinking," said Simon softly, "that Angelos saw something that told him Michael had found the cache. It's probably in some cave or other—Parnassus is honeycombed with them; and supposing that Michael, after he left Stephanos' house, had taken shelter in the one where the stuff was hidden? He'd stay there a few days till the Germans left the area, and then Angelos, doubling back to his treasure chest, would see the British officer coming out of the cave, his cave. . . . It could be, you know. And if Michael didn't see Angelos, as seems obvious, the Greek waited and took his chance and tried to wipe him out then and there. Which means—"

"Which means that, if you're right, the cache was very near the place where Michael was murdered," I said.

"Exactly. Well, we shall see."

"If there was anything, it'll have been taken long since."

"Probably."

"Angelos would come back and take it. If not immediately, then later."

"If he lived to come back. Three months after Mick's death he was out of the country for good."

I said, as casually as I could, "Was he? And what if Niko was possibly—just possibly—right? If he were still alive? Now, I mean?"

Simon laughed. "It's on the lap of the gods, isn't it?" One of the coins spun in his hand as he tossed and caught it. "What do you say? Shall we offer gold to Apollo if he'll bring Angelos back to Delphi now?"

"Aegisthus to Orestes' knife?" I tried to speak equally

lightly, but in spite of myself the words sounded harsh and hollow.

"Why not?" The coin dropped into his hand again and his fingers closed on it. He was a shadow in the starlight, watching me. "You know, I told you the truth when I said the tragedy was over. I don't feel chewed up or dramatic about Mick's death, even after what I've learned tonight. But, damn it all, he was murdered, in a filthy way, and—if I'm right—for the filthiest of motives. And the murderer got away with it, and possibly with a fortune into the bargain. I've no particular desire to find the fortune, but I want to know, Camilla. That's all."

"Yes, I see."

"I came here to talk to Stephanos and see Michael's grave, and to leave it at that. But I can't leave it now, not till it's really over, and I know why it happened. I don't suppose there'll be anything left to tell me, after all this time, but I have to look. And as for Orestes"—I heard the smile in his voice—"I've no particular ambition for revenge, either, but if I did meet the murderer . . . don't you see that I'd quite like a word with him?" He laughed again. "Or do you share Niko's opinion of my abilities?"

"No. No, of course not. But this man Angelos . . . well, he's—" I floundered and stopped.

"Dangerous? So you don't think that—if I do meet him— I ought to have it out with him?"

"An eye for an eye?" I said. "I thought we didn't believe in that any more."

"Don't you believe it. We do. But in England there's a fine, impersonal, and expensive machinery to get your eye for you, and no personal guilt except your signature on a cheque to the Inland Revenue. Here, it's different. Nobody's going to do the dirty work for you. You do it yourself and nobody knows but the vultures. And Apollo."

"Simon, it's immoral."

"So is all natural law. Morals are social phenomena. Didn't you know?"

"I don't agree."

"No? You stick to that, Camilla. This is the loveliest country in the world, and the hardest. Much of it, and you're apt to find yourself thinking in its terms instead of your own. There are times, I'd say, when you have to. . . . But you stand by your guns." He laughed down at me. "And for a start, don't believe a word I say. I'm a normal law-abiding citizen, and a most upright and solemn schoolmaster. . . . Now, enough of this Orestean tragedy. Michael's dead these fourteen years, and Delphi's been here three thousand, so we'll let Delphi bury its dead. It does it just here, incidentally; that's the graveyard just beside the path, under the trees. And now, if you're to get any sleep at all tonight, what about chasing up that drink? That's the studio there."

Without another glance in the direction of the graveyard, he led the way at a quickened pace over level ground towards the lights of the studio.

CHAPTER

8

Whom the gods love . . .
Menander
(tr. Lord Byron).

The studio was a big rectangular building situated on top of the bluff behind the village of Delphi. Later, in daylight, I was to see it as a big ugly box of a place, set down on a flat plateau quarried out of the living rock, so that, while its front windows commanded a magnificent view of the valley, its back looked out onto a wall of rock as high as its second storey. On this, the north side, were the big "front" doors, impressive affairs of plate glass which were never used. The tenants got in and out by a small door in the east end, which gave on the corridor running the length of the ground floor.

Inside, the place was as bare and functional as possible. Corridors and stairs were of marble, and spotlessly clean. On the lower floor, and to the left of the corridor, were the artists' bedrooms, facing south over the valley. These were simple in the extreme, each bedroom holding nothing but an iron bedstead with blankets and pillows, a washbasin with h. and c. both perpetually c., a small and inevitably unsteady table, and hooks for hanging clothes. Opening off each bedroom was a marble-floored shower stall—also, presumably, c. Opposite the bedrooms were other doors which I never saw opened, but which I imagined might be some sort of kitchen premises, or rooms for the caretaker. The resident artists worked on the upper floor where the light was better; here a row of rooms on the north side of the corridor served as studios and storerooms for their work.

But all this I was to discover later. Tonight the building was merely an ugly oblong box of a place planted down in a small quarry, with the light from a bare electric bulb showing us the door.

We had hardly got into the echoing corridor, when a door

a short way along it opened, and a young man came out like a bullet from a gun. He caught at the jamb of the door as he catapulted out and hung on, almost as if he felt the need of the door's support. He said in a high excited voice, "Oh, Simon, I was just—" Then he saw me and stopped, disconcerted, still theatrically posed in the stream of light that came from the door.

There was something about this method of appearance that was very like Niko's but there the resemblance ended. The young man—who I supposed was Nigel—had none of Niko's beauty or promise of strength, and very little, in consequence, of Niko's assurance. There was no conscious drama in his actions, and indeed now he was looking miserably embarrassed, almost as if he would have liked to retreat into his room and lock the door. He was tallish, and thin, and fair. His skin had taken the sun badly, and his eyes, which were that puckered blue that you see in sailors and airmen and men who habitually gaze into the distances, looked as if they had had too much sun. He had a straggling little beard that made him look young and rather vulnerable, and his hair was bleached to the colour and texture of dry hay. He had a weakly sensual mouth and the strong ugly hands of the artist.

Simon said, "Hullo, Nigel. This is Camilla Haven, who's staying at the Apollon. I've brought her up for a drink, and she wants to see your drawings. Do you mind?"

"Oh. No. Not at all. Delighted," said Nigel, stammering a little. "C-come into my room, then. We'll have a drink here." As he stood aside for me to pass him, slightly more flushed than before, I found myself wondering if he had been drinking alone in his room. There was that queer look about his eyes, a sort of sense that he was clutching at himself as really, as physically, as he had clutched at the door jamb, and in the same effort to control.

His room, basically as bare as the rest of the building, was frantically but rather pleasantly untidy. It was as if the artist's personality, far richer than it appeared from the look of him, had spilled over without his knowing it into the monastic-looking little cell. At the foot of the bed a rucksack stood on the floor, its contents bursting out in confusion. I saw two shirts, as brightly but rather more respectably coloured than Niko's, a tangle of rope, some dirty handkerchiefs which had obviously been pressed into use as paint rags, three oranges, and a copy of the *Collected Poems of Dylan Thomas*. The towel which was flung over the edge of the washbasin was as brightly yellow as a dandelion. Nigel's pyjamas, in a huddle on the bed, were striped in wine and turquoise. And everywhere on the cracked white walls there were sketches, drawing-pinned haphazardly; they were in a variety of styles, so that, looking from the bold to the delicate, from the pencil sketches to the water-colours curling up at the edges as they dried, I remembered what Simon had told me.

But I had no time to do more than glance, because our host had dived past me, and was dragging forward the room's best chair, a canvas affair of grubby orange.

"W-won't you sit down, Miss—Er? It's the best there is. It's quite clean really."

I thanked him and sat down. Simon had wandered over to the window, and hitched himself up onto the wide sill, where he sat, one leg swinging. Nigel, still with that air of disconcerted fussiness, was rummaging rather wildly among bottles on the floor of the shower stall. In a moment he emerged clutching two tumblers and a large bottle of ouzo.

"Do you like this stuff?" he asked me anxiously. "It's all there is."

There was something about Nigel that disarmed me into a deliberate lie. "I love it," I said, and waited resignedly while he poured a generous dollop into one of the tumblers, and handed it to me. "Would you like water with it?"

Now, ouzo is the Greek absinthe. It is made from aniseed, and tastes fairly mild and (to my mind) incredibly unpleasant. I find it quite undrinkable neat. On the other hand, if you add sufficient water to make it swallowable, there is a lot more to swallow.

I said bravely, "Yes, please."

Nigel grabbed a carafe from above the washbasin. Again it struck me sharply that his movements were a parody of Niko's. They were swift and abrupt and angular, but where Niko's had the grace of a striking cat, Nigel's were clumsy and almost uncoordinated. It was odd for an artist to be clumsy, I thought, then as I watched Nigel pour water into my glass, I saw that his hand was shaking. That was still odder.

The liquid misted, clouded, and went entirely beastly like quinine. I said, "When. Thanks," and smiled at Nigel, who was watching me with an anxious-puppy expression that made him look younger than ever. He was, I judged, about twenty-three, but the beard made him look nineteen. I smiled bravely and lifted the glass.

"*Gia sou, Kyrie* Nigel," I said. "I'm sorry, but I don't know your other name."

"Make it Nigel," he said unhelpfully, but with apparent pleasure.

As I drank carefully, I caught Simon's eye, to see that he knew quite well what I felt about ouzo. I scowled at him and took another drink, reflecting yet again that *Kyrie* Simon Lester saw a damned sight too much. I controlled the shudder that shook me as the liquor went down, and then watched fascinated as Nigel filled Simon's tumbler two thirds full, grabbed a glass for himself and filled that, and then raised it to his lips, and "*Gia sou*" quickly, and drank half of it at one fell gulp, neat.

"Cheers, comrade," said Simon. "Have you had a good day?"

Nigel, choking a little over the liquor, managed to say, "Yes. Oh, yes, thanks. Very."

"Where did you go?"

The young man waved a vague hand, which almost knocked the ouzo bottle off the table, but unfortunately didn't quite. "Up there."

"You mean up in the precinct?"

"No. Up the hill."

"Onto Parnassus again? Did you go up over the old track to hunt up some shepherds after all?" He turned to me. "Nigel's got a contract for a series of drawings of 'Hellenic types'—heads of peasants and old women and shepherd boys and so forth. He's done some quite striking ones in a sort of heavy ink line-and-wash."

Nigel said suddenly, "It's exciting. You can't know how exciting. You see a grubby little boy watching the goats, and when you really start to draw him you realize you've seen him a dozen times already in the museums. And I found a girl last week in Amphissa who was pure Minoan, crimped hair and all. It makes it difficult, too, of course, because try as you will, it looks as if you're copying the original Grecian Urn."

I laughed. "I know. I've met one Zeus and one rather wicked Eros and a couple of dozen assorted satyrs today already."

"Stephanos and Niko?" said Simon.

I nodded. "Nigel ought to meet them."

Nigel said, "Who are they?"

"Stephanos is a shepherd from Arachova and he's straight out of Homer. Niko's his grandson and he's—well, simply a beauty, American-Greek style. But if it's only the head you want, you could hardly do better." I reflected, as I spoke, that Simon had apparently told Nigel nothing about Michael or his mission that evening.

Nor did he tell him now. He said, "You may meet them yet. Stephanos is usually somewhere up between Delphi and Arachova—near that track I took you over yesterday. Is that the way you went again today? How far?"

"Quite a long way." Nigel looked round him vaguely, as if embarrassment had descended on him again, and added quickly, "I was sick of sitting about in the precinct and the valley. I wanted a walk. I got up above the Shining Ones and onto the track and then—well, I just went on walking. It was hot, but up there, there was a breeze."

"No work today?"

Simon's question was no more than idle, but a flush had crept up under Nigel's raw sunburn. It made him look cagey, but I guessed it was only shyness. He said, "No," very shortly, and buried his nose in his glass.

I said, "No shepherds playing pan-pipes to their flocks? On Parnassus? You shake me, Nigel."

He grinned at that. "No, more's the pity."

"And no gods?" I said, thinking of the starlit temple.

But his shyness asserted itself here completely. He said, almost snappily, "No! I tell you I did hardly anything! I was just walking. Anyway those heads are a bore. They're only bread and butter. You wouldn't like them."

"I'd love to see some of your work, though, if you could be bothered to show it. Simon's been telling me how awfully good your drawings are—"

He interrupted in a voice so quick and hoarse that it gave the effect of a small outburst of temper. "Good? Simon's talking bilge. They're not good. They please me, but that's all."

"Some of them are, very good," said Simon quietly.

Nigel sneered at him. "The niminy-piminy ones. The sweet little Ruskin-and-water ones. Can't you just hear the Sunday-paper critics turned loose over them? They're useless and you know it."

"They're first class and *you* know it. If you could—"

"Oh God, if, if, if," said Nigel rudely. He set his glass down on the table with a sharp click. "You know damn well they're useless."

"But they're what you want to do, and they show the way

you want to go, and that's the point, isn't it? They are 'Nigel Barlow,' and what's more, they're uncommon."

"*They're useless.*" The repetition was emphatic.

"If you mean they're not easy to make a living out of here and now, I agree. But I still think—"

" 'To thine own self be true'?" said Nigel, on a high-edged note that might have been excitement but sounded like bitterness. "Oh God, don't be a prosy old bore! And anyway it doesn't matter a damn. Not a damn, do you hear me?"

Simon smiled at him. I think it was then that I first really saw what lay behind that good-tempered and apparently unruffled self-command of Simon's; what made it so very different from the more flamboyant self-confidence I had envied. Simon cared. He really did care what happened to this casually-met, troubled, and not very attractive boy who was being so wretchedly rude. And that was why he had come back after fourteen years to find out what had happened to Michael. It was not a present tragedy, and he was not, after all, an Orestes. But he cared—for his father's sake, for Stephanos', for the woman's. "Any man's death diminishes me, because I am involved in Mankind." That was it. He was involved in mankind, and, just at this moment, that meant Nigel. "One takes it for granted," he had said, "that one is there to help." I suppose one gets to know men quickest by the things they take for granted.

He had set his glass down and now laced his fingers round one knee. "All right. Exit Polonius. Well, d'you want us to find you a selling line, Nigel?"

Nigel said, not rudely now, but still with a touch of that hot and slightly sulky impatience, "You mean a gimmick to make people come and look at them? A bloody little quick-sales trick to crowd a one-man show somewhere in the wilds of Sheffield or something? Two pretty drawings sold and my name in the local press? Is that what you mean?"

Simon said mildly, "One has to start somewhere. Couldn't you count it as part of the fight? And at least it might mean you hadn't to fall back on the ultimate degradation."

"What's that?" I asked.

He grinned. "Teaching."

"Oh. Well, I do see what you mean," I said.

"I thought you would."

Nigel said sulkily, "It's all very well to laugh, but I wouldn't be any good at it and I should loathe it, and that would be dreadful."

"The final hell," agreed Simon cheerfully. "Well, we must find you a gimmick, Nigel. Make them come to mock and remain to pay. You must make your pictures out of sequins, or do all your painting under water, or get yourself into the popular press as the Man who Always Paints to the Strains of Mozart."

Nigel gave him a reluctant and slightly shamefaced grin. "Count Basie, more likely. All right, what shall it be? *Art trouvé*, or bits of rusty iron twisted any old way and called 'Woman in Love,' or 'Dog eat Dog,' or something?"

"You could always," I said, "travel through Greece with a donkey, and then write a book, illustrated."

Nigel turned to me at that, but with the look of someone who has hardly been listening. I wondered again if he had been drinking too much. "What? A donkey?"

"Yes. There was a Dutch boy in Delphi this evening who'd just got in from Jannina. He'd been walking over the hills like Stevenson, with a donkey, and painting on the way. I gathered that he'd done a lot of sketching in the villages and more or less paid his way with them."

"Oh, that chap. Yes, I've met him. He's here now."

"Of course, I forgot. Simon told me he'd come up here to sleep tonight. Did you see his work?"

"No. He was too tired to bother. He went to bed at about nine, and I think it'd take an atom bomb to wake him." His look lingered on me as if he were with difficulty bringing me into focus and himself back into the conversation. He said slowly, "Being true to oneself . . . knowing that one can do a thing if only the world will give one the chance . . . but having to fight for it every step of the way. . . ." The blurred blue gaze sharpened and fixed itself on Simon. "Simon . . ."

"Yes?"

"You say a gimmick would be 'part of the fight,' because, in the first place, it would make people stop and look? If my stuff's not really good, no gimmick will get it anywhere beyond the first hurdle. You know that. But if it *is* good, then once people have stopped and paid attention, the *work itself* is what'll count. That's true, isn't it?"

"It could be. In your case I imagine a lot might depend on the gimmick." Simon smiled. "I have a feeling that quite a few good artists have been driven along a path they never intended in the first place as anything but an odd deviation —a wallop in the public's eye. Naming no names, but you know who."

Nigel didn't smile. He seemed still hardly to be listening,

but very busy following his own thoughts. He hesitated, then said suddenly, "Well, and that's being true to oneself, isn't it? And don't you think *that* means, come what may, one should take what one wants and needs? Go straight ahead the way you know you have to go, and the devil take the hindmost? Artists—great artists—work that way, don't they? And doesn't the end justify them?" As Simon seemed to hesitate, he whipped round on me. "What do *you* think?"

I said, "I don't know specially about great artists, but I've always imagined that the secret of personality—I won't say 'success'—was one-track-mindedness. Great men *do* know where they're going, and they never turn aside. Socrates and the 'beautiful and good.' Alexander and the Hellenizing of the world. On a different level, if I may—Christ."

Nigel looked at Simon. "Well?" His voice was sharp, like a challenge. *"Well?"*

I thought, There *is* something going on here that I don't understand. And I don't think Simon understands it either, and it worries him.

Simon said slowly, those cool eyes vividly alive now, watching the younger man, "You're partly right. The great men know where they're going; yes, and they get there, but surely it's a case of driving themselves without pause, rather than juggernauting over all the opposition? You think Polonius was a prosy old bore—you brought him in, remember, not me. I don't agree with him, but do him the justice of looking at the end of the quotation. 'To thine own self be true, . . . Thou canst not then be false to any man.' If being true to oneself means ignoring the claims of other people then it simply doesn't work, does it? No, your really great man—your Socrates—doesn't drive along a straight path of his own cutting. He knows what the end is, yes, and he doesn't turn aside from it, but all the way there he's reckoning with whatever—and whoever—else is in his way. He sees the whole thing as a pattern, and his own place in it."

I quoted, thinking back, " 'I am involved in Mankind'?"

"Exactly."

"What's that?" said Nigel.

"A quotation from John Donne, a poet who became Dean of St. Paul's. This comes in one of his Devotions . . . 'No man is an island, entire of itself.' He's right. In the end it's our place in the pattern that matters."

"Yes, but the artist?" said Nigel almost fiercely. "He's different, you know he is. He's driven by some compulsion:

if he can't do what he knows he *has* to do with his life he might as well be dead. He's got to break through the world's indifference, or else break himself against it. He can't help it. Wouldn't he be justified in doing almost anything to fulfil himself, if his art were worth it in the end?"

"The end justifying the means? As a working principle, never," said Simon. "Never, never, never."

Nigel sat forward in his chair. "Look, I don't mean anything dreadful like—like murder or crime or something! But if there was no other way—"

I said, "What are you planning to do, for goodness' sake? Steal the donkey?"

He swung round on me so sharply that I thought he was going to fall off his chair. Then he gave a sudden laugh that sounded very much to me like the edge of hysteria. "Me? Walk to Jannina and write a book about it? Me? Never! I'd be scared of the wolves!"

"There aren't any wolves," Simon's voice was light, but he was watching Nigel rather closely, and I saw the shadow of trouble in his face.

"The tortoises then!" He grabbed the bottle again and turned back to me. "Have some more ouzo? No? Simon? Here, hold your glass. Did you know, Miss Camilla I've-forgotten-your-other-name, that there were tortoises running about on the hills here? Wild ones? Imagine meeting one of those when you were all alone and miles from anywhere."

"I'd run a mile," I said.

"What *is* it, Nigel?" asked Simon from the windowsill.

For a moment I wondered just what was going to happen. Nigel stopped in mid-movement, with the bottle in one hand. He was rigid. His face went redder, then white, under the peeling sunburn. His ugly spatulate fingers clenched round the bottle as if he were going to throw it. His eyes looked suffused. Then they fell away from Simon's, and he turned to set the bottle down. He said in a curiously muffled voice, "I'm sorry. I'm behaving badly. I was a bit high before you came in, that's all."

Then he turned back to me with one of his quick angular movements that were like those of an awkward small boy. "I don't know what you must think of me. You must think I'm a pretty good heel, but things were getting me down a bit. I —I'm temperamental, that's what it is. Great artists are." He grinned shamefacedly at me, and I smiled back.

"It's all right," I said. "And all great artists have had a horrid struggle for recognition. As long as it doesn't come after you're dead, it's all the sweeter when you get it, and I'm sure you will."

He was down on his knees, lugging a battered portfolio from under the bed. "Here," he said, "I'll show you my drawings. You can tell me if you think they're worth anything. You can tell me." He was dragging a sheaf of papers out of the portfolio.

I said feebly, "But my opinion's no use. I really don't know anything about it."

"Here." He thrust a drawing into my hand. "That's one of the ones Simon talks about. And this." He sat back on his heels on the floor, and sent Simon a look that might almost have been hatred. "I'll be true to myself, Polonius. You can be bloody sure I will. Even if it means being true to nobody else. I'm not involved with mankind, as your old parson friend puts it. I'm myself. Nigel Barlow. And some day you'll know it, you and all the rest. Do you hear?"

"I hear," said Simon peaceably. "Let's see what you've done, shall we?"

Nigel pushed a drawing toward him, and then a handful at me. "This. And this. And this and this and this. They may never set the Thames on fire, but given a push and a bit of luck they're good enough to make me. . . . Aren't they?"

As I looked down at the drawings on my knee I was conscious of Nigel's fixed stare. For all the wild and whirling words the vulnerable look was there again, and on that final question the overemphatic voice had broken into naïve and anxious query. I found myself hoping with ridiculous fervour that the drawings might be good.

They were. His touch was sure and strong, yet delicate. Each line was clean and definite and almost frighteningly effective; he had managed to suggest not only shape, but bulk and texture, by pure drawing with the minimum of fuss. Somehow the technique suggested the faded elegance of a French flower-print combined with the sharp, delicate, and yet virile impact of a Dürer drawing. Some were mere sketches, but over others he had taken greater pains. There were rapid studies of the ruined buildings—part of a broken arch with the sharp exclamatory cypresses behind it; Apollo's columns standing very clear and clean; a delightful drawing of three pomegranates on a twig with shiny drooping leaves. There were several of olive trees, lovely twisted shapes with heads of blown silver cloud. In the plant and flower studies he used colour, in faint washes of an almost Chinese subtlety.

I looked up to see him watching me with that anxious-puppy stare from which all trace of belligerence had gone. "But Nigel, they're wonderful! I told you I didn't know much about it, but I haven't seen anything I liked as much in years!"

I got up from my chair and sat down on the bed, spreading the drawings round me, studying them. I picked one of them up; it was the drawing of a clump of cyclamen springing from a small cleft in a bare rock. The textural differences of petal, leaf and stone were beautifully indicated. Below the flowers, in the same cleft, grew the remains of some rock plant that I remember having seen everywhere in Greece; it was dead and dry-dusty, crumbling away against the rock. Above it the cyclamen's winged flowers looked pure and delicate and strong.

Over my shoulder Simon said, "Nigel, that's terrific. I haven't seen it before."

"Of course you haven't. I only did it today," said Nigel rudely, making a quick movement as if to snatch it back. Then he appeared to remember, as I had, that he'd told Simon he had done no work that day, for he dropped his hand and sat back on his heels, looking uncomfortable.

As usual, Simon took no notice. He lifted the drawing and studied it. "Did you mean to use colour in it? What made you change your mind?"

"Simply that there wasn't any water handy." And Nigel took the paper from him and put it back in the portfolio on the floor.

I said, rather quickly, "May I see the portraits?"

"Of course. Here they are—my bread-and-butter drawings." There was a curious note in his voice, and I saw Simon glance again at him, sharply.

There was a whole sheaf of portraits, done in an entirely different style. This was effective in its way, the beautiful economy of his drawing telling even in the thick, dramatic, and overemphatic line. His brilliance of execution had here become a slickness, the clever blending of a few stock statements into a formula. In a way, too, the originals of the portraits might have come from stock. What Nigel had been doing was, of course, to find "types" and to set these down; but, while some of these were discernibly living people, others could have been abstractions of well-known "Hellenic types" taken from statues or vase paintings or even from the imagination. There was one fine-looking head that might have been Stephanos, but it had a formal and over-typed air like an illustration to a set of Greek myths. A girl's face, all eyes, and deep shadows thrown by a veil, could have been captioned, "Greece: the Gate to the East." Another portrait —more familiar in type to me and so possibly more alive— was that of a young woman with the Juliette Gréco face, large lost eyes and a sulky mouth. Beneath it was the drawing of a man's head that, again, seemed purely formal, but was oddly arresting. The head was round, set on a powerful neck, and covered with close curls that grew low on the brow, like a bull's. The hair grew down thickly past the ears, almost to the jawline, as one sees it in the heroic vase paintings, and these sidepieces were drawn in formally, like the hard curls on a sculptured cheek. The upper lip was short, the lips thick, and drawn tightly up at the corners in the fixed half-moon smile that shows always on the statues of the archaic gods of Greece.

I said, "Simon, look at that. That's the real 'archaic smile.' When you see it on crumbly old statues of Hermes and Apollo you think it's unreal and crude. But I've actually seen it on men's faces here and there in Greece."

"Is that new too?" asked Simon.

"Which? Oh, that. Yes." Nigel gave him a quick upward glance, hesitated, then appeared to abandon his pretences, whatever they were. "I did it today." He took the drawing from me and studied it for a moment. "Perhaps you're right; it's too formal. I did it half from memory, and it's gone a bit too much like a vase painting. However."

"It's the Phormis head to the life," said Simon.

Nigel looked up. "Yes, so it is! That's it. I wondered what he reminded me of. I suppose I drew it in. Still, it makes a 'type' for the collection, and as Camilla says, it does exist. She's seen that queer fixed grin here and there, and so've I. Interesting. I thought."

"What's the Phormis head?" I asked.

Simon said, "It's a head found, as far as I remember, at Olympia, and is supposed to be that of Phormis, who was a playwright. That head is bearded, and this isn't, but it's got the same heavy wide cheeks and tight curls, and that typical smile."

I laughed. "Oh dear, and it's still walking these mountains. It makes me feel raw and new and very, very Western. That face, now—"

My hand was hovering over the Juliette Gréco girl.

Simon laughed. "That's real enough, and very Western indeed," he said. "That's our one and only Danielle, isn't it,

Nigel? You're surely not going to put her in among the 'Hellenic types'?"

"Danielle?" I said. "Oh, she *is* French, then? Somehow I thought she looked it."

Nigel had taken the drawing from Simon, and was stuffing that, too, away. He said in a muffled voice. "She was here as secretary to a chap attached to the French School."

"French School?"

"Of archaeology," said Simon. "It's the French School which has the 'right' or whatever they call it to excavate here at Delphi. They've been working here again recently on the site—there was some talk of a hunt for a lost treasury fairly high up the hill. You'll see a lot of exploratory pits dug on both sides of the road, too, but all they found there was Roman."

"Ah, yes. Modern stuff."

He grinned. "That's it. Well, they've had to pack up, because I believe funds gave out. Some of their workmen are still here tidying up—there are trucks and tools and what-have-you to be removed. But the archaeologists have gone, more's the pity."

I saw Nigel throw him a sidelong glance, and remembered suddenly something that Simon had said to me earlier. "He's been here in Delphi too long, and got tied up with a girl who wasn't very good for him."

I said, "Yes. I'd rather have liked to watch them at it. And think of the excitement if anything did turn up!"

He laughed. "*That* sort of excitement, I believe, is the rarest kind! Most of the long years are spent shifting tons of earth a couple of yards, and then putting them back again. But I agree. It would be terrific. And what a country! Did you see that glorious thing of the Negro and the horse that the workmen dug up when they were mending the drains in Omonia Square a few years ago? Imagine wondering what you might find every time you set out to dig your garden or put a plough to the hillside! After all, even the Charioteer—" He stopped, and turned his cigarette over in his fingers as if he were admiring the twist of blue smoke that curled and frothed from it.

Nigel looked up. "The Charioteer?" He was still kneeling on the floor, shuffling the drawings in the folder into some sort of order. "The Charioteer?" he repeated mechanically, as if his mind was on something else.

Simon drew on the cigarette. "Uh-huh. He wasn't dug up till eighteen ninety-six, long after the main shrines and treasuries had been excavated. Not long ago I read Murray's *History of Greek Sculpture,* and wondered why the author was so sketchy about Delphi, till I realized that, when he wrote his book in eighteen ninety, the half was not told him. Who knows what else is still up there in the odd corners under the trees?"

Nigel had sat back on his heels, his hands moving vaguely and clumsily among the drawings. If they were indeed his bread and butter he was, it occurred to me, remarkably careless of them.

He looked up now, the drawings spilling again from his hands.

"Simon." It was that strung-up voice again.

"Well?"

"I think I—" Then he stopped abruptly and turned his head. The studio's outer door had opened and shut with a bang. Rapid footsteps approached along the corridor.

To my surprise Nigel went as white as a sheet. He swung round towards me, swept the rest of the drawings off the bed into an unceremonious heap, then hastily gathered them all together to shove back into the folder on the floor.

As unceremoniously, the door burst open.

A girl stood there, surveying the untidy and crowded little room with an expression of weary distaste. It was the girl of the portrait, Gréco-look and all. It was also, I thought with a lightly quickened interest, the girl whose jeep, outside Thebes, had bullied the bus into submission in such a masterly way. She looked as she had then, completely in control of the situation, and rather bored with it.

She drawled, without removing the cigarette from the corner of her mouth, "Hullo, Simon, my love. Hullo, Nigel. On your knees praying over my picture? Well, the prayer's answered. I've come back."

CHAPTER

9

A girl—
No virgin either, I should guess—a baggage
Thrust on me like a cargo on a ship
To wreck my peace of mind!

SOPHOCLES: *Women of Trachis*
(tr. E. F. Watling).

Danielle was slightly built, of medium height, and had made the most (or the worst, according to the point of view) of her figure by encasing it in drainpipe jeans and a very tight sweater of thin wool, which left nothing to wonder at except how in the world did she get her breasts that shape and into that position. They were very high and very pointed and the first thing that one noticed about her. The second was her expression, which was very much the weary-waif look of Nigel's picture. Her face was oval, and palely sallow. Her eyes were very big and very black, carefully shadowed with a blend of brown and green that made them look huge and tired. She had long curling lashes that caught the smoke wisping up blue from the cigarette that appeared fixed to her lower lip. She wore pale lipstick, which looked odd and striking with the sallow face and huge dark eyes. Her hair was black and straight and deliberately untidy, cut in that madly smart way that looks as if it had been hacked off in the dark with a pair of curved nail-scissors. Her expression was one of world-weary disdain. Her age might have been anything from seventeen to twenty-five. She looked as if she hoped you would put it at something over thirty.

I should perhaps say here that her eyelashes were very long, quite real, and quite beautiful. This is in case it should be thought that my description of Danielle smacks of prejudice. The only reason that I had then for prejudice was the expression on Nigel's face, stuck there on his knees on the floor with his ungainly hands full of the delicate drawings, turning to face the door, and saying *"Danielle!"* in a cracked young voice that gave him away immediately and very cruelly.

He shoved the drawings clumsily into the folder and got to his feet.

After that first greeting she had ignored him. Nor, after one cool glance, had she looked at me. Her eyes were all over Simon.

She said again, "Hullo." I don't quite know how she made the simple dissyllable sound sexy, but she did.

"Hullo," said Simon, not sounding sexy at all. He was looking ever so slightly amused, and also wary, which annoyed me. Why it should, I'm not prepared to say, and didn't try at the time.

Nigel said hoarsely, "What are you doing here? I thought you'd left Delphi."

"I had. But I came back. Aren't you going to ask me in, Nigel dear?"

"Of course. Come in. It's wonderful—I mean I didn't expect you back. Come in. Sit down." He darted forward and dragged out the best chair—the one I had vacated—for her. But she walked past it towards Simon, who was standing by the window. She went very close to him. "I'm sleeping in the studio, Simon. I got tired of the Tourist Hotel, and anyway I can't afford it now. You don't mind me coming here, do you . . . Simon?"

"Not in the very least." He looked across her at me. "You'd better be introduced. Camilla, this, as you'll have guessed, is Danielle. Camilla Haven; Danielle Lascaux. I told you that Danielle was here for some time with the French School. She was Hervé Clément's secretary. You probably know the name. He wrote *Later Discoveries at Delphi.*"

"I read it not long before I came here. How d'you do?" I said to Danielle.

She gave me a brief stare, and a barely civil nod. Then she turned, and with what looked like very conscious grace, sat down at the opposite end of the bed from me, curled her slim legs up under her, and leaned back against the bedhead. She tilted her head and sent Simon a long look between narrowed lids.

"So you've been talking about me?"

Nigel said eagerly, "It was your portrait—the one I did of you." With one of his ungraceful gestures he indicated the untidily stuffed portfolio lying on the bed beside me.

"Oh, that."

"It's very good, don't you think?" I said. "I recognized you as soon as you came in."

"Uh-huh. Nigel's quite a clever boy, we know that." She sent him a smile that was a shadow of the one she'd given Simon, then reached out an idle hand and pulled two or three sheets out of the folder. I saw Nigel make a small sharp movement, as if of involuntary protest, then he sat down in the orange canvas chair, his hands dangling between his bony knees.

"Yes, I suppose it's a good enough portrait. Are my eyes really as big as that, Nigel?" She was leafing through the drawings: her own portrait; the one we had called the "Phormis head," with the close curls and tight smile; the cyclamen; and a drawing I hadn't yet seen, of a man's head and shoulders. "Flowers?" said Danielle. "Are they *paying* you to do things like that, Nigel? . . . *Who's this?*"

Her voice had changed on the query, so abruptly that I was startled. I saw Simon turn his head, and Nigel almost jumped. "Who? Oh, that. That's a chap I saw today on Parnassus. We were just saying before you came in that he was like—"

"No, no!" She had been holding the Phormis head and another drawing. She dropped the former abruptly, and thrust the other forward. "Not that one. This."

Something in her voice suggested an effort for self-command, and to my surprise her hand was unsteady. But when I said, "May I?" and leaned forward to take the drawing gently from her, she let it go without protest. I looked at it with interest, and then more sharply. It showed the head and bared throat of a young man. The face was beautiful, but not with Niko's vital and very Greek beauty; this was remote, stern, perhaps a little sad. He was not, I thought, a "Hellenic type" at all, though something about him was oddly familiar. But it appeared that he was not intended to form part of Nigel's gallery. This was the only portrait I had seen where Nigel had used what I might call his "flower technique." It was in his own style; the work was delicate, sure and arrestingly beautiful.

"Why, *Nigel* . . ." I said. "Simon, look at this!" Danielle let the others fall to the coverlet. She appeared abruptly to have lost interest, only asking, "Did you do these today?"

"Yes." And Nigel, before Simon had time to do more than glance at the drawing, had finally and this time effectively swept every drawing back into the folder and shoved it under the bed. He looked flustered, and every bit as resentful as he had earlier. But Danielle didn't pursue the subject. She leaned back again and said in her usual slightly bored tone, "For God's sake, Nigel, *are* you going to offer me a drink?"

"Of course." Nigel dived for the bottle of ouzo, put it down again so that it rocked and nearly spilt, then dashed to rinse a tumbler out in the basin.

I put my own glass down and made as if to get to my feet. But at that moment I caught Simon's eye, and I thought he shook his head very slightly. I sat back.

He looked down at the girl. "I thought you'd gone, Danielle. Hasn't the 'dig' packed up?"

"Oh, that. Yes. We got to Athens last night, and really I thought it would be rather a *thing* to be back in civilization again, but I had the most dreary scene with Hervé and then I thought to myself I really might as well be back in Delphi with . . ." she smiled suddenly, showing very white teeth . . . "back in Delphi. So here I am."

Nigel said, "You mean you've got the sack?"

"You could call it that." She watched him for a moment through the cigarette smoke, then she turned to me. "Simon told you the polite fiction," she said. "Actually, of course, I was Hervé Clément's mistress."

"*Danielle!*"

"For God's sake, Nigel!" She hunched an impatient shoulder. "Don't pretend you didn't know." Then to me, "But he was getting to be a bit of a bore."

"Really?" I said politely.

I thought her look was calculating under the long lashes. "Yes, really. They all do, sooner or later, don't you think? Do you find men bore you, Camilla Haven?"

"Occasionally," I said. "But then so—occasionally—do women."

That one went straight past her. "I hate women anyway," she said simply. "But Hervé, he was honestly getting to be the utter *end*. Even if he hadn't quit the 'dig' here and gone back to Athens, I'd have had to leave him." She blew out a long cloud of smoke, and turned her head to look up at Simon. "So back I came. But I'll have to sleep here, at the studio. I'm on my own now, so I haven't got the cash for the Tourist Pavilion, or anywhere else for that matter. . . ." She smiled slowly, still looking at Simon. "So I'll have to sleep rough."

What it was in her intonation I do not know, but somehow she managed to say the last simple sentence as if it meant sharing a bed with a sadist, and that meant Simon. I

felt another spasm of intense irritation. I knew I should have
wanted to feel sorry for Danielle, or even amused, but somehow it wasn't possible. I was beginning to suspect that she
was not trying to ape a pathetic maturity; the *weltschmerz*
wasn't a pose, it was real, and rather dreadful. So was the
weariness in the big lost eyes. But the pity I should have
owed her I felt for Nigel, now feverishly drying the tumbler
and saying rapidly:

"It's wonderful to have you back. You know that. And of
course you must stay in the studio. We'd love to have you,
and you'll be quite all right here. There's only me and Simon
and a Dutch painter—"

"A Dutch painter?"

Simon said smoothly, "A boy of about twenty who has
walked from Jannina and is very, very tired."

She shot him a look up under the fabulous lashes. "Oh."
She threw the half-smoked cigarette into the washbasin where
it lay smouldering. "Give me another cigarette, Simon."

He obeyed. "Camilla?"

"Thank you," I said.

Nigel pushed past me with a tumbler three parts full of
neat ouzo. "Here's your drink, Danielle." His face was anxious, concentrated. He might have been carrying the Holy
Grail. She took it from him and gave him a brilliant smile.
I saw him blink, and the flush on the burnt cheek-bones
deepened. She lifted the glass towards him.

"*Gia sou,* Nigel darling. I'm glad I came back. . . . But
you're not drinking with me."

It should have been corny, but it wasn't. The expression
on the boy's face was naked. He turned and grabbed the bottle and poured an inch or two of liquor into his empty glass.
But even as he turned back, the girl yawned, stretched, tilted
her head back on its long neck, and put out a hand towards
Simon. Her fingernails were very long and very red. Her
fingers ran caressingly down his sleeve. "Actually," she said,
still in that bored, velvet voice, "actually, you know, I'm Simon's girl. Aren't I, Simon?"

I must have jumped about a foot. Simon looked down
through the smoke of his cigarette, and said lazily, "Are you?
Delighted, of course. But perhaps in that case you'll tell me
why you hired a car for me in Athens this morning?"

The hand froze, then withdrew quickly. The thin body
twisted on the bed in the first movement she had made un-
consciously since she came in. It wasn't sexy in the least. It
was plain startled. "What are you talking about?"

"The car you hired in my name this morning. The car you were to have picked up at the Alexandros restaurant."

The black eyes held his for a moment, then dropped. "Oh, that." Her voice was calm and husky as usual. "How did you find out?"

"My dear Danielle, you hired it for me, didn't you? And you failed to pick it up. Naturally the people at the Alexandros got in touch with me."

"But that's impossible! How did they know?" She was scowling up at him now.

"Never mind how. Tell me why."

She shrugged and drank ouzo. "I wanted to come back to Delphi. I told you that I hired a car. They never take any notice in Greece of a woman, so I gave your name."

"And said it was a matter of life and death?"

"What? Don't be silly. Of course I never said that." She laughed. "You're very dramatic, Simon."

"Perhaps. A dramatic place, this. It gets into the blood. But you did hire the car."

"Yes."

"And came without it."

"Yes."

"Why?"

I thought unhappily, Because a fool of a girl called Camilla Haven had already taken it. Why couldn't Simon let well enough alone? Somehow I didn't particularly want to tangle with Danielle Lascaux. And she had every right to be mad with me if she had hired the beastly car—in whatever name—and had then presumably had to hunt up other transport for herself when she found it gone. All the same, she would have to be told sooner or later. . . .

"Why?" asked Simon.

She said sulkily, "Because I got the offer of the jeep from Hervé. It was more convenient."

I said, "I was right, then. I thought I recognized you. You were the girl in the jeep that overtook me just before Thebes. I remember you particularly. You were driving on the wrong side of the road."

She yawned, showing her tongue between her teeth. She didn't even look at me. "Probably. I find it more exciting that way."

Simon said, "Then you got up here well before Camilla did. Where've you been?"

She said, almost bad-temperedly, "What's it matter? Around."

I said, "In Itea?"

Danielle shot upright on the bed. Some ouzo spilled. "What are you talking about?" I saw a look of surprise touch Simon's face, then the familiar expressionless mask shut down. With the faintest quickening of the blood, I thought, He's interested. This means something.

I said, "I saw the jeep in Itea this evening. It was parked beside a house that stands right away from the village in the olive woods. I hadn't realized till this minute that it was the same one, but now I remember. It had a little tinsel doll hanging in the windscreen—where they usually have the icons. I remember noticing that when you passed me near Thebes."

She wasn't drinking. The smoke from that eternal cigarette crept up in a veil hiding the expression of her eyes. "This evening? How can you be so sure? Wasn't it dark?"

"Oh, yes. But there was a man with a torch tinkering with the engine, and the light caught the tinsel. Then the lights went on in the house."

"Oh." She drank a gulp of neat ouzo. It didn't appear to affect her. "Well, I expect it was the same jeep. I was down there, with . . . someone I know." Again that intonation, that glance up towards Simon. Nigel was watching her like a lost dog. I thought it was some—surprising—impulse of mercy that made her add, "I always go down to Itea in the afternoons. I've done it for weeks. I go to swim. Nigel knows that."

Nigel responded instantly, almost as if the last sentence had been a plea of proof. "Of course I know. But—did you really go there today before you even came up here?"

"Uh-huh." She gave him a narrow, glinting smile. "You were out, weren't you?"

"Yes."

"I thought you might be. And I'd brought Elena a present from Athens, so—"

"Elena?" said Nigel quickly.

"My friend in Itea. She often bathes from the same place as me, so I went back to her house with her."

"Oh!" said Nigel.

I thought she watched him for a second before she turned back to me. "And you, Camilla Haven? *You* went down to Itea first, before you came up here?"

"I only came up here an hour ago. I'm only visiting. I'm staying at the Apollon."

"But you went straight to Itea." The words were sharp,

almost, and sounded so much like an accusation that I said quickly, "I called at the hotel first " Then I added, ' I went down to Itea to find the hirer of the car."

There was a little silence "The . . . hirer of the car?" repeated Danielle.

"Yes. I—it was I who brought the car up from the Alexandros in Omonia Square. I—I was looking for the 'Monsieur Simon' who was alleged to be wanting it."

She blew out a small cloud of smoke and leaned back against the head of the bed, regarding me through it. "I . . . see. You brought my car up here? You?"

"Yes," I said unhappily. "I was in the Alexandros restaurant when the man from the garage came, and he mistook me for you. He gave me the keys and told me it was urgent, and that 'Monsieur Simon' wanted the car at Delphi as soon as possible. I—we got in a muddle of cross-purposes, and he vanished, leaving me with the key, and no idea of the address of the garage. I didn't know what to do, but I wanted to come here myself, and—well, he'd been so insistent that it was a 'matter of life and death' that—"

"That stuff again," said Danielle.

"That stuff again." I added, "I'm glad I don't seem to have inconvenienced you after all. You must have got here well before me. I told you you passed me before Thebes."

She said quite sharply, "And why did you have to go to Itea to find Simon?"

"Oh, I didn't. I—well, he found me quite easily. But of course as he didn't know anything about the car, that didn't help. We went to look for another 'Simon,' actually a Simonides who keeps a baker's shop near the cinema."

"That's not," said Danielle, "in the olive woods."

"No. I went to see the Pilgrims' Way."

"The Pilgrims' Way?" she said blankly.

Simon said, "Yes. You ought to know all about that, Danielle."

She said quickly, "Why?"

"My dear girl. Because you've worked here as an archaeologist's secretary."

"Mistress," said Danielle automatically.

Nigel said suddenly from behind me, "I wish you wouldn't talk like that."

She opened her mouth as if to say something blistering, but shut it again, and gave him one of her slow smiles. I didn't look at him. I said quickly, "Look, Danielle, I really am terribly sorry about this car. I suppose I—yes, I did think I might be doing the right thing, but it seems I was a bit hasty. I do hope it isn't going to cause any inconvenience *now*, because—"

"You brought it up here." She turned her head to give me a narrow look through the curling smoke. "You keep it."

I looked at her for a moment. Then I said slowly, "I suppose that is fair enough."

"You weren't asked to bring it here. I don't want it. You're stuck with it, and I hope you can afford to pay for it." She turned away to flick ash towards the washbasin. It missed and fell to the floor.

There was a short silence. I said carefully, "Whom do I pay?"

Her head came quickly back to me. "What d'you mean?"

"What I said."

"Well, me, of course. Didn't they tell you the deposit had been paid?"

"Oh, yes, they told me that."

"So what?" said Danielle.

I stood up and picked up my handbag. "Only that it surprises me a bit that you didn't call in on the garage after you'd got the jeep, and cancel the car. If you're as short of money as you've been telling us, I'd have imagined the deposit would have come in very handy. In fact, I can't see why you should have hired a car at all. The bus is cheaper. Perhaps you'll let me have the receipt, with the address of the garage?"

She sounded sulky. "Tomorrow. I have it somewhere."

"Very well." I turned to smile at Nigel. "I really must go, Nigel, or it'll be dawn before I get to bed. Thank you very much for the drink, and for letting me see the drawings. I think they're wonderful—I honestly do; and that last one is . . . well, a masterpiece. That isn't trite; it's true. Good night."

Simon was on his feet. As I turned to go, he made as if to move forward, but Danielle came off the bed in one quick wriggle. It brought her very close to him.

"Simon"—the claws were on his arm again—"my room's the one at the end, and the shower's stuck, or something. The damned thing drips and I'll never get to sleep. D'you suppose you could fix it for me?"

"I doubt if I'd be much good with it. In any case I'm seeing Camilla home now, and then I—"

I said stiffly, "There's not the slightest need to see me home. I can find my way quite easily."

"—and then I've got to go back and pick the car up. We left it below the shrine."

Nigel had opened the door for me. I looked back at Simon, with Danielle clinging to his arm. "You really needn't trouble. The car is my responsibility . . . as Danielle has pointed out."

His eyes, amused, met mine. I bit my lip, and said, "All right. I—it's very kind of you."

"Not at all. After all, if the car was hired in my name I've a sort of responsibility myself, wouldn't you say, Danielle?"

She flashed me one look of pure venom, under her lashes, then lifted them again to him. Her voice was all honey. "Not really. But if that's how you feel. . . . You'll come and fix that shower later, won't you? It really is a bore."

"Not tonight," said Simon. "Good night. Good night, Nigel, and thanks a lot. See you later."

On the way down to the hotel—which took about twelve minutes and was very steep and rough—we concentrated on not breaking our ankles and on not talking about Danielle. For me, the first was the easier task of the two.

At the hotel Simon said, "Camilla."

"Yes?"

"Come off it."

I laughed. "Very well."

"I grant you every right to the highest horse, or deepest dudgeon, or whatever it is, in Christendom. All right?"

"Perfectly."

"Don't worry about the damned car. I didn't pursue it in front of—well, back there, but I'll be very glad of it myself now that it's here, so don't give it another thought."

"I will not," I said clearly, "allow you to pay for my—my folly."

"We will not," said Simon calmly, "argue about it now. You should be in bed. You've had a long day, and tomorrow will probably be longer."

"I shall probably have to go tomorrow."

"Tomorrow? My God, the dudgeon isn't as deep as that, is it?"

"Dudgeons are high. No, it's not that. But there may not be a room at the hotel."

"Oh, I forgot. Well, look here, why not come up to the studio? You've seen it. It's plain, but clean, and very convenient. And now it seems"—the grey eyes crinkled at the corners—"that you'll be chaperoned."

"I'll think about it," I said, without much enthusiasm.

He hesitated, then said, "I hope you will. I—please don't go tomorrow. I was hoping you'd come with me."

I stared at him. "But—I thought you were going up Parnassus with Stephanos?"

"I am. I want you to come. Will you?"

"But Simon—"

"Will you?"

I said huskily, "This is absurd."

"I know. But there it is."

"It's your own very private business. Just because I—I bulldozed you into my affairs it doesn't mean you have to ask me to tag along in yours."

The amusement was there again. "No. Will you?"

"Yes. Of course."

"It'll be a long trek. An all-day job. If the hotel say they can't keep you you'll let me ring up Athens for you and get you into the studio?"

"Ring up Athens?"

"It's the property of the University Fine Arts Department, and you're not an accredited artist any more than I am. You'll have to come in as a student."

"Oh, of course. And Danielle?"

He grinned. "Maybe archaeologists count. If she gives my name to hire a car, she may give Hervé's when she wants a room in the studio."

"I suppose so. Well, please ring up Athens for me and I'll move in tomorrow night. What time do we start?"

"I'll call for you at half past eight." He gave me his sudden smile. "Good night, Camilla. And thank you."

"Good night."

As he turned to go, I said, before I could prevent myself, "Don't forget to go and fix the taps, will you?"

"Taps," said Simon gently, "bore me. Good night."

CHAPTER

10

What a personage says or does reveals a certain moral purpose; and a good element of character, if the purpose so revealed is good. Such goodness is possible in every type of personage, even in a woman.

ARISTOTLE: *The Art of Poetry*
(tr. Ingram Bywater).

Next morning I awoke early, so early that, when I found I couldn't easily go to sleep again, I decided to get up and see the ruins on my own before the day's adventures started. The thought made me, with a wry little smile, remember that I hadn't yet posted my letter to Elizabeth. When I was ready to leave my room I fished it out of my bag, opened it, and added a hasty postscript.

"Did I say nothing ever happened to me? It's started as from yesterday. If I live I'll write and let you know what you're missing.

"Love, Camilla."

The sun was already hot and bright, though it was only just a little past seven o'clock. I walked along the village street to post my letter, then turned into the steep way that climbs between terraced streets to the mountainside above.

This was a flight of wide steps, bounded by whitewashed walls from which the sun beat back. The already blinding white was muted everywhere by greenery; from every wall and roof spilled vines and hanging ferns, the vivid pinks and scarlets of geraniums, and brilliant cascades of marigolds and black-eyed Susans. At my feet hens pecked and scratched about. Now and then I stood aside as a donkey or a mule picked its dainty accurate way down the steps, while a black-veiled peasant woman, following it, smiled and gave me a soft "Good morning."

The steps took me eventually clear of the village, on to the hillside where piles of rubble and kerbstones indicated that a new road was being built. I made my way carefully along this, watched by the friendly and curious stares of the workmen, and, before I was aware that I had come so far, found myself clear of the last house, and out on the open hillside above the studio.

The climb had been steep, and the sun was hot. The path led along the foot of a low cliff-wall, which cast, at this early hour, a narrow shade. I found a flat rock in a recess of shadow, and sat down to recover from the climb.

The path that I was on seemed to be a continuation of the one that Simon and I had taken last night. It passed above the studio, then slanted down into the knot of pines that I remembered, and vanished thence more steeply towards the ruined temple precincts. Not far from where I sat, below me now and to the right of the path, I could see the studio, dumped down raw and square and ugly in its quarried plateau. Beyond it the valley of the olives swam and shimmered in the immense liquid distance of light, and beyond that again mountain after mountain, and the sea.

Then my attention was taken by a movement near the studio.

Someone was as early abroad as I. I heard the scuffle of footsteps mounting the rough path that led up from the plateau. Then I saw him, a thin, fair-haired figure carrying a rucksack, and clambering at a fair speed but with very little noise towards the path where I sat in the shadow. He hadn't looked in my direction; he was making for the knot of pines above the shrine, and moving away from me rapidly.

He reached the path. He was about seventy yards away from me, near the fence that marked the graveyard. He stopped, and turned, as if to pause for breath and survey the view.

I was just about to get my feet and hail him, when something about the way he was acting caught my attention, and I stayed still. He had taken a couple of quick steps back and sideways, into the shadow of a pine tree. The dappled shade netted and hid him, maculate, invisible. He stayed there, stock-still, and he wasn't looking at any view; his head was bent as if he studied the ground at his feet, but I knew, suddenly, that he was listening. He didn't move. There was no sound in the lovely bright morning but the chime of a goat bell from the other side of the valley, and the crowing of a cock down in the village. No sound from the studio; no movement.

Nigel lifted his head, and was looking about him, still with
those wary, abruptly stealthy movements. It was quite obvious that, wherever he was going, he didn't want to be followed and, remembering Danielle, I thought I saw his point.
And I wouldn't interrupt his getaway either. Smiling to myself, I stayed where I was. I didn't think he would see me
unless I moved, nor did he. He turned suddenly, and, leaving
the path, plunged uphill through the pines towards the
higher levels where the ancient stadium stood, and, beyond
it, the track that led above the Shining Ones and away into
the upper reaches of Parnassus.

I gave him a minute or two, and then I got up and went
on. Soon I, too, was under the shadow of the pines, and to
my right was the tumbledown fence, and the thicket of dried
weeds that edged the graveyard.

I don't quite know what made me do it, except that somehow, already, Michael Lester's affair was my own. I pushed
open the creaking gate and went in among the stones. When
I found it I had to spell it out very slowly to be sure it was
the one.

ΜΙΧΑΕΛ ΛΗΣΤΗΡ

This alien cross, an alien epitaph . . . and in my ear Simon's voice, claiming him still. " 'My brother Michael.' "
And behind that again I could hear the ghosts of other
voices, other claims: " 'The woman of my house, the cousin
of Angelos, the brother of Michael' " . . . " 'No man is an
Island, entire of itself.' "

I stood there in the hot early-morning silence and thought
about Simon. Today, I was committed to Simon's quest. I,
too, had answered a claim. He was going to see the place
where Michael had died, and he had wanted me to go too.

And I? Why had I said that I would go? I had said last
night that it was absurd, and so it was. . . . But I had a
queer feeling that, quite apart from Simon's need of me, I
had a need of my own. I, too, had something to find.

A bird, small and bright as a blown leaf, flew across the
hot stillness. I turned away and made my way between the
dusty mounds towards the gate.

I was thinking now, not of Simon, but of myself. Not of
the self, the identity I had felt it so necessary to assert when
I had sent back Phil's ring, but of the identity I had assumed so lightly yesterday and which, it seemed, I could not
yet put off. Not Camilla Haven, but just "Simon's girl."

I let myself quickly through the gate and hurried down the path till it brought me out above the ruins of the great shrine.

I've already written enough of Delphi, and indeed it's not easy to write about. The place takes the heart and the senses and wrings them dry. Eyes and ears and the instinct of worship are all that is needed there.

I walked slowly downhill in the sunlight. Here was the little pomegranate tree, clinging to a cleft in the marble of the theatre. Its leaves hung now without a rustle, dark green and still. The fruit was flame-coloured and as glossy as witchballs. Here were the breakneck steps . . . and here the stage of the theatre, where Simon had spoken last night; I could see the mark at the centre, where one's voice was taken and flung high up the mountainside. And now the steps to the precinct . . . that must be the monument of Alexander . . . and this the temple floor of Apollo.

The six great columns stood up like fire against the immense depths of the valley.

No one was about. I crossed the temple floor and sat down at the edge with my back to one of the columns. The stone was hot. Above my head the crumbling capitals were alive with the wings of martins. Far below the olives shimmered along the valley. In the distance Helicon was blue, was silver, was grey as Aphrodite's doves. Everywhere were the voices of songbirds, because Delphi is sanctuary. Somewhere in the morning distance sheep bells were ringing. . . .

It was still only eight o'clock when I left my seat and walked down the Sacred Way from the temple to the edge of the precinct, where a thick rank of pines keeps it from the road below. I went along the path under the pines, then down to the museum which sits in a curve of the road. I already seemed to have been up and about for so long that it was a surprise to find the doors still shut. There was a man in guide's uniform sitting under the trees on the other side of the road, so I crossed over to speak to him.

"The Museum?" he said in answer to my query. "I am afraid it doesn't open till half past nine. But would you like a guide now for the ruins, no?"

"Not this morning, thank you," I said. "I've just been up there. But possibly tomorrow, if I'm still in Delphi. . . . Will you be about here?"

"Always, at this time." He had a dark square face, and,

surprisingly, blue eyes. His look was sophisticated, and he spoke very good English.

I said, "I wanted to see the Charioteer."

"Of course." He grinned, showing very white teeth. "But there are other things too, here in Delphi."

"Oh, yes, I know, but isn't he the first thing everyone looks for in the Museum?"

"Of course," he said again. "If you come with me tomorrow I will take you also round the Museum myself."

"I should like that very much." I hesitated. "Do you—I wonder if you know the young English artist who is staying up at the studio? Thin and fair, with a little beard?"

"Yes. I know him. He has been here in Delphi for quite a time, no?"

"I believe so. Does he—has he been to the Museum much?"

"Indeed, yes. He comes very often to draw. Have you seen any of his drawings, *kyria?* They are very good, very good indeed."

"He showed me some of them last night, but not, I think, any of the statues and antiquities. I imagine he would do those well. Did he do any of the Charioteer?"

"Of course. Did you not say yourself that he is the first thing one looks for? And certainly in our small Museum he is the *pièce de résistance.*"

"Was he—did you notice if the artist was here yesterday?"

The guide didn't seem to be at all surprised at the odd catechism. His experience of tourists must have bred in him a vast tolerance. He shook his head. "I do not think so. I was here all day, but he may have been down here while I was up in the ruins. The tour takes nearly an hour. If you wish to see him, he sleeps up at the studio above the site, where they are building the new road."

"Perhaps I'll see him later." I judged it time to drop that particular catechism. "What new road are they making away up there above the village? Where can it possibly go?"

"To the stadium. Have you seen that yet?"

"Not yet."

"It is high above the shrine. Many tourists who come to Delphi never see it at all, because the climb is too steep. It is very beautiful—just the old oval race-track with the tiers of seats, exactly as it was in ancient times, and with the view . . . always that view of the olives and the valley and the sea. So now they make a road to let the cars and buses take the tourists up."

I stifled a pang at the thought of yet another wild and lovely sanctuary invaded by cars and buses, and said, "Ah, yes. I suppose anything that will bring money into Greece is a good thing. You are a native of Delphi, *kyrie?*"

"No. I am a man of Tinos."

"Oh. Then . . . I suppose you weren't here during the war?"

He smiled. "No. I was busy—very busy—on my island."

My island. There it was again. *A man of Tinos.*

Then he would not remember Michael Lester. It was possible that he had never heard of him. In any case—I caught at myself—I must not let myself go beyond even Simon's claim on my interest. I said merely, "Of course."

He was rolling a cigarette with neat, quick movements.

"There was certainly no need *then* for guides in Delphi, *kyria.* No one was troubling then about the shrine and the sanctuary and the Charioteer! We may say, if you like, that it is a pity—if men had had the time to come, as they came here in the days of the Oracle, when Delphi was the centre of the world, no doubt they would have found their quarrels healed." That quick sophisticated look, and the sudden grin again. "That, you understand, is what I always say when I show my tourists round. It is a very effective bit of patter. The Amphictyonic League of Delphi. The League of Nations. The U.N. Very effective."

"I'm sure it is. Do you add the bits about the fights between Delphi and her neighbours, and the laying waste of Crissa, and the monuments for Athenian victories over the Spartans, and Spartan victories over the Athenians, and the Argive monument stuck down just where it would annoy the Spartans most, and—"

"Sometimes." He was laughing. "I shall have to—what do you say?—watch my step when I show you round tomorrow, shall I not?"

"Not really. I read up an awful lot specially before I came. It makes it more exciting to *know* what happened here. I looked at a lot of photographs too." I hesitated again. "The Charioteer . . ." I said slowly.

"What of him?"

I was carrying a guide-book in my hand; *A Concise Guide of Delphi*, it was called, and on the cover there was a photographic reproduction of the head of the famous statue. I held it out. "This. I've heard so much about him, but I can't help wondering if I'll really like him. Those eyes; they're inlaid with onyx and white enamel, aren't they? And there are long metal eyelashes? They do look alive, I admit, but—look, you see what I mean?" I indicated the print. "That narrow forehead and the heavy jaw; it's not strictly a beautiful face, is it? And yet everyone says he's so wonderful."

"And so will you. No picture gives the true impression. It's the same with the great Hermes at Olympia. In photographs he is effeminate, the marble too smooth, and shining like soap. But the statue itself takes away the breath."

"I know, I've seen it."

"Then prepare yourself to see the Charioteer. It is one of the great statues of Greece. Do you know the thing that comes to me first whenever I see him again—which is every day?"

"What?"

"He is so very young. All that gravity, that grace, and so young with it. It used to be thought that he was the owner of the team—the winner of the race—but now they say that he was probably the driver for some lord who owned the chariot."

I said hesitantly, "There's a bit in Pausanias' account of Delphi, isn't there, about a chariot of bronze with a naked 'lord of the car' who might have had a driver, a youth of good family?"

"I believe there is, yes. But it could hardly apply to our Charioteer, *kyria;* the evidence is that he was probably buried in a great landslip during an earthquake in three seventy-three B.C., and, without being uncovered again, was built into the—what do you call it?—the supporting wall— the 'earth-holder' is the Greek word—that was erected to stop the rocks and earth from engulfing the temple again."

"Retaining wall," I said.

"Ah, thank you. The retaining wall. Well, you see, our Charioteer had vanished a few centuries before Pausanias came to Delphi."

"I see. I didn't know that."

He had finished rolling the cigarette. He put it between his lips and lit it with a spluttering of loose tobacco.

He said, "They say now that the Charioteer was part of a victory group erected by one Gelon, the winner of a chariot race, but anything may be true. So much was lost or destroyed or stolen over the centuries that the truth about our discoveries is only guesswork. And Delphi suffered much, because she was so rich. I think it is reckoned that there were six thousand monuments here—at any rate that is the number of inscriptions that have been uncovered." He smiled. "The landslide that broke and hid the Charioteer was an act of the gods, because it kept him out of the hands of the robbers. The Phocians laid the sanctuary waste barely twenty years after he was buried, and of course in later times countless treasures were destroyed or stolen."

"I know. Sulla and Nero and the rest. How many bronzes do they reckon Nero took to Rome?"

"Five hundred." He laughed again. "I *shall* have to watch my patter tomorrow, I can see!"

"I told you I only read it up just before I came. And there's so much—"

A sudden clatter and a volley of shouts from somewhere behind the Museum startled me, and I stopped and glanced over my shoulder. "What on earth's that?"

"Nothing. A little disagreement among the workmen."

"A little disagreement? It sounds like a major war!"

"We are always a fighting race, I am afraid. There is trouble today among the workmen. There are still men here from the 'dig' of the French archaeologists—the 'dig' is finished, but workmen have remained to clear up, and to remove the rails that the trucks ran on, and things of that kind. A mule strayed during the night, and now they have discovered that some tools are missing, and they are accusing the men who work on the stadium road of theft, and so —well, you hear that there is a little disagreement."

"Some tools and a mule?" I listened to the uproar for a moment or two. It sounded like the battle of El Alamein in stereophonic sound. I said drily, "Perhaps they haven't heard of the Amphictyonic League and the peace of Delphi."

He smiled. "Perhaps not."

"And now I really must go. I'll let you know if I can come with you tomorrow. You say you'll be here at this time?"

"Always."

I had a sharp inner vision of a life where one would be— always—serenely on the Delphi road in the early morning sun. "I'll try and be here by eight if I'm coming. If I can't—"

"It does not matter. If you come, I will take you with the greatest of pleasure. If not, it does not matter. Are you staying at the Apollon?"

"Yes."

"It is very nice, yes?"

"Delightful." I lingered for a moment, looking at the

closed door of the Museum. He was watching me through the smoke of his cigarette with that shrewd, incurious blue gaze. I said, "*Kyrie* . . . you weren't here during the war, of course, but you'll know what happened to the statues and things from the Museum? The Charioteer, for instance? Where was he? Hidden?"

"Only in a manner of speaking. He was in Athens."

"Oh. Yes. I see."

Behind me a shabby black car slid to a halt. Simon grinned at me over the door and said, "Good morning."

"Oh, Simon! Am I late? Have you had to hunt for me?"

"The answer to both those is no. I was early and they told me you'd come down here. Have you had breakfast?"

"Hours ago."

"Why people should adopt that disgustingly self-righteous tone whenever they manage to achieve breakfast before eight o'clock I do not know," said Simon. He leaned across the car and opened the door for me. "Come along, then, let's go. Unless of course you'd like to drive?"

I didn't bother to answer that one, but slipped quickly into the passenger's seat beside him.

As the car turned the corner and gathered speed along the straight stretch below the temple I said, without preliminary, "The Charioteer was in Athens during the war. Presumably in hiding."

He gave me a quick glance. "Oh. Yes, it would be, wouldn't it?" I saw him smile.

I said, almost defensively, "Well, you did get me into it, after all."

"I did, didn't I?" A little pause. "Did you come down through the temple this morning?"

"Yes."

"I thought you might do that. I've been up there myself most mornings by about six."

"Not today?"

He smiled. "No. I thought you'd like it to yourself."

"You're very—" I began, and stopped. He didn't ask me what I'd been going to say. I said, not quite irrelevantly, "Do you ever lose your temper, Simon?"

"What in the world makes you ask that?"

"Oh, come, I thought you were a thought-reader!"

"Oh. Well, let me see. . . . Last night?"

"That didn't take much guessing. Yes, of course. Nigel was abominably rude to you. Didn't you mind?"

"Mind? No."

"Why not?"

"I don't think I'd have minded from Nigel anyway, because he's not very happy. Life isn't easy for him, and on top of everything he has to fall for that girl, and she's led him the hell of a dance. But last night—" He paused, and I saw again that pucker of worry round his eyes. "Last night there was something wrong. Really wrong, I mean; not just Nigel's too-usual brand of nerves and temperament and frustrated talent, and that little she-witch playing him on a very barbed hook. There was something more."

"Are you sure he wasn't just a bit drunk? He said he was."

"Possibly. But that's part of the trouble—he doesn't drink much as a rule, and last night he was fairly putting it away, though he's like you—he doesn't like ouzo. No, there was definitely something very wrong, and I'd give quite a lot to know what it was."

"I take it he didn't tell you anything after you got back to the studio? I got the impression he was going to come out with something just as Danielle interrupted."

"Yes, so did I. But I didn't see him again. His room was empty when I went back. I waited a bit, but eventually went to bed. I didn't hear him come in."

"Perhaps," I said a little drily, "he was fixing the taps."

"That did occur to me. But no. Danielle's door was standing open. She wasn't there either. I think they'd gone for a walk, or down to the village for another drink, or something. And Nigel had gone when I got up this morning."

I said, " He went up the mountain. I saw him."

"You saw him?"

"Yes, at about seven o'clock. He went up past the graveyard through those pines, as if he were going farther up the hill."

"Alone?"

"Yes. In fact, he looked rather as if he wanted to be left very much alone. I didn't speak to him, and I don't think he saw me."

Simon said, "Well, let's hope he does some work today, and draws it out of himself, whatever it is. I expect I'll see him tonight." He glanced at me, smiling. "Did you make any more discoveries this morning?"

"Only one," I said, before I thought.

"And that?"

I found myself telling him, quite simply. "It was just my own discovery. We talked about it last night, with Nigel. It's something we're taught from childhood, but I'd never really had it brought home to me till now."

"What is it?"

"That saying of 'your parson friend,' as Nigel called him."

"Ah, yes, that." He was silent for a moment, then he quoted it softly, as if half to himself, " 'No man is an Island, entire of itself; every man is a piece of the Continent, a part of the main; if a Clod be washed away by the Sea, Europe is the less, as well as if a Promontory were, as well as if a Manor of thy friends or of thine own were; any man's death diminishes me, because I am involved in Mankind; And therefore never send to know for whom the bell tolls; It tolls for thee.' . . . Terrific piece of writing, isn't it? One should remember it more often."

The car slowed down and drew out to pass a little group of three donkeys pattering along in the dust at the edge of the road. On the foremost an old woman sat sideways; she had a distaff in her left hand, the spindle in her right, and as she rode she spun the white wool ceaselessly, without looking at it. She ducked a smiling salute to us as we went by.

Simon said, "What brought that home to you this morning?"

I hesitated, then said flatly, "Michael's grave."

"I see." And I thought he did.

I said, "It's this confounded country. It does things to one—mentally and physically and, I suppose morally. The past is so living and the present so intense and the future so blooming imminent. The light seems to burn life into you twice as intensely as anywhere else I've known. I suppose that's why the Greeks did what they did so miraculously, and why they could stay themselves through twenty generations of slavery that would have crushed any other race on earth. You come here thinking you're going to look at a lot of myth-haunted ruins and picturesque peasants and you find that . . ." I stopped.

"That what?"

"No. I'm talking piffle."

"It's good piffle. Go on. What do you find?"

"You find that the grave of Michael Lester is as moving and as important as the 'tomb of Agamemnon' at Mycenae, or Byron or Venizelos or Alexander. He, and the men like him, are a part of the same picture." I stopped, and then said helplessly, "Greece. Damn it, what is that it does to one?"

He was silent a moment, then he said, "I think the secret is that it belongs to all of us—to us of the West. We've learned to think in its terms, and to live in its laws. It's given us almost everything that our world has that is worth while. Truth, straight thinking, freedom, beauty. It's our second language, our second line of thought, our second country. We all have our own country—and Greece."

We sailed round a bend of the road and ahead of us the deep valley opened to show a great rounded beauty of a mountain, silver-green, blue-veined, cloud-grey.

"Why, damn it all," said Simon. "That hill in front of us. That's Helicon. *Helicon.* And then you wonder why this country gets you in the wind?"

"Not any more," I said.

And we didn't speak again till we came to Arachova and found Stephanos and Niko waiting for us in the café on the corner.

"Do you like my socks?" asked Niko.

"They're wonderful," I said truthfully. They were, indeed, in that landscape, something to be wondered at. They were luminous, and of a startling shade of shocking pink. They shone among the bleached hot stones of the mountain track like neon signs against a clear sky.

"They light up," explained Niko.

"I can see that. Where did you get them?"

"In Athens. They are the latest thing from New York."

"Do you go to Athens often?"

"No. I went to work there when I was fourteen. I was a page boy at the Acropole Palace Hotel."

"I see. Is that where you learned your English?"

"Some of it. I also learn it here in the school. Is good, huh?"

"Very good. Why didn't you stay in Athens?"

"Is better here." Niko looked back along the track we were climbing. Away below us Arachova had dwindled to a toy waterfall of coloured roofs. Niko turned back to me almost as if he were puzzled. "Here there is nothing. Is no money. But is better here. Arachova is my village." Again that look. "You think I am crazy? *You* come from London where there is plenty money. All Greeks are a little crazy, huh? But you think I am stupid to leave Athens?"

"There is a sort of divine madness about all the Greeks

I've met," I said, laughing. "But you're not crazy, Niko.
It's better here, certainly, money or no money. Don't ever
live in a town unless you have to! And I don't live in
London. I live miles away from it, in a country village,
just like you."

"Like Arachova?" He was vastly surprised. I had long
since discovered that to all Greeks England meant London
and nothing else. London, the huge, the golden-pavemented,
the jacinth-gated.

"Not quite like Arachova."

"And that is your village, as Arachova is mine."

I said, "Not quite, Niko. We've lost that way of feeling,
I'm afraid. How far is this place that we're making for?"

"Making? *Oriste?*"

"Going to. The place where Michael died." I said it softly,
with my eye on Simon's back where he walked with Stephanos a few yards ahead of us.

"About an hour from here. More, perhaps. It is nearer to
Delphi than Arachova. It is in a . . . I do not know the
word: a hollow place, a—" he stopped and made a scoop-
ing gesture.

"A corrie? Like this?"

"Yes. That is it. A corrie, where the rocks have fallen
near the foot of a cliff. My grandfather know the way. He
tell me it looks to the northwest—that is, away from Delphi
and Arachova, towards Amphissa. This track goes along
the face of the mountains and then we leave it and climb
up towards these cliffs where the corrie is. I think that many,
many years ago there was a road for beasts, but not now.
I do not know how far. I have never been, me. My grandfather, he know the way. You are tired?"

"No. It's rather hot, but I'm not tired."

"In Greece," said Niko reflectively, eyeing me, "the
women are very strong."

I thought of the village cafés, with their day-long comple-
ment of cheerfully idle men. "I imagine they have to be," I
said.

"Oh, yes." Niko misunderstood me, probably deliberately.
"In Greece the men are tough. Oh, very tough."

Somehow, at that moment, Niko's racy beauty managed to
look very tough indeed. His swagger, and the look he gave
me, were the plainest possible invitation to the kind of sug-
gestive verbal sparring that the Mediterranean men seem to
love. But two could play at the game of misunderstanding. I

said cheerfully, "Then if we do meet the shade of Angelos on the hill, I shall feel quite, quite safe with you, Niko."

"How?" He was momentarily thrown off his stride. "Oh, yes! But of course you will be safe with me! I should kill him, you understand. He helped to kill my great-grand-father's brother's son Panos, so of course I should kill him. And"—the swagger gave way again to Niko's own brand of youthful and artless high spirits—"it would be easy, because he is old and I am young."

"I suppose he's all of forty," I agreed. "And just how old are you, Niko?"

"I am seventeen."

I said mendaciously, "Really? I'd have thought you were much older than that."

He flashed me his delighted smile. "Would you? Would you really? And how old are you, beautiful miss?"

"Niko! Don't you know the rules better than that? I'm twenty-five."

"So old? But you do not look like twenty-five," he said generously. "It is a good age to be, not? See, this bit is rough. Take my hand, miss."

I laughed. "I'm not as old as all that, Niko. And I'm truly not a bit tired. Just hot."

It was indeed very hot. As we climbed steadily northward, the sun beat down on the right, throwing shadows sharp and hard as graphite along the white rock. The track where we walked was only by courtesy a track. It was not steep, cutting at a slant along the great flank of the mountain, but it was very rough, and some of the stones were sharp. We had long since left any trees behind, and the mountainside, unpunctuated now by pine or cypress, stretched one great wing of burning white from the high hard blue sky down to the dry watercourse deep on our left. Beyond the tortured path of this dead stream, the rock rose again, this time violently blocked in with cobalt shadow. High above, so that to glance at them hurt the eyes, three birds hung, circling slowly and with moveless wings, like some mobile toy on invisible threads. I thought I could hear their faint, sweet mewing. Nothing else broke the silence except the scrape and clink of our feet, and the sound of our breathing.

The track ran straight up to what looked like a wall of fallen rocks and rubble, and there stopped, obliterated. Stephanos, in front, had halted, and turned to speak to Simon, who was just behind him. He said something, gesturing towards the barricade of rock.

It looked like a landslip, a great torrent of red and ochreous earth frozen even as it poured down the steep wing of the mountain. It was spiked with broken rock and great white slabs of fallen limestone. Further down the mountainside it fanned out like the delta of a red river. Enormous blocks of stone had hurtled down with it, flung carelessly, as by the hand of an angry god, to dam the narrow gash of the watercourse.

Stephanos had turned aside to climb rather painfully up the steep hill-face beside the landslide.

"Is this where we leave the track?" I asked.

Simon turned. "No. That's still with us. This stuff's just lying across it. If we follow Stephanos up a little there's a place where it's safer to cross."

"It must have been quite a storm," I said, surveying the torrents of rocks in front, and the gigantic flung boulders far below us.

"Not storm. Earthquake," said Simon, then laughed at my expression. "Yes, one forgets, doesn't one? I told you this was a savage country. And this, I believe, is a baddish area. They've had quite a history of tremors hereabouts. The miracle is that any of the shrines and temples have a single pillar left standing. Can you manage?"

"Yes, thanks. Don't help me, Simon. I've got to keep my end up with Niko."

"Of course—and mine too, I think. . . . That's it. We cross here. It seems stable enough, but watch yourself."

We made our way slowly across the detritus of the earthquake. From higher up I could see where a whole slice of the mountain cliff above us had been torn away and thrown down. It had splintered into great white spearheads, against which the smaller fragments were piled in the drift of dark-red earth. We scrambled down this uncomfortable ramp towards the path which had shaken itself clear of the debris.

"I suppose the Earth-Shaker turned over in his sleep," I said, "and not so very long ago, either, by the look of it. The cracks look fairly fresh, don't they?"

Stephanos must have understood the drift of what I was saying. He had turned to wait for us on the track, and now spoke to Simon. "What does he say?" I asked.

"He says that there were two or three small shocks—this, by the way, is a small shock—about twelve years ago. A little further on, the mountain has been shifted about much more drastically. He says that only someone who was out on this part of Parnassus almost daily would still know his way about, once he had left the track. He also says that the place we are making for is almost completely changed since he found Michael there. It was just an open space at the foot of a low cliff, and now it's closed in by fallen rock into a kind of corrie, or hollow."

Stephanos nodded as he finished. He gave me a look from under his magnificent white brows. He asked Simon a question.

"Are you tired?" asked Simon.

"No, thanks."

Simon smiled. "Don't exhaust yourself keeping Britain's end up, will you?"

"I'm not. It's only the heat."

There was a flash of shocking-pink socks beside me as Niko dropped off the rubble to land as neatly as a goat. He dragged a water bottle out of a large pocket and unscrewed the top. "Have a drink, miss."

I drank thankfully. The bottle smelt ammoniac, like a nice donkey, but the water was good and still reasonably cool.

"Greek peasant women," said Niko, watching me with that limpid look of his, "can go for hours over the roughest country without food or drink."

"So," I said, stoppering the bottle and handing it back to him, "can camels. Thank you, Niko, that was wonderful."

"It was a pleasure, beautiful miss." Niko turned to Simon and held out the bottle. His look and gesture expressed, somehow, the most tender solicitude.

Simon, smiling, shook his head.

"Good," said Stephanos, and turned to go on. He and Simon forged ahead once more, and Niko and I took up our positions in the rear.

It must have been getting on for noon when we neared the corrie.

We left the track some way beyond the fall of rock and turned, in Stephanos' unfaltering wake, up into a markless desert of rock and dry earth. Sometimes we trudged upwards through sienna-coloured dust strewn cruelly with small boulders, and sometimes we walked more easily across great serrated flanges of the white and living rock. The sun was at its height and the heat was intense. The air wavered with it till the whole vast sweep of rock seemed to pulsate. If it hadn't been for the cool breeze that blew steadily at that height, it would have been insupportable.

By the time we were two-thirds of the way to the corrie,

and had done most of the climbing, I had got my second
wind, and was walking fairly easily. I was, I felt, upholding
British Womanhood not too badly.

"The Greek peasant women," said Niko, beside me, "used
to carry great loads of wood and grapes and things across
here. Regularly."

"If you tell me one more thing about Greek peasant
women," I said, "I shall scream and lie down and refuse to
move another step. Besides, I don't believe you."

He grinned. "It is not true," he conceded. "I think that
you are very wonderful."

"Why, Niko, that's nice of you!"

"And very beautiful too," said Niko. "Would you like an
apple?"

And he fished an apple out of his pocket and handed it to
me with very much the air of a Paris presenting the prize to
Aphrodite. His look of intense and dazzled admiration was,
one felt, one that had been tried before and found to work.

It still worked. My morale soared. I laughed and took the
apple and thanked him, and then a diversion was created
because neither he nor Stephanos would allow me to eat it
without peeling it, and Niko wanted to peel it for me and
Stephanos had the knife, so, being Greeks, they plunged into
a passionate discussion about this while Simon peeled the
apple and then handed it to me.

"For the fairest," he said.

"There's not," I said, "a lot of competition. But thank
you all the same."

Soon after that we reached our destination.

CHAPTER

11

That ground will take no footprint. All of it
Is bitter stone. . . .

EURIPIDES: *Electra*
(tr. Gilbert Murray).

The corrie did not lie at any great height. Arachova itself is almost three thousand feet above sea level, and we had climbed no more than eight or nine hundred feet in all since we had left the village. We were still only in the foothills of the vast highland of Parnassus, but we might have been lost, a million miles from anywhere. Since the village had dwindled out of sight we had seen no living creature except the lizards, and the vultures that circled and cried so sweetly, high in the dazzling air.

The place wasn't, properly speaking, a corrie. It was a hollow scooped out of a line of low cliffs that topped a steep, mile-long ridge like the crest along a horse's neck. From a distance the cliff looked fairly uniform, but on approach it could be seen that it had been split and torn into ragged bays and promontories where half a hundred winter torrents had gouged their headlong way down the mountainside.

Here and there lay evidence of a swifter and more wholesale violence. Earthquakes had wrested great chunks from the crag, quarrying back into the limestone face, throwing the enormous debris down, so that for hundreds of feet below the jagged cliffs, a loose and sometimes dangerous scree valanced the sloping hillside.

As we neared the edge of this, Stephanos turned aside, into a short steep detour that took us out above the level of the cliff top, and we approached the line of crags at a long slant that brought us eventually to the edge.

The old man stopped then, leaning on his crook, and waited for us to come up with him.

Simon stood beside him, looking down.

"This is the place?"

"This is the place."

It could have been a quarry hacked out of the cliff face during countless patient years. It had probably taken five seconds of earthquake for the Earth-Shaker to tear that semi-circular scar back into the cliff and fling the wreckage down before it in still formidable walls of jagged rock. The result of the earthquake's action was to make a roughly circular hollow, a sort of irregular crater some seventy yards across, which was walled to the north by the living cliff on which we stood, and shut in almost completely for the rest of its diameter by the vast sections of tumbled rock.

The centre of the crater floor was clear, but the encircling walls were piled in the now familiar way with red dust and rock debris. In spring, I thought, it would probably be beautiful, for it was sheltered, and I could see the dead remains of some scrubby plants and bushes where the melting snows and then the rain must have fed some alpine vegetation. Below us clung the lovely green of a little juniper, and just beside my feet the rock held two thick bushes that looked like holly, but which bore, incongruously, acorns with enormous cups as prickly as sea urchins.

To the right, on the west side of the corrie, was what appeared to be the only way out. This was a break in the wall of rock, towards which the smooth crater floor lifted in a rocky ramp. From the height where we stood I thought I could see, beyond and below this "gate," the ghost of an old track, leading westwards to vanish round a spur of the mountain.

Stephanos caught the direction of my glance. "That is the way he went."

He spoke in Greek, of course, and Simon translated for me, at the time in snatches, and more fully later; but once again I shall put the old man's words down directly, as they came.

"That is the way he went, down the old track towards Amphissa. It comes out above a disused quarry near the Amphissa road, behind the olive groves." He fell silent for a moment or two, looking down at the hollow beneath our feet. No one spoke. The sun beat on the back of our necks, and I felt, suddenly, very tired.

Then the old man spoke again, slowly, reminiscently. "I came to the head of the cliff just at this point. It was different then, you understand . . . here, where we stand, there was a pinnacle of rock, like a cat's tooth. It disappeared in the earthquake, but then it was a landmark that even an

Athenian could not have missed. And below the cliff, then, there was no hollow, as you see it now, walled and gated like a fortress. There was only the cliff, and below us some big rocks lying, and a space of clean stone. It was there that I saw them, Michael and Angelos. And the place is not covered. I marked it, and I know. It was there." The crook pointed. Almost in the centre of the dazzling floor of smooth stone, a little pile of stones, a cairn, threw a small triangular shadow. "I put those there later," said Stephanos, "after the earthquake had moved the cliff and the place was altered beyond recognition." There was another pause of silence, then he glanced sideways at me. "We will go down now. . . . Will you tell the lady to be very careful, *Kyrie* Simon? The path is steep, and made only for goats, but it is the quickest way."

As Simon transmitted the warning, I saw that there was indeed a path down into the corrie. It left the cliff top just beside us, between the two bushes of holly oak, and wound steeply down past more mats of holly and the dusty ghosts of thistles, into the bottom of the hollow. It was down this way that the dog must have raced to attack Angelos, and then Stephanos himself, to run to Michael's side as he lay dying in the sun. . . .

The sun was so high that almost the whole of the corrie bottom was shadowless. But where the cliff path debouched onto the level, a wing of rock cast a comforting angle of blue shade. I stopped there, and sat down with my back against the warm stone. Stephanos moved forward without pausing, and Simon followed him. Niko flung himself down beside me on the dusty ground. I hoped he wouldn't speak, and he didn't. He broke off a piece of a dead thistle and began scratching patterns in the dust. He wasn't paying much attention to his drawing; his intent gaze never left the other men.

Stephanos led Simon across the floor of the corrie, and stopped beside the little cairn. He was pointing down at it and talking, rapidly now. His hand moved and gestured, then came back to the same spot. Almost I could see the dying man lying there in the baking sun, the shepherd coming to the cliff top where a fang of rock stuck up like a cat's tooth, the dog dashing down that snaking path, the murderer turning to bolt out of the "gate" and down the track towards Amphissa and the sea. . . .

Then Stephanos turned heavily and trudged back to where we sat. He lowered himself down beside me with a sigh, then said something short to Niko, who got out a battered packet of cigarettes and handed him one. He gave his grand-father a light, then turned, with his brilliant smile, to offer a cigarette to me. We lit up in silence.

Simon was still standing in the centre of the corrie, but he wasn't looking down at the cairn where his brother had died. He had turned, and that cool appraising stare of his was slowly raking the sides of the corrie . . . the tumbled wall of rock that hemmed us in . . . the great sections that had fallen outward from the crag, and now made the two side wings of the corrie, piled high in vast slabs and wedges against the old solid rock of the cliff . . . the hollow curve of a shallow cave exposed in the scooped segment of broken crag, a cave that had been deep before the front of the cliff had fallen away and left its recesses naked to the air. . . .

My cigarette was mild and loosely packed and tasted slightly of goat; there was something about the beautiful Niko, I reflected, that harked back fairly consistently to the lower animals. I had half-smoked it, and Niko's was gone entirely, when Simon's shadow fell before us.

"What about lunch?" he asked.

The slight tension—of Stephanos' making, not Simon's—was broken, and we chatted over lunch as if it had been a normal picnic. My tiredness was rapidly dissolving, with the rest in the pleasant shade, and the solid excellence of the food we had bought in Arachova. We had rolls—a little dry after their progress in Niko's rucksack—with generous pieces of cold lamb sandwiched in; cheese in thick juicy slices; a paper full of olives that felt as if they were warm from the tree but were really warm from Niko; a hard-boiled egg, a very solid and very sweet chunk of some sort of cake made with fresh cherries; and a large handful of grapes, also warm and slightly tired-looking, but tasting ambrosially of the sun.

I noticed that Simon, as he ate, still looked about him, his eyes returning time after time, thoughtfully, to the recently torn cliff behind us. "This was done in the earthquake you spoke of, soon after the war?"

Stephanos said, through a mouthful of cake, "That is so. There were three or four shocks that year. It was nineteen forty-six. The villages were not affected, but a lot of rock was moved up here." He jerked his head towards the cliff. "This is not the only place of its kind. All along this ridge there are places where the tremors, and then the weather, have taken bites out of the hill. What the earthquake starts, the ice and snow don't take many winters to finish. There are three, four, five hollows, much like this one, where very little trace of the original cliff face remains. Only the goat track that we came down on . . . see? . . . there the cliff itself has not been moved. but you see the rocks piled against it as high as a ruined church. Oh. yes. I told you, *Kyrie* Simon, that a man who was not always out on the hill would soon miss his landmarks.''

"The pinnacle, for instance, that used to stand above the cliff?''

"I told you about that? Yes, I did, I remember. It was not so very high, but it served as a landmark for kilometres around. It was what guided me to Michael on that day. He knew of a cave here, he said, near the Cat's Tooth, and he meant to lie up in it until the German drive was over. I came up bringing him food, and to try and make him come back to Arachova where his wound might be cared for. But this I have spoken of already.''

Simon's eyes were on the shallow apse of the exposed cave. They were narrowed slightly, as if against the sun, and his face gave nothing away. "A cave? That one? It would be deep enough before half of it fell in.''

Stephanos lifted his heavy shoulders. "I do not know if that was the one or not. Possibly. But you must understand that the cliff is full of caves . . . some parts of Parnassus are a honeycomb of such places where an army could hide in safety.''

Simon had taken out cigarettes. "Camilla? I think I'd like to take a quick look around, all the same. Cigarette? Catch, Niko. . . .'' He got slowly to his feet, and stood looking down at the old man sitting heavily in the shade. "And you carried Michael from here to Delphi?''

Stephanos smiled. "It was fourteen years ago, and I was younger. And the way to Delphi is much shorter than the way we came . . . but steep, you understand, because Arachova lies nearly four hundred metres higher than Delphi. That is a big start on a climb like this, so we came by Arachova today.''

"I still think it was . . . well, quite a feat. And now I'm going to poke around for a bit. I want a good look at that cave. It looks as if there's another small opening at the back of it. Will you come, or are you resting?''

"I will come.''

"Niko?''

One swift graceful wriggle, and Niko was on his feet and brushing dust from his trousers. "I come. I have very good eyesight, me. If there is anything to be seen, I will see it. I can see in the dark, as well as any cat, so if there is an inner cave, I shall guide you, *Kyrie* Simon."

"We'll follow your socks," said Simon drily, and Niko grinned. The socks flashed across the corrie at a run, and were dimmed in the shadow of the cave's recess. Stephanos was getting slowly to his feet. Simon looked down at me and raised his eyebrows.

I shook my head, so he and Stephanos left me, and went more slowly in the wake of the luminous socks. A buttress of shadow swallowed them.

I finished the cigarette and stubbed it out, then sat relaxed and still, enjoying the shade and the silence and the bright dazzle of heat beyond my shadowed corner. The men were out of sight, either in the cave or somewhere beyond the piles of massive debris that buttressed the far side of the corrie. I couldn't hear them now. The silence was intense, thick as the heat. I was part of it, sitting as still as a lizard on my stone.

Some movement, real or imagined, at the head of the cliff path, caught my eye, and I turned to look, wondering half idly if Niko had found some way back to the cliff's head while I had been sitting there half-asleep. But there was nothing there, only the sun hammering on the white rock. The shadows, purple and anthracite and red, seemed themselves to flicker with movement. Against the violent patterns of light and shade, the green of the holly oaks and the cool curve of the juniper arching out from the face of the cliff were as refreshing as the sound of a spring. I remembered, suddenly, that as I had clambered down past them, there had been other green things below us, hardly noticed in the hazards of that steep exhausted scramble down the cliff.

Where there was green, there must certainly, in September, be water . . . cold water, not Niko's tepid bottle that smelled of goat. The thought brought me eagerly to my feet. A shadow at the cliff top flickered again, but I hardly noticed. My eyes were on the corner below the slim bow of the juniper, where, like a mirage, showed a glimpse of vivid emerald. . . .

I got up, skirting the corrie's edge, picking my way between the enormous fallen blocks. I slid between two rough rocks that caught at my clothes, bent my head to pass under a wing of limestone that shored up the cliff like a flying buttress—and there was the grass. The colour was so startling, and so beautiful after the dazzling changes rung by sun and stone that I must have stood quite still, gazing at it, for a full minute. It flowed in a deep and vivid ribbon of green between two boulders streaked liberally with the red of waterborne iron. But there was no water now. There might be some spring, I thought, that was dependent on intermittent showers high on the peaks; perhaps, like snow on the desert's face, the grass sprang up in the wake of a shower and faded with the next day's sunset. . . . It lay there, itself like a small pool of cool water, a green thought in a green shade, moist to the touch, and lending the corner of the corrie a freshness that the shadowed rock had not had.

I sat gratefully down, with my hands spread on the ground and the soft grass springing up between my fingers. Among the green were tiny flowers, bells of pale blue, like pygmy harebells. Some of these grew on the face of the cliff itself, and their seeds had, in the last decade, flown and rooted everywhere in the fallen debris of earthquake. Only here in this moist corner were they still in flower, but I could see fading clumps of seeding stems on all sides among the boulders. Other alpines had grown here too; there was something with a pale furry leaf and a thin dry flower-stem left sticking out like a hummingbird's tongue; a tuft of tendrils dried into hexagonal shapes till they looked like bunches of brown chicken-wire; a tiny plant of the acorned holly, rooting purposefully in a thin crack. Then with another shock of pleasure I saw one more flower that had not yet died of drought. In a cleft just above eye level there was a plant of cyclamen. The leaves, blue-green and veined palely, were held out in stiff formal curves on their red stems. The flowers were soft rose-pink, a dozen of them, and clung like a flight of moths to the dry cliff. Below the flowers, in the same cleft, grew the remains of another rock plant, dead, fraying away to dust in the drought. Above it the cyclamen's flowers looked pure and delicate and strong. . . .

Something was fretting at the edge of my mind. I stared at the cyclamen, and found I was thinking of the Dutch painter and his donkey surrounded by the laughing village lads, and I wondered, without knowing why, what Nigel was doing now.

We went back by the shorter route.

It appeared that the search of the cave had yielded nothing, and apparently Simon didn't want to delay Stephanos and Niko by making a more prolonged investigation. We left the corrie by the gap in the west side, and scrambled down the steep slope below the scree.

We had nearly reached the bottom of the dry valley that

lay below the ridge, when we came on the barely visible track that I had glimpsed from the top of the crags. Even this was appallingly rough going. We made our careful way along it for some hundred yards or so, and then it forked. The right branch fell steeply away, curling out of sight almost at once round a spur of cliff. The left-hand branch turned downhill for Delphi. We took this, and in just over half the time the outward journey had taken, we saw ahead of us the edge of the high land and, beyond it, the gap where the Pleistus valley cuts its way down to the sea.

Stephanos paused and spoke to Simon. The latter turned to me.

"Stephanos has come back this way because he thinks you may be tired. This path will lead you straight down to Delphi. It comes out above the temple, and you can get down behind the Shining Ones, and then through the stadium. The drop down to the cliff top is steep, but there's no danger if you take care. I'll come down with you if you like, but you can't possibly miss the way."

I must have looked slightly surprised, because he added, "The car's at Arachova—remember? I thought I'd go back along the top with Stephanos now, and collect it. But there's no need to drag you the whole way."

I said gratefully, "Oh, Simon—that car! I'd forgotten all about it. I don't really see why you should have to shoulder all the responsibility for my bit of nonsense, but I must confess I'll be awfully glad if you will! Don't tell Niko, but I really am beginning to feel I'd like to be home."

"Well, it won't take you long from here, and it's all downhill. No—look, dash it, I'll come with you."

"I wouldn't dream of letting you, if it means your trailing back later on to Arachova for the car. I can't possibly get lost between here and Delphi, and I promise to be careful on the cliff path." I turned to hold out a hand to Stephanos and thank him, then did the same to Niko. It was like Stephanos, I thought, virtually to ignore me all the time, and yet to lead the whole party some hour or so out of its way to show me the quick way home. The old man nodded gravely over my hand and turned away. Niko took it with a melting look from those beautiful eyes and said, "I will see you again, miss? You come to Arachova often?"

"I hope so."

"And you will come to see the rugs in my sister's shop? Is very good rugs, all colours. Local. Is also brooches and pots of the very best Greek style. For you they are cheap. I tell my sister you are my friend, yes?"

I laughed. "If I buy any rugs and pots I'll come to your sister's shop, Niko. That's a promise And now good-bye. and thank you."

"Good-bye, miss. Thank you, beautiful miss."

The luminous socks plunged away along the path after Stephanos.

Simon grinned. "His grandfather'd have the hide off him if he could understand half he says. Is there such a thing as innocent depravity? Niko's it if there is. A little of Athens superimposed on Arachova. It's a fascinating mixture. isn't it?"

"When it's as beautiful as Niko yes. . . Simon was it true that you didn't find anything in the cave? Or was there something that you didn t want to talk about in front of the others? You didn't see anything at all?'

"Nothing. There was a small inner cave, but it was as blank as a scoured pot. . . . I'll tell you about it later on; I'd better be off after them now. I'll be in to the Apollon for dinner and I'll see you then. Afterwards we'll get you installed at the studio. You'll dine with me, of course?"

"Why, thank you. I—"

"Take care of yourself, then. See you at dinner." And with a lift of the hand he was gone in the wake of the shocking pink socks.

I stared after him for a few seconds, but he didn't look back.

It occurred to me, with a slight sense of surprise, that this time yesterday I hadn't even met him.

I turned and began to make my careful way down towards Delphi.

CHAPTER

12

Seize her! Throw her from Parnassus, send her bounding down
the cliff-ledges, let the crags comb out her dainty hair!

EURIPIDES: *Ion*
(tr. Philip Vellacott)

It was late afternoon, and the sun was straight ahead of me
when at length I came out on top of one of the great cliffs
that stand above the Shrine at Delphi. Far below me and to
the right lay the temple precinct, its monuments and por-
ticos and its Sacred Way looking small and very clean cut in
the sun, like the plaster models that you see in museums.
The pillars of Apollo were foreshortened, and tiny as toys.
Directly beneath me was the cleft of the Castalian Spring.
The tangle of trees filled it like a dark waterfall. Already,
beyond the tree-filled cleft, the Flamboyant cliff was taking
the late afternoon sun like flame.

I moved back a few feet from the edge, and sat down on a
stone. To one side of me grew a thicket of tallish juniper.
Beyond and all around this was the usual dusty expanse of
hot stone. The path to the stadium led off to the right past
the bushes, but I was tired, and here at the cliff top a cool
breeze from the sea allayed the still-hot blaze of afternoon.

I sat quietly, chin on hand, looking down at the dreaming
marbles of the shrine below, at the blue-and-silver depths of
the valley where hawks circled below eye level, at the great
cliff beside me burning in the sun. . . . No, I thought, I
could not leave Delphi yet. Even if it meant sleeping in the
studio near the intolerable Danielle, in order to save what
I must owe on the car, I couldn't leave. There must be tomorrow—and the day after, and the day after . . . how long
a succession of days would it take before I had begun to
learn and see and taste what Delphi had to show? I must
stay. And my decision (I told myself quickly) had nothing
to do with Simon Lester and his affairs. Nothing. Nothing

whatever. On the thought I found myself wondering just what Simon would have decided that we should do tomorrow. . . .

"What are you doing up here?"

The question came from close behind me. I turned sharply. Danielle had come out from behind the thicket of juniper. Today she had on a wide bell of scarlet skirt and a turquoise-coloured blouse that was open at the neck. Very open. The inevitable cigarette clung to her bottom lip. Her mouth was rouged a pale pink against her sallow skin. Today her fingernails were pale pink too. On the thin brown hands it looked odd and slightly improper.

"Why, hullo," I said pleasantly. If I was to be the girl's neighbour tonight in the studio, it didn't do to let last night's irritation with her bad manners reappear.

But Danielle had no such scruples. It was quite obvious that manners, bad or good, had no place in her scheme of things. She simply was, and if others didn't like it, they had to endure it. She repeated in that sharp voice that sounded as if she really wanted to know, "What are you doing up here?"

I said, letting a note of mild surprise creep in, "Sitting looking at the view. And you?"

She came towards me. She moved like a model, hips thrown forward and knees close. She stood between me and the edge of the cliff in one of the attitudes you see in fashion drawings—one hip out, toes at twenty past seven, one thin hand gesturing with the cigarette. Any minute now she would open her mouth and let the tip of her tongue appear.

She said, "It's a long climb from the shrine on a hot afternoon."

"Isn't it? Has it tired you very much, or did you just come round the top from the studio?"

She gave me a glittering glance. I couldn't see for the life of me why she should care what I was doing up here, but she obviously did. And I certainly wasn't going to tell her where we had been. That was Simon's pilgrimage, and no one else's. If he chose to take me along, well, that was his affair. But I wasn't going to tell Danielle.

She said, "Where's Simon?"

"I don't know," I said truthfully. "Were you looking for him?"

"Oh, not really." To my surprise she came forward and sat down not two yards from my feet. She swore once, viciously, in French, as her hip met a thistle, then she settled herself gracefully on the dusty ground and smiled at me. "A cigarette?"

"Why, thanks very much," I said, before I thought.

She regarded me for a while in silence, while I smoked and tried not to feel annoyed that now I could hardly get up and leave her, which I very much wanted to do. Really, I reflected, when faced with this sort of person why do we hold madly on to our own tabus; why could my careful manners not allow me to get up—as Danielle certainly would have done in my place—say, "I'm bored and you are a mannerless little trollop and I don't like you," and then walk away down the hill? But there I sat and looked pleasantly noncommittal and smoked her cigarette. I must admit that it was a good one, and—after Niko's—nectar and ambrosia. I wondered why she had offered the olive branch, and eyed her warily. "I fear the Greeks, even when bringing gifts. . . ."

"You weren't in to lunch at the Apollon."

"No," I agreed. "Were you?"

"Where did you have lunch?"

"I had a picnic. Out."

"With Simon?"

I raised my eyebrows and tried to register cold surprise at the inquisition. It had no effect whatever. "With Simon?" she repeated.

"Yes."

"I saw him go out in the car."

"Did you?"

"He picked you up somewhere?"

"Yes."

"Where did you go?"

"South."

This set her back for half a minute. Then she said, "Why don't you want to tell me where you went and what you've been doing?"

I looked at her rather helplessly. "Why should I?"

"Why shouldn't you?"

"Because," I said, "I don't like being catechized."

She digested this. "Oh?" She turned those big tired eyes up to me, and asked, "Why? Have you and Simon been up to something?"

Said by Danielle, the harmless question could only mean one thing. I said explosively, "My God!" Then I began to laugh. I said, "No, Danielle. We have not. We took the car down to Arachova and left it there, then we walked back over the hill towards Delphi. We had a picnic at a place where there is a lovely view of Parnassus. Then I came on towards home and Simon went back for the car. If you sit here long enough you'll see him drive past below you. In case you don't know it by sight, the car you hired is a big black one. I don't know the make. I know very little about cars. Will that do? And thank you for the cigarette. I must be going." And I stubbed out the two-thirds-smoked cigarette and got to my feet.

She made a little movement without getting up, a sinuous little wriggle in the dust, like a snake. She smiled up at me. The cigarette had dropped from her lip and was smouldering on the ground beside her. She made no attempt to retrieve it. She was smiling and showing pretty white teeth with her tongue between them. The tongue was pale like her lips and nails. "You're annoyed with me," she said.

I felt suddenly very old with all the adult weight of my twenty-five years. "My dear girl," I said, "what could possibly lead you to imagine that?"

"You see, it's only," said Danielle from the dust, "that I'm jealous about Simon."

I wanted passionately to turn and run, but this gambit hardly provided me with a good exit line. I merely shed most of those adult years at one go and said feebly and childishly, "Oh?"

"Men," said the voice of the dust snake, "are all the same, mostly. But there really is something about Simon. I expect even you feel it, don't you? On the whole my lovers bore me, but I want Simon. I genuinely do."

"Really."

"Yes. Really." The flat little voice held no inflection. "And I can tell you just what it is about Simon. It's—"

I said sharply, "No, really, Danielle!"

She shot me a look. "You're in love with him yourself, aren't you?"

"Don't be absurd!" To my horror I sounded almost too emphatic. "I hardly know him! And besides, this is not the—"

"What difference does that make? It takes me two seconds to know whether I want a man or not."

I turned away. "Look," I said, "I must go. I expect I'll be seeing you later. Good-bye."

"Are you seeing him again tomorrow?"

The question was said idly, in that same flat voice; but

it was not quite idle. Something made me pause and turn
back to her.

She didn't meet my look. She was tracing a line in the
dust with a pink-tipped forefinger. "What's he doing tomorrow?"

Definitely not quite idle. I said, "How do I know?" as
coldly as I could, before it occurred to me that I did know,
quite well. He would certainly go straight back to the corrie,
to look for Michael's hypothetical cave. And he just as certainly wouldn't want Danielle tagging after him. The whole
of this embarrassing interview seemed to indicate that she
was prepared to do just that.

I said in the tone of one conceding a point to a stubborn
adversary, "All right. I'll tell you. I am seeing him. We're
going to Levadia for the day. There's a horse fair, and
gipsies, and he wants to take photographs."

"Oh." She was looking away over the valley with eyes
narrowed against the sun. Then she sent another of those
glinting looks up at me. "But what a bloody waste," she
said.

Though I was used to her by now, I didn't quite manage
to control the little flicker of anger that ran through me. I
said, "So he didn't come to repair the taps last night?"

The beautiful eyelashes fluttered, and her eyes narrowed
over a look of the most intense venom. "You're very out-
spoken, aren't you?" said Danielle.

"My bad manners," I said. "I'm sorry. And now I must
go if I'm to get a bath before dinner. See you later. Did you
know I was to come and stay at the studio from tonight?"

Her eyes opened wide. The dislike was still there, and
now annoyance, and then both were suddenly, curiously,
overlaid by what looked like calculation. "That'll be convenient, won't it?" said Danielle, meaning what only Danielle
could mean. Then I saw her look change again. It slid over
my shoulder and I saw surprise in her face, and something
else.

I turned quickly.

A man had come out from behind the clump of juniper. He
was obviously a Greek, dark, broad-cheekboned, with crisp
curled hair that showed a hint of grey, and a smudge of a
moustache over a mouth at once thin-lipped and sensual. He
was of medium height, and stockily built. I guessed his age
to be around forty. He was dressed in a grey striped suit,
rather shabby, and a dark crimson shirt with a vermilion tie

that would have clashed if the colours had not been harmlessly faded.

He spoke in French. "Why, hullo, Danielle."

It was as if he had told her quite plainly, *"It's all right."* I could see the look of surprise fade. She relaxed. "Hullo. How did you know I was here?"

I thought, Because you've just been together behind the juniper bushes and I interrupted you. Then I shook the thought away with the wry reflection that this was what contact with Danielle did. Five minutes with her, and a full half-pound of civet would hardly sweeten the imagination.

Danielle said idly—too idly—from the dust, "This is Camilla Haven. She's been out with Simon this afternoon and she's sleeping at the studio tonight." Then to me, "Dimitrios is a guide."

The man bowed and sent me a smile. *"Enchanté."*

"He doesn't speak English," said Danielle. "Do you know French?"

"Yes," I said, and murmured something polite.

Dimitrios said, "Mademoiselle has been to see the shrine this afternoon?"

"No. I went this morning early."

"Ah. And now you come up to the top of the Shining Ones to see the last of the sun."

I said, "It'll be some time still till dark, surely?"

"Perhaps not so long," said Dimitrios. I saw Danielle turn her head to look at him. Her head was on a level with my thigh, and I couldn't see her eyes for the curtaining lashes. Something crept along my spine like a cold-footed insect. The man, no less than the girl, gave me the creeps.

I gave myself another of those hearty mental shakes. "I must be going. If I'm to have a bath before dinner and arrange about—"

"These rocks," said Dimitrios, "are called the Phaedriades, the Shining Ones. Always I tell my tourists the story of the Shining Ones. Between them flows the Castalian Spring, whose water is the best in Greece. Have you tried the water of the spring, mademoiselle?"

"No, not yet. I—"

He came a step nearer. I was between him and the edge of the cliff. "They stand over the shrine like guardians, do they not? Because that is what they are. They were not only the protectors of the holy place, but they were themselves the place of execution. There were people executed on these cliffs—for sacrilege, mademoiselle. Did you know that?"

"No. But—"

Another step. He was smiling, a smile of great charm. He had a pleasant voice. Beside me in the dust I saw Danielle lift her head. I saw that her eyes now watched me, not the man. She was smiling at me with the utmost friendliness, her eyes for once bright, not tired at all. I moved back from him a step or two. It brought me within four feet of the edge.

Dimitrios said suddenly, "Be careful." I jumped and his hand came out to my arm. It was gentle on the flesh. "You are not here for execution as a traitor to the god, mademoiselle." He laughed, and Danielle smiled, and I thought suddenly, wildly, Why the hell can't I just pull my arm away and run? I hate the pair of them and they frighten me, and here I stand because it isn't polite to go while the damned man's talking.

"I always tell my tourists," he was saying, "one particular story. There was a certain traitor who was brought up here for execution. Two of them came with him to the edge . . . just there . . . to throw him over. He looked over . . . yes, mademoiselle, it is a long way down, is it not? . . . and then he said to them, Please will you not send me over face first, please will you let me fall with my back to the drop? One understands how he felt, mademoiselle, does one not?"

His hand was still on my arm. I pulled back against it. It slid gently up the flesh to the inside of my elbow. I noticed that his nails were bitten to the quick and that his thumb was badly cut and crusted with dried blood. I started to turn from him and to pull my arm away, but his fingers tightened. His voice quickened a little in my ear, "So they threw him over, mademoiselle, and as he fell, he—"

I said breathlessly, "Let me go. I don't like heights. Let me go, please."

He smiled. "Why, mademoiselle—"

Danielle's voice said, dry and thin, "Are these your tourists, Dimitrios?"

He gave an exclamation under his breath. His hand dropped from my arm. He turned sharply.

Three people, a man and two women, were coming slowly along the path from the direction of Arachova. The women were plain, dumpy, middle-aged; the man was stoutish, and wore khaki shorts and had an enormous camera slung over one perspiring shoulder. They looked at us with incurious red faces as they plodded past like beef cattle in a row, like angels of heaven.

I shot away from the brink of the cliff the way a cork

leaves the very best champagne. I didn't bother to say anything polite to Dimitrios, and I didn't even fling a good-bye at Danielle.

I hurried down the path in the wake of the three tourists. Neither the Greek nor the girl made any move to follow me, and after a while I slackened my pace and walked more slowly, trying to control my thoughts. If Danielle and her damned lover—for that the Greek was her lover I had no doubt at all—had tried for some reason to frighten me, they had succeeded. I had felt both frightened, and a fool, and it was a beastly mixture. But there had surely been nothing more than that . . . a spiteful trick and a distorted sense of humour? It was absurd to imagine anything more. I had only done so because I had spent an exacting and physically tiring day. I disliked Danielle and I had shown it, and she had wanted to frighten and humiliate me because I had interrupted her sordid meeting with the Greek behind the junipers. And even, perhaps, because of Simon. . . .

I had reached the stadium. The flat racetrack lay empty and silent in the sun, cupped in its tiers of marble seats. I almost ran across the bare dust, hurried between the columns of the starting gate, and down in the path that led to the shrine. I found that my heart was still hammering in my breast, and my throat was tight. The path dipped, dropped, twisted past a well where water trickled, and came precipitously down onto the smooth track above the theatre. There were my three tourists, still comfortably trudging along, talking something incomprehensible that might have been Dutch. There were people, too, in the theatre just below me, people on the steps, people everywhere on the floor of Apollo's temple. It was quite safe to stand here under the trees and wait for my heart to slow down. Quite safe. . . .

The slanting sun was golden on the quiet stones, was apricot, was amber, was a lovely liquid wash of light and peace. A bee went past my cheek.

Beside me was the pomegranate tree. The fruit glowed in the rich light. I remembered the cool feel of it in my hand last night, and Simon's voice saying: "Eat it soon, Persephone, then you'll have to stay in Delphi. . . ."

Well, I was going to stay. I was still going to stay.

My breathing was back to normal. Apollo the healer had done his work.

I went composedly down the steps, across the sunbaked circle of the theatre, down through the scented pines that rim the shrine, and along the main road to the hotel.

Even when, washing for dinner, I saw on my bare arm a streak of dried blood—Dimitrios' blood from that cut thumb —I felt only a brief moment of disgust. I had been stupid and imaginative and had had a fright; that was all.

But I felt a curious reluctance to go down to dinner before Simon appeared, and I wished with a quite startling fervour that I was not committed to sleeping in the studio that night.

CHAPTER

13

... With hollow shriek the steep of *Delphos* leaving.

MILTON: *Nativity Hymn.*

It must have been close on three o'clock in the morning when something woke me. My room was second from the end of the long corridor, next to Danielle's, and at the opposite end from the outer door, near which were the rooms of the two men. The Dutch painter had gone that day, so we four were the only occupants of the studio.

For some time I lay in that heavy state between sleep and waking where it is hard to disentangle reality from the trailing clouds of dream. Something had woken me, but whether I had heard a noise, or whether it was the dream itself that had startled me awake, I couldn't tell. There was no sound outside. The quiet air of Delphi wrapped us round. I moved my cheek against the hard pillow—pillows in Greece are always made like bricks—and prepared to drift back into sleep again.

From the next room came the sound of a movement, and then the creak of the bed—two sounds so completely normal and expected that they should never have roused me further. But with them came a third sound that brought my eyes wide open in the dark and my cheek up off the pillow, and made nonsense of the normality of the night. Someone was talking, very softly: a man.

My first thought was embarrassment of having heard, my next irritation succeeded by disgust. If Danielle had to have her lover in her room I didn't want to be pilloried, sleepless, on the other side of a too-thin partition. I turned over with as much fuss of bedclothes and creak of bedsprings as I could, to let them know how thin the wall was, then I pulled the sheet—it was too hot for blankets—over my head, and tried to stop my ears to the sounds that succeeded the whispering.

Sleep had gone for good. I lay rigid under the sheet with my eyes wide open in the darkness and my hands as hard as I could bear to hold them over my ears. It wasn't that I'm particularly a prude; but being forced to listen in on anyone's more private moments isn't pleasant, and I didn't want any part or parcel or hint of the more private moments of Danielle. Her public moments were quite embarrassing enough.

I wondered how the unpleasant Dimitrios had got into the place. Even though he was only here to visit Danielle, I didn't one bit like the idea of his being free to come and go. I supposed that he might have climbed in by her window, and if so, sooner or later he would go out the same way. I would no doubt hear him scramble out and drop the twelve feet or so to the floor of the rocky platform where the studio was built. I waited, furious with Danielle for subjecting me to this, furious with myself for minding, furious with Dimitrios for pandering to her monstrous egotism. It was a beastly experience.

How long it was before there was quiet from the next room I don't know. It seemed an age. But after a while all was silent, except for the whispering again, and then I heard someone moving furtively across the floor. I waited for the sounds of the window, and the cat-foot drop to the ground outside. But they didn't come. I heard the door to the corridor open, and steps went stealthily past my door.

That brought me upright in bed with a quick nervous jerk of the heart. If Danielle wanted to let a man in and out of her room, very well. But she had no damned right to let a man like Dimitrios loose inside the place. Had she—*had she?*—given him a key?

Then, out of the dark, came another thought that kicked through those nerves again.

Perhaps it wasn't Dimitrios at all.

Perhaps it was Nigel.

I was out of bed and had thrust my feet into my slippers, and was shrugging my way into the light summer coat that also served me for a dressing gown, before I quite realized myself what I was going to do. Then I had fled across the little room and had, very softly, opened my door and was peering out into the corridor.

I suppose this bit isn't pretty. It wasn't any business of mine if Nigel had gone to Danielle's room and got what had

been so patently his heart's desire. But when I had thought
of him I had had a memory, sudden and bright and clean, of
the young eagerness of Nigel's face; the vulnerable eyes and
the weak mouth and the silly boy's beard. And I had seen his
drawings, the visions of tree and flower and stone that he had
translated with such impeccable and yet impassioned skill.
If this, too, was Nigel . . . I had to know. Call it sheer, vul-
gar, woman's curiosity if you like, but I had to know if the
impossible Danielle could really annex him like that—if she
was really prepared to make Nigel, whom she despised,
squander himself in worship at her shoddy little shrine.

I believe I was thinking, incoherently, that something
must be done to stop her ruining Nigel, and then, even more
incoherently, of Simon. Simon must be told tomorrow.
Simon would know what to do. . . .

I slipped softly out of my room. The outer door at the end
of the corridor had its upper half of glass, and outside it the
dark was slackening off into dawn. The pane was grey.
Against it I saw him.

He was almost at the end of the corridor, standing outside
a door—Nigel's door—as if he had paused there waiting for
something. I shrank against the wall, but even if he had
looked back he could not have seen me against the darkness
at my end of the passage. I stayed still, pressed against the
cold marble, and felt humiliated and angry and ashamed all
at once, wishing I hadn't known, wishing I was still fathoms
deep in sleep, wishing I could remember Nigel by his work
and not, as now, through the smudgy little whispers of Danielle. . . . "Men are all the same anyway . . . it bores me
. . . I want Simon . . . I genuinely do. . . ."

The silhouette at the corridor's end moved at last. He
took a step forward and put his hand to the knob of the door.
Then he paused again, momentarily, with his head bent, as
if listening.

I thought I must have made some sound and that he had
heard me, because I could see, now, that it wasn't the Greek:
it was too tall. It wasn't Nigel either. It was Simon.

If I had been in a condition to think, the swift and complete rebellion of every nerve and muscle in my body, and of
every drop of blood in my brain, would have told me finally
about myself and Simon. But I had hardly realized what I
had seen, when the night broke open rather more really, and
very much more noisily.

Simon pushed open Nigel's door. I saw him reach up as if

for the light switch, but even as he moved the beam of a powerful torch speared out of the darkness of the room to catch him full on the face and chest. I saw his fractional check and recoil, as if the light were a physical blow in the eyes, but the pause was less than momentary, no more than the tensing before the spring. Before he had even blinked once he had launched himself forward along the beam of light, with the speed of a bullet. I heard an impact, a curse, the swift stamp and flurry of feet on the stone floor, and then all hell seemed to break loose inside the room.

I ran down the corridor and paused in the doorway. The little room seemed to be a pandemonium of violently struggling bodies. In the weaving, flashing beam of the torch the two men looked enormous, and their shadows towered and waved grotesquely over ceiling and walls. Simon was the taller, and seemed to have a momentary advantage. He had the other's wrist in one hand and seemed to be struggling to twist the man's arm so that the torch would light his features. The beam swung wildly, erratically, as the other fought to resist him, the light sweeping in violent, broken arcs through the darkness. It caught me, standing in the doorway, and raked a brilliant curve across my feet and the skirt of the nightdress below my coat. Someone snarled something incomprehensible in Greek, and then the man had wrenched his arm free from Simon's grip and, with a grunt of effort, brought the heavy torch down in a vicious blow aimed for Simon's head. Even as the blow whistled down, Simon jerked aside, so that the torch came down with a sickening sound on the side of his neck. It must have struck a muscle, for his grip seemed to loosen, and the Greek tore free.

It must, after all, have been Dimitrios. I saw the stocky body and broad shoulders in the erratic light before Simon was on him again, and the torch flew wide, to strike the wall beside me and fall to roll somewhere near the foot of the bed. Darkness stamped down. I had no time to wonder about Dimitrios—why he had come to Nigel's room, why Simon had followed him, or even—strangest of all—why Nigel himself didn't appear to be here, when the two men, at grips again, hurtled past me to come violently up against the door of the shower stall. There was a crack as a wooden panel gave way; somewhere on the floor was the sharp explosion of breaking glass; one of the flimsy chairs went over with a splintering sound; then the bedsprings crashed and whined as the two bodies went down on the bed together.

I flung myself to my knees not two feet from the heaving bed, groping wildly for the torch. Somewhere here I had heard it roll . . . not far, surely? . . . these things rolled in semicircles . . . ah! . . . there it was. I clutched it, groping at the metal to find the catch, wondering if the fall had broken the bulb. . . .

It was a heavy torch and the catch was stiff. The bed, rocking like a ship in a storm, shot away a foot from the wall on screaming castors, hurtled back again with a crash that should have brought the plaster off the walls. The springs creaked, strained, gave again with an appalling noise as the men slithered to the edge and then fell to the floor.

A moment of gasping stillness, and then they were on their feet again. A pause, filled with the sound of heavy breathing. I jumped to my feet, still wrestling with the torch, and suddenly the thing flashed on in my hand. For the second time that night it caught Simon full in the eyes. And this time the Greek, seizing the advantage like lightning, charged down the beam, out of the blinding light. Simon went down with a crash that shook the room. I saw him catch the edge of the bed with his shoulder as he fell. The blow must have momentarily crippled him, but, surprisingly, the Greek didn't follow it up. Nor did he turn to deal with me. He had his back to me, and the light waveringly pinned for a moment the heavy bull-like shoulders, the dark curled hair. . . . He didn't even look round. I heard a gasping snarl in French, *"Put the bloody thing out, will you?"*

I hit him as hard as I could over the head.

I missed him. Just as the blow fell, something warned him. He didn't turn into the light. He lashed backwards with a crooked elbow that caught the torch, knocking it flying, then swept on to strike me full across the breast in a heavy blow that sent me staggering to fall at the foot of the bed. The torch hurtled wide a second time and went out for good. As I went down I saw, in one swift flash of the flying light, the Greek turn and leap for the doorway, with Simon after him in a lunge. And in the doorway stood Danielle, fully dressed, with wide brilliant eyes and parted lips.

She whipped back to let the man past. Then, with a languid-seeming movement that was nevertheless as swift as a snake's, she stepped into the path of Simon's rush. I heard the other man running up the corridor towards her room and the open window, as Simon came violently up against her body. I heard her gasp as his weight jammed her hard against the doorpost. He stopped short.

I couldn't see more than the dim outlines of movement against the grey light of the corridor, but she must have been clinging to him, for he said, harsh and breathless, *"Let me go!"* and she laughed in her throat. Along the corridor a door slammed. Simon moved sharply and I heard him say, very softly, "Do you hear me? Take your hands away, or you'll get hurt."

I hadn't heard him even sound ruffled before; now I realized with something like a sharp little shock that he was angry. Danielle must not have set much store by it, for I heard her murmur, with the breath hurrying through the husky voice, "Go on doing that. I like it. . . ."

There was a second of frozen silence, then in the near-darkness the group by the door exploded into movement. The girl was flung aside against the other door jamb with a violence that sent the breath out of her in a sharp cry that held more surprise than anything else. Before she could recover herself Simon was back in the room, hurling himself across it towards the window, tearing at the catch.

The casement was rusty, and it must have been stiff. As it screeched wider I heard, like an echo at the other end of the building, the shriek of rusty hinges, and the thud as a heavy body dropped to the ground. Steps clattered and slithered away into the darkness.

Simon was up on the sill, a dark bulk against the greying sky. But before he could swing himself out and after the quarry Danielle flew after him like an arrow and clung to his arm.

"Simon . . . Simon, let him go, Simon dear, what a fuss. . . ." In spite of his recent violence she clung to him still, pleading in that voice which under its overtones of sexiness might have held a touch of fear. "Simon, no! He was with me. Don't you understand? *With me.*"

I saw his hand fall from the window catch. He turned. "What? What d'you mean?"

"What I say. He was in my room. He only came to see me."

I said from the floor beside the bed where I was still sitting, "It's true. I heard them."

I heard her laugh again, but the sound didn't hold its usual assurance. Simon shook her off as if she didn't exist and dropped lightly back into the room, "I—see. He's gone, anyway . . . Camilla? Are you all right?"

"Perfectly. Is there any light?"

"I think the bulb's out. Half a minute." He seemed to be

feeling in his pockets. "What are you doing down there? Did that brute hit you?"

"Yes, but I'm all right. I was just—I was keeping out of the way." I got up a bit unsteadily and sat on the bed, just as Simon found matches and struck one. He surveyed me by its light. I smiled rather waveringly up at him. I saw then that he was dressed only in a pair of grey flannels. In the light of the match I could see the gleam of sweat on his chest and a shining dark trickle of blood from a cut at the base of the neck, where a deep V of sunburn showed. He was breathing a little faster than usual—not much, but perceptibly a bit faster—and his eyes for once didn't look cool and amused at all. But the match burned steadily in a tremorless hand. I asked anxiously, "What about you?"

"Don't give it a thought. Honours were about even . . . more's the pity."

Danielle said petulantly, "What did you have to fight for?"

He said crisply, "My dear girl, he attacked me. What would you expect me to do?" He had lit another match and was looking round the room for the light bulb.

I said, "That was Dimitrios, wasn't it?"

Simon gave me a fleeting look of surprise as he picked the light bulb up from the washbasin. Danielle turned her head as if startled, then smiled that cat-and-cream smile of hers. "You recognized him? Of course."

Simon had dragged one of the wooden chairs forward, and now mounted it to fit the light bulb into its socket. The light flashed on, harsh on the disorder of the bare little room. He got off the chair, looking at me.

"Are you sure you're all right?"

"Quite. But, Simon—where's Nigel?"

"I've no idea. He hasn't been to bed; that much is apparent." In spite of the tossed state of the bed, the sheet still lay tucked flatly in. No one had slept there. Simon hesitated, then turned to Danielle. She was standing near the door, leaning against the wall in a pose of lazy grace. Her eyes looked long and sleepy again under the thick lashes. She had taken a cigarette out of a pocket and was lighting it. She dropped the burnt-out match on the floor. All through the operation the narrow glinting gaze had been on Simon . . . all over him.

He said flatly, "You say that man was with you? How did he get in?"

"I let him in."

"By the door?"

"No. By my window."

"Come off it, Danielle. Your window's twelve feet from the ground. Don't tell me you plaited sheets or let down your hair for him. Did you unlock the door for him, or has he got a key?"

She said sulkily, under the coldness of his voice, "I don't see what the hell it's got to do with you, but yes, I did unlock it."

"It's got everything to do with me that your visitor was apparently prowling round where he's no damned right to be. And there's the little detail that he went for me with apparent intent to do damage, if not worse. What was he doing in Nigel's room?"

"How do I know?"

"He jumped out of your window in the end. He could have gone that way in the first place. Why didn't he?"

"It was easier to get out through the door, and quieter. The key's in the lock."

"Then why did he come in here?"

She shrugged. "He must have heard you moving and dodged in so that you wouldn't see him. I don't know."

"He couldn't have known there was no one in the room."

"I'd told him they were nearly all empty. I expect he took a chance. And now I'm tired of this, and tired of the inquisition, and I'm going to bed." She straightened, yawning deliberately and daintily, like a cat, showing all her pretty teeth and that pale pink tongue. Then she turned her head and let the big sleepy eyes move insolently over me. Simon had found the end of a battered pack of cigarettes in his trouser pocket and had given me one. He bent over me to light it. His breathing was quite even again now. If it hadn't been for the cut where the torch had hit him, and that thin glaze of sweat drying on his skin, you would never have guessed that a few minutes ago he had been fighting for his life in the dark.

Danielle said, sounding suddenly waspish, "What are you doing here anyway, Camilla?"

"I heard a noise and I came along."

She smiled. "And got knocked down. Did he hurt you?"

"I hope not as much as I hurt him."

She looked momentarily startled, and this gave me a quite absurd prick of satisfaction. "You hurt him? How?"

"I hit him over the back of the neck with the torch. Hard."

She stared at me for a moment longer, a very queer look.

"*You hit him?*" Her voice sounded quite shaken. "I can't see—you have no business. . . . He is my lover, and if I wish to let him come here—"

I said sharply, "He was doing his best to kill Simon. And besides, I owed him something."

She looked at me almost stupidly. "You—owed him something?"

"Yes. And don't play the innocent, Danielle. You didn't look so innocent on the Shining Ones this afternoon."

"I . . . see."

She let out a breath. Simon said sharply, "What are you talking about? What happened?"

"Nothing. It was Camilla's imagination. She thinks Dimitrios—oh, it's so silly that I won't speak of it. It was a joke. And now I'm sick of this. I'm going." She dropped the half-smoked cigarette on the floor and turned quickly. I got to my feet.

"Just a minute," said Simon pleasantly. "No, please don't go yet, Camilla. We're forgetting Nigel. Danielle, have you any idea where he might be? Did he say anything last night to—?"

She said viciously, "Why should I know where the fool went? I don't know and I don't care. He could be dead as far as I'm concerned."

I said, "I think I know where he went."

Simon was dabbing at his cut neck with a handkerchief. I saw his brows shoot up. "You seem to know an awful lot tonight."

"Doesn't she?" Danielle had stopped in the doorway, and turned her head sharply. Her voice was not, like his, amused. "All right, you tell us."

I said, "It's only a guess. But . . . well, Simon, d'you remember our talk in here the other night, about Nigel and his work, and needing a gimmick, and the Dutch boy walking from Jannina and all that?"

"Yes. You're not suggesting that Nigel has taken a leaf out of that boy's book, are you?"

I said, "There's been a mule stolen from the excavations above the shrine. I know because the guide told me this morning . . . yesterday morning, I suppose I should say. And I saw Nigel early the same morning, and he was trying not to be seen—"

"Where?" asked Danielle.

"Just outside the studio here."

"Which way was he going?"

"I didn't see. He seemed to be making farther up Parnassus—towards the stadium."

"Ah well," said Simon, "you may be right. I suppose what Nigel does is very much his own affair, and he was certainly feeling thoroughly unsettled. He may easily have cut loose for a few days." He turned to rinse his bloodstained handkerchief out under the tap. "I think we'd better just tidy his room up and get out of it. There's blood on the washbasin here, and I'm afraid the floor isn't all it should be. We'd better have a look at the damage and do what we can."

I said, "Leave that. I'll clean the basin up. But let me have a look at that cut, will you? Danielle, perhaps you'll be good enough to clear the floor and pick up that broken glass?"

She sent me one of those looks of glittering dislike, which was, this time, quite justified. "It won't take you long. I'm tired. You forget, I haven't been to sleep yet tonight, and oh, how I need that sleep. . . ." She yawned, sent another narrow-eyed look at me, and went out rather quickly, shutting the door behind her.

Seconds later, from the other end of the corridor, came like an echo the slam of her bedroom door.

CHAPTER

14

Courage is a thing
All men admire. Think what it will mean
For your good name and mine, if you do this.

SOPHOCLES: *Ajax*
(tr. E. F. Watling).

In Nigel's room there was the sort of silence that is usually
called pregnant. But at least, I reflected, there was no longer
any need to suppress the urge to discuss Danielle. . . .

My eyes met Simon's in the mirror. "You wanted to get
rid of her, didn't you?"

"You're coming on with that thought-reading, aren't you?
I did indeed."

"Why?" I added, carefully, "Apart, that is, from the obvious reasons."

The brief amusement in his eyes vanished as he turned
and looked down at me. His look was grave, sombre even.
"Because I don't like the feel of this thing, Camilla."

"The feel of it?"

"Yes. Too much is happening. Some of it may be irrele-
vant, or it may matter the hell of a lot. Danielle and this
man, for instance. . . . And Danielle and Nigel. I've begun
to wonder."

"Then I was right. Turn round towards the light and let
me have a look at that cut . . . you didn't want me to go on
talking about Nigel in front of her?"

"No."

"It's not deep, but you're going to have a bruise and a stiff
shoulder, I think. Have you any antiseptic in your room?
You don't think he's gone off with a Modestine into the
mountains?"

"Yes. No, I mean. No, I don't believe he's off on a trip,
but yes, I have some antiseptic."

"Then don't forget to put it on. The wound's quite clean and it's stopped bleeding." I stood back and looked at him inquiringly. "Then what have Danielle and Nigel and this Greek of hers got to do with us—with you, I mean?"

He said slowly, "This Greek—this lover of Danielle's . . . you said his name was Dimitrios?"

"Yes. I met him yesterday on the way back from the corrie. He was with her above the Shining Ones."

"Ah, yes. The Shining Ones. What happened there, incidentally? What did you 'owe' Dimitrios?"

"Oh, it was nothing, really. He was unpleasant in a greasy sort of way, and talked a lot about people being thrown off the cliff and so on. We were awfully near the edge and he could see I didn't like it, and it amused him. . . and Danielle too. It was just a nasty little trick to make me look a fool—which I did, I may say. I bolted."

There was a frown between his eyes. "I see. Camilla, has nothing occurred to you about this—Dimitrios?"

"Occurred to me? What sort of thing? I don't like him, and I think—" I stopped short. I said, on a long breath, *"Dimitrios!"*

"Exactly. You remember? Angelos had a cousin called Dimitrios Dragoumis, who had gone to live at Itea. At Itea, mark you."

"And I saw the jeep down at Itea . . . Danielle had driven it straight down there when she got in from Athens! If it's the same Dimitrios . . . then Dimitrios Dragoumis is Danielle's lover, and that was his house I saw. She wasn't visiting any friend called 'Elena,' she was visiting him, and I'll bet, if the jeep's anything to go by, that she was there when I passed the house!"

"You're certain it was the same jeep?"

"Quite. I told you I recognized the doll hanging in the windscreen. There was someone tinkering with the engine, and that wasn't Dimitrios, but all the same, I've a feeling we're right. It's the same Dimitrios. That would explain why Danielle's so darned interested in you." I added, "Or partly."

He passed that one.

"Well, then, say we're right, and let's look at what we have . . . Dimitrios Dragoumis is Danielle's lover. Whether there actually is anyone called Elena or not, it's quite true that Danielle has been in the habit of spending her afternoons down near Itea, swimming. She told me once she'd found a secluded little cove where the water was clean (it's filthy in Itea itself) but she wouldn't tell me where it was. My guess is that she met, not 'Elena,' but Dimitrios, on these swimming expeditions, and took up with him. He may have been there to fish—he's a fisherman, did I tell you, and owns a caique?"

"He told me he was a guide."

"There's no guide in Delphi of that name, that I do know; and if he took the trouble to lie . . ." He didn't finish the sentence. He was frowning down at his cigarette. "Well, let's go on. Dimitrios, the cousin of Angelos, sends Danielle into Athens to hire him a car—on a matter of life and death. In other words, in a hell of a hurry."

"Well?"

His eyes lifted. "An expensive need. And he's a sailor. Why would he want a car?"

I sat down again on the bed. "I don't know. Go on."

Absently, he flicked a gout of ash into the washbasin.

"Danielle hired a car for him, but then got the better offer of a jeep from her French friend Hervé Clément, and came up in that. She didn't revisit the garage to let them know . . . and she hadn't given them Dragoumis' name—hence all the nonsense about 'Monsieur Simon,' and the interfering but well-meant efforts of Miss Camilla Haven. But Danielle's actions do spell something, don't they?"

"Urgency," I said slowly, "yes. And secrecy?"

"Exactly. And I could bear to know what's urgent and secret about Danielle, and Dimitrios the cousin of Angelos," said Simon.

A pause. A beetle blundered in through the open casement, hit the wall with a crack like a pistol shot, and zoomed out again into the dark.

"But—the car?" I said, seizing on what was still my own piece of the mystery. "Why the car? You said Dimitrios Dragoumis was a fisherman. What would he need a car for, from Athens, with all that hush-hush nonsense about it?"

"That's just it," said Simon. "He is a fisherman, and he owns a boat. And now he has a jeep . . . got from Athens and kept very quiet locally. To me, that adds up to one thing. Transport."

I said, in a voice that sounded queer, "Urgent, secret transport . . ." Then, sitting up briskly, "But—*no*, Simon. It's absurd."

"Why?"

"I can see what you're getting at . . . the reason why Angelos' cousin might need this urgent and secret transport.

You mean that you think Dimitrios has found Angelos' cache—whatever it was that Michael found on Parnassus? And the jeep and the caique are to carry—oh!"

"Well?"

"*The mule!* Simon—the mule!"

He nodded. "You can't take a jeep up Parnassus, can you? The mule was stolen the night I saw Stephanos. Danielle brought the jeep up the same day. I'll bet you anything you like that Dimitrios' caique will shortly be lying carefully invisible in one of the tiny inlets beyond Amphissa."

I said, "Look, hold on, Simon. You're only guessing. It *could* have been Nigel who took the mule. He's gone off somewhere, and we were talking about the Dutch boy to him, and—"

"And it would have been very much simpler for Nigel to have bought the donkey—which went dirt cheap—off the Dutch boy," said Simon, "than to have stolen a mule from the excavations. He wasn't all that hard up, and there really wasn't all that need of secrecy for *him*. In fact, if he was off on a trek of that sort, you'd even have thought publicity was necessary."

"Yes, I suppose so. All the same, he looked pretty secretive when I saw him sloping off yesterday morning."

"Oh? But I still don't think he took the mule. It vanished on Monday night, and that night Nigel was up here. Of course he did go out later for a walk with Danielle, but I hardly think—"

I said tautly, "You're right. It wasn't Nigel. I've just remembered something. When we were in the theatre, and you were reciting, I was up near the top row of seats, and I heard something moving up the hillside about me. You know how you hear something without really taking it in consciously, until, later, something reminds you? Well, it was like that. I thought nothing of it—if I heard it at all, I thought it was just the breeze, or a stray goat or donkey or something. But I remember now that I heard metal—a small chinking of metal, like a shod hoof, or the nails of a boot."

Simon smiled slightly. "The beasts here aren't shod. Hadn't you noticed? And the locals wear rope-soled espadrilles on the hill. If you heard movement and the chink of metal, Camilla, then you heard a beast's bridle. It sounds to me as if you really might have heard the mule being stolen. Friend Dimitrios, taking the mule off up the hill. Well, well."

I said sharply, "Simon, if he was above the theatre when you were reciting, he'd hear us, wouldn't he?"

"Almost certainly." He laughed. "Though I'm afraid he'd hardly appreciate *Electra*. He's not likely to know any classical Greek."

"Not only that," I said uneasily, trying to remember. "We talked about Michael, and—"

"In English, though. It's very probable he doesn't understand that well enough, either. Let's hope not."

I cried, "He doesn't! Danielle told me so yesterday—and there'd be no reason for her to lie to me then. . . . But look, Simon, you can't be right; about the reason for all this, I mean. It really is absurd. Maybe Dimitrios is up to no good, and maybe Danielle is in it, and maybe they did steal the mule and hire the car to transport something, but it can't, it just can't, be Michael's 'treasure'!"

"Why not?"

"Because it's too much to swallow that Dimitrios should have spent fourteen years or so looking for the stuff, and just have found it now. Oh, I grant you he could have searched a thousand years and never found it, especially if he didn't have precise information from Angelos—and he probably didn't, because you can be sure Angelos meant to come back when things had simmered down enough for him to leave Yugoslavia and come home. He may not have told Dimitrios at all. Dimitrios may merely have guessed that Angelos had hidden something, and not have known where to start looking. But what I can't swallow is the assumption that he should have found Angelos' cache *now,* this week, the very week you're in Delphi. That's too much of a coincidence, and I don't believe it."

"But is it?"

"How d'you mean?"

He said slowly, "You've got it the wrong way round. Supposing those two things *have* happened at the same time: I am here in Delphi, and Dimitrios finds Angelos' cache on Parnassus. You call it coincidence. I call it cause and effect."

"You mean—?"

"That the two incidents are certainly related, but not by chance. Dimitrios found the hiding place, not just while I happen to be here—but simply *because* I'm here."

I stared up at him. I passed my tongue over my lips. "You mean—that he followed us up to the corrie yesterday?"

"Precisely that. He could have found out when we were going and he could have come to spy."

I said hoarsely, "He did. When I was sitting there in the corrie and you were in the cave with the other two men, I thought I saw something move at the top of the cliff. It could have been someone watching."

His gaze sharpened. "Are you sure of that?"

"Not really. But I thought there was movement, and looked up, but couldn't see anything. The sun was in my eyes."

"I see. Well, it might have been Dimitrios. And then he followed us down, intending to meet Danielle on top of the Shining Ones. Could be."

I said, "I did her an injustice. I thought they'd been together, and I'd interrupted them."

"He'd hardly have had time to get down there before you. Most of the way it's pretty open, and we might have seen him." He thought for a few moments. "Well, let's look at the sequence of events, shall we? Dimitrios, you'll remember, did try to find out from Stephanos—the only man who knew anything definite about the place where Michael died—anything he could about Michael's death. He didn't get anything out of Stephanos. Perhaps he did try to find the place himself. Perhaps he did gather a slender clue or two from his cousin before he left the country. But even with definite instructions from Angelos he still could have been raking the mountain all this time and found nothing. All the marks, like the Cat's Tooth pinnacle, have gone, and anything could lie buried under that earthquake rubble for fourteen years—or fourteen hundred—undiscovered. Angelos himself, if he were still alive, and if he came back to look, would be in exactly the same case."

I said, rather breathlessly, "Niko said there were ghosts on the hill . . . lights . . . d'you remember?"

"Niko talked a lot of rubbish, but he may well have told the truth there. Dimitrios may have been seen searching. But, to go on with the story—supposing he *had* searched all that time, and had had no luck in locating the cache, then, after years, he heard that I, Michael Lester's brother, was coming to Delphi. This might prove to be his chance. What is more likely than that Stephanos would show me, Michael's brother, the place? When I arrived, Stephanos was away in Levadia, but Dimitrios could easily find out when he was coming back. It's quite some time since I planned this visit; Dimitrios could have known, and taken time over his prep-

arations. Supposing we were right, and he had noticed
Danielle driving down almost daily to Itea with the jeep to
bathe? Here was transport of the kind he would need. He
wouldn't dare buy or hire transport locally; he's well known,
and people would ask questions. But it would be easy
enough to scrape acquaintance with Danielle, and buy her
silence—and her help—with a promise to cut her in on the
final haul. It would only remain to collect a mule or a donkey, and there again Danielle was the answer. I'll bet you
she took the mule; she'd worked with the archaeologists for
weeks, and she knew just where everything was kept and
how to get at it. . . . What is it?"

"I've just remembered. It wasn't only a mule. I remember.
The guide said 'some tools and a mule.' "

"*Did* he?" His voice was still quiet, but the light-grey eyes
blazed in his brown face. "Well, well, well. . . . Does it
make sense, or not? Or am I jumping ahead too fast?"

"Pretty fast. They're rather scrappy bricks, and made
with awfully little straw, but they could be solid. Go on."

"Where was I? Yes: Dimitrios has everything lined up
for the day when Simon Lester should arrive and lead him
straight to the spot where Michael died. But then he—
Dimitrios—has a stroke of bad luck."

"Danielle's boss leaves Delphi, and she has to go too—
with the jeep?"

"Exactly. She went on Sunday, perforce. She must have
gone straight to the garage in Athens and arranged to pick
up a car next day, as soon as she could get free of Monsieur
Clément." He grinned. "We know what happened next. Her
error. But luck came in again, as she persuaded Hervé to let
her have the jeep. And she came back. She took the jeep
down to Itea. Whether she brought Dimitrios up that night
with her we can't know, but she probably did. She—or he—
took the mule and a crowbar or so from the workmen's
sheds above the shrine, *et voilà*."

I said, "And then all Dimitrios had to do was to wait and
follow us. Too easy."

"Much too easy. I should have thought of it after what
Stephanos told me, but I admit it never seriously occurred to
me—till I saw the earthquake damage up there—that anything that Mick found might still be hidden. However, there
it is. You can bet your boots he was up there yesterday, and
now all he has to do is to hunt that fairly small stretch of
cliff, and then he and Danielle are made for life." He smiled
down at me. "I admit it *is* a lot of bricks to make with very

little straw, but where else is the straw to go? We have certain facts, and we must fit them in somewhere with the knowledge that friend Dimitrios is up to no sort of good."

"And he is the cousin of Angelos. . . . Yes, I see what you mean. But why did he come here tonight? Just to see Danielle again?"

He said soberly, "Ah, that . . . that's what I meant when I said I didn't like the feel of this affair. What we've discovered—or guessed, if you like—so far, is straightforward enough, but Nigel . . ." He paused, then turned to pitch the stub of his cigarette out of the open window. "Nigel. He's in this somewhere and I want to know where."

"You mean that Dimitrios came to see *him?*"

"No. Dimitrios came here looking for something. And I could bear to know what." He glanced round the room. "And I could also bear to know where Nigel is."

I said, "The drawings have gone."

"What? Oh, the ones on the wall. So they have. Well, the sooner we find out what else is gone the better. . . ." He began to move round the bare untidy little room as he spoke. "We'll soon see if he intended—no, don't you bother, Camilla. Sit still. There's not much searching to be done in a place this size, even if a couple of gorillas have turned everything upside down first. . . ."

"Dimitrios didn't take anything with him, anyway," I said.

"No, he didn't, did he? One might say he hardly had time. That's one satisfactory thing about tonight's affair."

"Perhaps Danielle was telling the truth. Perhaps he did only come in here to hide from you when he heard you move."

"Not on your life." He had opened the shower stall and was rummaging inside. "He didn't have time, after he'd heard me move, to take that light bulb out. He did that as soon as he got into the room, and to me that means he had some business in here that was going to take a minute or two, and he didn't want to risk being surprised and recognized. I must have heard him almost straightaway—I'd been lying awake wondering where the blazes Nigel was, and as soon as I heard the movements I got up. It didn't take me long to roll off the bed and grab my flannels and get into them, and then to get to the door. He hadn't quite shut the door—for quietness' sake, I suppose—and when I saw torchlight moving beyond it I knew it wasn't Nigel, and I went carefully. As I shoved the door open, I saw the light swinging round the room as if it was looking for something. That was all, because of course he turned on me."

I laughed. "Yes, and you told Danielle he attacked you—which, sir, was a lie. I was watching, and you went bald-headed for the poor chap before he even had time to say 'Good evening!'"

He grinned. "And for a very good reason. He whipped round when he heard me at the door, and he pulled a knife. I thought it best not to give him time to think about using it."

I drew a long breath. "I—see. You were right about the feel of this thing, weren't you? All I can say is, that for a member of our staid and slightly stuffy profession, your reactions are—well, fairly rapid, not to say decisive."

He was still smiling. "Two strenuous years' conscription in the tough end of the Artists' Rifles . . . besides what Michael taught me all unofficial-like. It bears fruit—besides, I'm rather afraid I enjoyed it. I like a good and dirty fight. . . . I say, Camilla."

"Yes?"

"His things *are* all gone."

"Everything? Not just his painting things?"

"Everything, I think. The rucksack—see, he used to hang it on this peg. I suppose he didn't carry a razor, but the towel's gone too, and the soap, and what clothes he had. And unlike me he was conventional even in this climate and wore pyjamas. Are they tucked down there under the sheet?"

"I don't think so. No, they're not."

He said, sounding at once puzzled and relieved, "Then he meant to go anyway. Damn the boy, he might have told me, and saved me a couple of sleepless hours. Well, at least he isn't sitting up on Parnassus somewhere with a sprained ankle, whatever else he's got himself into. I'll just make sure there's nothing down here. . . . ah, there's the Greek's knife. I thought I heard it fly under the bed. And that hellish clanging noise we made was Nigel's apology for a wastepaper basket. . . . Lord, what a mess! Orange peel and pencil shavings and all the dud drawings he's thrown away. I really think we'll have to bribe our way out of this, Camilla my girl."

"For goodness' sake, let me help." I slipped from the bed to the floor and gathered up a handful of papers. I dropped them into the biscuit tin that served Nigel for a wastebasket. "I'll clear this stuff up. You see if that chair'll mend, and straighten the table. There's no damage except the broken glass, and we better leave that till morning and see if we can find a brush and—*Simon!*"

He was busy straightening the furniture. He swung round. "What is it?"

"These papers . . . they're not 'dud drawings' at all. They're—they're the finished things, his Hellenic types!" I shuffled them through my hands. "Yes, look, here they are! There's that head that's a bit like Stephanos, and the smiling one that looked like a statue, and that must be the Minoan girl he told us about—and here's a shepherd boy. And more . . . look." I began to leaf through them rapidly. My hand wasn't quite steady. I said, "I know he was doing them under protest, and he *was* feeling at odds with life, but surely, Simon, he can't afford to throw them away? What in the world—?" I stopped short.

Simon said sharply from above me, "What is it?"

I said shakily, "This one. This is the head, that lovely, lovely head. The young man with the strange face. And look, he's torn it up. Not the others, but this. It's torn right across." I looked down at the fragments on my lap and said sadly, "He needn't have torn it up. It was beautiful."

He stooped to take the pieces from me, and studied them for a few moments in silence.

At length he said, "What else is there? Not the flower studies, surely?"

"No. No. They're all the 'types,' except that lovely head."

I heard him take a breath, as if of relief, and when he spoke I knew he had had the same fleeting stab of fear as I myself. "Then—whatever made him go—I don't think we need worry overmuch. That fit of the blues hasn't made him plan anything foolish after all; he's taken the good stuff with him. Except this . . ." He opened his fingers, and let the fragments drift down onto my lap. The action was like a shrug; a sigh. "Ah, well, we can't guess what's biting the boy. But I'll be thankful when I know—"

I said abruptly, "*The cyclamen.*"

He said, suddenly sounding very weary, "Is that there as well, after all?"

"No. It's not here. That's not what I meant. But I've remembered something, Simon, and I think it's important. Yesterday, when we were up in the corrie—Michael's corrie —I saw a plant of cyclamen growing in the rock. I didn't realize it at the time—at least I think I must have subconsciously, because I know I was thinking about Nigel as I looked at it—but it was the same plant that was in the drawing. I tell you, I didn't connect it then; but now, when we were talking about his drawings, I somehow saw it again. And it was the same. I'm sure of it. And that means that Nigel's been up in that corrie too!" I drew a deep breath. "And perhaps, if *Nigel* had found Angelos' cave, that would explain some of the things he said on Monday night. Simon, Nigel was in that corrie, and, if you ask me, Nigel found the cave! And Angelos' hoard was still there!"

Simon said, hard and sharp, "Then if Nigel found anything in that corrie, he found it on Monday. He did that drawing on Monday."

"Yes, and he told you he'd done no work, till we found that he'd slipped up over the Phormis head and the cyclamen!"

He said slowly, "It could be. I went up some of the way over the track with him on Sunday. He might have gone back on his own and stumbled on the place. One of those weird freaks of chance, but they do happen. Oh, my God, suppose he did?"

We stared at each other. I said, "And yesterday morning I saw him setting off again . . . and looking secretive about it. Simon, perhaps it was *Nigel* who took the mule. Perhaps we're wrong about Danielle. Perhaps Nigel's trying to move the stuff, whatever it is, himself."

Simon said, in a harsh voice that was anything but casual, "And if he is? If he's got across that damned Greek in the process? Don't forget he's somewhere in this too."

"Perhaps he's working with that damned Greek," I said. "Perhaps."

I said, "Simon, don't worry so. One thing's obvious; he did mean to go. He's cleared up here, and he's scrapped the stuff he didn't want. Whatever he's up to, and even if his affairs *have* tangled with Dimitrios', he's gone deliberately. He may have got himself into something illegal, or at most immoral, but he meant to, and—well, you can't really be his keeper to that extent, can you?"

He hesitated, then suddenly smiled. "I suppose not. At least, not till it's daylight."

I said, making a statement of it, "You're going up there, of course."

"Of course. I intended to anyway, and now it seems I shall have to."

He looked down at me for a moment. That unreadable mask had shut down again over his face. I don't know what

I expected him to say. I know what nine men out of ten would have said—and Philip would have said it twice.

Simon didn't say it at all. He said merely, "I'll come and call you. And now you'd better go and sleep. We'll have to make an early start."

I got to my feet. "Will you take Stephanos and Niko?"

"No. For one thing it would take too long, and for another, if there's anything to be found that Nigel and/or Dimitrios haven't already found and moved, I don't want witnesses till I know where Nigel comes in, and whose property it is. If it is arms and gold, the ownership might be a rather delicate political question under present circumstances."

"Heavens, yes. I hadn't thought of that."

"And now let me see you back to your room. . . . By the way I haven't thanked you yet for bashing friend Dimitrios over the head for me."

"I'd never have got near him," I said truthfully, "if he hadn't thought I was Danielle. And I missed him anyway."

"All the same it was a stout effort."

He opened the door, and I went past him into the chilly corridor.

"They taught us a lot," I said sedately, "in the tough end of St. Trinian's."

CHAPTER

15

"Tell the Emperor that the bright citadel is fallen to the ground; Apollo has no longer any shelter, or oracular laurel tree, or speaking fountain. Even the vocal stream has ceased to flow."

The Delphic Oracle to the Emperor Julian.

It can't have been much after six when Simon woke me. I had sleepily answered "Come in" to his knock before I remembered that I was no longer in the hotel, and this was not likely to be a chambermaid with a cup of tea. As I turned my head, looking, still sleepy-eyed, towards the door, it opened. Simon didn't come in, but I heard his voice.

"Camilla."

"Mmm? Oh—Simon. Yes?"

"Could you bear to get up now, d'you suppose? I think we ought to move. I've got coffee on a Primus if you would like to come along and get it when you're dressed."

"All right."

"Good." The door shut. I shot, fully awake now, out of bed, and began to dress quickly. From my window I could see the morning sunlight sliding like apricot bloom over the rounded top of Mount Cirphis.

In my room it was still cool, for which I was grateful. I wasn't so grateful about the icy gush of water from the taps—both taps—but in any case washing at Delphi is a penance; the water is as hard as pumice stone, and just about as good for the skin . . . but it woke me up fully and finally, and it was with a tingling sense of new adventure that at length I went quickly along to Simon's door and tapped.

"Come in."

I noticed that he was making no attempt to keep his voice low this morning, and he must have seen a query in my face as I entered, because he looked up from the Primus he was tending and said briefly, "Danielle checked out an hour ago."

"Oh?"

"I followed her down as far as the upper road. I didn't see where she went in the village, but I did see a jeep drive off north."

"That means she's either making for Itea or further along towards Amphissa?"

"Yes. Coffee?"

"Lovely. Simon, this smells like heaven. Rolls too? You're very efficient."

"I went along to the baker's after I'd seen Danielle off the premises. Here's the sugar."

"Thank you. Where do you think she's gone?"

"God knows, and there's not much point in guessing. Probably to pick Dimitrios up in Itea—though if the jeep was in Delphi it seems odd he didn't take it last night when he got out of the studio. How d'you feel today?"

"I'm fine, thanks. And you? How's the shoulder? You're sure that was all the damage?"

"Certain. And it's really hardly stiff at all. I feel ready for anything."

He was sitting on the edge of his bed, a cup of coffee in one hand and a roll in the other, looking, as ever, completely relaxed and at ease. "And you?" he said. "Ready for your adventure?"

I laughed. "I can hardly believe that two days ago I was writing to my friend that nothing ever happened to me. Is it Goethe who says somewhere that we ought to beware what we ask the gods for, because they might grant it? I asked for adventure, and it seems I got it."

He didn't smile. He appeared to consider what I'd been saying for a minute or two, then he said, quite seriously, "I ought not to let you come, you know."

I didn't ask why, I drank coffee and watched the sunlight wheel a fraction to touch the edge of the window-frame. A butterfly hovered, then winnowed down to cling to the strip of sunlit stone. Its wings fanned gently, black velvet shot with gold.

Simon said, "Don't mistake me. I don't think we—you, are in any danger; but it'll be a hard day, especially following after yesterday and last night. The only possible danger is running unexpectedly into Dimitrios, who'll certainly be up there, but if we're reasonably careful, that

can be avoided. I don't think he'll be expecting us. He
probably thinks that, now I've seen the place, that closes
the account for me."

"In any case I told Danielle we were going to the fair
at Levadia."

"*Did* you? Good for you. Was she showing interest,
then?"

I smiled. "Yes, she showed interest. She asked me flat
out where you were going today. I—well, I'm afraid I just
mistrusted her on principle, and told her a lie." I set down
my coffee cup. "It seems it's just as well. Dimitrios certainly won't be looking out for us."

"Excellent," said Simon. "Of course, there's no reason
anyway why he should have expected me to go up there
again, is there? He doesn't know I know of the existence
of any 'treasure.' If Michael had sent any information
home, Dimitrios might well imagine I'd have come long
ago. Cigarette?"

"Thank you."

He leaned forward to hold his lighter for me. "No," he
said, "I think Dimitrios will see it as a pilgrimage for me;
and that's over. All the better. But we'll be very careful,
just the same. With any luck we'll see what's going on, and
where Nigel comes in—and then we can think about
possible reinforcements." He sent me a grin as he got up
off the bed and reached for his haversack. "In any case,
don't worry. All things being equal, I can deal with friend
Dimitrios. And I refuse to be afraid of Nigel. Even if he
has got himself mixed up in anything for the sake of the
cash, he'd never in a million years do violence for gain. Or
so I think."

"I agree."

"Apart from those two there's Danielle." That swift
grin again. "Well, I wouldn't like to swear that I could
precisely 'deal with' Danielle, but let's say I'm not afraid
of her."

"We might be wrong about them," I said. "There may
be nobody up there at all, except Nigel."

"It's possible"—he was packing the haversack as he
talked: more of the fresh rolls, some fruit, chocolate,
water: Spartan fare, but nonetheless appropriate for that—
"it's quite possible that we are wrong about Dimitrios and
Danielle, but in any case I'm not concerned at the moment
with Michael's 'find' except as it touches Nigel." A look.

"You're convinced about those flowers in the drawing, aren't you?"

"Absolutely."

"Well, that's one thing we're sure of in a maze of guess-work. We don't really know a damned thing about Dimitrios and Danielle, but we do know Nigel has been in that corrie, and we do know he was wildly excited about something that same night. And Dimitrios came here, for some purpose, to visit Nigel's room. We'll freeze on to those facts, and let the rest develop as it will. . . . Are you ready to start?"

"Yes."

"Then let's go."

Already the morning sun was warm overhead, but the rocks were still cool from the night. The path past the graveyard was wide enough for us to walk side by side.

Simon said, "All I'm hoping today is that—if you're right—we run across Nigel and see what he's up to, and knock some sense into his silly young head before he gets himself involved in something he can't get out of. And incidentally—this is the path off to the stadium—and incidentally, find the cave."

He had stopped where the narrow path left our track, and waited for me to precede him. I paused, and looked at him straightly. "Tell me one thing. Why *are* you letting me come?"

For the second time since I had known him, he seemed oddly at a loss. He hesitated, as if looking for the right words.

I said, "Granted that you don't want Stephanos and Niko along. But you'd get along much faster and do much better alone, *Kyrie* Lester, and you know it. You also know quite well that if we *do* run into Dimitrios it might develop into quite a sticky party. Why don't you leave me at home to get on with my knitting?"

A pine branch cast a bar of shade across his face, but I thought I saw a smile behind the light-grey eyes. "You know the reasons quite well, *Kyria* Haven."

"Reasons?"

"Yes."

"Well, I know the first. I wished a little too hard for an adventure, so I can darned well take what comes, and four eyes are better than two if we want to find Nigel and the cave?"

"Not quite. I had the idea that you were looking rather hard for something on your own account."

I turned abruptly and led the way up the narrow path between the pines. I said, after a bit, "Perhaps I was." Then, later still, "You—do see rather a lot, don't you?"

"And you know the second reason."

It was shady under the pines, but my cheeks felt hot. I said, "Oh?" and then felt furious with myself because the syllable seemed to be inviting an answer. I added hastily, "I can show you where the cyclamen is, of course."

"Of course," said Simon agreeably.

We had reached the stadium. We crossed the slanting shadows of the starting gate and left the trees. Behind us in the holly oaks and cypresses the birds flashed and sang. The singing echoed and rang up the limestone cliffs.

We crossed the stadium floor in silence and took the steep path that led to the rocky reaches of Parnassus.

We saw no one on our way to the corrie.

Most of the way from Delphi the track was easy to follow, and, apart from one open stretch soon after we had left the top of the Shining Ones, it wound along rocky valleys which would have offered plenty of cover in case of alarm. But the hot desert of broken rocks seemed as empty as yesterday. We travelled in short bursts, going fairly fast, but with frequent pauses in the shade to get our breath and to scan the surrounding country for signs of movement.

At length, as we made our way up a steep dry watercourse, I looked upwards to the right and saw the line of cliffs that held the corrie. Simon, who was ahead of me, stopped and turned.

"We'll wait here, I think, and eat. Look, here's a good place, in the shade between these two boulders. We can't be seen, and we can keep an eye on the valley and on those cliffs. I'd like to be quite sure no one else is about before we make our way up."

I sat down thankfully in the place he indicated, and he produced food from the haversack. The rolls didn't taste quite as good as they had in the cool of the morning, but as I ate I began to feel better. The tepid water was a benison, and the fruit was ambrosia itself. . . .

I let Simon do the watching. After I had eaten I relaxed against the rock with eyes half-shut against the light, and he lit a cigarette for me. He showed no sign of hurry or impatience, or even curiosity. We smoked in silence, and I saw his eyes move almost idly across the landscape, up to the corrie, along the cliff, down the scree, back to the corrie.

At the very edge of my vision there was a movement. I turned my head sharply, eyes fully open now. I could see nothing. But there had been a movement; of that I was sure. I was just about to touch Simon's arm when I saw it again; it was as if one of the rocks of the scree had moved . . . a goat. It was only a goat. As it walked forward, taking shape against the void of tumble rock, I saw others with it, two, three of them, moving purposefully along some age-old track of their own. I was wondering half-idly if there was a goatherd with them, and if perhaps they had strayed from the troop, when I thought I heard, far away over the cliff top, the sound of a pipe. Even as I heard it and strained my ears to catch the notes, it faded, and I dismissed it as fancy. The thin, broken stave had been purely pastoral, something from a myth of Arcady, nymphs and shepherds and pan-pipes and green valleys. But this was Parnassus, home of more terrible gods.

I relaxed again and watched the smoke from my cigarette wind up in the sunlight. I remember that I didn't think at all about the business of the day. I thought about Parnassus, and the gods who lived there, and Simon. . . .

I stole a look at him. He was looking almost dreamily up towards the cliffs. He looked about as tense and vigilant as in the fifth hour of the House Cricket Match. He caught my look and smiled, and moved his hand lazily to knock ash from his cigarette. I said, "A penny for them?"

"I was wondering if there was anyone with those goats. I don't think so."

"I thought I heard a pipe being played, away over there," I said, "but I expect I imagined it. Did you hear anything?"

"No. But it's possible. I don't think those three would be up here on their own. You must have very good hearing. I never heard a sound."

He crushed out his cigarette and got up, reaching a hand down to me. "Shall we go up now? I think we're un-observed, but I don't want to cross that big open stretch towards the corrie 'gateway.' If we skirt it, and go up that gully there, I think we can get round without the risk of being seen, and it'll bring us out above the cliff where

we were yesterday. It'll be a bit of a stiff pull, I'm afraid.
Are you tired?"

"Not a bit."

He laughed. "One up to British womanhood. Come along.
And keep down. This is where the real stalk starts."

Simon lay flat at the corrie's lip, looking downwards. I
crouched behind him, a little way back from the cliff edge.
I waited, watching him for a signal.

It seemed an age before he moved. Then he turned his
head and lifted a hand, with a slow cautious movement
that carried its own warning.

In spite of myself, I could feel tension pull my nerves
taut, like cold wires touching the skin. I inched forward
until I lay beside Simon. I was screened by one of the
low holly oaks. I lifted my head slowly till my eyes were
above the level of the edge. I looked down into the corrie.
There was no one there.

As I looked at him, with surprise in my face and a
question, he put his lips to my ear. "Dimitrios is here."

Again that coward jerk of the heart. Every vein in my
body was contracting, little thrilling wires tightening till
my muscles wouldn't obey me. I found I had ducked my
head down again behind the holly oak, and my cheek was
on my hand in the hot dust. The hand was cold.

Simon breathed, just beside my ear, "He's just vanished
somewhere underneath us. I saw him duck under that piece
in the corner." He jerked his head slightly towards it. "Is
that where you went exploring yesterday?"

I nodded. I swallowed, and managed to say quite evenly,
"What was he doing?"

"I don't know. He just seemed to be hanging about.
Waiting for someone or something. Nigel, perhaps, or—"

He broke off and seemed to go lower into the ground. I
shrank down beside him. The holly oak hid me, and I
peered down.

Then I saw Dimitrios. He came out from somewhere
below us, ducking his head as he passed under the flying
buttress that seemed to shore up the cliff. He was smoking,
and his eyes were frowning and narrowed against the high
blaze of the sun. He walked carefully over the rocky floor
of the corrie towards the northern gap in the wall. Every
now and again he stopped, and slanted his head as if to
listen.

He reached the corrie entrance, and stopped there, look-

ing down towards Amphissa. Once he turned his head and
looked the other way, the way we had come, from Delphi.
Then he came back into the corrie. He flung down the
butt of his cigarette and lit another. I noticed sweat on his
dark face and dust yellowish-white on his clothes. He
wasn't in the dark suit today; he was wearing dungarees in
dull faded blue, and a khaki shirt with a red kerchief
knotted at the neck.

The cigarette was lit now. He dropped the match, then
looked round him for a few moments as if undecided. He
took a few steps into the corrie and I thought he was
going back towards the corner where the cyclamen was, but
he stopped suddenly, as if impatient of waiting, turned
sharply on his heel, and walked, rapidly now, as if his mind
was at last made up, out of the corrie.

Simon said in my ear, "Gone to meet Nigel, or Danielle,
do you suppose? Give him a minute or two."

We gave him five. They seemed very long minutes.
There was no other sound in the hot morning but our own
breathing. The sun beat down on us as we lay on the bare
earth. I was thankful when Simon moved at last.

We got quickly to our feet, and went down the twisting
little path like a couple of mountain goats. We almost
ran across the corrie floor and ducked under the fallen
rock into the corner.

There it was, the patch of brilliant green, and the drifts
of tiny blue bells, the lovely traces of the mountain rain.
But today it was different.

Simon had checked. "Is this the place?"

"Yes, but—" I caught my breath and pushed past him,
to stand staring at the cliff.

The cyclamen had gone. Where it had clung to its crack
in the rock there was now a black fissure. The crack had
widened, split, and gaped open, as pressure had been
exerted on the weather-rotted rock. I could see the raw
white marks where the crowbars had gained their leverage.

A slab, similarly marked, lay at our feet, newly fallen,
and crushing the fresh grass. Yesterday it had been leaning against the rock face, masking what lay behind from
my casual glance. Today there was a split in the face of
the rock, some seven feet high by a foot and a half wide—
a narrow fissure which angled sharply up to a point at the
top. It opened onto darkness. The cave. Michael's cave.

My mouth was dry. I said hoarsely, "Yesterday that slab
was leaning up against the cliff, at an angle. There was a

crack behind it, very narrow. I remember now. It didn't look like an entrance to anything, but that must have been it."

He nodded, but he wasn't looking at me, or at the mouth of the cave. He looked past me, up at the cliff top, the corrie walls, all round us.

No movement; no sound.

There was a pile of mule droppings on the grass, that hadn't been there yesterday. I pointed to them silently, and Simon nodded. He said softly. "We were right, then. . . . We'll go in. You wait here a moment. And keep those ears of yours open. I won't be long."

He disappeared into the darkness of the cleft. I waited. Once again, far away, I thought I heard that little thread of music, the ghostly echo of the pan-pipes. Heard now, in this hot cruel corrie, the sound spoke no longer of Arcadia, and the kindly god of flocks and herds. It was a panic prickle along the flesh.

It had gone. I had imagined it again. I stood with my hands tightly clasped together in front of me, and made myself wait without moving.

Simon showed in the darkness of the cleft, like a beckoning ghost. I almost ran towards him into the cool darkness of the cave.

After the glare of day the place was dead-dark. It was like running against a black velvet curtain. I stopped, blinded. I felt Simon's arm come round me, guiding me in out of the light, then he switched on a torch. The light seemed feeble and probing after the blaze of day, but we could see.

We were in a widish passage which sloped gently downwards for some five or six yards and then turned abruptly to the left. The original entrance must have been wide, but it had been blocked by successive falls of stone to leave only the narrow cleft through which we had come. The passage itself was clear enough, and smelt fresh and cool.

Simon said, "The slope gets steeper. There's another twist down to the right, and then the cave itself . . . Here. Quite a place, isn't it?"

It was indeed. The main cave was huge, a great natural cavern the size of a young cathedral, with a high curved ceiling that vanished into darkness, and clefts and recesses that swallowed the feebly-probing torch-light. Stalactites and stalagmites made strangely shaped, enormous pillars. Fallen rock lay here as well. In some of the dimly seen

apses there were boulders and masses of rough stone showing, in the elusive light, like the massive tombs that lie
betwen the columns of a cathedral. Somewhere I could hear
the faint drip of water. The place was impressive, magnificent even, but it was a ruin. Dust and rubble lay everywhere, some of it recent-looking, some of it apparently
undisturbed for centuries.

The torch-light moved, swept, checked. . . .

Simon said, "There."

He said it softly, almost idly, but I knew him now. My
heart gave that painful little jerk of excitement. The light
was holding something in its dim circle, a circle which
seemed to have brightened, sharpened, focussed. . . . There
was a pile of rubble by a column to the left of the cavern
mouth. It looked at first like any of the other heaps of
fallen debris, then I saw that among the shapes of the
broken rock, more regular shapes showed . . . a cubed
corner . . . the dusty outline of a box. . . . And beside them
in the rubble the dull gleam of metal: a crowbar and a
shovel.

The torch-light swept further. "See that? They've shifted
some of it already. See where it's been dragged through the
dust?" He sent the light skating quickly round the rest of
the great cavern. Nothing. Another time I would have ex-
claimed over the ghostly icicles of rock, the arches, the
chambered darknesses that the corners held, but now my
whole interest, like the torch-light, was centred on that
pile of rock debris and what it contained.

Simon paused for a moment, cocking his head. No sound
except the drip of water somewhere, very faintly. He moved
forward with me beside him, and bent over the exposed
corner of the box.

He didn't disturb it. The torch worked for him. "There's
the government stamp. This isn't gold, Camilla. It's guns."

"Guns?"

"Uh-huh. Small and useful Sten guns." He straightened
up and switched the light out for a moment. In the thick
darkness his voice was soft and grim. "There's an excellent
market for this sort of thing at several points in the Med
just now. Well, well."

I said, "I don't believe that Nigel would do that."

The torch flashed on again. "Come to think of it, neither
do I. I wonder . . ." He moved off round the pile, exploring
deeper into the darkness behind the big stalagmite.

"Simon," I said, "d'you mean these were flown in here during the war?"

"Yes. I told you. Gold and arms galore."

"But that was nineteen forty-two, wasn't it? They wouldn't keep, surely?"

I heard him laugh. "You talk as if they were fish. Of course they'll 'keep.' They're packed in grease. They'll come out as good as new. . . . Ah. . . ."

"What is it?" In spite of myself my voice sharpened.

"Ammo. Stacks of it. My God, this'd take a couple of days to shift, this stuff. No wonder . . ." His voice trailed away.

"Simon? What is it?"

He said without a trace of inflection, "The gold."

I moved forward so fast that I tripped over a root of the stalagmite and almost fell. *"Where?"*

"Steady there. So this is what treasure trove does to you. Here." The torch-light was steady on the pile of broken rock. Among the dust and splintered fragments the corners of two small boxes showed. They were of metal, but the corner of one had been smashed open, and under the dusty gaping metal was the living gleam of gold.

Simon was saying, "That's Michael's little find, Camilla. That's why Mick was murdered. But I still don't quite see. . . ." He paused, and I saw his brows draw together, but after a while he went on in his even voice, "Well, we were right, as far as it went. Two boxes, at least, and there may be more under the rubble."

"They're very small, aren't they?"

"One of them would be one man's work, all the same. Did you know that gold was almost twice as heavy as lead? They'll have quite a job shifting what they've got here."

I said, "They?"

He answered my look. "I'm afraid you were right about Nigel. I think he *was* on his way up here yesterday morning, and it's Nigel who's been working here while Dimitrios was in Delphi."

I said apprehensively, "But we still don't know they're working together. If Dimitrios came up last night, or early today, and found Nigel here, and set about him the way he did with you—"

He shook his head. "No. Think it out. There must be two of them in it. Look at this stuff again; look how it's buried. Angelos probably did throw a bit of rubble and small stones over it to hide it, but he never put this pile of rock over it. This has come down in an earth tremor—probably the one that shut the cave and broke the cliff above us. Shifting this kind of thing is sheer hard work, and Dimitrios just hasn't had time to do everything alone."

"You mean—?"

"Work it out. There must be two men on the job, Camilla. If Nigel found the cave, it still hadn't been opened up yesterday, enough to let those boxes be carried out. Whether Nigel showed it to Dimitrios, or whether Dimitrios found it himself as soon as we left the corrie yesterday, the man simply hasn't had time single-handed to do all this. Remember he followed us almost straight down to Delphi; he wouldn't have had time to get his tools from where they were hidden, and shift that slab. And even if he came back to do that later, he was down in Delphi again in the middle of the night."

"What about Danielle?"

"She couldn't have got up here and then back again between the time you saw her on the Shining Ones, and the time she went to bed last night. What's more she couldn't, physically, do this sort of job."

He paused for a moment, as if listening, and then went on. "And look at the situation just now. We know Danielle went north with the jeep. She won't have had time to get up here from the Amphissa road. Dimitrios is waiting for someone, but it's not Danielle. The mule's been here, hasn't it, and gone? At a guess, Dimitrios is waiting for whoever has taken the mule over, loaded, to meet the jeep. Nigel."

The torch flashed again, momentarily, over the gold. He said, "You remember Stephanos saying that the old track leads to a disused quarry near the Amphissa road? It sounds the sort of place where they might park the jeep out of sight while they ferry the stuff across the hill with the mule. They seem to have made a start on the guns. I imagine they'll stack the loot somewhere down near the road till they can get it all away together; and if they've any sense they'll leave the gold safely here till the last minute. . . . Did you hear anything?"

We stood very still with the light out. "No," I said. Then, slowly, "You know, I—I don't trust Dimitrios."

I heard the ghost of a laugh in the dark. "Today's great thought, Camilla, my darling? You surprise me."

He had surprised me too, but I hoped my voice didn't show it. I said, "I was thinking of Nigel. Even if they are working together now, it's only because Nigel found the stuff first, and Dimitrios wants help to shift it. Once the work's done—" I stopped, and licked dry lips.

"I know." No trace of amusement now. "Well, we're here now, so that should be taken care of."

"Yes. But Simon"—even to me the whisper sounded thin and miserably uncertain—"Simon, what are we going to do?"

"Wait. What else can we do? We don't know the score yet, but no doubt we soon will."

He switched on again, and the light flicked round the cavern. "There's plenty of cover here, and we'll hear them in good time—or at least you will. If Nigel comes up alone, all the better, but if it should be Dimitrios coming back . . ."

He grinned down at me, but some quality in the grin brought the reverse of comfort. I said suddenly, accusingly, "You *want* him to come back."

"And if I do?" The smile deepened at the expression on my face. "By God, Camilla, don't you see? I pray he does come back. There's your score to settle as well as mine, and now there's that idiotic boy to straighten out. . . . It would be better if Dimitrios came. Don't you see?"

"Oh, yes, I see."

His hand came out, momentarily, to touch my cheek, a moth-light touch. "Don't be scared, my dear. I'm not going to get myself killed and leave you alone with the wolves." He gave a little laugh. "I've not the slightest intention of fighting fair . . . and two can play at the game of attacking down a torch-beam."

I said, I hoped steadily, "He may be armed."

"I'm pretty sure he's not. There wasn't room for a gun in those dungarees."

"He's probably got himself another knife."

"Probably. And I've got his. Two can play at that game too."

"Simon!"

I heard him laugh again as he moved away. "Poor Camilla. . . . Now, half a minute. Stay where you are. I'll be back."

He slid, with wary flashes of the torch, out of the cave, and the small light dwindled and vanished into the curve of the passageway. He was gone perhaps two minutes. I stayed just where I was, with the gold at my feet, and one hand in my pocket nervously fingering the bulk of the

Greek's torch, which I had picked up in Nigel's room last night, and found to be still serviceable. Then the will-o'-the-wisp light danced back along the passage wall, and Simon was beside me.

"Not a sign of either of them, so we'll have a closer look at this stuff, I think."

"Do you want any help?"

"No, thanks. Scout around and find a bolt hole to make for when he comes." He was already busy, crouching beside the pile of rubble, his hands moving gently over the dusty surfaces.

I left him to his task, his hands moving among the dust just as Michael's hands must have moved fourteen years ago when he made the same discovery. I flashed my torch back momentarily as I moved away. It showed his crouching body, the quiet intent face, the hands. . . . Michael Lester finding evidence of treachery to the Allies. For some reason I gave a little shiver. They said ghosts walked, didn't they? And the ghost of Angelos, who smiled as he killed? "If ghosts are true," Niko had said, "then he still walks on Parnassus. . . ."

The cave was even bigger than I had thought. I passed between pillars of stalagmites as massive as Apollo's columns at Delphi, and into an anteroom as deep as a private chapel. There was ample cover. Simon and I could lie hidden almost anywhere, when Dimitrios came. . . .

The light was uncertain in my hand. Its beam touched the walls, the fallen masses that blocked the antechamber, and diffused itself into nothingness among the dark recesses. But even as I turned back, the edge of the light shimmered momentarily with a sliding, liquid gleam. I paused. There was the drip of water again, more clearly now. I went forward, the torch exploring ahead of me. The floor lifted a little, and there was a streak of damp on it that caught the light. I could feel the freshness in the air, above the dead dust-smells of the cave, and there was the drip of water, closer now and clearer; there must be some spring in the cave—perhaps the same spring whose overflow fed the grass and flowers outside. I went forward quickly now, the light flicking over the rock in eager search. There was the now-familiar pile of broken rock against the rear wall of the cave; there the wall itself, streaked with damp and seamed with black fissures; there a wrecked stalagmite leaning drunkenly against a slab that lay at an angle to the wall. . . .

There was something very familiar about the slab. It only took me a couple of seconds to realize why. It was the same shape, and leaned in the same way, as the slab that yesterday had barred the cave mouth, and today lay tumbled in the grass outside.

I approached it slowly, knowing what I would find. As I paused beside it I could hear the drip of water plainly. Then I felt the skin prickle cold again along my arms and back.

With the drip of water came another sound, a sound that I had heard already twice that day and disbelieved, as I disbelieved it now. The sound of a pipe. Pan's pipe . . . it played a delicate little fall of notes; another; again. Silence, and the drip of water.

And the sound had come from behind the leaning slab.

With the hair lifting along my arms I bent to peer behind it. I was right. There was a gap, narrow, perhaps eight inches wide, but still a gap. And it didn't, like the other cave mouth, give onto darkness. Beyond it, the darkness slackened.

I think I had forgotten Dimitrios. I said softly, and even to me the echoes of my voice sounded queer, "There's a way through here. I'm going to see."

I don't know if Simon answered. I was squeezing through the narrow gap. The rock scraped me, caught at my clothes, then let me through. I was in a widish passage which led upwards in a gentle curve. The floor was smooth. Round me the darkness slackened further, and more clearly through the torch-light the walls of the gallery took shape. Ahead of me it curved more sharply to the right, and beyond the curve I could see that the light grew clearer. The drip of the water was clear and loud.

Then it came again, the sound I had been listening for above the trickle of water; a little stave of music, hauntingly off-key. . . .

I rounded the corner. Ahead was the light, the arch of the gallery framing a blaze muted by moving green. I caught a glimpse of grass, and the hanging boughs of some slender tree dappling the sunlight at the mouth of the tunnel.

I almost ran the rest of the way. I ducked under the arch and came suddenly, blindly, into a little dell.

It wasn't a way out. It was a small enclosure, like a lightwell. Centuries ago this had been a circular cave into which the gallery had run, but the roof had fallen in and let in the sun and the seeds of grass and wild vines, and the spring had fed them, so that now, in the heart of the mountain, was this little well of vivid light roofed with the moving green of some delicate tree.

The music had stopped. The only sound was the drip of the spring and the rustle of leaves.

But I had no thought to spare for Pan and his music. Apollo himself was here. He was standing not ten feet from me as I came out of the tunnel. He was naked, and in his hand was a bow. He stood looking over my head as he had stood for two thousand years.

I heard Simon coming along the tunnel behind me. I moved aside. He came quickly out of the dark archway into the dappled light. He was saying, "Camilla, I—" then he stopped as if he'd been struck in the throat. I heard him say, "Oh, God," under his breath. He stopped just behind me.

Some draught moved the curtain of leaves. Light flickered and burned from the bow, and shifted along the bronze of the throat and face. A broken arrow of gold lay in the grass at the statue's feet.

After a lifetime or so I heard myself saying shakily, "This . . . *this* is what Nigel found. He was here. Look."

I stopped and picked up the little water pot from where it lay in the damp moss at my feet.

CHAPTER

16

Apollo shows himself not to everyone, but only to him who is good. He who sees him is great; he who sees him is not a small man. We will see thee, O far-striker, and we will never become small!

CALLIMACHUS: 2.9.

"Yes." Simon turned the pot over in his hand. "That's out of Nigel's sketching-box. He may have heard the water when he was drawing the cyclamen outside, and that led him into the cave and then through here . . . to this." His eyes, like mine, were fixed on the statue. The face was god-like; remote, wise, serene, but young, and with a kind of eagerness behind the level brows.

I said breathlessly, "It's the face in the drawing, isn't it? —the lovely drawing he tore up. . . . I said it looked like a statue. D'you remember how he snatched it back from us?"

Simon said slowly, "That was when Danielle was there. But before that—d'you remember my saying that he seemed to be on the verge of telling me something, and then when Danielle came in he stopped short and shut up?"

"Of course. Then she *can't* have recognized it, can she? He'd only found the cave that day, and it's obvious he wasn't going to tell her about it!"

"And by God he was right," said Simon. "Guns and gold is one thing; in a way that kind of treasure trove is legitimate prey for greasy thugs like Dimitrios, and if the boy thought he could get something out of a spot of gun-running, well, that's his affair. But *this* . . ." he went down on one knee in the grass. Very gently he lifted the golden arrow. Where it had lain the whitened grass roots showed a clear print. He put it down again. "As I thought. Nothing's been touched. You can't tell me friend Dimitrios could have kept his paws off a bit of loose gold." He got to his feet with a breath of relief. "No, the boy's kept his mouth shut, and there's quite enough in the outer cave to fix Dimitrios' interest there. Thank God for the artist's conscience. But I think the sooner I get hold of Nigel the better."

"You—you don't think Dimitrios'll come exploring, like I did, and find it?"

He laughed under his breath. "I'd bet on it that he won't; he's far too busy, for one thing, and for another, now that I come to think of it, even if he was dying of thirst he'd never squeeze through the gap."

"I suppose not. But how in the world did *he* get in here? And why?" I put a hand to my head. "I—I can't seem to think straight about anything just at the moment. I feel knocked kind of sideways."

"I'm not surprised. No wonder Nigel was 'high' that night. He must have been half out of his mind with excitement. And no wonder Mick—well, never mind that now. I doubt if we'll ever know just how and why the Apollo got here, but we can make a pretty good guess, I think. You know that the sanctuary at Delphi, after it ceased to be able to protect itself and its vast wealth, was plundered again and again. We don't know where a fraction of the stolen statues went. It was the metal ones that were taken; gold went first, of course; and then bronze, to be melted down for weapons. . . . From the look of this one, with that gold on it, it would be one of the most precious, and it's certainly one of the most beautiful. Why shouldn't some priest, or some small band of devotees, have decided to save it; cart it out of Delphi and find sanctuary for it till the troubled times were over?"

"But—why here? And *how?*"

"There used to be a track this way—the natives refer to it as 'the old track,' and, in these parts, God knows how old it might be. We came along it part of the way. Even so, it must have been quite a trek. Myself, I'd have brought the thing up in a mule litter. I suppose the plan was to retrieve the statue later when things were safe, or even, if this happened at a very desperate time, to set up a sort of small secret sanctuary high on the mountain. If they'd just wanted to hide the statue, after all, they could have buried it, but they've *placed* it, haven't they? And with the Greek instinct for drama, they've put it at the end of a dark tunnel, in the blazing light, and all its trappings round it. . . . Did anything strike you about the cave, Camilla?"

"You mean that it was a bit like a cathedral—or a temple?"

He nodded. "It's a common enough quality in big vaulted places with stalactites and so on, but nonetheless impressive. The priests who were so fanatical to save this statue must have known of the cave for long enough. Not only that . . . there was this inner shrine, full of light, the perfect 'bright citadel' for the god—so here he is. Look at that vine, Camilla, and that tree."

I looked at him stupidly. "The vine? It's a wild vine, isn't it? And the tree—is that a sort of laurel?"

"A bay. Apollo's laurel," said Simon softly.

"But Simon, after two thousand years—"

"Trees live a long time, and when they die they leave seedlings. And vines run wild. Those were planted, Camilla. You notice how the Apollo is just under the lip of the overhang, and the vines and that spindly tree make a screen? I don't know if you *can* get to the top of this light-well and look down, but you'd see nothing. . . . And there is the spring. Yes, I think this was a sacred cave, with a sacred spring, and what more natural than that the priest who was so eager to save his god should house him here? And I'll bet that if we look closely we'll find that the entrances to both inner and outer caves were artificially blocked up—"

"They were. I noticed that. The slab that Dimitrios had moved was the same as the one that was across this inner tunnel."

"And then, after God knows how many years, the earthquakes opened the doors again . . . for Angelos. And Michael."

"*Michael!*" I looked at him almost guiltily. I had forgotten Michael. "Of course. The letter. The bright citadel. Oh, Simon."

He gave a little smile, and quoted softly: " 'Tell the Emperor that the bright citadel is fallen to the ground; Apollo has no longer any shelter, or oracular laurel tree, or speaking fountain. Even the vocal stream has ceased to flow.' Yes, Mick proved the Delphic Oracle wrong. That's what the letter meant."

I said, "You know, I didn't say anything, but I thought your brother wouldn't have written quite the way he did about a cache of arms, or even gold. All he'd have had to do, surely, was to divert them back to their proper uses?"

"I know. That's what got me too. But I never thought of anything like *this*." His voice didn't change, but suddenly I got the sharp impression of intense excitement. "My God," said Simon, "who could have imagined this?"

We stood side by side staring at the statue. I think it was the loveliest thing I have ever seen. The shadows played over the bloomed bronze of the body; the eyes dwelt on some remote distance beyond and above our heads, as the eyes of lions do. They were curiously alive, carefully inlaid with enamel and some black stone, so that the dark pupils seemed to flicker and glow with the movement of light and shade. I knew of only one other statue that had eyes like that.

Simon echoed my thoughts, softly, "The Charioteer."

I said, "You think so? You think he's by the same hand?"

"I don't know a darned thing about it, but that's what he makes me think of."

"That's what he made Michael think of," I said.

He nodded. "And Nigel too, if you remember. . . . It was when we were talking about the Charioteer that Nigel seemed suddenly to make up his mind to tell me about this. It may only have been because we were talking in general about discovering statues, but I don't think so. I seem to recollect some tension when the Charioteer was mentioned."

"It's not only the eyes," I said, "but the whole impression of strength going along with grace . . . a sort of liquid quality—no, that's the wrong word, it sounds too weak, whereas this is—well, terrific. Simon, why shouldn't he be not only by the same hand, but part of the same group? It's only so much guesswork, isn't it, that the Charioteer was part of a victory statue for some potentate or other? Heavens above, if there were six thousand statues there, you'd think there might have been a chariot statue of Apollo somewhere in Apollo's own sanctuary? And why shouldn't the Charioteer be the driver, and this—the god himself—the Lord of the Car?"

"Why not indeed?" said Simon.

"What are you smiling at? I can't help getting excited, can I? And why shouldn't I have a theory? It seems to me—"

"No reason at all. And it seems to *me* that one theory's as good as another. Yours at any rate is the most exciting one that comes to hand. . . . No, I was smiling at something quite different. Dimitrios."

"Oh!" It was like being jerked out of the sunlight into cold water. "I—I'd forgotten all about him."

"I should like to . . . now," said Simon. He had never taken his eyes off the statue. "But I'm afraid we must deal with that little matter before we come back to this."

"What do we do about it?" I asked, rather blankly.

He gave it one long look before he turned away. "We

leave it here in its bright citadel, and we get back to the land of shadows, my dear. We know now what Michael found, and we also know what Michael was murdered for. That chapter's closed, I think, with the death of Angelos. But the one that's still open is what we've got to deal with now. Nigel found the bright citadel too, and I admit to feeling rather strongly that Dimitrios and Danielle shouldn't really be let in on . . . this."

I said almost violently, "They'll not touch it if I can stop them."

"Then we'd better get back into the cave and play watch-dog. Camilla . . ."

"Yes?"

He stood for a moment looking down at me. The guarded look was there again, with some expression behind the cool eyes that made me wonder what was coming. But he only said, rather lamely, "I shouldn't have let you come."

I didn't answer.

He said, "You're frightened, aren't you?"

Still I said nothing. I wasn't looking at him. I wondered fleetingly why I didn't mind his knowing. All at once he was very close to me, and his hand came under my chin, gently lifting my face to meet his gaze. "You know why I brought you, don't you?"

"Yes."

"And I was right."

"Yes. I know."

"You underrate yourself so shockingly, Camilla. You're not to play second fiddle any more. Understand?"

"Yes."

He hesitated, and then said rather abruptly, "You made a discovery yesterday; remember? 'No man is an Island.' It's true in more ways than one. Don't go on hating yourself because there are some things you can't do and can't face on your own. None of us can. You seem to think you ought to be able to deal with anything that comes along, much as I might, or someone like me. That's absurd; and it's time you stopped despising yourself for not being something you were never meant to be. You'll do as you are, Camilla; believe me, you will."

I didn't quite trust myself to answer. After a second or so I said lightly, "All I ask the gods is that one day I'll see you, too, shaken right out of that—that more-than-sufficient calmness of yours, onto the plane of mortals like me! The day that happens, I'll sacrifice to Apollo myself!"

He grinned. "I might have to hold you to that. But meanwhile you can be sure that it won't be friend Dimitrios that'll do it. I'm going back now to see if he's around—or Nigel. Would you rather stay here?"

"No. I'll come with you. I—I'd like to know what's going on."

His hand touched my cheek as it had once before, a moth's touch. "Then don't be scared, please. I'll not let Dimitrios get near you."

"All right. What do I do?"

"Nothing yet. Just keep out of sight, and do as you're told before you're told to do it."

"What could be simpler? Very well."

"And now we'll go back."

The Apollo looked serenely over our heads as we turned and left the sunlight.

The cave was still empty. We waited in the shelter of the cleft, listening, and then Simon squeezed his way through without using the torch. After a minute or two I heard his voice softly in the dark. "It's all right. You can come through."

I slid through the narrow opening. The beam of Simon's torch lit the way for me, and then played over the tilted slab. "See? Those are chisel marks. You were right. The slab was hacked to fit across the opening. And that crack above . . . that'll be where the rock shifted in the tremor that opened up the cave again for you and me . . . and Michael."

I ran a slightly unsteady finger along one of the marks. "Two thousand years. . . . Oh, Simon, I wish we could know—" I stopped abruptly.

"Mmm?" The torch was still moving over the old tool marks. He seemed absorbed.

I managed to whisper calmly enough, "He's coming back. I can hear him."

The torch snapped out. A moment's unbreathing silence. "Yes. You get back through the cleft and wait till we see what he's up to. I hope to God it's Nigel."

As the breathed sentence ended I felt his hand on my arm. I obeyed him, slipping back through the narrow opening to wait, heart beating jerkily again, against the rock on the other side of the slab. I felt him beside me, pressed close to the edge of the cleft.

The steps came closer, hesitated at the door of the cave, and then came in. The sounds were at once dulled by the dust and made hollower by the cave's echoes. They were succeeded by other sounds: the dull thud of a spade hacking at the pile of rubble; the chink as it struck stone, and then metal; the sounds of breathing and effort; a soft expletive in Greek and then the splintering of wood and a thud; a dragging sound. . . . He had uncovered a box and was dragging it nearer the mouth of the cave in readiness for transportation.

I felt Simon's body, close to mine, tense like a runner's at the starting tape. His arm was across me, holding me still against him. It was like a steel bar. I wondered if he would attack Dimitrios now, out of the dark. . . .

But he didn't move, except to shift his shoulders and head slightly so that I thought he could see round the edge of the slab. He stayed like that for what seemed an age, rock-still. I could feel the pulse beating in the hollow of his elbow; it was unhurried. Mine, under it, was tumbling along anyhow, like a faulty engine.

The arm relaxed. I felt him turn his head, and his breath was on my temple. I heard the barest thread of a whisper, "He's gone out again. Did you hear a mule?"

"I don't think so."

"Stay here. I'll come back."

A swift, compelling pressure of the arm round me, then it lifted. A movement beside me, the scrape of cloth on stone, and he was gone. The cleft felt cold and damp. I shifted my shoulders with the sudden chill and hunched my arms close to my sides and waited, listening. The echo of my coward pulses seemed to fill the cave. . . .

I heard his steps in the dust just before he reached the cleft again and slid through. It was warmer with him there. He bent his head and said softly, "He's left the box just inside the entrance and gone out again. He seems uneasy; I think he's wondering if anything's happened to whoever's coming with the mule. I think I'd better go after him."

He wasn't touching me, so he didn't feel the jerk of my heart. He just heard me say, "Yes?" quite calmly.

"It's just on the cards something has happened to delay Nigel, and I'd like to know what. And I want to know the way they're taking. That track peters out very soon. I'll follow Dimitrios down till I see where he's bound, and then if a chance occurs I'll . . . well, deal with him."

"You mean you'll *kill* him?"

"Good God, no. But I'd like him put safely out of action while we get time to work this thing out our own way. . . . And now I must go, or I'll lose the blighter."

I hadn't realized that my hand had gone up to the breast of his shirt. His came up to cover it, warm and steadying. I said, and I couldn't quite keep the shake out of my voice, "Simon, take care."

"Be sure of that. Now, don't worry, my—don't worry. I'll be all right, and so will you. Stay here, under cover. You'll be as safe as a house in this part of the cave, and anyway I promise you I won't let Dimitrios out of my sight. Right?"

"R-right."

His other arm came round my shoulders, and momentarily he pulled me against him. It was a gesture of comfort and reassurance, no more. . . . But I thought his lips brushed my hair.

For the second time the arm dropped from my shoulders and he turned away as swiftly and lightly as a ghost. This time he switched on his torch, and I saw his shadow leap back, gigantic, along the wall of the cleft as he slipped through. I pressed forward till I could see into the cave. The little circle of light danced away through the faintly echoing spaces of darkness; the pillars and buttresses and masses of rock sent towering shadows reeling up the walls to stretch and lose themselves into the blackness of the vaulted roof. Simon, moving swiftly, himself like a shadow, dwindled across the empty darkness and was gone like a wraith into the outer tunnel. A shadow flickered back momentarily over the rock, then darkness swallowed it.

My hands were spread flat against the inner side of the slab. My eyes ached with the darkness. It was cold again. I had to exert all my self-control to stop myself running out and across the cave after him into the blessed sunlight.

At length I turned and made my way rather drearily back to the bright solitude of Apollo's sanctuary.

How long I waited there I don't know. At first I sat quietly enough in a corner where the sun fell unmasked by leaves, gazing at the statue of the god and trying to empty my mind of all worry about what was going on outside.

But after a while the very beauty and stillness of the place began to oppress me. I found I could sit still no longer, and, getting to my feet, I picked up Nigel's waterpot and carried it over to the spring. Under the thin trickle I rinsed it carefully, and drank. I rummaged in Simon's haversack and found what remained of our food, half of which I ate. After that I got myself another drink. Then I fidgeted about the little glade, examining the statue more closely, looking—but without touching them—at the broken pieces of gold in the grass, fingering the leaves and ferns. . . .

When I found myself stooping for a third time to drink at the spring, I realized that fear had given place to a sort of impatient irritation. Sunlight and peace had done their work too well: I was now thoroughly on the fidget. I found myself glancing almost second by second at the watch on my wrist —an automatic act which irritated my nerves still further, as I hadn't the remotest idea what time it had been when Simon left me. I hovered near the mouth of the tunnel, fingering my torch. . . .

After all, I told myself, I was perfectly safe. Simon was with Dimitrios, and I wasn't in the least afraid of Nigel. I wanted something to do; I wanted to know what was going on; I wanted Simon's presence. . . .

I went cautiously along the tunnel, back into darkness, hesitated in the shelter of the slab, then let myself through into the main cave.

I, too, used my torch this time. A last absurd jump of the nerves made me send the light skating once round the vaulted darkness, almost as if I expected to find that, after all, Dimitrios had not gone. But the place was empty. There really was nothing to be afraid of; if he came back I would hear him, and would have ample time to take sanctuary again. Moreover, Simon was on his tail, and if Dimitrios returned I could depend on Simon to come with him.

The torch-beam was steady now. I went softly across to the arch of the outer tunnel, and then turned off the light. I felt my way carefully along the wall of the curving passage, until, as I rounded the first bend, the darkness slackened, and I could see my way.

There was no box standing beside the entrance. Dimitrios must have set off carrying it. So much the better, I thought, vaguely. It meant he did intend to go right down to the jeep; and it would slow him down and make it easier for Simon to follow him.

I edged forward until I could see out into the corrie.

Here, too, that faint sense of surprise assailed me to see it unchanged; dazzlingly hot, still, deserted. . . .

The glare hit at the eyes. I could smell the dust and the mule dung and some dried aromatic plant that crumbled to powder under the hand I put up to the rock beside me. There was no sound at all. Nothing moved; even the hot air hung still.

I hesitated. The temptation to get out of the cave was

strong, to climb the cliff path above me, and take refuge somewhere higher up the mountain where I could at once be free and yet hidden, and, more important, see any movement that there might chance to be near the corrie. But Simon must know where to find me, and he had told me to stay here. I must stay.

I went back into the cave.

I remember that I stood there for some minutes, looking round me almost idly. I was trying to picture the place before the earthquake that had first shaken down some of the stuff that blocked the aisles and recesses between the pillars. It was very possible that this had been a sacred cave. Here the Apollo had been carried by hasty, reverent hands; here, perhaps, sacrifices and other acts of worship had been made before the holy place had been finally sealed and hidden and left to its two thousand years of silence.

The beam of my torch suddenly dimmed, then brightened again. But the warning spurred me into movement. With only one brief glance back at the entrance, and a couple of seconds' pause to listen for sounds of Dimitrios' approach, I set myself to a careful exploration of the cave.

I don't quite know what I was looking for. I certainly wasn't consciously hoping to find further "treasure"—either of the kind in Angelos' hoard, or relics of Apollo's worship. But it wasn't very long before I did in fact come on evidence of another cache. In a deep bay between two pillars, at the edge of the cave not far from the stack of boxes, a pile of rubble—a shallow barrow of the stuff heaped away in a bay of rock—looked as if it had been recently disturbed.

I approached it and bent over, sending the now perceptibly dimming beam probing among the broken fragments.

I could see nothing that suggested boxes or articles concealed there, but, quite clear in the dust at my feet, was the print of a rope-soled shoe, and the marks beside it as of something being dragged.

I went closer and stooped to peer. The beam slid over the pile, caught on something, and halted. It jerked in my hand once, then fixed, still, and far too bright now, on what lay behind the pile of rock and dirt.

The murderer hadn't bothered to bury Nigel. His body had been dragged and then flung into this meagre hiding, and now lay, stiff and horrible and indescribably grotesque, between the heaped rubble and the wall of the cave.

In the paralyzed moment before I dropped the torch from a numbed hand, and let the merciful darkness loose again, I saw what had happened to Nigel. You can see an awful lot in a split second's acute terror and shock; the picture your brain registers then is complete, the stuff of a million lingering nightmares still to come. Nothing is missed; every bestial detail is there for the mind to come back to, turn over, re-picture without ceasing.

He had been tied. The rope had gone now—no doubt the murderer had need of it—but the boy's wrists were scored raw where he had struggled. He had been tied, and tortured. In that one glance I had seen the shabby green shirt ripped down off one thin shoulder, and, on the upper arm, shocking against the peeling skin, a series of marks whose sickening regularity could mean only one thing. He had been burned four or five times, deliberately. Other things I saw that, at the time, meant nothing, but which, in nightmare recapitulations of that second's horror, I have since seen and recognized a score of times. I don't intend to describe them. Let it remain that Nigel had died, in pain. His eyes were open. I remember how they gleamed in the light of the torch. And his teeth clenched, grinning, on some fragment that might have been skin . . . Dimitrios' bitten thumb . . . the filthy murderous hand that had slid down my arm yesterday at the Roseate Cliff.

It was on that flash of realization that the torch dropped and the dark stamped down. I don't know what happened then. I remember, one moment, the picture in the torch-light, vivid, terrible, complete, then the next moment it was dark, and the rock was cold; it was crushing me, tearing my clothes, tripping my running footsteps; it was soft to my falling, whimpering body. . . .

I was lying at Apollo's feet on the damp moss. My hair was wet, and my hands, and the breast of my frock. Something was hurting my right hand where it pressed deeply into the grass. It was the broken end of the gold arrow. I sat looking at it for a very long time before I even saw it.

Dimitrios, I was thinking stupidly, confusedly; Dimitrios . . . he had murdered Nigel yesterday. While we had been here in the corrie, in the bright sunlight, Nigel had been in the cave with his murderer, tied and hurt and—no, that wouldn't do; he hadn't been gagged, and we'd have heard him. He was dead before we got up here, and then Dimitrios had come down to Delphi to search his room. . . .

I stared down at the beautifully worked fragment of gold in my hand, and tried to think. . . . But all that would come to me was that Nigel, poor muddled, eager young Nigel, who was a good artist, had been murdered by Dimitrios. . . .

Dimitrios! This time the thought came anything but confusedly; it whipped into my brain with a point as sharp as the one that pricked my palm. I was on my feet, and the gold arrow spun, glittering, forgotten, to the grass. Dimitrios, whom Simon and I had casually dismissed as someone who could easily be "dealt with"—Dimitrios was out there on the hillside, and Simon was tailing him, waiting for a chance to attack him, unconscious of the fact that the Greek was a murderer as vile and ruthless as ever his cousin Angelos had been. . . .

Momentarily I had forgotten poor Nigel. I ran back into the tunnel with never a thought of what lay there in the cave.

The darkness came up against me like a tangling net. As I rounded the first bend in the tunnel I had to stop short, then feel my way forward slowly, my hands shaking and slipping on the cool rock.

I reached the slab. I pressed my body into the narrow cleft, craning to peer forward into the cave. But I couldn't see at all; the darkness boiled still against my wide-open eyes with shapes and spangles of a million fizzing colours. Without my torch, and blinded like this with my swift dive back out of the light, I would be helpless to cross the cave. I shut my eyes and waited there for the swarming dark to clear. The slab felt cold and damp under my flat-spread hands.

Then I heard him.

I thought at first it was the surge of the knocking pulses that nailed me to the rock, but then I knew it was the soft tread of rope-soled shoes in the dust.

I stayed where I was, frozen to the rock, and opened my eyes.

I could see now. Light was moving in the cave, a powerful light. Not Simon—Simon's torch, like mine, had begun to fail . . . and in any case, the steps had not been Simon's. But at least where Dimitrios was, Simon would be. And from the way the Greek came forward into the cave with unhurried confidence, he still didn't know of Simon's presence.

Even as the thought came, I heard a tiny sound outide the cave. My eyes flew in apprehension to the Greek. He was behind the light and I couldn't see him, but the moving beam never faltered. He hadn't heard. The sound came again, and now I knew it for what it was; the chink of metal was a bit jangled. Dimitrios had brought the mule.

The Greek passed out of my small range of vision. I waited till I heard the familiar scrape and shift of a box and the clatter of settling stones, and the grunts and short breathing of effort. Then I inched my way nearer the edge of the slab and peered round it, a centimetre at a time.

He had put the torch down in a little niche above him, so that the beam was directed onto the rock pile. His thick powerful body was stooping over this. His back was towards me; he had laid his jacket down beside him, and under the blue shirt I could see the bulge and play of his muscles as he heaved at one of the half-buried boxes. Then he dragged it out into his arms, and straightened up, holding it. I hadn't before realized how immensely strong he must be. He carried the box slowly over to the cave mouth and went out of sight with it up into the tunnel. I heard him dump it there. I heard him coming back. Still with that unhurried soft tread he came out of the tunnel mouth, into the steady beam that illumined the cave.

For the second time in those few minutes, I felt the kick of shock over the heart.

It wasn't Dimitrios. It wasn't anyone I had seen before. But hard on the moment of shock and confusion, I knew that I was wrong. I had seen him before, and more than once. Now, faced in the queerly lit darkness with that heavy head, the thick dark curls tight like a bull's and crisping down the swarthy cheekbones towards the smiling thick-lipped mouth, I knew him. This was the Phormis head of Nigel's drawing: this was the face like an archaic statue's, with the wide fleshy cheekbones and the up-cornered, tight-lipped smile. More—this was the face I had seen, unnoticing and unremembering, bending over the engine of the jeep outside Dimitrios' cottage. And it must have been *this* face, not the Apollo (which it was certain she had never seen), that Danielle had recognized among Nigel's drawings. . . .

But before I could follow this further, two other memories flashed, sparks into the dry tinder of fear . . . Nigel saying to Danielle, "That's a chap I saw today on Parnassus," and Simon's voice in the dark, translating for me something Stephanos had told him, "He'd kill, and smile while he did it. Always that smile. . . ."

Angelos. Angelos himself. And Dimitrios was God knows where. And Simon was with him.

Angelos turned back to the pile of rubble. The torch-light

slid over the thick skin, shiny with sweat. The smile never altered. No doubt he had smiled as he and Dimitrios killed Nigel between them. No doubt he would smile when Simon, having disposed of Dimitrios, came openly up to the cave to find me. . . .

Angelos straightened his thick body and stood still, as if listening. He turned his head. There were sounds outside, not metal-shod this time, but the sounds of someone hurrying towards the cave.

I remember thinking, with a kind of numbed calmness, that if I screamed, it would warn Simon—but it would warn Angelos too. He was expecting Dimitrios, and he could have no idea that Simon and I were here. He had made no move to douse the torch. But on the other hand, if Simon had dealt with Dimitrios, Simon too would be off his guard. . . .

The steps came closer; were in the tunnel. Angelo's hand went to his pocket. I took in my breath.

With a stumbling rush and a flurry of breathing, Danielle hurried into the cave.

CHAPTER

17

Ah there is Justice in heaven,
And fire in the hand of God,
The reckoning must be made in the end.

SOPHOCLES: *Electra*
(tr. E. F. Watling).

The man relaxed, but his voice, pitched low, was angry. "What the hell are you doing here?"

She had stopped at the edge of the torch-light. She looked at once younger and much prettier than I had seen her. She had on the turquoise blouse and scarlet cotton skirt, and her haste had flushed her face and hurried her breathing, making her seem more normal and less cynically in control of herself. She hadn't looked at Angelos. Her eyes were riveted on what remained of the cache of boxes.

"So that's it!" Like him, she spoke in French.

"That's it." He regarded her sourly. "I told you last night we'd located it, didn't I? So why the devil didn't you do as you were told and stay out of sight till I came for you?"

She walked forward slowly while he was speaking, her eyes still on the stuff at his feet. Now she looked up under her lashes with that provocative gamine grin. "I wanted to see for myself what was going on. Don't be angry . . . nobody saw me come."

"Did you see Dimitrios on your way up?"

She shook her head. She was stooping over the pile, prodding with a toe at the broken box that showed the gleam of gold. I saw her breasts rise and fall quickly, as if with excitement. He said sharply, "No sign of him?"

"No."

He swore and struck the spade almost savagely into the stones. "Then where the hell is he? I came by the high way —it's shorter if you know your road . . . and if you didn't see him either—"

"I came by the high way too." Again that smiling look up through the lovely lashes. "How did you think I found my way here? I waited where I thought you'd come, and then I followed you."

He grunted. "Clever, eh? Then that means he's gone down the other way to look for me. Blast the man; he's as jumpy as a bean on a griddle, and about as much use. And you—you should have stayed away till I came for you. I told you I didn't want you up here."

She laughed. "Maybe I didn't trust you, Angelos. Maybe you wouldn't have come for me."

He gave a short laugh. "Maybe."

"Well, I wanted to see *this*," she said, amost childishly, "and besides, I didn't want to hang about down there all day. That damned jeep's dynamite anyway."

"Why? The stuff's not in it."

"No, but—"

"Did you park it where I told you?"

"Of course I did. Angelos, why d'you have to do this in daylight? You're crazy."

"I know what I'm doing. There's next to no moon just now, and this country's murder with a mule on a black night, and I daren't use a light. There'll be nobody about between here and the place where I'm stacking the stuff, and we can ferry the whole lot from there to the jeep in a couple of hours after dusk." He added, with a sort of heavy irony, "Always providing, of course, that you do as you're told, and that my cool-headed cousin gets back in time to give me a bit of help with the hard work!"

She laughed. She had recovered her breath now, and with it her own particular brand of throaty charm. She straightened up and gave him one of her long-lidded glinting looks. "Well, I can help instead, can't I? You won't send me back now? Don't you think, Angelos *mou*, that you might pretend to be a little bit pleased to see me?"

She moved up close to him as she spoke, and he pulled her to him and kissed her in a way that managed to be perfunctory and yet lustful. I saw her press her thin body against him, and her hands crept up to move among the thick curls on the back of his head.

I drew back a little in my crevice, shutting my eyes momentarily as if against this new discovery. *Angelos* her lover. *Angelos*. Through the whirl of fear and confusion the facts twisted and readjusted themselves into a different pattern. It had been Angelos, not Dimitrios, who had scraped acquaintance with Danielle on those long afternoons at Itea; this deliberately, not only to while away the boredom of inaction, but because she had the use of the jeep, whereas to buy or hire other transport would involve enquiries later, and provoke the very gossip the cousin had to avoid.

And by the same token it had been Angelos, not Dimitrios, who had broken into the studio last night. I remembered now, quite clearly, that the hand which had reached back for the torch had not had a torn thumb. And I remembered Danielle's little smile when I had so swiftly identified her lover as Dimitrios. . . .

Angelos pushed her away, not too gently. "You know damned well you should have stayed away. There's no room in the games I play for anyone with baby-nerves."

She was lighting a cigarette. She said, almost snappishly, "It wasn't nerves; it was curiosity, and I've a right to know what's going on. Baby-nerves, indeed, after what I've done for you! You'd never have got the jeep but for me, and I got you the tools and the mule on Monday night, didn't I? And I've played spy on the Englishman and that wretched girl he's taken in tow—and all you do is walk in last night out of the blue, stay with me half an hour, and tell me damn all except that today's the day, and I'm to get the jeep to the quarry, and you expect that to be that! You might have landed me in a hell of a jam last night, but you never said a word to me!"

"What d'you mean?" He was working again, levering at a solid lump of rock that was wedging down a couple of boxes. The dislodged dirt and small stones hissed down to the floor. He seemed hardly to be listening to her.

She said sharply, "You know quite well what I mean. When you came to my room last night, you said you hadn't seen Nigel, and—"

"Nigel?"

"The English artist. I told you. He was throwing out hints on Monday night about getting rich and famous, and he was drunk. After the others had left I gave him another couple of ouzos and took him for a walk. . . . Did I tell you that?" She was watching the man through the wisping smoke of her cigarette, and her tone was provocative. He neither looked up nor took the slightest notice.

She tapped ash off with a sharply pettish movement. "Well? It was obvious he'd found something up here on the hill. You said you were going to wait for him yesterday and find out what it was, and where—"

"So what? We didn't need to, did we? Your English friends came and showed us the way."

"They showed you the cave too?"

He laughed shortly. "Hardly. If they'd found the cave yesterday we'd not have been able to get near it now for troops three deep round the door!"

She moved impatiently. "I didn't mean that way. Of course they didn't find it, or they wouldn't be trailing harmlessly off to Levadia today. But you *did* find it pretty quickly, didn't you? Dimitrios told me at the Shining Ones that you'd found the place, and that you were working on it then while he came down to do some final clearing-up."

He had laid aside the crowbar, and was using the spade to shift some of the smaller debris. The thud of digging echoed dully. He didn't look up. He said, "When Stephanos showed them the spot where I broke Michael's neck I knew where the cave lay. Everything was changed, but I knew the crack must open on the cave. I couldn't get through it the way it was; but after I'd sent Dimitrios down I got to work and opened it up."

"I know. You told me this last night." She wasn't, as usual, letting the cigarette hang from her lips as she talked. She was smoking in jerky movements that spoke of tightly strung nerves. She said, making it sound like an accusation, *"But you never mentioned Nigel."*

He straightened up from his work, eyeing her, his head thrust forward like a bull's, and his look at once formidable and wary. The fixed half-moon smile on the thick mouth was in its own way terrifying. He said roughly, "Come on. What is all this? Why the hell should I mention Nigel?"

She blew a long plume of smoke, then said flatly, "When you left me last night, you went to Nigel's room. Why?"

"That's simple enough, isn't it? You'd told me he'd done a drawing of me as like as a photograph. I wanted to destroy it."

"But he'd cleared out—packed up and gone. You knew that. I'd told you that. I'd been in myself that evening to try and find the drawing, and all his stuff was gone. He'd taken it with him."

"Oh, no," said Angelos, "he hadn't."

"What d'you mean? You never saw him. How d'you know what he had on him?"

She stopped. I saw her eyes widen as they met his look. Her lips parted so that the cigarette fell to the ground and lay there smouldering. She ignored it. She was staring at him. He was standing very still, leaning on the spade, watching her. I could see sweat on the heavy face and on his hairy forearms.

He said again, softly, "Well?"

Her voice was shaken clear of any of its carefully affected overtones. It came clear and thin, like a little girl's. "You did see him? Yesterday? He *did* tell you where the cave was?"

"Yes, we saw him. But he didn't tell us anything. I told you the truth about that."

"Then—then—why did you lie about seeing him?"

The smile deepened as the thick lips parted. "You know why. Don't you?"

There was a long pause. I saw the pink tongue come out to lick once, quick as a lizard's, across her rouged lips. "You—killed him? Nigel?"

No reply. He didn't stir. I saw her throat muscles move as she swallowed. There was no horror or regret or fear in her face; it was blank of expression, with parted lips, and wide eyes fixed on the man. But her breathing hurried. "I . . . see. You didn't tell me."

His voice was soft, almost amused. "No, I didn't tell you. I didn't want to scare you away."

"But—I still don't understand. Didn't he know about the cave? Wasn't I right?"

"He knew; you can be sure of that. But he didn't tell us. We tried, but he wouldn't come through with anything that made sense."

She swallowed again. She hadn't taken her eyes off him. She might have been a waxwork but for the eyes, and the convulsive muscles of the throat. "Did you—have to kill him?"

He shrugged his heavy shoulders. "We didn't, in a manner of speaking. The bloody little pansy died on us. A pity." His head sank lower. The smile seemed to thicken. "Well? Scared? Going to scream and run?"

She moved then. She came close to him again, and her hands came up to the breast of his shirt. "Do I look as if I wanted to run, Angelos *mou*? Would I be the sort you'd want along with you if I was that kind of baby-nerve?" The hands slid up his shoulders and over them to the back of his neck. She pressed closer. "I know all about you, Angelos Dragoumis. . . . Don't think that I don't. They still tell quite a few stories about you, here in Delphi. . . ."

A laugh shook him. "You surprise me."

She pulled his head down, and said, against his mouth, "Do I? Does it surprise you to know that that's why I'm here? That that's why I like you?"

He kissed her, lingeringly this time, then thrust her away from him with his free hand. "No. Why should it? I've met women like you before." He still held the spade in his other hand, and now he turned back to his task. Danielle said, eyeing the broad back a little sulkily, "Where is he?"

"Near enough."

I saw her eyes show white for a moment as she gave a quick over-the-shoulder look into the shadowed corners. Then she shrugged and reached in her pocket for another cigarette. "You may as well tell me what happened."

"All right. Only stand back out of the way. That's better. Well. . . . We waited beside the Delphi track for the boy, but he didn't come that way. He must have started early and gone some other way round, because the first we saw of him was when he was away beyond us and almost up to these cliffs. We got up as close as we could without his seeing us, but when we'd worked our way up that gully that lies east of here, he'd vanished. We got up above the line of cliff, and separated; then waited. After a bit we saw him, just appearing walking out of the corrie here, as cool as you please. So we came down the cliff and got hold of him."

"Why did you have to do that? The English couple were coming. Once you saw the place where Michael died—"

"A bird in the hand," said Angelos, and I saw the thick grin deepen again. "For all I knew, Stephanos wouldn't remember the exact spot, and it was certain that your artist friend had just come out of some hiding place. Besides, he'd done that drawing of me. He'd seen me."

She was lighting another cigarette. The flame of the match wasn't quite steady. Her eyes looked wide and brilliant above it. "What did you do?"

He sounded indifferent. "We tried to scare him into talking at first, but he wouldn't come through. To tell you the truth I began to think you were wrong and he hadn't found a thing, only then he began to babble something about a cave and 'something beyond price' and he was damned if he'd let us touch it. Then we really got going. . . ." He straightened up and got out a cigarette. He thrust it between his lips, and leaned forward to get a light from hers.

I thought, I shall see that smile in my dreams. . . .

"But he still wouldn't say anything that made sense," said Angelos. "Babbled about water, and some flowers. . . ."

The contempt in the thick French made the words sound
obscene. "My English is fair enough. but I couldn't get all
the words. In the end there was something about gold, I'm
pretty sure, but just as we were getting to that, he died on
us. God knows we'd hardly started. It looked to me as if he
had a groggy heart."

"What happened then?"

"We'd hardly finished with him when we saw Stephanos
and the boy from Arachova bringing the English couple
along. We threw the body behind some rocks and waited
and watched till the old man took them to the corrie and
showed them the place. It's altered completely; I might
have looked for a thousand years, let alone the last two. As
soon as they'd gone, I got down into the corrie and started
looking round. It was dead easy. Your Nigel helped us after
all with his crazy blathering; there was only one place where
grass grew, and flowers, and it was much where I expected
the cave to lie, if Stephanos had been accurate. We soon
saw where the entrance was. Getting into it was another
matter, but of course with the boy dead on our hands we
had to be sure there'd be no enquiries until we'd got clear
off and no traces left. So I got on with the job alone while
I sent Dimitrios down to see you as arranged. I told him
not to tell you about Nigel, but to get quietly into the
studio and clear the stuff out of his room as if he'd packed
up and gone. He did that. You'll find all the boy's stuff in
the back of the jeep under the sacking. Dimitrios brought
a big folder of drawings, but like a fool he was in too much
of a hurry to check them, and he never saw that the picture
of me wasn't there. . . . It mightn't have mattered, but that's
the sort of detail that can sometimes matter the hell of
a lot. I thought it worth attending to, anyway. I'm officially
dead, and by God I'm staying that way, and no rumours!"

"Did you find it?"

"No. I didn't have time. There was a lot of paper with
the rubbish in a tin on the floor in his room. That fool
Dimitrios hadn't thought it worth bothering about. But in
fact if that's where the drawings are, nobody's going to take
any notice of them. They'll just think he's tidied up and
left."

"They do. The English couple think he's gone on a trek
over the hills—with the mule."

"Do they?" He sounded amused. "Then that's that, isn't
it?"

He had cleared the boxes now of their covering of stones.

He stooped to work one of them clear of the pile. She watched the play of the great muscles for a few moments in silence. Then she said again, "Where is he?"

"Who?"

"My God, Nigel of course! Did you just leave him out there for the vultures?"

"Not likely. They'd have given us away more quickly than anything else. He's here."

For the first time I saw some strong feeling move her. It was like a spring tensing. *"Here?"*

He jerked his head sideways. "Over there." He jerked the box free at last, straightened up, and carried it out of the cave. The torch still shone strongly enough from its niche on the pillar. Danielle stood still for a moment, staring towards the dark corner where Nigel's body lay, then, as if with an effort, she walked forward, took the torch down from its niche, and went over to the pile of rubble that hid the pathetic body. The light shone down on what lay, mercifully, beyond my range of vision.

It was at that moment that I remembered my own torch, dropped near Nigel's body. If she saw it . . . if the light from her torch picked up its glint in the dust. . . .

Angelos was coming back. He said irritably, "Still no sign. He seems to have taken one of the small boxes down himself by the lower track. Or else we'd have seen him." Then he looked across and saw where she was. She still had her back to him. The heavy face watching her didn't change its expression, but something in the look of the eyes made my blood thicken. "Well?"

She turned abruptly, "Are you going to leave him here?"

"Where else? Take him in the jeep to the bay at Galaxeidion?"

She ignored the irony. "Aren't you going to bury him?"

"My God, girl, there's no time. I've got enough to do shovelling half Parnassus off this stuff. You can throw some dirt down over him if you like, but it hardly matters. Something for you to do while I load up."

She came quickly back into the middle of the cave. "I'm not staying here."

He laughed. "As you wish. I thought you weren't squeamish, *ma poule?*"

"I'm not," she said pettishly, "but can't you see it won't do to leave him here, even if we do cover him? It's obvious already there's been someone at work here, and if anyone does come up they're bound to see—"

"Why should anyone come?"

She hesitated, eyeing him. "The Englishman, Simon—"

"What of him? You told me yourself he'd gone off to Levadia."

"I know, but—well, I was still thinking about what happened in the theatre, on Monday night."

In the theatre, on Monday night . . . I leaned back against the rock, trying, through the mists of tension and fear, to remember . . . the sounds I had heard as I sat there: the tiny jingling . . . it had after all been Danielle, taking the stolen mule off to meet the men. And Simon and I had talked, down there in the theatre. . . . It wasn't only the speech from *Electra* that those wonderful acoustics had sent up to Danielle, above us in the dark. And Danielle understood English . . . What had we said? *What, in heaven's name, had we said?*

It appeared that, whatever it was, she had reported it to him before. He laughed. "Oh, that. It's no news. Of course he knows Michael was murdered. D'you think Stephanos wouldn't tell him that? What difference does it make? Nobody knows *why.*"

"But if he suspected you were still alive—"

"Him?" The thick voice held nothing but amused contempt. "In any case, how should he? Nigel's dead, and no one's going to recognize that picture now."

"There was the gold," said Danielle.

The dark was boiling round me. As clearly as if he were just beside me, I heard Simon's voice again. *"It's not over . . . till I find what Michael found . . . the gold."*

"Gold, gold, gold—you see it everywhere, don't you, *ma poule?*" He laughed again. For some reason his spirits seemed to be rising. "You didn't *see* it was gold, now, did you? She picked something up and you saw it glitter, and your imagination did the rest."

"I tell you it was gold. I saw her staring at it."

The dark slowly cleared. Against it I saw a picture—not the one they were speaking of, but later; Simon, coming away from the centre-mark just before he spoke. . . . She hadn't heard. By the mercy of the gods of the place, she hadn't heard.

Angelos had turned away and was lugging another box clear of the pile. "There. That's as much as the poor bloody mule can take on one trip. . . . Now, forget that nonsense for five minutes, and you can give me a hand loading up. He found no gold yesterday, and that's a fact. He's got no reason to come back here. He's been, and seen all he can. Why should he come again? To bring a posy for Michael?" He laughed again, unpleasantly. "By God, I almost wish he would! . . . I owe him something, after all."

She said, with a sort of spite, "And her. She hit you."

"She did, didn't she?" he said cheerfully. "I think we'll wait till Dimitrios comes. He can't be much longer." He paused, looking round the cave. "It's queer to be back . . . and it looks just the same. Just the same. These pillars, and that bit of rock like a lion's head, and the drip of water somewhere. I never found the spring. . . . Can you hear it?"

She said impatiently, "But Nigel. You must do something about the body. Can't you see—?"

"You may be right." His voice was almost absent. It was clear that Nigel had long since ceased to matter at all. "In fact he may do us a better turn dead than he did alive. . . . *He* can go over the cliff with the jeep. Yes, there's the water. I thought so. It's over here somewhere. . . ."

Danielle's voice stopped him as he moved. There was a note in it that I hadn't heard before. "The jeep? Over the cliff? I didn't know you planned to do that."

"You don't know all I plan to do, my fair lady," he said. He turned back to her as he spoke, and I couldn't see his face. I saw hers. It looked suddenly thinner, and sharp, like a frightened urchin's. He said, "What is it now? We've got to get rid of the jeep somehow, haven't we? If the boy's found in the sea with it that accounts for him as well."

She said, almost in a whisper, "It's mine. Everybody knows I brought it up from Athens."

"So what? Everybody'll assume you were in it too, and that will be that."

Still she didn't move, but stared up at him. She looked very childish in the turquoise top, and scarlet bell of skirt. He went towards her till she had to tilt back her head to look him in the eyes. He said on a note of impatience, and something else, "What is it now? Scared?"

"No. No. But I was wondering—"

"What?"

She spoke still in that hurried whisper. "What you were going to do with the jeep if you . . . if you hadn't had Nigel's body to send over the cliffs with it?"

He said slowly, "The same, of course. They'd have thought you were in it and had been—"

He stopped abruptly. Then I heard him laugh. His big

hand went slowly out and ran down her bare arm. It looked very dark against her pale olive flesh. There were black hairs on the back of it. "Well, well, well . . . My poor little pretty, did you really think I'd do a thing like that to you?"

She didn't move. The thin arm hung slack by her side. Her head was tilted back, the big eyes searching on his face. She said in that flat little voice, "You said '*He* can go over the cliff in the jeep. . . .' as if you'd planned it for someone else. As if—"

He had an arm round her now, and had pulled her close to him. She went to him unresisting. His voice thickened. "And you thought I meant you? *You?* My little Danielle . . ."

"Then who?"

He didn't answer, but I saw her eyes narrow and then flare wide again. She whispered, *"Dimitrios?"*

His hand came quickly over her mouth and his body shook as if with a laugh. "Quietly, little fool, quietly! In Greece, the mountains have ears."

"But, Angelos *mou*—"

"Well? I thought you said you knew me, my girl? Don't you see? I had to have his help, and his boat, but when did *he* earn the half share of a fortune? The stuff's mine, and I've waited fourteen years for it, and now I've got it. D'you think I'm going to share it—with anyone?"

"And—what about me?"

He pulled her unresisting body closer to him. He laughed again, deep in his throat. "That's not sharing. You and I, *ma poule*, we count as one. . . ." His free hand slid up her throat, under her chin, and then forced her head up so that her mouth met his. "And I still need *you*. Do I still have to convince you of that?" His mouth closed on hers then, avidly, and I saw her stiffen for just a moment as if she was going to resist, then she relaxed against him and her arms went up to his neck. I heard him laugh against her lips, and then he said hoarsely, "Over there. Hurry."

I shut my eyes. I turned my head away so that my cheek, like my hands, pressed against the cool rock. It smelt fresh, like rain. I remember that under my left hand there was a little knob of stone the shape of a limpet shell. . . .

I don't want to write about what happened next, but in justice to myself I think I must. As I shut my eyes the man was kissing her, and I saw his hand beginning to fumble with her clothes. She was clinging to him, her body melting towards his, her hands pulling his head down fiercely to meet her kisses. Then when I couldn't see any more I heard h'm talking, little breathless sentences I couldn't catch—didn't try to catch—in a mixture of Greek and his thick fluent French. I heard him kick a stone out of the way as he pull⁻d her down onto the dusty floor of the cave near the rubble pile . . . near Nigel's body. . . .

I only heard one sound from her, and it was a little half-sigh, half-whimper of pleasure. I'll swear it was of pleasure.

I was shaking, and covered with sweat, and hot as though the chilly cleft were an oven. Under the fingers of my left hand the stone limpet had broken away. I was holding a fragment of it in my curled finger, and it was embedded in the flesh, hurting me.

I don't know how long it was before I realized that the cave was quiet, except for the heavy breathing.

Then I heard him getting to his feet. His breathing was deep and even. He didn't say anything, and I didn't hear him move away. There was no sound from Danielle.

I opened my eyes again, and the dimming torch-light met them. He was standing beside the pile of rubble, smiling down at Danielle. She lay there, still looking up at him. I could see the glint of her eyes. The sweat on his face made the wide fleshy cheeks gleam like soapstone. He stood quite still, smiling down at the girl who lay at his feet staring back at him, her bright skirt all tossed-looking in the dust.

I thought, with crazy inconsequence, How uncomfortable she looks. Then, suddenly, She looks dead.

Presently Angelos stooped, took her body by the shoulders, and dragged it across the cave to pitch it down in the rubble beside Nigel.

And that is how Danielle Lascaux was murdered within twenty yards of me, and I never lifted a finger to help her.

CHAPTER

18

Go while the going's good,
Is my advice. . . .

SOPHOCLES: *Philoctetes*
(tr. E. F. Watling).

By the mercy of providence I didn't faint, or I'd have pitched straight out into the torch-light. But the narrow cleft held my body up, and my mind (numbed, I suppose, by the repetition of shock), seemed only very slowly to take in what had happened.

It was as if some sort of mental censor had dropped a curtain of gauze between me and the scene in the cave, so that it took on a kind of long-distance quality, the murderer moving about his dreadful business at a far remove from me, as a creature of fiction moves on a lighted stage. I was invisible, inaudible, powerless, the dreamer of the dream. With light would come sanity, and the nightmare vanish.

I watched him, still in that queer dead trance of calm. I think if he had turned in my direction I would hardly have had the wit to draw back, but he didn't. He dropped Danielle's body down in the dust beside Nigel's, and stood for a moment looking down at them, lightly dusting his hands together. I wondered for a moment if he was, after all, going to shovel the dirt over the bodies, then it occurred to me that Danielle's useless spark of instinct had been right; his plan for disposing of Nigel in the jeep had come a little too pat. It was Danielle who had brought the jeep; it was Danielle who was to be found with the wreck of it. . . . That had been his plan all along. I saw it now clearly. I didn't believe for a moment that he intended to kill his cousin Dimitrios—but even if that were true, he had certainly never intended to share anything with Danielle. What she had to offer was only too easily found elsewhere. What was equally certain was that he hadn't wanted to kill her here. He must have intended to save himself the transport of her body by killing her when the job was over, but her half-frightened queries had aimed just a little too near the mark for comfort. Better kill her now, and risk the extra load to be ferried down after dusk.

He had turned back now to the pillar where the torch was lodged. I watched him, still as if he were an actor in a play—a bad actor; there was no expression on his face, no horror or anxiety, or even interest. He reached up a hand, picked up the torch, and switched it off. The darkness came down like a lid on a stifling box. He seemed to be listening. I could hear his untroubled breathing, and the tiny rustle of settling dust under the girl's body. There was no sound from outside.

He switched on the light again and went out of the cave. A bridle jingled as the mule moved, but it appeared that he hadn't untied it. I heard him move off, his soft footsteps unaccompanied by the sharper ones of the beast. He must have decided to reconnoitre the corrie before daring to lead out the mule. . . .

The footsteps dwindled steadily. I couldn't hear them any more. I waited, straining my ears. Nothing but the soft movement of dust in the cave, and the restless shifting of the mule's hoof in its corner. He must have left the corrie—perhaps to look for Dimitrios' approach.

One thing was certain: Angelos had no idea that Simon had any reason for further curiosity about the corrie. He felt as safe from discovery in this remote stretch of Parnassus as he would on the mountains of the moon.

And Simon? Simon, too. . . .

I was out of the cleft and flying across the dark cave. There was no light, but I don't remember that I needed it. My body was acting of itself, like a sleepwalker's, and like a sleepwalker's it must have dodged every obstacle by instinct. My brain, too . . . I had no conscious plan, not even any coherent thought, but at some queer submerged level I knew I had to get out of that cave, to Simon. . . . There was something about Dimitrios coming back, and Simon . . . something about warning Simon that here was not one shifty little crook to deal with, but two men who were murderers . . . something important to tell Simon . . . and more important than anything, I had to get out of the darkness, out of that stifling cage of rock, into the blessed light . . .

The sun struck down at me like a bright axe. I put a hand to my eyes, flinching as if at an actual blow. I was blinded, swimming in a sea of light. My other hand, groping out before me, touched something warm and soft, that moved. I jerked away with a little gasp of terror and in the same moment I realized that it was the mule, tethered in the narrow corner outside the cave. Its muzzle was deep in the grass, and it hardly paused to roll a white eye back at me before it resumed its eager cropping. The warm ammoniac smell of its coat brought a momentary, comfortless, memory of Niko. I thrust past it, ducked heedlessly under the buttress, and ran out into the corrie.

There was no sign of Angelos. I turned and ran for the foot of the cliff path.

The heat in the bottom of the corrie was palpable. I felt the sweat start out on my body as soon as I left the shade. The air weighed on me as I ran. My lungs laboured to drag it in, and dust was burning and rough in my throat. The corrie was a well of heat, in which nothing moved except me, and I thrust through it blindly, with the whip of panic on me. . . .

I reached the foot of the cliff. I believe I realized that if Angelos had gone to meet his cousin, he would have gone by the gateway, and not up the cliff. But this again was not a conscious thought. I only knew that I had to get up, out of the hot enclosing walls of rock, out onto the high open stretches above the cliff.

The afternoon sun shone full on the cliff where the path lay. The brightness of the white limestone splintered against the eyes. As I plunged up the steep, twisting little goat-track I felt the rock burn the soles of my shoes like hot metal. When I put a hand to the face of the cliff it seemed to scorch the flesh.

I climbed as fast as I dared, trying to make no sound. The dust hissed like sand under my feet. A pebble rolled and fell to the foot of the cliff with a crack like a pistol shot. My breathing was as loud in the still air as sobbing.

I was a little less than halfway up when I heard him coming back.

I stopped dead, pilloried against the naked rock, clamped to it, like a lizard on the bare stone. The rock burned through my thin dress. As soon as he got to the gateway he would see me. I couldn't possibly get to the top in time. If there were somewhere to hide. . . .

There was nowhere to hide. A bare zigzag of goat track; a couple of steep steps of natural rock open to the sun: a ledge holding a low tangle of brown scrub. . . .

Regardless now of noise I scrambled anyhow over the rocky steps, pulled myself off the path onto the ledge, and flung myself down behind the meagre shelter of the dead bushes.

There was one small holly oak, shining green, among a mass of foot-high tufted stuff like a tangle of rusty wire netting. This was prickly to the touch, but as I dragged myself nearer its shelter, pressing against it, it crumbled under my desperate hands. I remember that it seemed quite a natural part of the nightmare, that the barrier between me and murder should crumble as I touched it.

I drew back from the dead bushes and pressed myself deep into the dust of the ledge, as if like a mole I could dig myself into the ground for safety. I put my cheek to the hot dust and lay still. Above me an overhang dealt a narrow shade, but where I lay the ledge was exposed to the sun. I could feel its cruel weight on my back and hand, but I hardly heeded it. Through the wiry scrub I was watching the corrie below me.

Angelos came up into the gateway and then walked quickly down the ramp and across the corrie. He didn't look up, but made straight for the cave, disappearing from my view in the corner.

I waited, pressed down in the burning dust. . . .

I was just getting ready to move, when I saw him again. He came out into the sunlight, moving very quietly now, and looking about him. He had brought his jacket out of the cave, and held it carefully over one arm. In the other hand he held something that shone in the sunlight. It was the torch I had dropped by Nigel's body. Angelos' own torch.

The black arched brows were drawn frowning over his eyes. The smile pulled the thick lips. He stopped in the centre of the corrie, turning the torch over in his hand.

I lay still. Invisible, the mule moved restlessly, and metal clinked.

Angelos raised his head and sent one long look round the corrie. It raked the cliff, touched me, passed me by. Then the massive shoulders lifted in a tiny shrug, and he thrust the torch into a pocket of the jacket. I saw him slide his hand into the other pocket and bring out a gun. He weighed this for a moment in his hand, thoughtfully, and then turned back towards the cave.

My hands braced themselves in the dust. He would have recognized the torch, no doubt of that. He was going back into the cave to search for whoever had dropped it. And this

time I didn't propose to linger till he came out again. I
wasn't going to wait here, to be brushed off the cliff by that
gun like a lizard off a wall.

I felt my muscles tighten up like vibrating wires. He was
moving deliberately across the corrie floor. Soon he would be
out of sight.

Something fell onto my hand with a sharp little rap of
pain that nearly made my cry out. A pebble. Then a shower
of dust and small stones, dislodged from somewhere above
me, rattled down the cliff like a charge of small shot.

Angelos stopped dead, turned, and stared upwards straight
at me.

I didn't move. I didn't think he could see me at that angle.
But my mind stampeded with another, and worse panic, as
I heard the sounds approaching the top of the cliff. Dimitrios, as yet scatheless, with Simon behind him? Or Simon,
coming cheerfully to tell me that justice had been done on
"last night's marauder"? Any hope I had had that Dimitrios
might have been forced into telling Simon himself about
Angelos, vanished now as I listened to that incautious approach.

I saw Angelos stiffen, then he whipped out of sight behind
a jut of rock.

The sounds came nearer. I turned my head till, by twisting my eyes in their sockets, I could see the cliff top. If it
was Simon I must shout . . . my mouth opened ready for the
cry, and I licked the dust off my dry lips. Then something
moved suddenly against the sky at the brim of the cliff, and
I saw what it was.

A goat. Another. Three big black goats, yellow-eyed, flop-
eared, peacefully intent on the dry scrub at the cliff's head.
. . . They turned aside at the brink of the cliff and moved
slowly across above me, outlined against the deep blue of
that translucent sky. As they went I thought I heard again
the sweet faraway stave of the goat-herd's pipe. The coolly
pastoral sound fell through the heat like the trickle of
Apollo's spring.

The relief was dizzying. The rock swam in the dazzling
light. I shut my eyes and put my head down beside the dusty
scrub. Something smelt sweet and aromatic—some memory,
wisping out of the dust, of potpourri and English gardens
and bees among the thyme. . . .

I don't know how long it was before I realized that the
afternoon held no sound at all.

When I looked again, Angelos had come out of concealment, and was standing where he had been before, in the centre of the corrie floor. He was standing very still, staring up, not at me, but at the edge of the cliff above me where the goats had been. Slowly I followed his gaze. I could feel the breath of the hot stone on my cheek.

The goats were still there. They, too, were standing stock-still, side by side, at the brink of the cliff. They were looking down, with ears forward and eyes intent and curious . . . six yellow satyrs' eyes, staring fixedly down at me, some forty feet below them.

Angelos dropped his coat onto a boulder beside him, and started for the foot of the cliff.

At his movement I heard the flurry of dust and pebbles as the goats fled. It echoed the quick jump and kick of my own heart. But I didn't move. Whether some instinct kept me clamped still like a hiding animal, or whether the flood of fear that washed and ebbed through my blood actually drained the power of movement from me, I can't tell. At any rate I lay flat for the few decisive moments during which the Greek crossed the corrie and plunged up the goat path towards me. And then it seemed that he was almost on me, and it was too late to escape. I remembered the gun and lay there, unbreathing, pressed flat to the hot earth.

I had a shelter of a sort from below, and from above the overhang might partly hide me. The path sloped sharply past the end of the ledge where I lay. It was possible—it was surely possible?—that he might hurry past it and never look back to see me lying there behind the crumbling scrub? My dress was of pale-coloured cotton, now sufficiently streaked with dust. Against the glaring rock and the red pebble-strewn dust he might miss me. He might yet—surely?—miss me.

He was just below me now. He stopped. His head was a few feet below the level of my ledge. I couldn't—daren't—look, but I heard the climbing steps stilled, and then his breathing close beneath me. He was looking up. My own breath hardly stirred the dust under my mouth.

He paused where he was for a few seconds, and then I heard the soft steps moving on. But they didn't come on up the track. They moved carefully away to the left, below my ledge.

Through the pathetic barrier of dead plants I could just see the top of his head. It was turned away now, and I knew that he must have left the track. I could hear loose pebbles slither and spatter down the rock, and the rustle of the dry

plants he trod over. He went very carefully, with pauses almost between each step.

I had to know what he was doing. I moved my head
slightly, and saw him better.

There was a ledge below mine, with a few sparse plants
and a tumble of loose fragments of stone. I had noticed it in
that second's wild glance round for shelter. It wouldn't have
hidden anyone larger than a child. But he searched it, gun in
hand, quartering it methodically, like a dog.

Then he left it, and came back carefully onto the track.
He paused there briefly once again, so that for a silly moment I wondered if he was satisfied, and would go down
again into the corrie, thinking perhaps that the goats had
been watching a snake. . . . But he turned without further
hesitation and started up the steep section that would bring
him up to me.

I don't even think I was frightened; not now. It was as if
fear had been raised to such a pitch that it killed itself, like
a light that goes vividly bright just before it goes out. I was
back in that dim-lit, remote theatre of unreality. This wasn't
happening to me.

I suppose that nobody, in their heart of hearts, ever believes that they themselves will die. Volumes of philosophies
have been written out of this belief alone. And I'm sure that
nobody ever believes that a foul thing like murder can over-
take them. Something will stop it. It can't happen. To others,
but not to them. Not to *me*.

I lay, almost relaxed, abandoned to fate and chance, in the
hot dust, and Angelos swiftly climbed the path towards me.
In a moment now he would reach the end of my ledge. He
might see me straightaway, or he might turn aside and beat
the scrub till he flushed me, scared and filthy with dust, from
my hiding place. He was there now. He couldn't miss me. . . .

I have read somewhere that when a man is hunted for his
life, one of the chief dangers he undergoes is the desperate
urge to give himself up, and have done. I had never believed
it. I had thought that fear would drive him till he dropped,
like a hunted hare. But it's true. It may have been that
something forbade me to let the man find me crouching,
dirty and frightened, at his feet; it may simply have been
the terrible blind instinct of the hunted. But the impulsion
came and I didn't attempt to resist it.

I stood up and began to brush the dirt off my frock.

I didn't look at him. He had stopped dead when I moved.

He was standing just where my ledge left the track. To get off it I would have to pass him.

I walked forward through the scrub and stones as if I were walking in my sleep. I didn't meet his eyes, but watched my feet on the rough going. He moved a little to one side and I passed him. I went slowly down the path again to the bottom of the corrie. He came just behind me.

When I got to the level ground I stumbled and nearly fell. His hand took hold of my arm from behind, and my flesh seemed to wince and shrink from the touch. I stopped.

The hand tightened, then with a jerk he pulled me round to face him. I think if he had gone on touching me I would have screamed then and there, but he let me go, so I kept silent. I knew that if I tried to scream I would be killed out of hand. But I backed away from him a step or so till a boulder touched the back of my legs. Without meaning to, I sat down; I couldn't have stood. I put both hands flat on the hot surface of the stone as if I could draw strength from it, and looked at Angelos.

He was standing perhaps five feet from me, legs a little apart, one hand thrust negligently into the belt of his trousers, the other arm hanging loose at his side with the gun dangling. His head was forward slightly, like a bull's when it is deciding to charge. The heavy face was terrifying with its tight, curved smile, the perfect arch of the black brows and the cruel eyes that seemed to be solid, opaque black, without pupils, and without light from within. The thick nostrils were flared and he was breathing fast. The bulls' curls along his forehead were damp and tight with sweat.

He had recognized me, of course. I saw that as his slow stare raked me. He must have seen me distinctly last night in the light of the torch.

He said, "So it's my little friend of the studio, is it?" He was speaking in the quick guttural French he had used with Danielle.

I tried to say something, but no sound came. As I cleared my throat I saw the smile deepen. My voice came back. "I hope I hurt you," I said.

"That score," said Angelos, very pleasantly, "will soon be quite even." My hands pressed hard on the warm stone. I said nothing. He said abruptly, "Where's the Englishman?"

"I don't know."

He made a small movement towards me and I shrank back against the boulder. His expression didn't change but his voice did. "Don't be a fool. You didn't come up here alone. Where is he?"

I said hoarsely, "I—we were sitting up there on the cliff and we saw a man hanging about . . . that chap Dimitrios. He's a guide . . . I don't know if you know him. Simon . . . my friend . . . went off to speak to him. He—he thought it was him last night at the studio and I think—I think he wanted to find out what he'd been after."

It was so near the truth that I hoped he might be satisfied as far as Simon was concerned. But it wouldn't help me. Nothing would.

"And you've been up on the cliff all this time?"

"I—why, no. I went over the hill a little way, and then I thought Simon might have come back, so I—"

"And you haven't been in the cave?"

"Cave?" I said.

"That's what I said. The cave."

The sun was cold. The rock was cold. I suppose even till this I had been hoping against silly hope, but now I knew for certain. Of course I was going to die. Whatever I had seen or not seen—the mule, the cave, the treasure, Nigel, Danielle—it wouldn't help me in the least to play the innocent. None of these things mattered beside the one fact that now I had seen Angelos.

He had taken two paces away to where his coat lay over a boulder. He slipped a hand in the pocket and brought out the torch. "You left this, didn't you?"

"Yes."

A gleam of surprise in the black eyes showed that he had expected me to deny it. I said flatly, "I dropped it when I saw Nigel's body. And I was in the cave just now when you killed Danielle."

The metal of the torch flashed as he made a sudden little movement. At least I had startled him into interest. If I could keep him talking . . . if I could keep alive for just a few more minutes . . . perhaps the miracle would happen, and I wouldn't die. Murderers were conceited, weren't they? They talked about their murders? But then Angelos took murder so for granted that it had hardly seemed to interest him to commit, let alone to discuss. . . . But he was a sadist, too; perhaps he would enjoy talking to frighten me before he killed me. . . .

I said hoarsely, gripping the stone, "Why did you torture Nigel? Did you really mean to kill Danielle?"

It wasn't going to work. He dropped the torch back on

top of the coat, and gave a quick glance round the encircling cliffs. Then he put the gun down gently beside the torch, and turned to me.

I did manage to move then, but the thrust of my hands that took me off the warm stone sent me a pace towards him. As I whirled to run he caught me from behind and pulled me back as easily as if I had been a rag doll. I suppose I fought him; I don't remember anything except the blind panic and the feel of his hands and the acrid smell of his sweat, and the appalling iron strength that held me as effortlessly as a man's hand holds a caught moth. One hand came hard over my mouth, crushing my lips against my teeth, but the palm was slimy with sweat; it slipped, and I wrenched my head away and managed at the same moment to kick him hard on the shinbone. I paid dearly for the moment of advantage, for as I twisted my body in a vain attempt to break away, he half-lunged forward to drag me close again and silence me, trod on a loose stone that rolled under his foot, and we fell together.

If I had fallen undermost I should probably have been badly hurt, if not stunned, for he was a heavy man; but he went down onto his side in a stumbling fall, dragging me with him. Even then the brutal grip never loosened, and as we hit the ground he moved like lightning, flinging himself over my body with a quick heave, and holding me down on the ground underneath him.

Then his grip shifted. I was on my back, my left arm twisted up under me, so that our double weight held it there, almost breaking. My right wrist was in his grip, clamped down against the rock beside me. His free hand flashed up to my throat. The heavy body held me down; I couldn't move, but frantic now with terror I screamed and twisted uselessly under him and jerked my head from side to side, trying to avoid the hand that slipped and groped on my throat for the hold he wanted. I screamed again. He cursed in Greek and hit me hard across the mouth and then as my head went back against the rock the hand gripped my throat at last, moved a little, tightened. . . .

I was still alive. It was years later and the boiling agonized black had cleared, and I was still alive. I was still lying on my back in the hot dust, and above me the sky arched in a great flashing, pulsating dome of blue. Angelos' weight was still on me. I could feel the heave of his heavy breathing; the smell of his sweat was rank; his hand was wet and sour and foul across my mouth; the other hand was still on my throat, but it lay loosely there, and now it lifted.

He didn't move away. He lay there quite still, with rigid muscles, looking up and away from me towards the entrance to the corrie. Then his hand slid from my face and went down onto the dusty rock beside my head, ready to thrust him to his feet. I remember that the hand was on my spread hair, and the tug as he put his weight on it hurt me. The tiny pain was like a spur. It pricked me back to consciousness. I stopped blinking up into the vibrating blue of the sky, and managed to move my head a fraction, to look where Angelos was looking.

He was staring straight into the sun. At first I could see nothing in the dazzle at the mouth of the corrie. Then I saw him.

I knew who it was straightaway, though he was only a shadow against the glare. But even so I felt the sharp cold thrill run up the marrow of my spine as I felt Angelos' heart jerk, once, in his body, and heard him say, thickly, "Michael?"

CHAPTER

19

I am come,
Fresh from the cleansing of Apollo . . .
. . . To pay the bloody twain their debt
Of blood.

EURIPIDES: *Electra*
(tr. Gilbert Murray).

Realization, shock, recognition—it must only have taken a few seconds, but it seemed an age.

One moment Simon was silhouetted in fractional pause against the glare of the gateway, the next, Angelos had swung himself off my body and onto his feet as lightly as a dancer. He must have forgotten that his gun had been laid aside, for I remember that his hand flashed, as if automatically, to his hip just as Simon, coming down the ramp with the speed of a ski-jumper, brought up not five yards from him in a flurry of dust and shale.

Angelos was standing right over me, hand still at hip, watching him.

Simon had stopped dead where he was. I couldn't see his expression, but I could see Angelos', and fear seeped back into my blood as agonizingly as warmth after frostbite. I stirred in the dust and tried to say something, to tell Simon who and what he was, but my throat was swollen and sore, and the brilliant light swam round me sickeningly as I moved, and I couldn't make a sound. Angelos must have felt me move at his feet, but he took no notice. Simon hadn't glanced at me either. The two men watched one another, as wary and slow as two dogs circling before a fight.

I waited for Simon to rush him as he had done last night. I didn't notice then how hard he was breathing, fighting to get heart and lungs under control after his rush up the steep track towards my terrified screaming. Nor did I realize that he still thought the Greek might be armed . . . and I was

227

lying where knife or gun could reach me, seconds before Simon could make contact. . . . None of this was I in any state to realize. I only knew that Simon didn't move, and I remember wondering, with a sick cold little feeling, if he was afraid. Then he took two paces forward, very slowly, and now that he was no longer between me and the sun, I saw his face. The cold feeling went, and I wasn't afraid any more. With the fear, the tenseness went out of my body, and I felt myself relax and begin to tremble. The bruises the Greek had inflicted began to hurt. I turned on my side and tried to pull myself a little further away from him. I couldn't have got up, but I dragged myself a foot or so away to crouch, shaking and still gasping for breath, against the base of the boulder where I had sat before.

He took no notice of me. He had dealt with me, and thrown me aside, and now he was going to deal with Simon. I could be finished after that.

Simon said pleasantly, "I take it you are Angelos?" His breathing was still over-fast, but his voice was level.

"The same. And you are Michael's little brother."

"The same."

The Greek said, on a note between satisfaction and contempt, "You are welcome."

Simon's lips thinned. "I doubt that. I believe, Angelos, that you and I have met before."

"Last night."

"Yes." Simon looked at him for a few seconds in silence. His voice went flat and uninflected. Knowing him now, I felt my heart tighten and begin to race. He added, "I wish I had known—last night."

I turned my head painfully and managed to say, "He killed Nigel . . . and Danielle." It was some seconds before I realized that I had made no sound at all.

"You murdered my brother Michael." Simon hadn't even glanced at me. He was breathing evenly now, his face wiped clean of all expression but that light, watchful look. I recognized it for what it was. Just so must Michael have looked when he faced Angelos here all those years ago. Just so must this blazing sky have looked down, those indifferent rocks throwing back its blinding heat. Time had run back. Angelos faced Michael again, and this time the odds were on Michael.

It seemed that Angelos didn't think so. He laughed. "Yes, I killed Michael. And I shall kill you, little brother. In your country they do not teach men to be men. It is different here."

Simon was moving now, very slowly, forward a pace; another.

"How did you kill my brother, Angelos?"

"I broke his neck." I noticed with surprise that the Greek was giving ground. He had lowered his head in that characteristic way he had. I could see the contraction of the flat black eyes against the light. I saw him blink rapidly once or twice, and he moved his head as a bull does whose horns pain him. Then he took a slow step backwards, sidling a little . . .

I thought for a moment that he was trying to get Simon out of line with him and the sun, and wondered fleetingly at the same time why he should have let the other play for time like this, when suddenly, like a flash out of a black night, I knew what he was doing. I remembered the gun, lying hidden from Simon in the tumble of Angelos' dropped coat.

Somehow I moved. It was like lifting a mattress stuffed with clay to lift my body from the scuffled dust, but I rolled over, kicked myself along the ground with one convulsive jack-knifing motion, like a fish, and grabbed at the dangling sleeve of the coat just as Angelos took a sudden, swift step aside, and stooped for the gun.

I had the sleeve. I yanked at it with all my strength. It caught at a bit of the rock, tore, and came with a jerk. The torch flashed over like a rocket and crashed on a stone by my head. The gun flew high and wide, hit a pile of stones three yards away, and slithered out of sight. It actually struck the Greek's hand as he reached to grab it. He whirled with a curse and kicked me and then went down sickeningly across the boulder as Simon hit him like a steam hammer.

Simon came in with the blow. The Greek's forearm, even as he went down over the rock, just managed to block the side-handed chop at the throat that followed it, and counter in the same movement with a wicked elbow punch that took Simon in the lower part of the stomach. I saw pain explode through him like a bursting shell, and as he recoiled the Greek, using the rock as a springboard, came away from it in a lunge with all his weight behind it. Simon's mouth disappeared in a smear of blood. His head snapped back in front of another blow that looked as if it had broken his neck, and he went down, but as he went he hooked one leg round Angelos' knee and, using the man's own momentum, brought him crashing down over him. Before the Greek hit the ground Simon had rolled aside and was above him. I saw the Greek lash out with a foot, miss, and aim a short chopping blow with the edge of a hand at Simon's neck; Simon hit him in the throat and then the two were locked, heaving and rolling in the dust that mushroomed up round them.

I couldn't see . . . couldn't make out . . . Angelos was on his back, and Simon seemed to be across him, trying to fix the man's arm in a lock, to drag it under him as Angelos had dragged mine; the Greek smashed again and again at his face; the shortened punches hadn't much force behind them but the blood was running from Simon's mouth. Then suddenly the flailing fist opened, clawed, came down onto Simon's cheekbone and slithered across it, the big spatulate thumb digging, digging, for his eye. . . .

I had dragged myself to my feet, holding on to the boulder beside me. He couldn't do it after all; he couldn't be expected to do it . . . he was the younger, and he knew how to fight, but Angelos had the weight, and all those desperate years behind him. . . . If I could help . . . if I could only help. . . .

I stooped giddily, and reached for a lump of rough rock, lifting it in hands that shook like leaves. I could hit him as I had last night . . . if I could find a weapon—perhaps the torch—

The gun.

I dropped the knob of rock and flung myself, with sobbing little breaths, at the pile of stones where the gun had gone. Here, surely, it had struck and slid out of sight? No sign. Then here? No. Here? . . . oh, dear God, *here.* . . .

There, white on the limestone, a scratch had marked its passage . . . I drove a shaking hand down between the jammed rocks. They scraped the skin and it hurt me but I hardly noticed. I thrust my arm down as far as I could. My fingers, stretching, touched something cold and smooth . . . metal. I couldn't reach it; the tips of my fingers slipped over it, no more. I could feel my lips trembling as the tears spilt salt onto them. I lay down hard against the stones and thrust my arm further into the narrowing crack. The cruel stone rasped at the skin and I felt blood running down my wrist. My fingers slid further, curled, gripped. I had the gun. I tried to withdraw it. But with my hand now curved round the butt I couldn't pull it back between the stones. I dragged at it, hopelessly, stupidly, and my hand hurt till I cried out with the pain, but I couldn't drag the gun out. . . .

Simon had twisted back from that gouging thumb. The Greek lunged violently to one side as the other's hold slackened, and then, somehow, was free. With a movement incredibly quick for a man of his build he had rolled aside and was bunching to jump to his feet. As he went I saw his hand close, like mine, on a cruelly jagged chunk of rock. But Simon was as quick. The same movement that threw him back and away from the clawing hand had brought him to his feet. He saw the Greek clutch the rock. Even as the fist closed on it and the arm muscles tightened Simon jumped. His foot stamped down on the man's hand. The rock was undermost, and I heard the man make a dreadful sound as his hand was smashed down onto it. But he whipped over and brought his foot up with what looked like appalling force into Simon's groin. Simon saw it coming, and tried to sidestep. The foot grazed the inside of his thigh. Simon's hand came up under the lashing ankle; I saw a heave and a twist, and the Greek crashed back onto his side like a felled ox, and Simon plummeted down onto him again in the smother of dust. Another blow, a sick sound of flesh and bone smacking together, and then Angelos was uppermost, his fist smashing down like a hammer. . . .

I opened my hand and let the gun go. I dropped to the base of the pile of stones, and began to claw at them with those useless, shaking fingers, trying to pull the heavy stuff aside. From behind me came the thud and slither of their bodies on the ground, the torn dreadful breathing, and, again, the sudden sharp sound of pain. I thought it came from Simon.

The stone under my hands gave way, and I threw it down and tore at the next. And the next. And then a pile of dry earth and small jagged pebbles.

Then I saw the blue-dark gleam of the gun.

I thrust the last lump of rock aside and pushed my hand through. The muzzle was towards me. I grabbed it and dragged the thing out. I didn't even think once of the danger of holding it like that. I just dragged it out between the rough stones and turned, holding it in my aspen hands. I remember thinking with surprise how heavy it was. . . .

I'd never touched a gun before in my life. But of course it was quite easy. You simply pointed it and pressed the trigger: I knew that. Provided I got close enough . . . and if the men would only break apart for a moment and let me see through that stifling dust. . . . One simply pointed the thing and pulled the trigger, and Angelos would be dead, blasted out of life in a fraction of time. It didn't occur to me that this was in any way a wrong or a momentous thing to do. I took a couple of faltering steps in the direction of the struggling bodies on the ground. . . .

It was funny, but it was difficult to walk. The ground was unsteady and the dust dragged at my feet and the gun was too heavy and the sky was far too bright but still I couldn't see properly. . . .

The locked bodies on the ground moved as the man underneath made a seemingly titanic effort. Both men were covered with dust: I couldn't see who it was lying prone with one arm twisted into that cruel lock behind his back . . . or who it was who lay astride him, shifting his grip now, straining in some final agonizing effort. If only they would break apart . . . if only I could see which was Angelos. . . .

The man uppermost lay clamped over the other, one hand hard round the wrist of the locked arm, his own free arm flung round the prone man's neck in a tight embrace. As I watched, the embrace tightened still further. . . .

The prostrate man's head came painfully back. The red dust was thick in the black curls. The broad cruel face was smeared red with it too, an archaic mask carved grimacing in red sandstone. It was Angelos who lay there in the dust, breath sobbing throught the grinning lips, trying with weaker and weaker movements to throw Simon off his body.

I stood there, the gun drooping in my hand, the driving purpose snapped in me, staring like someone in a dream at the two bodies that heaved, breathing as one, on the ground at my feet.

A muscle bunched in Simon's shoulder. The Greek's head moved back another fraction. The grin was a rictus, fixed, horrible. His body gave one last desperate heave to rid itself of its killer, threshing sideways across the dusty rock. But Simon's grip didn't shift. Even as the two bodies, still locked, slithered a yard or so across the dusty rock to fetch up hard against the cairn where Michael had been murdered, I saw Simon's arm tense, and jerk tightly back, and heard Angelos' breath tear out of his throat in a sort of whistling gasp that broke off short. . . .

I knew then that Simon didn't need me or the gun. I turned aside and sat down on the boulder. I leaned back very wearily against the hot rock and shut my eyes.

After a while there was silence.

Angelos lay still, sprawled face downward against the little cairn. Simon got very slowly to his feet. He stood for a moment looking down. His face was filthy with dust and blood, and lined with fatigue. I could see how his muscles slumped with weariness as he stood there. He put up the back of his hand to wipe the blood from his face. His hands were bloody too.

Then he turned away and for the first time looked at me. He made as if to speak, and then I saw his tongue come out to wet the dust-caked lips. I answered his look quickly.

"I'm quite all right, Simon. He—he didn't hurt me." My voice had come back, hoarse and not too steady. But there was nothing to say. I whispered, "There's a rope on the mule. It's down by the cave."

"Rope?" His voice wasn't his own either. He was coming slowly towards me. "What for?"

"Him, of course. If he came round—"

"My dear Camilla," said Simon. And then, as he saw the look in my face, in a kind of anger, "What else did you expect me to do?"

"I don't know. Of course you had to kill him. It's just— of course you did."

His mouth twisted. It wasn't quite a smile, but nothing about him seemed, just at that moment, to be like himself. It was a stranger who stood in front of me in the blazing sunlight, with a stranger's voice, and something gone from his face that I remembered there. He stood there in silence, looking down at his hands. I still remember the blood on them.

The nausea had gone, and the world steadied. I said quickly, almost desperately, out of a rush of shame, "Simon. Forgive me. I—I guess I can't think straight yet. Of course you had to. It was only . . . coming so close to it. But you were right. There comes a time when one has to . . . accept . . . things like this. It was damnable of me."

He did smile then, a trace of genuine amusement showing through the weariness. "Not really. You were right too. But—just exactly what were you planning to do with that?"

"With what?" Following his look, I stared stupidly down at the gun in my hand.

He leaned forward and took it from me gently. The blood-stained fingers avoided mine. They were shaking a little. He laid the gun carefully to one side. "I think perhaps it's safer there."

Silence. He stood over me, looking down still with that stranger's look.

"Camilla."

I met it then.

"If you hadn't got rid of that thing," he said, "I should be dead."

"And so should I. But you came."

"My dear, of course. But if he'd got to that gun . . ." A tiny pause, so slight it didn't seem that what he said could be important. "Would you have shot him, Camilla?"

Quite suddenly, I was shaking uncontrollably. I said, with a sort of violence, "Yes. Yes, I would. I was just going to, but then you . . . you killed him yourself. . . ."

I began to cry then, helplessly. I reached out blindly with both hands, and took his between them, blood and all.

He was sitting beside me on the boulder, with his arm round me. I don't remember what he said; I think part of the time he was swearing under his breath, and this seemed so unlike him that I had to fight harder to control the little spurts of laughter that shook me through the sobbing.

I managed to say, "I'm sorry. I'm all right. I'm not hysterical. It's—it's reaction or something."

He said with violence, the more shocking because it was the first time I had heard it from him, "I'll not forgive myself in a hurry for dragging you into this, by God! If I'd had any idea—"

"You didn't drag me in. I asked to be in, so I had to take what came, didn't I? It wasn't your fault it turned out as it did. A man does what he has to do, and since you *did* feel like that about Michael, after all, you did it. That's all."

"About Michael?"

"Yes. You said the tragedy was over, but of course once you knew Angelos was still alive—"

"My dear girl," said Simon, "you didn't imagine that I really killed him for Mick, did you?"

I looked up at him rather numbly. "No? But you told Angelos—"

"I was talking the language he'd understand. This is still Orestes' country, after all." He looked down at the scuffled dust between his feet. "Oh, I admit it was partly Mick— once I found myself here, and facing him. I felt murderous enough about him when I knew he was still alive, even before Dimitrios told me the rest."

"Dimitrios? Of course. He told you?"

"He was persuaded to, quite quickly. Niko turned up and helped me." A pause. "He told me what the two of them had done to Nigel."

"Then you know. . . ." The breath I drew was three parts

relief. I remembered that look in Simon's eyes, and the smooth single-mindedness with which he had killed Angelos. I shivered a little. "I see."

"And then," he said, "there was you."

I said nothing. My eyes were on two—no, three specks in the bright air, circling slowly, high above the corrie. Simon sat beside me without moving, looking at the trampled dust. He looked all at once unutterably weary. If it hadn't been for the evidence sprawled across the stones one might almost have thought that he, not Angelos, had been beaten. "Any man's death diminishes me, . . ." I thought of Nigel, tumbled grotesquely behind the pile of dirt, and understood.

The silence drew out. Away somewhere on the mountain I thought I heard something, the clatter of stones, a breathless call. Simon didn't move. I said, "Tell me about Angelos. How did he get into it? Why did he wait till now to come back?"

"He's been before. We were right in our guesses about the search for the gold—the lights and voices, and Dimitrios' questions—but we were wrong about the name of the seeker. It wasn't Dimitrios himself. He knew nothing about the cache originally. When Angelos left Greece for Yugoslavia at the end of nineteen forty-four, he intended to come back as soon as he could. But he committed murder—political murder this time—in his adopted country, and was put away for 'life.' He was released two years ago, and came secretly back to look up his cousin. He let him into the secret, since he had to have somewhere to hide, and an agent to help him. They looked for the stuff—just as we guessed —but failed to find it. Dimitrios did his best to pump Stephanos, and the two of them must have searched desperately over the earthquake area at intervals through the spring and summer, then they gave up for the time being, and Angelos went back to live in Italy. I imagine he intended to come back again in the spring of this year, as soon as the snows had melted, but by then I had written to Stephanos, and the rumours were going about that I was coming to Delphi. He decided to wait and let us show him the place. That's all."

He glanced down at me. "And now, what happened to you? Why on earth did you come out of the cave? Surely he never found you in there, in sanctuary?"

"No." I told him then all that had happened since he had left me to follow Dimitrios. I found that I could tell it all quite calmly now, with that queer detachment I had felt in the cave, as if it were a play; as if these things had happened, not to me, but in some story I had read. But I remember being glad of the feel of Simon's arm round my shoulders, and of the heat of the sun.

He listened in silence, and when I had finished he still didn't speak for some minutes. Then he said, "I seem to have rather more to forgive myself for than just bringing you in on—that." For the first time his eyes went back to the cairn where the body lay. They were as I first remembered them, vivid and hard and cool. "Quite a score," he said. "Mick, Nigel, poor silly little Danielle. And then, of course, you. . . . It would almost take an Orestes, wouldn't it?" He took in his breath. "No, I doubt if the Furies, the Kindly Ones, will haunt me for this day's work, Camilla."

"No, I don't think they will."

There was a shout from the gateway behind us. With a clatter of stones, Niko hurled himself into the corrie and raced down towards us.

"Beautiful miss!" he yelled. *"Kyrie* Simon! It's all right! I'm here!"

He slithered to a halt in front of us. His startled gaze took us both in—my torn and filthy dress, the bruises, my scraped wrists and hands, and Simon covered with blood and dust and marks of battle. "Mother of God, then he *was* here? Angelos was here? He got away? He—"

He stopped abruptly as he caught sight of the body lying against the cairn. He gulped, and flashed a look at Simon. He looked at me as if he were going to speak, but he just shut his mouth again, tightly, and then went—it seemed reluctantly—across to where Angelos lay. There was the sound of slower footsteps from the gateway of the corrie, and Stephanos came into sight. He paused there for a moment, just as Simon had done, then came deliberately down the ramp towards us. Simon got stiffly to his feet. The old man stopped at my elbow. His eyes, too, were on Angelos. Then he looked at Simon. He didn't speak, but he nodded, slowly. Then he smiled. I think he would have spoken to me then, but Niko had straightened up and now came running back. A flood of Greek was poured out at Simon, who answered, and presently seemed to be telling his story. I caught the name "Michael" several times, and then "the Englishman," and "the French girl," and the word *"speleos,"* which I took to mean "a cave." But I was suddenly too tired to pay any attention. I leaned back into a bar of shadow and waited, while the three of them talked across me. Presently, with a word from Simon, he and Stephanos left me and went towards the cave.

Niko lingered for a moment. "You are not well, beautiful miss?" he asked anxiously. "That one—that Bulgar—he hurt you?"

To call anyone a Bulgarian is the worst term of abuse a Greek can think up; and they have quite a range. "Not really, Niko," I said. "I'm a bit shaken, that's all." I smiled at him. "You should have been here."

"I wish I had been!" Niko's sidelong glance at the cairn was perhaps not as enthusiastic as his voice, but apparently it took more than murder really to dim his lights. He turned his look of dazzled admiration on me. "I should have dealt with him, me, and not on account of my grandfather's cousin Panos, but for *you,* beautiful miss. Though *Kyrie* Simon," he added generously, "did very well, not?"

"For an Englishman," I said deprecatingly.

"Indeed, for an Englishman." He caught my look and grinned, unabashed. "Of course," he added, "I help him with Dimitrios Dragoumis. I, Niko."

"He told me so. What did you do with him?"

The black eyes opened wide. He looked shocked. "I could not tell you *that*. You are a lady, and—oh, I *see*." The devastating smile flashed out. "Afterwards, you mean? I take him down to the road, but not to Delphi, because I want to get back and help *Kyrie* Simon, you understand. There is a truck, and I explain to the men, and they take him to Delphi to the police. The police will come. I shall go presently to meet them and guide them here. And so."

"And so." I said it very wearily. It seemed as good a period to the day as anything.

Beyond my bar of shadow the sun seemed white-hot. Niko had on a shirt of vivid electric blue, patterned with scarlet lozenges. The effect was blinding. He seemed to shimmer at the edges.

I heard him say cheerfully, "You are tired. You do not want to talk. And the other men will be needing me, not? I go."

As I shut my eyes and leaned back, I heard him crossing the corrie at his usual impetuous gallop.

It seemed a long time before the three of them came out of the cave again into the sunlight.

Niko came first, leading the mule. He seemed subdued now, and a little pale. He didn't come over to me again, but swung himself onto the mule's back, kicked it into reluctant motion, and, with a wave to me, clattered out of the corrie.

Stephanos and Simon stood talking for a few minutes longer. Stephanos looked sombre. I saw him nod to something Simon said. then he gestured upwards towards the blazing arch of sky where those black specks still hung and circled. Then he turned and trudged slowly across to a patch of shade near the body. He sat down there, and settled himself, as if to wait, leaning forward with his head against the hands clasped on his staff. He shut his eyes. He looked suddenly very old—with that Homeric head and the shut eyes as old as time itself.

It was a picture I was never to forget, that quiet tailpiece to tragedy. There was the blue arch of the brilliant sky; there the body that the Kindly Ones had hunted down and killed on the very spot where he himself had shed blood; there the old man, bearded like Zeus himself, nodding in the shade. At the head of the cliffs stood the black goats, staring.

From somewhere, not too far distant now, came the little stave of music; the goat-herd's pipe whose sound, drifting down through the light-well, had led me to the Apollo of the holy spring. At the sound the goats lifted their heads and, turning, moved off, black against the sky, an Attic frieze in slow procession.

Simon's shadow fell across me.

"Niko's gone to guide the police here. He wanted to escort you to Delphi, but I told him you wouldn't be fit for the trek quite yet. You and I have something still to do, haven't we?"

I hardly heard the question. I said, apprehensively, "The police?"

"Don't worry. There'll be no trouble for me. Apart from everything else, and God knows he's done plenty, he was trying to kill you." He smiled "And now, are you coming? Stephanos is asleep, by the looks of it, so he won't wonder where we've gone."

"You didn't tell him and Niko about the shrine?"

"No. The question of what to do about the guns and gold is out of our hands now, thank heaven, but the other question's our own to answer. Do you know the answer?"

I looked at him inquiringly; perhaps a little doubtfully. Then he nodded, and I said, slowly, "I suppose so."

He smiled and put down a hand to me.

We went into the cave in silence. Simon's torch was almost dead, but it showed the way. It was not strong enough to probe too far into the shadows. He paused just outside

he entrance, and I saw him step aside and stoop over some-
hing that lay near the pile of rubble where the boxes had
een. He straightened up with one of Angelos' crowbars in
is hand. I didn't look further, but followed the mercifully
imming light through the pillared vaults until the slab
arred the way.

The light paused on the old marks of tooling in the stone.
There," said Simon softly. "It should slide back easily
nough. Even another three or four inches should block the
ntrance. . . . I'll leave this here for the moment."

He laid the crowbar down and we went through the cleft
or the last time, and up the curving tunnel that led to the
right citadel.

He had stood there without move or change for more than
wo thousand years; now, it seemed a miracle that in the
ast hour he had remained untouched, unaltered. The sun
ad slid further towards the west and the light fell more
lantingly through the leaves; that was all.

We knelt at his feet and drank. I cupped my hands under
he spring and splashed the water over my face and neck,
hen held my wrists under the icy runnel. It stung on the
ruises and the scraped flesh of my wrists, a sharp remedial
tinging that seemed to signal my body's return from what-
ver numb borderlands of shock I had been straying in.
 sat back, flicking the cool drops off my hands.

I noticed then that the mark had gone from the third
inger of my left hand. There was no sign at all of the pale
ircle where Philip's ring had been.

I sat looking at my hands.

Simon was leaning forward, putting something on the
tone plinth at the statue's feet. There was the gleam of
old.

He caught my look and smiled, a little wryly. "Gold for
Apollo. I asked him to bring Angelos back, and he did it,
ven though it was done in that damned two-edged Delphic
way that one always forgets to bargain for. However, there
t is. It was a vow. Remember?"

"I remember."

"It comes to me that you made a vow, too, in this very
hrine."

"So I did. I'll have to share your coin, Simon. I've noth-
ng here to give."

"Then we'll share," he said. That was all, in that casual
easy voice with no change in it; but I turned quickly to

look up at him. The vivid grey eyes held mine for a moment, then I turned from him almost at random and picked up Nigel's little water pot. "We'll leave this here too, shall we?"

Something glinted, deep in the grass, down beside the edge of the stone plinth. I smoothed the long stems aside and picked it up. It was another gold coin.

"Simon, look at this!"

"What is it? A talent? Don't tell me Apollo's provided a ram in the thicket for—" He stopped short as I held my hand out towards him.

I said, "It's a sovereign. That means Nigel did find the gold as well as the statue. He must have left this here."

"Must he?"

"Well, who else—?" Then I saw his face and stopped.

He nodded. "Yes. Of course. Michael made an offering, too."

He took it from me gently and laid it beside the water pot, at the feet of the god.